IN THE FALLING LIGHT

by

JOHN L. CAMPBELL

For Heather,

Readers are the Best Sort
of Proof!

[signature]

Wild Highlander Press © 2012

John L. Campbell

IN THE FALLING LIGHT Copyright © 2012 by John L. Campbell

 Wild Highlander Press ® is a registered trademark.

The following were previously published in another form; "Avoiding Miranda" & "Pet Shop Tarantulas" at *SNM Horror Magazine*, "Muse" at *Static Movement*," "Eater of Stars" & "Zero Tolerance" at *Death Head Grin*, "Lyme Disease" at *Deadman's Tome*, "The Houe on Mohawk" in *Conceit Magazine*, "Chained," "Trophy Wife," "Ten Rules of Walter" & "Salty" at *Necrology Shorts*, "Wildfire," "Texas Rising," "Of Crimes and Crows," & "King of the Monster House" at *Schlock! Webzine UK*, "Courageous Little Philomena's Wondrous Bait" in *Gargoyle Magazine*, "Barringer Road," "Trail of Breadcrumbs," "Someplace the Wind Blows Through," "Embracing Neptune," "Taillights," "Jack's Folly," "Rejection," & "American Tragedy" at *MicroHorror,* "Corn of Cortez" in *Timeless Worlds.*

Cover design and illustration by Keith Haney/Haney@xmission.com

Printed in the United States

ISBN-13: 978-1478262114

For Linda and Daniel, the center of my world.

Special thanks go to the following people, who made this collection possible; Albert Carlos, who took the time to explain the inner workings of a prison, and corrected me when things didn't make sense; Keith Haney, for his magnificent artwork, unvarnished feedback and eternal patience with artistic revisions, and to his wife Laura for letting me steal away his time; James Polisky, whose art I fell in love with at a street festival, and whose piece, "The Town Secret," inspired me to write about Courageous Little Philomena; To Al and Ginny, for enduring rough draft readings without my glasses; To my wife, my primary reader and most important critic, who not only supports my endless keyboard tapping and dares me to dream, but who also provided the title for "Corn of Cortez;" And to the readers and editors, both online and print, who gave me their time, their criticism and encouragement. Thank you all.

Additional titles by John L. Campbell

Red Circus: A Dark Collection

The Mangroves

CONTENTS

Chained
Playthings
Barringer Road
Texas Rising
Rejection
Muse
Avoiding Miranda
Lyme Disease
Taillights
Wildfire
Trail of Bread Crumbs
Zero Tolerance
Trophy Wife
Pet Shop Tarantulas
Embracing Neptune
Courageous Little Philomena's Wondrous Bait
The House on Mohawk
Someplace the Wind Blows Through
Rising Sun, Setting Sun
Girl on a Platform
American Tragedy
Salty
Grand Central
A Ranch in Nevada
Eater of Stars
Of Crimes and Crows
Society
Jack's Folly
Corn of Cortez
Ten Rules of Walter
King of the Monster House

CHAINED

It was one of countless failing farms in the West Virginia hill country, fields lying fallow and gone wild because there was no money for planting, a rusting tractor sinking into the earth because there was no money to fix it. The barn had collapsed in the center, looking like an old swayback horse, and hadn't been rebuilt. A pickup which only ran when it wanted sat in the weeds beside a two story house with peeling paint and plastic stretched over those windows missing glass. In the dooryard, a small dog harried a clutch of scrawny chickens.

A quarter mile behind the house a line of elms straddled a narrow stream, and a large, time-worn rock jutted out of high grass at the base of one old tree. It was here that father and son sat side by side in the shade, looking out at the sun-warmed meadow between the creek and the house. Dragonflies flitted and hovered over grass and wildflower which were still in the unmoving air, and blue skies sailing overhead.

Leo McClellan was rolling a cigarette – he couldn't afford store bought, couldn't afford much of anything these days – while his son Matthew watched. Matthew was twelve.

"McClellan's have been on this land since my great-granddaddy's day." Leo waved vaguely towards the overgrown fields, the house which was falling apart. "It wasn't always like this. McClellan's have grown up in that house for over a hundred years. I'd hoped you and your sister would do the same." He looked down at his worn out boots for a long time. Matthew said nothing.

When he looked up, Leo squinted into the bright sky and rubbed a hand across the rough whiskers on his chin. "Lots of things happened here. Right *here*, in fact." He slapped the rock they were sitting on. "Like Earl. I tell you about Uncle Earl?"

"No, Daddy." His voice was cautious, respectful.

Leo grunted. "Well, it ain't the kind of story you tell a boy, but I suppose I should. You deserve to know. He was my great uncle, lived in a little shack out past the barn. It's long gone now. He helped my daddy with the farm." He was silent then, staring out at the meadow, then softly said, "We take care of our own." He looked back down at his boots, and Matthew thought he might not tell the story after all. Then Leo looked at him and smiled with bad teeth. There was no money for a dentist, either.

"It was June, 1967. I was seven years old. No one could say exactly when it happened to him, or how long he had it before it started to show. I hear it's different with everyone. But I remember it. Some things you can't forget, no matter how much you'd like to." Leo finished rolling his smoke and took a long, measured moment digging a wooden kitchen match out of his pocket, striking it on the rock and holding it to the tip. Cheap tobacco smoke hung around him in the still air.

"Uncle Earl got himself bit. Raccoon or fox or some such, we never did find out. Most likely a coon. Earl wasn't too particular about where he dumped his trash, and the little bastards was always nosing around. Anyway, he got bit on the arm and caught the rabies. You know about the rabies."

Matthew nodded. Farm kids were taught early on about the dangers of wild animals, what warning signs to watch for, and were told that if they ever had to shoot an animal they thought might be infected, not to shoot it in the head, so its brain could be tested. In school they learned about the effects, learned that it drove a person crazy before it killed them, but that shots at the hospital could save your life.

Leo squinted at the sky again, not seeing the sweep of white clouds over the startling blue field, seeing only his childhood. "I was pretty young, don't recall everything that led up to what happened, but I remember Uncle Earl was sick a lot, and some days he had so much pain he couldn't work the fields. You better believe that made my daddy plenty mad. Lazy don't sit well with McClellan's.

"Earl got worse. He started shuffling around the dooryard like he was lost or didn't know where he was, or he'd sleep a lot. When he wasn't sleeping sometimes he'd just up and scream for no reason, or flap his arms like a frightened hen. I remember thinking he was funny, but my daddy told me to keep away from Uncle Earl or he would blister my ass. He and my mama, they knew what was happening."

"Didn't anyone take him to the doctor, Daddy? They could have fixed him."

Leo looked sideways at his son. "Doctors. Bunch of damned bloodsuckers looking to get rich off poor folk. Besides, my daddy didn't have a pot to piss in." He looked at the fallen barn, the shabby house. "Like us." He smoked and watched a touch of breeze catch the little cloud and carry it away. "McClellan's take care of their own."

There was another long silence, and Matthew shifted, uncomfortable on the rock. The tree had actually grown around the big piece if field stone, the thick trunk curving slightly, and Matthew settled his back against its bark. His daddy didn't seem to mind, and he was thankful for that.

"Wasn't long before things got even worse for Earl. Instead of sleeping, he was up all night, walking around the outside of the house and carrying on, yelling and pissing himself, talking to people that wasn't there, jumping like he'd been goosed. By that time I didn't need daddy's promise of an ass blistering to keep away from him. He scared me. One afternoon I was out by the barn, playing with a little truck in the weeds, and I turned around. Earl was standing not three feet away in nothing but his underwear, standing real still, arms hanging at his sides, not saying a word but smiling all big, like something was funny. But his eyes didn't say funny. His eyes said he wanted to do something bad. Something *really* bad. See, he'd started getting sneaky, moving real quiet. That was worse than all the noise. It meant you never could tell where he was."

7

Leo looked at his son. "He'd gone crazy. You understand?"
Matthew nodded slowly.

"I told mama what happened by the barn, and then it wasn't just me scared. That night I heard mama and daddy whispering in the kitchen. They said Earl was dangerous, and something had to be done."

"Did they call the sheriff, Daddy?"

Leo shook his head. "Ain't you been listening? I told you we take care of our own. We sure don't hand family over to the law, or ship them off to a pack of doctors. Earl was family, and there's nothing more important than that. My daddy, he was a good man, and he did what he did to protect mama and me." He crushed out his smoke. In a softer voice he said, "Daddy didn't have no choice."

Neither one spoke for a while, then Matthew asked in a small voice, "Did grand-daddy...kill Uncle Earl?"

Leo didn't answer, just went back to squinting at the sky. "Daddy didn't have no choice," he repeated, and Matthew couldn't tell if he was speaking to the past or trying to convince himself.

"At the end of it, Earl was scared of water. Couldn't drink it, throat closed right up, and near pitched a fit any time daddy tried to give him some. Thirsty as he was, he wouldn't touch a drop."

"Hydrophobia," said Matthew. "We learned it in school."

Leo turned and grinned, ruffled his son's hair. "You're a smart boy." Then he tipped his face back to the sky and closed his eyes. "No, daddy didn't kill Uncle Earl. Killing a man goes against God. What daddy did was chain old Earl by the neck to this tree right here, the one you're leaning on. Earl used to sit on this very rock like we are now, raving mad and yanking on his chain and screeching like a cat in heat. I guess daddy never figured what it was doing to Earl, being so close to the creek and all."

The stream rippled past within arm's length of the tree, sunlight dropping through the leaves to dapple the water.

"Daddy chained him to this tree so he couldn't hurt no one. Then he let the rabies run its course." He opened his eyes, and tears began trailing down his weathered cheeks. "Earl lasted three days, and I don't think he was quiet once during that time. Screamed until he could only make little raspy noises, thrashed about and rolled on the ground, tore his hair out of his own head. Wouldn't go near the creek, though. And the unholy things that came out of his mouth, sweet Jesus. I had nightmares for years. Sometimes I still wake up in the house and think I hear him back here, crying and cursing and begging and wishing all manner of hate and death on my daddy. He would have torn us all apart with his hands and teeth if daddy hadn't been such a strong man, hadn't made that hard decision."

Leo sighed. "And daddy stayed with him through it all." He pointed to an old stump fifteen feet away. "Sat right there keeping watch, keeping Earl company, talking when the man would listen. You don't walk out on family, Matthew, not ever."

"What…what happened to Uncle Earl?"

"One morning he was quiet, so I walked out here, thinking he must've gotten better. Daddy was sitting on the stump, crying. The only time I ever saw him cry. Uncle Earl was dead."

Matthew looked at his father, anxious. "He died from the rabies?"

Leo shrugged. "In a way, I guess. Uncle Earl bashed his own head apart on this rock." He set a palm down on the grainy surface. Matthew's eyes went to his father's hand, then back to his face.

"Madness can make a person do near anything, son. That's what the rabies is, madness. So now you understand, don't you?"

Matthew started to cry. "Daddy, doctors can fix rabies."

Leo shook his head. "Not when it's so far along. I'm sorry."

Matthew jerked at the chain that was padlocked around his neck, the same chain that then encircled the tree and was secured with another padlock. He tried to grip the collar of links, but it was so tight his fingers could barely get between flesh and steel. He pulled at the chain where it met the tree, but it held firm. "But Daddy," he wept, "I'm not bit."

Leo stood and moved a few feet away, watching his son yank uselessly at the chain. He rubbed his hands at the tears which wouldn't quit, the skunk bite on the back of one rough hand a pink, infected bloom. "The rabies is making you crazy, Matthew, just like Earl. I'm so sorry, son, it's the only way to keep you from hurting anyone."

"Daddy!" Matthew strained against the steel, making a wheezing sound. "Doctors can fix it! I'm not bit! None of us are!"

Leo blinked through his tears and looked at the two adjacent trees, staring as if he was seeing them for the first time. His wife Emma was neck-chained like her son, sitting splay-legged with a dazed look on her face, uncomprehending. Locked to the next tree over was Jamie-Lynn, nine years old, slumped and sagging, only the chain holding her up. Jamie-Lynn's face was purple, her tongue was thick and sticking out, and her eyes looked like cloudy marbles. Her chain collar had been locked down just one link too tight.

"The rabies makes you think things that aren't true," he told his boy, tapping the side of his head with a finger. "Even make you think you don't have it."

"I'm not bit!" Matthew pulled again and again at the chain. "I'm not bit! You are! You are you are *YOU ARE DADDY!*"

Leo's heart was breaking to see his son like this, for what he was about to go through. But his own daddy had been strong and so he would be strong too. But dear God, it hurt so much. He walked to the stump and sat down, resting his hands on his knees, his left eye beginning to develop a tic. He didn't like the sound of the creek, didn't even want to look at it, and certainly wasn't going to go near it. The creek was a bad thing, though he wasn't sure why.

"Daddy, *please!*" There was more screaming and rattling of chain.

"Gonna stay with you through this, Matthew. Ain't gonna walk out on you, gonna stay right here."

Leo wiped at his mouth.

His hand came away wet with foam.

PLAYTHINGS

The woman was old. Ancient. Like a collection of dried, dead leaves held together in a hunched, human shape with straggles of long white hair. If the heat kicked on, that first rush of warm air would cause the leaf-person to blow apart with a crackle and disintegrate into tiny, fluttering pieces.

How old was she exactly, Cesar wondered? The agency said it didn't know. Close to a hundred, if not more. She looked more like a thousand, like a mummy in a faded black dress, with an old afghan over her knees.

Rosalyn Acre sat in her rocking chair, feet barely touching the floor, curved so far forward by osteoporosis that her head was closer to her knees than the back of the chair. Her skin was cracked and lined like a desert mudflat, and her eyes were runny and pale with cataracts. She wore high, pink hospital socks with white strips of rubberized tread, and diapers which required frequent changing.

Cesar watched as she raised her cup and saucer to pinched, lined lips, making crude smacking noises with her tongue in a mouth where teeth had not resided for three decades. The hands holding the saucer, spidery and veined blue, trembled and made the cup rattle against the china, slopping out tea. She slurped. Cesar was careful not to let his disgust show.

11

"Toys go mad when they're not played with," she announced into the tea, her raspy voice sounding hollow and thin against the china.

"Right, Mrs. A."

"May I have a cookie?"

"They're on a plate right next to your chair, Mrs. A." Cesar pointed, and the old woman slowly turned her head to look. *Slow,* he thought, *the seasons move faster than this old broad.* She set the saucer in her lap and began to reach for a macaroon, her twig-like arm extending in excruciating inches. Cesar didn't have the patience to watch, and sighed as he rose, stepped to her side table and handed her a cookie. She made the same, sticky smacking noise as she dipped it into the tea until it was soft enough to gum, then crammed it into her toothless maw.

The heat did kick on then, but she didn't blow away. Cesar was glad it had, as the sprawling, Victorian mansion was prone to all sorts of drafts and chills. He wore two shirts under his pale blue scrubs, the first a simple white undershirt, the next a long-sleeved thermal. Sausalito sat on the north side of the bay, and the house rested on a cliff-side property overlooking the water, San Francisco visible to the south when it wasn't shrouded in fog. It got chilly up here, much cooler than Southern California, but the long-sleeved shirt wasn't just for the cold of the climate and the house. It was as much to conceal his tattoos, especially the ones he had picked up at Chino. The baggy scrubs also went a little ways to hide his build; broad-shouldered and solid, like a boxer. He had been hard when he went inside the last time, but four years work on the weights in the yard had made him harder, and bigger too.

"They get so lonely," the woman mouthed as she gummed her soggy cookie, "and then they lash out, like angry children. Do you understand?"

"Sure, Mrs. A."

"Please, Lyle, call me Rosie."

"Okay, Rosie," said Cesar. He didn't know who Lyle was. It could have been one of the many home health care workers who had gone before him, or a person remembered over the century of her life, or maybe just someone she invented. He didn't care. He did know a few things, though.

12

He knew he despised changing her soiled diapers, despised the noises she made, her raspy voice and breath, her dead eyes. He knew she was frail, and that nearly anything could finish her off; a fall, a choking spasm in her sleep, a sickness. Hell, by now even Death had to be tired of waiting around for this artifact to check out from old age. Yet she clung to life, never deteriorating beyond her current state, as if she had pulled out of a dive and was now circling just above death in a holding pattern. Essentially, despite her vulnerability, she was healthy, and Cesar had to keep her that way.

Not because it was his job. That was a joke.

He had to keep her healthy because she was loaded. Rosalyn Acre was said to be worth in the neighborhood of two-hundred-forty million. No living heirs, her vast fortune scheduled to be distributed among a wide variety of charities – including the State of California, the biggest fucking charity case of all – upon her passing. Cesar imagined there was a phone book worth of people marking off days on the calendar towards that great payoff moment. Not Cesar. He needed her alive, because he believed she kept a lot of her wealth right here in the house, in cash.

And he hadn't found it yet.

If the old broad died, he would be immediately out of a job and out of the house, unable to continue his search. It was in his best interest to keep her warm and properly medicated and living.

Cesar knew one other thing. Once he found her stash, he was gone.

Killing the old bitch then would just be an added bonus.

Rosie's head was drooping even further, and Cesar quickly snatched the cup and saucer away before she could drop them. He had no worry she would topple forward out of the chair. He always belted her in. Ragged snoring now, so Cesar headed to the kitchen with the china.

He passed through a room big enough to handle banquets of a hundred plus, then stepped out the back door and lit up a smoke. The bitch flipped out if she smelled cigarette, so he was careful to always go outside, and kept mints in his pockets just in case. Behind the mansion was an expansive green space of manicured lawns and flowerbeds bursting with color, all leading to a walled drop-off and the water beyond. Although it was well over a hundred feet down to where the surf rolled and crashed against rocks at the base of the bluff, it could still be heard as a soft, rhythmic shushing. It was peaceful. Tall pines provided shade for walkways meandering through the greenery, which Rosalyn frequented when the weather was fair, Cesar always in attendance, bringing the wheelchair in case she needed it. She usually didn't, relying on an aluminum cane – not even a walker! She was strong for her age, and he smirked through his cigarette smoke. All those motherfuckers sitting around waiting for their big "Rosie's-dead-now-pay-up" moment were going to be waiting a long time.

At least until Cesar got what he wanted.

She wouldn't nap long in the chair, so there would be no searching until later. Cesar lit another smoke, leaning against the wall. He wondered what it cost for the landscapers to take care of this place, and shook his head. All that fucking money to cut grass and trim hedges. What a waste. He had better things to do with cash.

Cesar had been on his last three months of a four year robbery bit – out early on good time – when he was given a new cellmate, a skinny black kid named Jevon who got himself jammed up in a bigger-than-average coke deal with weapons present. He'd landed a fifteen year stretch, and this was his first taste of hard time. Jevon was scared and ill-equipped for what awaited him. Cesar made the kid his bitch immediately, satisfying his own needs and renting him out for smokes and protection.

Jevon talked a lot, and that was what originally set Cesar on the path which would bring him here. Before moving south to LA and getting busted, the kid had worked for the Youngman-Price Healthcare Agency in San Francisco. The agency provided live-in health workers who cared for those who were not yet ready for – or refused – full time residential placement, and could afford to have someone stay with them four or five days a week to see to their medication, feeding and cleaning. Jevon explained what it took to get that kind of gig, and Cesar had been shocked. Three months of training in basic first aid and geriatric care, a clean background check, and some prior experience preferred. That was it. Fucking California, man. It was that same, half-assed system which allowed so many pedophiles to slip undetected into the education and daycare system. It made him sick.

Jevon talked about when the agency had sent him to look after this rich old broad in Sausalito, all alone in a big, drafty house and worth millions. Completely batshit as well, but she refused to live in a rest home and had high power lawyers to keep her out of one. Jevon said the place creeped him out, that there were strange noises and things moving at the corner of your eye and laughter like from a little kid. He said no one lasted on the job more than a couple months, and lots of them just took off and never came back to the agency. Superstitious nonsense. But then he started talking about the cash.

He didn't know where the stash was, even admitted he'd made an attempt to find it, but he swore it was there. People would come to visit her sometimes, charity people, and she'd always have a fat envelope of bills for them.

"Where's she get the envelopes?"

Jevon looked at him with those stupid eyes and said, "I dunno, Staples?"

Cesar broke his nose for that one.

Later he asked, "No, dumbfuck, where'd the cash come from?"

Jevon shrugged, looking over his icepack, and his voice was thick and nasally. "She just had it. I'd go to get something for her, and when I came back she'd have it in her lap, waiting for the charity people."

"So she kept it close by."

Jevon shook his head. "Nah, man, I looked all over. She's too old to use the stairs, sleeps in a little room on the main floor, but I searched that whole level. Never found nothing."

Now, seeing that Rosalyn Acre was a good deal more agile than she appeared, and could probably manage stairs, although slowly, Cesar knew a much broader search was required. Jevon was just lazy.

Just before his release, Cesar brought a sharpened piece of Plexiglas into the showers and stabbed Jevon to death, holding the kid by the throat and staring into his surprised and frightened eyes while he did it. No one was able to put the killing on him, and he was released as scheduled. Jevon wouldn't be telling anyone else about the rich old lady with fat envelopes of cash.

Cesar crushed out his butt and slipped it into a Pepsi can he kept concealed inside the spout of a drain pipe, then headed back in, popping a mint and stopping in the kitchen to wash his hands and scrub his face. When the water stopped he could hear tiny snorts and wheezes, the sign she would be waking up soon. He went back to the parlor.

It took six months of muling heroin for Cat Santos in Orange County, living like a monk and saving every cent, until he had enough money put away to relocate north and get what he needed from some specialists he met in prison. The cost of the health worker training was nothing compared to what he spent on a new identity, fabricated background and phony job references. It wiped out his savings, but within a year of leaving Chino he had completely disappeared from the system, left his parole officer behind, and became a clean-cut employee of Youngman-Price. He had considered the quicker and less expensive route, simply doing a night-time home invasion and grabbing what he could. But if what Jevon said was true, that the money was hard to find, then a couple hours in the house might not be enough. Instead, Cesar decided he'd be smart about it.

It was surprisingly easy to land the Rosalyn Acre gig. As Jevon had said, no one wanted it, no one lasted long, and most never came back. And the stories! Holy Christ, the bullshit that floated around about the house being haunted and the old woman being a witch. He heard plenty of that, but nothing about large amounts of cash hidden away.

Cesar had been here three weeks now, on duty and staying overnight five days straight, then off for two when Rosie went into the medical center for a couple days as the doctors ran tests and verified she would live another week. Only a few people came to the house, including the gardeners who showed up once a week, but they stayed outside. A cleaning service came every other Wednesday, grocery and pharmacy delivery was on Friday, and one time a Youngman-Price supervisor had dropped in unannounced to check up on his employee. The visit was brief, and the supervisor left satisfied. Cesar wasn't allowed to stay in the house while she was away at the medical center, and had to return to his dumpy apartment in Oakland until she came back.

Those were frustrating days, since it was lost time, time which could be spent searching the house.

Though there were plenty of bedrooms on the upper floors, he slept in a narrow, converted hall closet not far from Rosalyn's first floor bedroom, a baby monitor on the floor beside him so he could hear her in the night if she went into distress. His room was simple and bare, cell-like, and the irony was lost on him.

He had to admit that Jevon was right, the place was creepy, more so at night than in the day. He was sure he'd heard running feet on the floors above, and what at first sounded like a child's giggle but was certainly just air in the plumbing. He'd caught movement out of the corner of his eye several times, but he suspected the old bag had a cat somewhere. She said she didn't, but shit, she was senile, probably wouldn't remember it even if she had one. Probably rats in a place this old. And of course there was the frequent, uneasy feeling of being watched. More than once he had awakened in the dark absolutely certain someone was in the room with him, watching as he slept. Cesar knew that was just holdover paranoia from being in the joint.

Three weeks of searching after she went down for the night, poking through room after room with a big six cell flashlight, checking under beds and inside closets packed with moth-eaten clothes and ancient hat boxes, looking in dressers and behind paintings. Nothing. No steamer trunk full of bills, no hidden safes or cubby holes. As big as the place was he had drawn a rough map and checked off rooms already inspected, and even after all this looking there remained unexplored areas. He was confident he'd find it.

Especially since he had seen the envelopes.

It happened on two occasions, once right before a visit from UNICEF, the other during a begging call from the Greater Bay Area Animal Rescue Shelter. One moment it wasn't there, but turn around for a second and look back, and there it was, a plump envelope resting on the afghan in her lap. And the hag hadn't *moved* from her chair.

Said hag was waking up now, snuffling and rubbing bony knuckles at weepy, pale eyes, smacking her lips. Cesar checked his watch and brought her some water and her medication, having to hold the glass for her as she choked it down. She looked up at him with dull gratitude, and he smiled gently back at her, imagining how wonderful it would be to punch her in the face, to hear those bones crack.

"I want my pictures," she announced.

Cesar just looked at her. What the fuck was she talking about?

"There," she pointed past him, and he turned towards a full bookcase against one wall. "My pictures. I want to look at them."

Cesar moved to the bookcase, eyes running up and down the many shelves of leather-backed books. They all looked old, and some were probably rare and worth a lot by themselves.

"On the bottom. My pictures." Her voice was petulant, like a child.

Cesar squatted and looked at the bottom shelf – something darted under a table on the left, out of the corner of his eye, but when he snapped to look there was nothing there.

"My *pictures!*" Now she was wheeze-shrieking.

"Okay, Mrs. A, I'm looking."

"Rosie!"

"Yes, Rosie. I'm looking." He spotted a cluster of photo albums, pulled one out and held it up. "This?"

"No! Cock asshole…" she shook her head, and seemed to lose interest as she poked at a mole on the back of her hand. Cesar wasn't surprised by the outburst or the language. She was batshit, after all, and he'd heard it from her before. He started to put the book back.

"The red one," Rosie said.

There was only one that color, a big book with a cracked, dark red leather cover. He pulled it as she unbuckled herself – *he didn't know she could do that* – and tottered towards a flower-patterned love seat, carefully lowering herself to the cushions as if the very act of sitting down could fracture her bones. And likely it could, he thought.

Rosie patted the cushion beside her. "It's very large, I'll need you to hold it for me, Lyle."

"Yes ma'am," he said, keeping from rolling his eyes. Now he'd have to sit for the next hour or so and look at old photos of people she wouldn't remember, listening to rambling stories about the ones she did, and all the while not giving a flying fuck. He sat and opened the book.

Cesar didn't know much about history, but the way people were dressed in the old black and white photos looked to be from the turn of the century. The *previous* century, and he wondered again just how old the bitch might be. The photos in this book appeared to be from her childhood, and he endured her stories, patiently turning the pages when she asked, holding back sighs when she trailed off into the fog of memory, having trouble recalling names or places, watching her get frustrated at times as she studied long-gone faces and tried to remember who they had been. He barely heard her.

"This is me with Pumpkin," she said as a new page was turned.

Cesar was thinking of a stripper he had known in LA with the tattoo of a tarantula on her inner thigh, and remembering the way she looked up and batted her long black eyelashes while her mouth was occupied. He glanced down at the page, and instantly forgot about the stripper, looking instead at where the old woman was pointing. It was a faded image, brown with time, of two little girls playing on a wooden floor with a collection of dolls and tin toys. Sunlight was streaming through an odd, circular window set in an alcove, dust motes heavy in the air and giving the scene a mystical look. In the background he could see a pile of trunks, a heavy wardrobe, a wire dress dummy with a frilly hat on it and a stack of paintings partially covered with a tarp. A large object stood just inside the shot on the far right, tall and smooth, a pair of side by side doors on heavy hinges, each with a large handle, and one with a big dial.

A vault. A big, free-standing vault.

Rosalyn was babbling about someone called Pumpkin, but Cesar didn't hear her. He was staring at the vault, at the objects in the room behind the girls, and at the window. He recognized the unusual shape and design of that window. The house had half a dozen of them which could be seen from the outside, all set in dormers. That was an attic window. Rosie's vault was in the attic.

"Such happy days," she crooned, fumbling to turn the page. Cesar let her do it, his eyes staying on the image of the vault until it disappeared into the book.

It was eight-thirty, and the old woman had been asleep for an hour. Cesar climbed the narrow stairs from the third floor to the attic landing, the baby monitor clipped to his belt, its red light flickering as she snored softly in the background. He carried the Maglite in one hand, and had a dozen pillow cases draped over the other arm.

The landing's boards creaked as he stopped before the single door, the flashlight throwing a white circle on the plain wood. He reached for the cut glass knob and turned, expecting it to be locked, fully prepared to shoulder it open if it was. It wasn't. The door swung in quietly, revealing a vast dark space. A breeze puffed through the opening, smelling of dust and mold and age. Cesar stepped inside, closing the door softly behind him, and panned the flashlight around.

The attic ran the length of the house, a ten foot central beam peaked overhead, the roof angling down on each side with exposed rafters. Moonlight glowed in the circular dormer windows, spilling washed-out light into some places and casting deep shadows in others. He checked for a light switch, found none, traced the flashlight beam along the walls and roof, saw no light fixtures. It was dusty, and he sneezed twice. A lot of junk had collected up here in the century since that photograph was taken, creating a maze of tarp-draped furniture, stacks of crates and trunks, decaying cane patio chairs and rotting umbrellas, more dress dummies and lots and lots of paintings. He heard a skittering noise to his right. Rats for sure.

The window he had seen in the photo was in front of him on the opposite wall, and he made his way past a lumpy couch and a pile of cracked leather suitcases, reaching a central aisle running both directions through the center of the junk. He panned the light right and immediately picked out the top of the vault, right where the photo had shown it, hidden behind a draped wardrobe. That it was still here was not particularly surprising, the thing must weigh a ton or more, and must have been a real bitch to get up to the attic in the first place. Cesar walked towards it, wondering how much stuff he would need to move to get to it, then wondering how he was going to get it open. He had no tools. Might have to wake the old bag up and shake her until she spit out the combo.

He needn't have worried on either count. There was a clear path to where the vault stood against a wall, and both doors were wide open. His powerful flashlight beam revealed multiple shelves running top to bottom on each side, and resting on every one of those shelves were stacks of tightly-bundled bills wrapped in colored, paper bands.

"Jesus," he whispered, walking slowly towards it. The flashlight moved up and down, side to side, revealing that the vault was deep, and every shelf was packed to the back with bundles. He stopped in front of it – the vault was taller than he was – tucked the flashlight under an armpit and took down a stack, riffling through it. Hundreds. The band read $10,000.00. And there were hundreds of them. Thousands. How much was here? Had to be millions, all in untraceable cash.

Cesar grinned broadly, then his mind started clicking. First off, the pathetic armload of pillow cases wouldn't be close to enough. He'd have to find luggage – plenty of that up here – and start loading. He would stage the cases near the attic door, then make trips downstairs. The mansion had a mini-van to be used for emergencies or light errands, and Cesar had the key. He would back the van to the kitchen door and start loading. How many trips? Didn't matter, he had all night. He'd try to be quiet so as not to wake the old woman, but if he did, what did that matter either? He could smother her easily, leave her in the bed, let the doctors wonder if she had simply died in her sleep. As for Cesar? They'd think he got scared when she died and took off, maybe try to charge him with negligence or car theft, but it wouldn't make any difference. It was only Tuesday, and she wouldn't be missed until Saturday. By then he'd have dumped the van and would be in South America, rich as a Latin dictator.

"Thanks, Jevon," he whispered, chuckling, and then noticed the ladder. It was small, too small for a child, something for a doll's bunk bed maybe, leaning up against the open shelving of the vault. The shelf it reached looked more depleted of stacks than the others. Was that the shelf where Rosie got her money? He pointed the flashlight in there and saw a stack of business envelopes. She could get to the attic? That was a lot of stairs, but he supposed she could, he had seen her walking virtually unassisted outdoors. But why the ladder? The shelf would only come to her waist, there'd be no need for it, and she probably couldn't climb it anyway.

Something bit deeply into his right ankle, and Cesar screamed, spinning, dropping the flashlight. It rolled to the base of the vault and stopped, the beam at floor level. A stuffed animal, a bear with patches of fur missing, was attached to his ankle, biting – *biting?* – deep into his flesh. He tried to kick it free but it hung on, small paws raking red furrows in his shin as it clawed for a better hold. Cesar shook his leg wildly, his breath coming fast, and then there was a metallic squeak and a new pain, this one sharper, his other ankle, a deep slice into the tendon. He screamed and had a moment to see a small figure beside him, something a foot tall and wearing a black cone for a hat, closing a long, gleaming pair of sewing scissors. Then his severed tendon took him to the floor.

"Eeeeeeee!" A high-pitched screaming came from all around as small shapes leaped upon him from atop boxes and furniture, landing and sinking nails and teeth into his hands and thighs and cheeks. He kicked out, hitting the flashlight and making it roll, and in the crazy white light he saw dolls and puppets and more stuffed animals, all old and worn from long-ago use. They were stitched and patched, missing eyes and limbs, but the eyes they did have blazed with a silvery light, and their mouths were filled with tiny, sharp teeth. They shrieked and squealed as they covered him, biting and biting.

The scissors plunged into his left thigh, and Cesar screamed again, arching his back like a wrestler on the wooden floor, the toys hanging on like obscene cowboys in a hellish rodeo. Cesar saw the thing with the scissors, a doll twelve inches high with a black cone hat, tiny black beads for eyes. It was grinning with evil little teeth. He recognized it, the toy which Rosie had been playing with as a child in the photo.

This is me with Pumpkin.

Pumpkin yanked out the bloody scissors with two hands, then drove them in over his head like a whaler with a harpoon, burying them to the handles in Cesar's belly just above his left hip. He gasped, eyes snapping wide as it pierced flesh and then organs. A dark jet of liquid spurted onto the vault door, spattering the grinning doll. It looked into his face with its silvery eyes and snickered.

Cesar tore the creatures off his face, and they took away bites of his flesh as they went. He pounded his fists at them, forcing them off, but they came right back, biting anew. He thrashed, his impressive strength sending toys flying, crushing several, ripping others apart with his hands. He was screaming nonstop now, his wails rising and falling, and he flipped to his stomach and started crawling. They leaped upon him, and he felt the scissors stab into one butt cheek, missing his scrotum by an inch. His only thought now was survival, safety. He saw a huge steamer trunk standing open in the gloom not far away, big enough for a man, big enough for him. He fast-crawled to it, leaving a bloody trail, then turned and began slapping and pulling madly at the dozens of toy creatures still biting at him. He threw them, he twisted off their heads, he pounded them with his big fists. With a last kick at a china doll with a fractured face, he heaved himself into the trunk and pulled it closed with a thump, landing in a thin layer of old dresses that smelled of mothballs. His searching hands found a pair of garment straps set in the interior of the lid, and he pulled down on them, hanging on to keep the trunk closed.

"*Eeeeeeee!*" A chorus of tiny shrieks from outside the trunk as dozens of little fists began pounding the walls in fury.

Cesar realized he was screaming, and forced himself to shut up. His breathing was ragged, his body afire with pain, and the deepest wound of all, the one in his side, was pulsing. That was a bad one, and it would kill him if he didn't get medical help soon. He pressed a palm against it, feeling blood sliding through his fingers.

And then it got quiet, the pounding and unholy screeching stopping suddenly. Silence except for Cesar's harsh breath.

A moment later he heard the soft shushing noise of rubberized hospital socks on a wooden floor. "What's this? What's this?" Rosie's dry voice floated through the trunk. The lid moved, someone trying to lift it, and Cesar held it down with both hands.

"Lyle? Are you in there, dear?"

He let go of the strap with a gasp of relief, and the old woman slowly lifted it open. In the muted glare of the flashlight she looked down at the shivering, bloody man curled in the bottom of the trunk. "Oh, my!"

"Rosie," Cesar gasped, tears in his eyes, "thank God you..."

23

"Oh, my, he's still alive." Rosie shook her head, as Pumpkin leaped into the trunk with a shrill little cry, scissors raised. Cesar screamed and held up his hands as the old woman let the lid drop back into place.

She was slumped in her chair in a doze, the morning sun beaming through lace curtains and warming the parlor. She snored lightly, and drooled into her afghan. A sound brought her around, and she lifted her head, focusing runny eyes on the small figure before her, standing a few feet away beneath a coffee table, hugging one of the legs. It had black bead eyes and a black cone for a hat.

"Hello, Pumpkin," she said, smiling.

The doll hid its face shyly behind the table leg, then peeked out again.

"I'll have the agency send over another one right away."

Pumpkin smiled with sharp little teeth.

"Would you like a cookie, dear?"

BARRINGER ROAD

Cheap carpet was making her nose itch, rubbing a slow burn across the side of her face as the van bumped and swayed. Zip ties at her ankles and wrists cut her skin, and the duct tape across her mouth reeked of the man who put it there. Cassie tried desperately to slow her racing heart as her mother's words came back to her.

"Predators hunt the Silver River Mall."

She should have listened a long time ago.

Terrence Cobb tried to focus on the road, but the twelve-year-old in back kept pulling his attention, the excitement giving him dry mouth. The snatch had been easy, the girl standing alone at the end of the sidewalk just down from the movie theatre, far from security lights. She'd been so surprised that she didn't even have a chance to put up a fight. Terrence watched his headlights sweep across the empty blacktop and endless trees, checking his mirrors, seeing they were clear. Focus, he told himself. He could relive it all later.

Barringer Road was a body dump. Terrence had used it three times before, but he wasn't the only one. People settling old scores, ending marriages with a shovel blade, even others like him had been leaving their problems out here for years. An eleven mile stretch of two lane asphalt tracing lazy curves through deep woods, Barringer Road cut across from US 14 to County Road 107 without a single inhabitant to disrupt the solitude. Dozens of turnouts, deserted camp sites and dead end logging roads ensured the privacy Terrence craved, and its distance from population made it impractical for the law to patrol with any regularity.

He had scouted his spot weeks earlier, an overgrown pair of ruts that dead-ended a mile in at a cluster of old stumps, long unused and out of screaming distance. Terrence had placed a yellowing deer skull on the shoulder near the turn-off to mark it. Now the headlights picked it out in the darkness ahead, lifeless sockets staring into the night like a harbinger of what was to come.

Cassie felt the van slow and turn, now lurching over a rougher surface, branches cracking under the tires. She was sweating, and her dark hair hung across her face in wet strands, her heart speeding. The zip ties were cranked down tightly. The man was strong, had thrown her effortlessly into the van.

Within minutes they reached the dead end, and Terrence shut off the headlights. He preferred moonlight for this part of it, the cold whiteness washing away all color. His hands trembled as he moved to the side door, patting his pants pocket for the reassuring weight of the big folding knife, his old companion.

He wiped the back of his hand across his lips and rolled open the door, gazing at the girl lying on her side. Her dark eyes were wide and watching him over the silver tape, her shallow chest heaving.

"Almost home, sweetheart," he said, smiling.

And then the girl arched her back and snapped the zip ties like they were paper instead of hard plastic. Her body contorted, enlarging with a ripple of muscle and an explosion of coarse hair, hands curling to talons, her face extending into a snapping muzzle.

Terrence stumbled backwards and started to scream, but the adolescent werewolf was on him in a second, bearing him to the ground, pulling his ribcage open and tearing into his throat with a violent thrash of her snout. Hot liquid sprayed across the side of the van, black in the starlight.

He died staring at the moon.

Later, her belly full and satisfied, Cassie loped through the forest on all fours, heading home. She couldn't wait to tell the pack about her first solo kill, and to hug her Mom, thank her for her good advice.

Real predators hunted the Silver River Mall.

TEXAS RISING

Hurricane Sophie, a Category-5 nightmare, swept in off the Gulf on September 16th, devastating the coastal regions. Everyone had seen the giant coming, swift and terrible, but despite widespread evacuations she savaged all she came in contact with, flinging her destructive arms wide. Corpus Christi vanished, and pieces of obliterated oil platforms as well as entire tankers were cast ten miles inland.

She tore north across the Hill Country, into the Big Country, and failed to drop to a Cat-3 as predicted by the time she reached Leesville, population 18,000, located in a county which averaged only seventeen people per square mile. Along with her merciless winds, Sophie brought rain. Lots of rain.

Everyone expected flooding. Central Texas was known as Flash Flood Alley, and every fire department was trained and equipped for swift water rescue. Most flooding deaths were the result of people trying to cross moving water, underestimating the force and weight of the currents, and every year the news ran footage of some fool standing on the roof of his pickup amid white water, waving his arms while people worked to save him. For the most part, this was the type of rescue firemen in rural Texas were trained for. Helicopter crewmen were similarly trained to descend on cables to pluck folks from rooftops and trees.

No one expected Sophie to come this far, with such force.

No one imagined what was approaching, and by the time her full fury was realized, it was too late.

Dell McCall straddled the peak of his roof as if he was riding one of his horses, facing his family. They were straddling too, all in a line like half-drowned crows. Above them the sky was a boiling mix of black and charcoal, clouds tumbling over one another as rain slashed down in dark curtains. Water poured down their faces, and they tried to wipe it from their eyes and hold onto the roof at the same time. The wind was a woman's scream.

Arlene, Dell's wife of twenty-two years, hugged their two-year-old Dylan to her chest as she looked at her other two children. Their seventeen-year-old was closest to her, and Ricky, eleven, rode the roof behind her.

"Bailey, I want you to climb over your brother and sit so you're facing me again."

"I'll fall!"

"You won't fall. I've seen you ride in the rain plenty of times. You just hold on tight, you can do it." Arlene said something else, but it was lost in the wind. When her voice came back it was firm. "Go on, now." Bailey nodded but stayed put.

"Once you're set, you're going to scooch backwards all the way to the chimney, put your back hard against it. You understand me?"

Bailey nodded again, wiping a clump of hair from her eyes. She was trembling. Dell wasn't sure she would move at first, thought she might freeze up, but then she started to her feet. She held onto her brother as she edged past him, her sneakers sliding over the wet shingles. Her legs were shaking and she began to whimper, gripping Ricky's shoulders hard while he in turn clung to the roof.

"Mama…"

Her right foot shot away and she went down with a scream, banging her chin, losing her grip on Ricky, and for one terrible moment Dell saw her sliding, sliding, falling and swept away. But one hand caught the roofline and the other snagged on Ricky's jeans.

"Mama!"

"Pull yourself up!"

"I'm falling!"

"You pull yourself up, Bailey McCall!"

The girl's sobs were torn away by the wind as she obeyed her mother's voice, clawing her way back to the roofline and throwing a leg over, hugging her brother's back and burying her face in his wet shirt.

"Now you get to scooching," Arlene commanded.

Bailey shook her head, hiding her face.

"Do it *right now*, girl!"

She pulled her face out of hiding. "I hate you!" she screamed, but did as she was told, easing her butt backwards six inches at a time, holding the roofline with both hands while Arlene cooed a steady stream of encouragement. "That's it, baby, you can do it, you're doing fine, honey, keep going..." Five endless minutes later she pressed her back against the bricks of the chimney.

"I'm sorry, Mama," she cried, wiping at her eyes.

"It's okay, baby, Mama knows. I'm so proud of you."

Dell gave his daughter a smile, and she managed a weak one in return. His wife's voice cut through the wind again. "Ricky, your turn, just like your sister."

The eleven-year-old needed no encouragement. He scooted backwards with the fearless agility of boys and crossed the distance in seconds, into Bailey's waiting arms. Arlene was murmuring to Dylan, keeping his face shielded from the biting rain as the toddler shivered close against her and cried. Dell looked away, at what had become of the world.

The McCall ranch sat twelve miles outside Leesville proper, the house and a cluster of outbuildings and trees alone on the flats of Gonzales County, not another structure in sight. It was sheep country, wide open and green, dotted in places with clumps of Texas oaks. Now, however, they might as well have been at sea, for eight feet of brown, turning water was moving across the flats like an ocean in every direction, endless, hammering at the gutters of their one story house. The white roof of Arlene's Durango could still be seen a quarter mile off as the SUV was carried away, and the wheels of Dell's Chevy poked just above the surface where the overturned pickup had floated to rest against the tree in what had been their front yard.

The water around them was fast and unforgiving.

29

Just beyond the house were the rooftops of the sheep shed and the second story of the barn. None of the smaller buildings could be seen. They were already underwater.

Arlene looked back into the wind and rain at her husband. "Together?"

He nodded, and they began to scoot forward across the space separating them from their children, slowly, carefully. Dylan was starting to squirm, and Arlene clamped him tight against her while she used the other hand to stay balanced and pull herself along. Dell kept close, prepared to grab them both if she should tip over one side or the other, not thinking or caring that he would most likely be pulled over with them if they went.

They stopped once, Dylan's squalling competing with the driving wind, and Arlene used both hands to rock and soothe him. Then they were off again, the rough shingles grating beneath them, knees gripping the wet roof like the withers of a bareback horse. Lightning split the sky, followed close by sharp, rippling cracks as they reached the far end, Arlene's knees touching Ricky's. They rested for a moment, his wife's forehead pressed against the toddler, Dell's against his wife's shoulder. A surge of wind rocked them and the rain fell harder, coming in sideways for a moment, both conspiring to send them off the roof. They hung on.

"Bailey," Arlene was shouting, "I want my hands free to grab anyone who might slip, so I'm going to pass Dylan forward. Ricky, you're going to help. Put him tight in between the two of you."

Both kids nodded that they understood, and whatever fear they might have had for themselves momentarily vanished as they undertook the deadly serious task of protecting their youngest. Within moments, Dylan was safely tucked between his brother and sister, Bailey covering him with her body. In the midst of the horror, Dell McCall felt a burst of pride for his children.

It was short-lived, as the situation and bitterness crashed back in on him. He could have evacuated them days ago, when Sophie was crossing Florida. They could have left when she brushed Louisiana, showing no signs of diminishing, then again as she made landfall on the Texas Gulf Coast. But everyone was so certain she would slow down and blow out in the Hill Country, even the TV weathermen, that it would just be hard rain and high wind by the time it reached them. What Texan picked up his family and ran from that? They had been through heavy weather before. Dell supposed that had been at the heart of it. Pride. Too proud to be chased off his land.

And then there she'd been in all her terrible glory, ripping overland at record speeds, and it had been too late. The wind and thunder had gotten them moving in the early hours, and the dreaded grumble of water rushing across the main road – cutting off any hope of driving out – had sent them up an aluminum ladder and onto the roof mere seconds before a dark tide bristling with uprooted trees had surged across the flats, surrounding their house.

He looked at the barn, with its safe, dry loft and much higher roof. I should have taken them there, he thought.

New gusts attacked out of the early morning, rain cutting hard through their clothes, making them all tuck and hunch against it, closing their eyes. Dylan cried loudly until a long barrage of thunder drowned him out.

You did this to them, Dell thought. You led them up here to die.

He clenched his teeth so hard he thought they might crack.

The wind lifted for a moment as the storm drew a breath, and he looked around once more. All gone. The horses drowned in their stalls, his fine Dall sheep either swept away on the Texas tide or drowned in their pens. The house. Arlene's photo albums. Troy's flag. All gone.

The thought of Troy McCall's flag – handed to Arlene two years ago by a somber Army colonel and later placed reverently over the mantle, now just another piece of floating debris – caused an ache in his chest. Nineteen-years-old and killed by a roadside bomb on some obscure, numbered highway outside Baghdad, dead in a war that began when he was still Ricky's age. It was Dell who had given his approval to the enlistment, caught up in his eldest son's excitement over adventure and patriotism and career possibilities, the chance to be more than a sheep rancher.

He looked at his family shivering in the storm. Troy wouldn't be the last McCall child to be led to destruction by their father.

Dell looked to the barn again, remembering a night shortly after they'd gotten the news, him alone in the dark, surrounded by the warm sweetness of hay and horses, alone with his shotgun

31

resting across his knees. He had been beyond crying, his body exhausted and drained, eyes distant and raw, a single shell in the chamber. It was this fine woman in front of him who came along in the dark, taking the shotgun and holding him, and he'd discovered he did have more tears, the two of them crying together. She had saved his life.

And as repayment for that gift, he had now sentenced her to death.

"Daddy?"

Dell squeezed his eyes shut, his fists tight and shaking.

"Daddy, look."

He opened his eyes to see Ricky pointing to the sheep shed, and Dell wiped away tears and rain as he saw what had caught his son's attention. An animal was scrambling out of the floodwaters, nails scratching and slipping as it clawed furiously up the corrugated tin slope, finally gaining purchase and moving on unsteady legs to the peak. It was a coyote, a female he had seen before, recognized by her drooping left ear. She gave herself a shake from tail to head, then stood there shivering, looking down at the brown sea churning all about the shed.

"She's alone," said Ricky, who remembered her too, and now they were all looking. "Where's her pups?"

Dell and Ricky had been out riding a few weeks ago, and saw her fifty yards off, loping across the grasslands, three little pups trotting behind her in a line. As a rule, sheep ranchers will shoot a coyote on sight, and Dell was no exception, in fact he'd had his rifle with him that day. He could have easily made the shot, but allowed her to go on her way, not sure why. Not because of Ricky, who was old enough to know what a plague coyotes were to a sheep herd, and not because of her pups. Every rancher Dell knew would have dropped each one in turn without hesitation, getting them before they got bigger and could do real damage. But he didn't, hadn't even wanted to. He had no explanation for his son or himself, other than a private suspicion it probably had something to do with Troy, but it was confused and they were thoughts he had no desire to explore.

Now, as he looked at her, scrawny and shaking and alone on a rooftop with no understanding of what was happening to her, he was glad he hadn't done it. "Her pups are gone," he told his son. "She couldn't save them."

Arlene reached back and squeezed her husband's knee. It was small comfort.

For a while no one said anything, just watched the animal pace from one end of the roof to the other, turning her head from side to side, tail tucked. Finally it was Ricky who asked the question.

"Are we going to get rescued, Daddy?" Behind him, Bailey looked up to see the answer.

"Of course we are." He had to raise his voice so they could hear him over the wind, and doing that allowed him to hide the way it cracked.

"Is a helicopter going to pick us up, like we saw them do on TV during Katrina?"

"They can't fly in this," Bailey said. "The wind's too strong." It was snapping her hair around her head and face as if she was being electrocuted.

Arlene shot her daughter a look. "They'll just have to use a boat, won't they, honey?" She gave her husband's leg another squeeze.

Dell said that yes, a boat would come for them. He couldn't see his wife's eyes, and that was just as well. They wouldn't have to watch each other lie.

Another rising surge of wind ended further conversation, and the McCall's tucked down as lightning flashed within the violent clouds, rain pelting them without relent while thunder rolled across the Texas sea. They were all shivering, the wind and rain turning cold. Only Dell kept his head up, looking at the coyote which had ceased pacing for the moment and stood midway along the rooftop, her pelt hanging in wet straggles. She winced at every crash of thunder, and though he couldn't hear her, Dell imagined she was whining as well. Wet and whining and hopeless.

He saw that the water was halfway up the shed's metal slope, and a glance down to the right showed him that the gutters of his house were gone, a good foot under now. The brown sea rolled against his roof, and a huge oak tumbled past, branches turning slowly as it floated quickly by. Some debris was tangled with it; a red cooler, a lawn chair, the bloated shape of an armadillo corpse, a telephone pole with a snarl of wire trailing behind, thumping briefly against the house before it was gone. Something swollen and gray with stiff legs sticking out of the water chased the debris, and Dell realized it was a dead mule.

Minutes later the white box of a delivery truck cruised past on the far side of the front yard tree, leaning at a sharp angle, and Dell recognized the logo of bright flowers on the side as Dawson's Orchids. Gonzales County was one of the biggest orchid suppliers in the U.S., and Dell knew the owner. The truck's cab was submerged, and with a chill he wondered if Lyle Dawson might not still be in the driver's seat, buckled in tight with his dead hands on the wheel.

While Dell watched Texas float by, the water climbed another foot up his roof.

Arlene was tugging at his pants leg to get his attention, and she half turned and moved her head close so the kids wouldn't hear her. "What are we going to do?"

Dell looked at her for a long moment. "We have to hang on as long as we can, and hope someone comes."

Her green eyes never left his. "No one's coming." It wasn't a question.

"Not in time to make a difference."

She turned back to face her children and said nothing more.

Dell silently cursed the storm, cursed himself, then just stared at the coyote. She was pacing again, looking and sniffing, back and forth, but nothing had changed except the water was closer. He wondered if she realized she was finished. He doubted she could grasp a concept like that, and didn't really expect her to start howling as if lamenting her fate. Animals didn't do that. He suspected she would go out with more dignity, anyway. She was lucky. She wouldn't have to stand there helplessly and watch the storm take her pups. The wind screamed at them then, the rain an endless lashing of needles, and they tried to become as small and tightly wrapped as they could. No one made a sound, not even little Dylan who just cowered and shook against his mother, and they waited. Waited for a salvation Dell knew wasn't coming.

The temperature dropped further and they were all shivering, the wind whipping their clothes and buffeting them, trying to push them off. Rain streamed off their bodies, down their cheeks, into their eyes and noses, and the volume of the torrent around them raised, more and more debris cracking off the edges of the roof. Out front, the branches of the big oak were whipping madly, and once in a while a larger limb would snap off with a sound like a gunshot, falling to be pulled away. Abruptly there was a great tearing noise, like a deck of giant cards being shuffled, and an entire section of shingles was ripped away, one after another in mere seconds, each spinning away into the sky.

Dell scanned the horizon as best he could. He had been through tornados, most Texans had, and twisters were famous for teaming up with hurricanes to add their own flavor of death and destruction. In this low light and masked by the constant shrieking, one could be upon them before they knew it. And there would simply be no way to hide from it.

He palmed the water off his face, rubbing it out of his eyes, squinting into the storm. The sheep shed was gone now, completely submerged and for all he knew, torn away completely. The coyote was gone as well, and no one had witnessed her passing.

The water had risen to within four feet of the peak and his family.

The crunching of another floating tree bumping and brushing against the house made him snap his head to the left, and for an instant he saw the oncoming arms of a hundred black branches, reaching to tear his family away, and then the tree rolled and swept past. Dell let out a gasp, realizing that it was only a matter of time before another tree arrived, floating higher, one that didn't turn away and brushed them off as casually as a man sweeping toast crumbs off a table.

A cracking of branches made him look right again, towards the front yard oak, and he saw his capsized pickup was still firmly wedged against it. Something else had floated up onto it and become stuck. Something wide and silver. Construction site material? It was hard to tell through the gray curtain of rain. After a full minute of staring he realized what it was.

Arlene saw it at the same moment and knew immediately. "My God, is that a boat?"

A wave rocked the silver object, turning it slightly and showing it to be the aluminum hull of a capsized fishing boat, the black prop of an outboard motor jutting out of the water. A red stripe ran down one side, and big, upside-down reflective letters read LEESVILLE FIRE RESCUE.

Arlene gripped her husband's knee in a fierce clench. "Ray Hammond."

Dell stared at the inverted hull. Ray Hammond was chief of the Leesville Volunteer Fire Department, and the crew leader of the town's swift water rescue team.

"What happened?"

Dell shook his head. "Nothing good." People's lives in small towns are hopelessly intertwined, everyone knowing everyone's business and all the little details of their lives. But that was also what made that sort of life so wonderful. Ray, his crew, their families were not strangers, and to the McCall's, were extensions of their own family. The sight of that empty boat shook them, because they both knew it hadn't floated off a trailer somewhere. Ray and his boys would have been aboard, out in the thick of the nightmare as soon as the water started rising, doing their duty and trying to help their friends in the community.

But Dell was thinking more about the boat.

He judged the distance, about twenty yards directly in front of the house, fast moving water in between. Water filled with debris that could sweep him away, providing the current didn't do it first. He could get a head start on it by going off the far end of the roof, buying maybe fifty feet of upstream advantage. Then swim like hell.

A tangle of barbed wire and fence posts rushed past.

Arlene was a better swimmer, no doubt about that, but she wouldn't have the strength to turn the boat upright once she made it. He wondered if he would. Dell was not an impressive swimmer, but twenty years of ranching had kept him fit. It would have to be enough. The current would fight against the boat, and despite his strength it might take it away before the job was finished. Even if he flipped it and held on, could he get the motor started? It was underwater now. Would it crank? He realized there was a time not so long ago when his biggest problem was lambing, a month-long season of labor and midwiving. He had always thought his life depended upon its success. Funny how quickly things changed.

Dell noticed Arlene was staring at him, and turned to look at her. She raised her voice over the wind. "How am I going to handle three children up here if you drown, Dell McCall?"

"What choice do I have?"

"You can stay alive. You can stay here with your family and hope for rescue."

He pointed at the boat. "Ray and his crew were the only rescue we were going to get. Bailey was right, they can't send up helicopters in this, and the water's going to be up here in two hours, probably less. No one is coming."

His wife pushed wet hair aside and stared at him, but it fell right back into her eyes. Then a gust hit them, making them both hunch, the force of it ripping away more shingles and creating whitecaps on the water's surface, howling across the rooftop, adding spray to the downpour.

He kissed her long and hard, then turned on the peak and started scooting towards the opposite end of the house. Bailey and Ricky saw him going, and cries of "Daddy!" came to him from behind, distant in the wind as he fixed his eyes on the edge ahead of him. Though it seemed longer, it took only minutes before he had crossed the rain-washed roof to where it dropped off at the end, turbulent waves spinning only a few feet below, smashing against the side of the house before flowing around it. He stared down at the turning current and wondered about whirlpools. Ahead, out over the stormy flats, all manner of debris was floating their direction, mostly trees, but also something big and flat and dark. He watched, entranced by the sight as it slowly rolled over in the water, wheels up.

A boxcar.

Dear Jesus. If that thing hit the house it would take it right out from under them.

He stood, one foot on either side of the peak, arms outstretched as he balanced against the wind, straightening slowly. A forceful gust drove him back into a crouch, but when it passed he straightened again. He didn't dare look back at his family, knowing that if he did he would lose his nerve and crawl back to them. He took several quick breaths and dove.

The sea welcomed him like an expectant killer.

The water was cold, faster than he had anticipated, and no sooner did his head break the surface that he slammed back against the wall of his house, instantly losing whatever distance the dive had given him. He heard a hollow, sucking gurgle and felt it carrying him to the corner, where it would pull him under and around, sending him speeding past his family in seconds.

Dell kicked out against the house and started swimming, pulling hard against the current, straight into it. The draft at the corner tore at him from behind, dragging, and he kicked to get away, to get distance from the suction before he tried turning towards the boat.

Rain and wind beat at his eyes, and he sputtered in the brown water. It was so damn strong, and he felt like he was swimming in place, going nowhere, like he was in one of those fancy motorized lap pools rich folks installed in their houses. Only here there was no switch to shut off the current. This was nothing like swimming in still Texas lakes or slow moving rivers. He tried to remember the lessons of his youth, swimming in the heavily chlorinated pool at the 'Y' in Brownsville. Face down, stroke, turn to the side and breathe, stroke, face down, stroke, breathe, kicking, kicking all the time, never stop kicking. Fight the urge to dog paddle.

He had moved only a few yards from the house, and still it sucked him back.

Dell began angling to get away from that deadly corner of the house, still into the current, stroke, stroke, kick, breathe. Something caught at his pants leg and tugged hard, a branch maybe, please, God, not more fencing, he would be like a fish in a net. The object pulled free. Stroke, stroke, kick, breathe, stroke *STROKE SWIM LIKE A MAN GODDAMIT!*

He lost track of where he was, didn't dare look. Had he already been carried past the house? Was he struggling towards nothing while his family watched him flailing away into the distance? Stroke, stroke, pulling harder, kick, kick, muscles burning, *oh my God why didn't I take off my boots?* Stupid! Kicking harder still, turning his face to the right for a breath. The long dark shape of the boxcar was closer, tall white letters down one rusting side reading SOO LINE. It was heading for the house. Couldn't think about that, swimming, pulling hard, hard, HARDER!

His shirt caught on debris, jerking him back, and Dell cried out, thrashing at the surface, coughing as water and leaves tried to choke him. He kicked and pulled, but it had him and his rhythm was broken. He curled up and reached back to free himself, knowing he was going to drown now, his head smacking against something, more debris.

He hoped Arlene and the kids wouldn't see him die.

Dell's knuckles rapped against metal and he tried to keep his head above the surface, shaking to clear his eyes. A big black shape was inches away.

A tire.

His shirt was hooked on the bumper of his submerged pickup.

Dell let out a thankful cry and ripped the shirt away, scrambling up onto the undercarriage, feeling the capsized vehicle bob under his feet. Ray Hammond's boat was close enough to touch, hung up on another tire. Branches cracked overhead, and he stood in a balanced, half-crouch in water up to his knees, seeing that the Chevy had lodged in the oak's main fork.

He didn't look for the boxcar, didn't want to. If it hit him, he'd never know it, and would prefer that to a miss, to seeing it tear his house and his family apart upon impact. He moved as quickly as the water allowed, examining the aluminum boat, seeing that the current had already put it on a helpful angle. He wouldn't have to flip it completely over, only about three-quarters.

And then what? Have the water rip it from his hands?

He moved along the truck's undercarriage to where the boat was actually sticking into the air a little, creating a dark, watery gap. Dell held his breath and ducked under, pulling himself up into the boat like a turtle in a shell. Darkness. No, not completely, a bit of gray light coming in through the gap. Flat seats now overhead, nothing else, all washed away. He felt the boat shift above him, the pickup shudder beneath him, and tensed.

It all held.

He pulled himself into the darkness towards the back, the space between the water and air narrowing. Dell had never been in Ray Hammond's boat before, but he had been in plenty similar. There, the center seat, more than just an aluminum plank across the hull, this one a storage box. Kneeling in the darkness, he felt for

39

the latches, found the one on the left, flipped it, cold hands slapping in the other direction. Found the second latch.

The lid spilled open, gear falling out as if from a ruptured piñata, dumping into the water. Dell's hands scrambled through it until they felt rope, a tightly rolled coil. He quickly wound one end around his waist several times, knotting it tightly. Then he crawled on his knees back towards the light and tied the other end to the front bench seat. Had there been a flashlight in the box? Probably, the kind that floated. He would need it to examine the outboard motor. He started back to look.

Tucked inside the turtled boat, Dell didn't see it coming.

A forest green dumpster, half filled with water, heavy and floating like a boat itself, washed into the rear of the Chevy, striking hard and dislodging it from the tree. The pickup slid away from the oak as the dumpster turned over, hitting the rear of the rescue boat before it sank, knocking it loose from the tire which had held it in place. The current caught the aluminum hull and sent it spinning away. Dell, trapped inside the capsized hull, was pulled with it, his head and shoulder slamming into a metal wall, casting him into deep water as the boat moved off, the rope dragging him along the bottom behind it.

Arlene and the kids screamed as they saw the dumpster break both the boat and the pickup free, and she shouted her husband's name into the storm as the current carried the aluminum shape away from the house and out of sight. Dell's head didn't appear.

Two feet below the family, the surface washed against the shingles as the hurricane sent waves of spray over their huddled figures. Arlene heard a metallic groan and looked over her shoulder to see the boxcar moving in the current, a rusting behemoth turning slowly on the surface, creaking as it moved past the house with only feet to spare. It rotated and then drove into the barn like a great torpedo, and in a splintering crash the structure was torn apart, the roof collapsing, a whole piece floating for a moment, then breaking up and slipping under. Hay and shattered planks vanished quickly downstream.

Arlene stared into the storm, the shock of seeing the barn torn away quickly replaced with grief for her husband, for the children she would not be able to save, for the life they would never know. Her tears were lost in the rain.

An hour passed, and the water was now touching their feet, the spray a relentless whipping, and all three kids were crying now. Arlene reached out to pull them to herself, and got them started with a prayer. Above them, around them, the storm closed in to finish the killing. In the end, the wind became the sound of a ripping chainsaw.

But it wasn't the wind.

And it wasn't a chainsaw.

Dell McCall's arms and back were a rage of pain from hauling himself underwater along the rope, pulling himself upwards to break the surface and gasp at wet air, clinging desperately to the slick aluminum. Lyle Dawson's orchid truck had gotten stuck against a line of oaks a mile and a half down from the ranch, and when the rescue boat slammed into its cab – the driver's seat was empty – it nearly flipped over. Half drowned, Dell crawled onto the cab's roof and then tore some shoulder muscle flipping the boat the rest of the way over, fighting against the pull of the water to hold onto it long enough to climb in. Ray Hammond had been a man who cared for his equipment, and despite being submerged, the big Mercury outboard fired on the first pull.

Now, that same Mercury growled against the shriek of the storm as Dell guided the craft against the current, one arm locked onto the throttle tiller. He stared with grim purpose at the line of little shapes still clinging to the roof of his house, and when Arlene saw him coming for them and raised one hand, Dell shot his own triumphant fist into the heavens.

The hell with Texas, he thought. We'll raise sheep in Montana.

REJECTION

If you looked at me, the first word which would come to mind is *cancer,* or more specifically *chemo..* I wouldn't blame you for making the assumption. With my taut skin, pronounced neck cords and arms like jointed pool cues, the next word would be *skeleton.* Hard to believe when this all started I tipped the scales at three-thirty and smoked like a fiend. Not cancer. Heart disease, the kind which requires either a new pump, or a pine box.

They found me a new pump.

I didn't ask where it came from until later.

I have a dim memory of lying in the recovery bed and seeing my surgeon in the room, speaking quietly with a man in an Air Force uniform and lots of chest ribbons. Strange, this was a civilian hospital and I'd never been in the Air Force. Some of my family had, but just as many had worked at McDonalds, and there wasn't a fry kid talking to the doc. Later they told me it was a hallucination brought on by the painkillers.

The transplant saved my life, and for a year I felt great. I ate well, exercised, and got fit. My doc – my regular physician, not the surgeon – was encouraging and pleased with my progress. His enthusiasm drained when I started getting sick again.

Rapid weight loss, nausea, hair falling out…it had to be the Big 'C.' The doc sent me to an oncologist, who pronounced me cancer-free. Fearing it was the new pump, he next paired me with a cardiologist, who declared the heart was strong and healthy. More testing followed; needles and stress tests and sonograms and physicals. No explanation, but I continued to deteriorate. Now there was joint and nerve pain, migraines, trouble with my equilibrium. No, not a tumor either. They checked for that.

"You've stopped your toxic behavior," my doc said. "I think it's the new heart."

"Is my body rejecting it, trying to kill it?"

He took a long time to answer. "It's the other way around. It looks like the *heart* sees the *body* as the intrusion."

That took some digesting. He sent me for more tests, and when I came back three days later he reversed his diagnosis. "Forget what I said about the heart, there's nothing wrong with it. You're experiencing some kind of cellular problem, or possibly a virus. We'll sort it out."

I didn't like the way he couldn't meet my eyes. I also didn't like the dark blue sedan with government plates parked across the street when I left.

My body was becoming weaker, looking like a stranger in the mirror, nearly hairless now with skin turning a corpse shade of gray. I went back to the surgeon for answers.

"Where did the heart come from?"

"I'm sorry, but health information confidentiality…"

"Doctor, please. Where?"

He must have felt my desperation, because he looked around his office before whispering, "Roswell, New Mexico." He wouldn't say more, and asked me to leave.

That evening, however, he called my house and apologized, said he wanted to talk, and asked me to come see him in the morning. When I got to his office there was a new receptionist, a young man with a military-style haircut who announced that the doctor had left on an extended vacation, and didn't ask if I wanted to see someone else. In the lot, a blue sedan with two men in it was parked two rows behind my car.

I haven't left the house in three weeks now. I weigh eighty-nine pounds, can barely make it to the bathroom without screaming, and the air feels thick and hard to breathe. When I dare to look in the mirror I see my head has enlarged, along with my

43

light-sensitive eyes. I don't dare look out the window, because I know they're watching, waiting to see what happens next.

So am I.

MUSE

She comes to me through shaded corridors
long legged and sleek
red satin sliding over her curves
I wait with pen suspended, a single drop of ink
falling to the page
black in the candlelight
Her fragrance touches the stillness, and I tremble
longing to feel her press against me
crimson lips at my ear
breathing darkness
My name whispered from the hall
and as the click of her footfalls approach I wonder
high heels
or hooves

AVOIDING MIRANDA

Excited shouts and the laughter of children bounced off the wall of the elementary school like a ball, rebounding onto the playground. Fourth and fifth graders staked their claims to swings and monkey bars and hopscotch grids, stormed colorful, half-buried concrete pipes and sat in small clusters playing games. Though they kept to their little groups, they remained a whole which belonged, and Emily remained on the outside.

She sat on the edge of a brick planter, hydrangea at her back, her body tensed as if to run, watching the children she wanted so badly to join, and searching everywhere else for the reason she couldn't. An observer might have said she looked haunted. Emily would have chosen the word hunted.

Miranda was out there, probably watching her right now.

Emily chewed at her thumbnail, a habit she'd picked up recently and one which her mother pronounced "nasty." Sometimes she gnawed her nails to the quick, making them bleed. She didn't notice anymore. Her eyes settled on three girls sitting in the shade of a maple, talking and giggling. Brittney, Shay and Addison – the Power Pack. She was supposed to be one of them, would have been, but now didn't even dare approach them for fear of their taunting, disgust and contempt. And not just from them, from all her classmates. It would be a while before the word *ostracized* appeared in the vocabulary lessons.

And it was all Miranda's fault.

The double doors banged open and Emily jumped, letting out a high squeak and snapping her head right. Miss Colon, the pretty blonde teacher in charge of the fourth grade, emerged with a bag of red balls over her shoulder and glanced briefly at Emily. She didn't smile, and looked away quickly without a word, heading onto the playground. Even the teachers didn't want to have anything to do with her.

"That's because I have a parasite," Emily said, watching the young woman trot away. Parasite was a word she knew.

"A pair of what?" said Miranda, sitting down on the edge of the planter to Emily's left.

Emily squeaked again, recoiling and sliding away, making a face. *God* she smelled so *bad!* "Parasite," she repeated through clenched teeth. "What you are. Something nasty that latches onto something good and sucks all the good stuff out of it."

Miranda's heavy brow creased as she tried to process the word, her normally bulging eyes – Emily didn't know the word *thyroid* yet – nearly closing with the effort. Then she opened them. "That's a bad thing." She stared hard at Emily for a moment, and then her face split with a broad, bucktoothed grin. "Aw, you're teasing me, Em." She spit a little when she said 'teasing.' "That's just another word for friend."

"You're *not* my friend," Emily hissed. "Because of you I don't *have* any friends. Because you leeched onto me and you're a troll and why don't you just go away and leave me alone!" She wrinkled her nose at the girl's limp, oily hair and Salvation Army clothes and slumped shoulders. "You're so *ugly!*" Emily said, on her feet now. She brushed at her sequined Ed Hardy top and Banana Republic jeans as if whatever horrid something Miranda had might be airborne, and might have settled on her.

Miranda just looked at her and wiggled a finger up her nose.

Emily's face lit with rage. "I hate you!" she screamed, pointing at this *thing* that insisted on talking to her and being around her every day, every minute, who had turned her into a social leper. "I wish you would just die!"

47

Some of the kids on the playground stopped to stare, including the Power Pack, who immediately began whispering and giggling. Emily flushed and her eyes welled, and she ran from Miranda, crashing through the school doors to find someplace to hide.

At 1:15, Miss Crane's fifth grade class was half way through their social studies section, a week-long module on the first fifteen presidents. Emily, seated in the back left corner, was listening and filling in information on a worksheet as she followed along in her textbook. She liked social studies. Sometimes she wished she lived in one of those long-ago times. Any time other than this one.

"Emily," Miranda whispered.

She ignored it.

A poke in the shoulder. "Em. Emily." Poke, poke. "Em."

"Stop it."

Miranda, big for her age and overweight – the biggest kid at P. Beckham Elementary by far – used an adult-sized desk. For reasons both unfair and incomprehensible, Miss Crane had placed the girl at the back, directly behind Emily. All day Emily had to listen to her stuffy nose and mouth breathing. When she had asked to be moved and explained why, Miss Crane told her she "wasn't going to put up with any nonsense," and sent her back to her desk. She hadn't asked again.

Another poke. "Emily. How many z's are in president?"

"Leave...me...alone," Emily whispered tightly.

Corbin Harding, a good-looking, dark haired boy sitting to her right, looked over and made a face. She didn't look up, just kept her head down and tried to pay attention to the lesson. In addition to being fat and ugly and smelly, Miranda was often disruptive in class, and Emily frequently took the heat for it, as if she was somehow encouraging the Beast in the Back. *Guilt by Association* was another phrase she hadn't learned yet, but she understood the concept well enough. What she didn't understand was why Miranda hadn't been put in one of the special classes. They had their own little trailers out on the edge of the parking lot. That's where she belonged, not here, hanging over Emily's shoulder and stinking up the air.

It just wasn't fair. Emily was pretty, she knew it, and popular with the other kids. The Power Pack had been sizing her up, checking to see if her clothes were cool enough, testing to be certain she listened to the right music – Bieber, of course – and knew all his lyrics, verifying that she knew the coolest phrases. Preparing to make her one of them. Emily did well in class, and even the teachers had all liked her. Then *she* butted in, this half-a-retard who could barely read and dressed like a hillbilly on a TV show. Miranda had decided they were friends, and that had been the end of everything. No Power Pack, no cute boys wanting to talk to her, no more teachers being nice to her. She was a pariah, a word which wouldn't appear until high school English.

And Emily couldn't get rid of her.

Miranda waited for her on her walk to school, insisting on following her. She came around at recess, and wanted to sit with her at lunch time, and even showed up on the weekends when Emily was playing in the neighborhood. The troll-girl with her cheap Wal-Mart shoes always found her and wanted to talk to her.

And that was the biggest problem of all.

Miranda was crazy.

The things she talked about...lighting little fires and melting doll faces with matches, and killing a cat she had lured into her back yard with a can of tuna. Emily wasn't sure that one was true at first, but the more crazy things Miranda said, the more she believed. The bigger girl said she heard people talking to her, people that weren't there. Lately, Miranda had been saying worse things, things that scared her and made her sick to her stomach and feel like she wanted to cry. And Emily had come to another realization.

Miranda wasn't just crazy.

Miranda was dangerous.

"Hey," she whispered, close to Emily's ear. "Brittney said if I took a knife and cut myself, peanut butter would come out. Is that true?"

Emily ignored her.

"I think if I cut Brittney's throat, Pez would come out. She eats enough of them. Do you think so?"

Emily struggled not to hear, to listen instead to Miss Crane.

The girl grunted "Pez," and chuckled.

Then there was a long silence, and Emily sighed, thinking she might get some relief, some distance from Miranda, a rare thing indeed. In order to keep away from her, she'd found herself running home from school each day, taking different routes, dodging through yards and peeking around fences like a soldier in a war movie. Sometimes it worked. And sometimes she felt a small measure of victory and felt good about being so clever, but usually she just felt tired, drained. Most people did not think children could feel stress, *real* stress. They were wrong.

Miranda leaned forward again, her breath hot and smelling like cheese crackers. "I took a knife from Mommy's kitchen."

Emily stopped writing, stopped listening to Miss Crane.

"The next time my baby brother Leo starts crying, I'm gonna push it into his tummy. I think he's full of spaghetti-o's."

Emily bolted to her feet, knocking her textbook to the floor, spinning to face the girl and clamping her hands to her ears. *"Shut-up-shut-up-shut-up!"*

"Miss *Green!*" the teacher yelled, slapping her lesson plan onto her desk and striding up the row. "You know we don't tolerate outbursts in class."

Emily was crying and started stomping her feet. "It's *her,* Miss Crane! She won't leave me alone!" She pointed at Miranda, who was staring down at her textbook as if she was innocent, one finger sneaking towards a nostril. "I hate you!" Emily screamed, wanting to slap her and pull her hair until she cried. Miss Crane snatched her by the upper arm and marched her through the class, and as she was pulled along Emily saw the shocked looks, the smiles, the whispering, the faces. A moment later she was alone in the hall with her teacher, who pressed her against a wall with both hands on her shoulders.

Miss Crane seemed out of breath and rattled, looking as upset as Emily felt. "Now you're going to stand here until I come get you, and you're going to calm yourself down." She straightened and took a deep breath, smoothing her hair back, her hands trembling just the slightest, then gave Emily a stern look before pushing back into the classroom.

Alone in the hall, Emily's crying soon stopped as she stared at the bulletin board on the far wall, bordered by green and blue twists of crepe paper with a blue background. A large school of multi-color construction paper fish covered it, and Emily saw the fish she had made, a neat, precise rendering of Nemo, complete with one fin smaller than the other.   Then her eyes fell on Miranda's, a giant, choppy red piranha with one bulging eye and a vast, open mouth filled with sharp teeth.   For the first time she noticed the positions of the fish, and her eyes widened.

Miranda's fish was moving in for the kill.

It was aiming for Nemo.

Class dismissed at 2:30, and by 2:33 Emily was into the straps of her Bieber backpack and headed briskly towards an exit, trying to stay ahead of the crush of children pouring into the hall.   She needed some lead time.

A hand caught hold of her pack, and Emily was jerked into a recessed doorway.

Miranda, nearly a foot taller and fifty pounds heavier, held her against the door with one hand pressed against her chest.   Her eyes were narrowed, and she kept licking her lips.

"You gonna tell on me?" she asked.   "You gonna tell what I said about my baby brother?"

Emily tried to speak, tried to say, no, she wouldn't tell, wanted to scream for a teacher to make the monster go away.   All she could do was shake her head violently.

Miranda seemed to think it over for a moment, then leaned in. "I think you're gonna tell."   She bit her bottom lip and chewed. "Can't let you tell.   Gonna have to make you be a quiet girl."

Emily screamed and kicked out, landing a blow on the bigger girl's shin, and Miranda howled, taking her hand off Emily.   She took the opening and darted past, into the hall, heading for the exit doors and the promise of sunlight in the windows, the safety of outside.   A moment later she was through and leaping down the steps, sprinting across the lawn, her backpack bouncing against her shoulders.

"Emily!" A bellow behind her, and then the thud of heavy feet pounding down the steps. Emily ran faster.

Taking the straight, direct route home was fastest but the bigger girl's longer legs would catch her out in the open.   Instead, she cut across Marshall Avenue and ran past a block of nicely kept homes, her pink Nikes slapping the sidewalk, then turned at the corner onto Douglas.   She zipped between a pair of parked cars, crossed to the other side and ran past more houses before cutting diagonally across a yard and sprinting up the side of a brick ranch. There were no fences, only a hedge across the very back and in seconds she had dropped to her knees and was scrambling under it. Her backpack snagged, and for a terrifying moment she was hung up, trapped, losing valuable seconds. Then she heaved, and with a tearing of nylon, was free.

Beyond was another yard with a turtle sandbox and a swing set, but thankfully no dog – she worried a little about dogs – and no one to yell at her for trespassing. Another run, this time under a rose trellis, and she was out on Palmer Street. Her street, only two blocks from home.

She was puffing hard, her heart at full gallop, and there were leaves in her hair. The hedge had cut a red stripe across one cheek, and though she felt the sting, she didn't care. Miranda would do far worse if she caught her.

And the pounding feet were close.

Emily didn't see the puddle until she was in it, a small brown pond at the corner where a clogged storm drain had backed up. Her right foot splashed into it, nearly to the knee, and she was slow to react. A slimy leaf shot out from under her sneaker and she went down, face first, arms pin-wheeling.

The splash was spectacular.

Sputtering, she fought to her knees, blinking brown water out of her eyes, and then Miranda smashed into her from behind, forcing her back down. She felt the girl's weight on her back, her hands in her hair, pushing her head under. She tried to scream, but only let out a burst of air and reflexively gasped, sucking in rain water that burned and made the world turn a quickly darkening red.

Someone leaned on a car horn, a long, blaring close by that scared Miranda off her victim. Emily felt the weight leave her back and she flailed for the surface, choking and pulling in ragged breathes as Miranda ran away. The smaller girl barely glanced at the old woman in the nearby car, the one who had saved her and who now just stared at her with a look of shocked horror. Emily staggered on the asphalt, dripping and daring a glance back, but Miranda had ducked away between houses. She limped the last block home as quickly as she could.

A few minutes later she banged through her front door and squeaked towards the kitchen, her shoulders hitching with a mixture of half sobs and relief. She didn't care that she left wet, brown footprints on the floor and the hallway runner, didn't care that she left a brown handprint on a wall. She had just escaped murder at the hands of a fifth grader. She was traumatized, her worst school day ever, and her mother would just have to understand.

"Mom?" she said as she entered the kitchen.

Emily Green, a single mom and a very worn-out thirty six, turned at the voice. She had a used-up look, her face long and lined, her eyes weary. Leo was riding her hip, his face covered in pasta sauce.

"For Christ's sake, Miranda, what have you been into?" She looked at her daughter, a heavy, hulking thing with a laundry list of imperfections, standing before her with arms limp at her sides and her mouth hanging open, wearing her usual dull expression. And now wet and muddy as well. "Did you track that through the house?"

Miranda said nothing.

Emily Green sighed as she took in the soggy, sack-like gray sweatshirt, the patched corduroys, the plain, yellow dollar store backpack with a big rip in it. All she could afford. She shook her head and looked away, putting Leo back in his high chair. "Go get cleaned up."

Emily stood in the doorway shocked, her designer clothes ruined and dripping. Get cleaned up? That was it? She had barely made it home alive, and this was her welcome? She turned and ran for her room, slamming the door behind her.

"Don't slam the door, Miranda," called her mother.

Emily shed her now-ruined Justin Bieber pack and walked into her closet, closing the door behind her and moving to the back, pressing against the wall, kicking a doll with a melted face out of the way. Sitting in complete darkness, she started chewing her thumbnail. Life was so unfair.

A match flared, white and intense at first, then warm and flickering. "Leo's gonna start crying soon," Miranda said. "Wanna see my steak knife?"

Emily began to scream.

LYME DISEASE

It got out.

This single thought kept repeating itself as Joanna Bishop stood in a room of frightened people, everyone seeming to be moving and yet no one able to take their eyes off the big, wall-mounted screens. And the fact that it had gotten out – as catastrophic as that was - wasn't the worst part. What it was doing was the real horror.

On screen, live images shot from news choppers over Southern Connecticut, and a few attempts at ground coverage that didn't last very long, brought home a central message. Groton Research Facility E-11 had become a monster factory.

A screen on the left showed a bumpy image shot from a fast-moving car, the driver trying to negotiate a street in New London lined with businesses. The reporter's narration came from off screen, and in the excitement of the moment whatever professional broadcasting skills he had learned no longer applied.

"...left turn, left, left! Brian, as you can see the destruction is widespread, and it looks like most people have evacuated. We're not seeing anyone on the streets, though there were some small groups fleeing the area a few minutes ago. At this point we don't even see police or other emergency services. There are fires…"

The jumpy video showed an overturned bread truck burning in an intersection, a dozen motionless bodies scattered around it on the pavement. The vehicle swerved to avoid running over one of them, and bounced over a curb.

"...Ow! Shit! Okay Steve, head up this way. I thought I saw lights from a squad car. Brian, it looks like they've already moved through this area, so we're heading east, into a more residential area. We're going to try to find someone in command, though around here it seems -"

A massive black shape with too many legs leaped from behind an abandoned bus, slamming head on into the news vehicle, starring the glass. There was a crunching of metal and the view tipped upside down as the car flipped over. The camera was still pointing forward, showing blood on the windshield, the driver slumped over with his head and neck flopped at an obscene angle. The view jerked as the camera was struck, rolling to show a cockeyed shot of a shattered window, then a man started screaming off screen, a bloody hand appeared, clawing for a grip as it was dragged away, and a moment later the video was lost to a blue screen.

Connecticut 12 cut back to its studio. Brian, the anchor, looked pale and mumbled something about technical difficulties.

Joanna looked at another screen, this one with the words RECORDED EARLIER scrolling across the bottom. A news chopper was sweeping low over I-95 outside Groton, above six lanes of divided highway packed with refugee traffic. A tide of black shapes spilled over the southernmost guardrail and poured across the slow-moving lanes. None of the cars were moving fast enough for dramatic wrecks, but collisions quickly piled up, and it all came to a halt. Helpless.

The larvae were the size of footballs.

The nymphs were as big as picnic tables.

Adults were the same size as the cars they ran at, struck and flipped over. All were hard-shelled and black, eight-legged with barbed claws. Some of the smaller ones were crushed by low speed crashes, but after being hit the larger ones simply flipped from their backs to their legs and attacked the cars, claws reaching through open windows, pincers ripping open car doors to get at the occupants. Hunting for blood meals.

"Lt. Jeffries," Joanna called, not looking away from the screen, "temperature reading?"

A man behind her responded at once. "The complex is reading a constant forty-one degrees, Colonel."

"Complex status?" This question was directed to the man standing beside her, a major with dark good looks and an impeccable uniform.

"We're on complete lockdown, Colonel."

"The lab?"

"On lockdown as well."

"Keep an eye on the temperature, Spencer. I don't want it above forty-two." It was an order she had repeated several times already, but the major affirmed it as if it was the first time, and Joanna looked around at the people in the bunker's command center. Most wore sweaters or jackets, and most wore gloves, except for those working keyboards, who had to stop and shake their hands every so often to keep the blood moving. Breath puffed in the air like little white ghosts, but no one complained about the cold. They had all been briefed on what happened at anything warmer than forty-five degrees.

Major Peck moved off to check on an officer, and Joanna took a seat at an unused workstation, her iPad in her lap. She ran her fingertips over the leather cover, tracing the letters stamped into it, smiling; *Bishop, Joanna C. Lt. Col. U.S. Army.* Olivia had given it to her last year, a gift to celebrate her promotion to light colonel. Olivia, her tough-minded sister who had survived both a divorce and breast cancer. She would have made an outstanding officer. Joanna wondered if Delaware was far enough away to keep her sister safe. And for how long?

She opened the iPad and brought up the facility app, tapping in a top-clearance passcode, then tapping her way through several menus until she brought up real-time schematics. The first was a satellite shot of the exterior. E-11 was a mostly underground complex at the edge of the Groton Boat Yards, having once been part of the naval facility but now taken over by the U.S. Army exclusively for Project Blackleg.

When one thought of secret, underground military research facilities, places like the Utah and Nevada deserts came to mind. Not coastal, heavily-populated Connecticut. It was both coincidental and ironic that this research should have been carried out so close to the town of Lyme, the original discovery point for the disease back in 1975. It *should* have been Nevada, she thought, as far away from people as possible. Someplace you could quickly nuke if something went wrong.

Her finger moved the screen around. A project like this should have never been.

She traced the perimeter fence and double tapped at each guard post, confirming that all the MPs had been pulled back into the safety of the bunker. She next scrolled through the floor-plans of the above ground structures, looking for the heat signatures which would indicate people who had missed the evacuation to the sub-levels. There was no sign of life. No human life, anyway. Her fingertips slipped and tapped through all three subterranean levels, no longer looking for heat sources (there were plenty of those) but checking to see that the Firebreaks were secure. These were triple-thick steel blast doors which, during lockdown, compartmentalized the complex much like watertight doors on a ship. As Major Peck had indicated, E-11 was secure.

She snorted.

Not secure enough, clearly. Not tight enough to keep L-2207 from escaping. And the little bastard was not only blood and fluid-borne as intended, but had also figured out a way to become airborne. That had *never* been intended. Nor had its side effects.

"Colonel?"

Joanna looked over her shoulder at Master Sergeant Jackson standing in a doorway, one of her communication people.

"Ma'am, ten minute warning for your call."

"Inform Major Peck, please."

"He's already in the conference room, Colonel."

Joanna nodded. "Carry on." She switched apps and pulled up data she would need for her call with the Pentagon. They had access to the same information, but she would be expected to give the brief. Data and an assortment of close-up color photographs appeared on screen. The images were disturbing.

Project Blackleg's objective had been the testing of accelerated biological processes, with the primary subject being *Ixodes Scapularis*, the North American Blacklegged Tick, selected for its durability and capacity to carry and transmit ten known diseases. The introduction of radical growth hormones showed early progress, and the scientific minds at the Pentagon quickly saw the potential for weaponization turn to reality with the development of Batch L-2207. Simply put, the goal had been to breed large specimens which could be infected with any number of nasty diseases, then release them in enemy territory or population and let them spread death. No exposure of American troops, no cruise missiles or carriers, and very, very cost effective. Technically, the project was a violation of international law and a breach of half a dozen treaties the U.S. had signed or even sponsored. And it was also just like many other nasty, top secret weapons programs her country developed. Although there was no immediate need and certainly no plans to use it, the generals and the White House liked to have options. Just in case.

So they had done as asked, and succeeded. And for whatever it was worth, not a single specimen had escaped the complex. In fact they had all been terminated in their breeding chambers the moment everything went wrong. None had gotten out.

It was L-2207 that snuck past her multi-layer security program.

Joanna closed her iPad and made her way to the conference room, finding Major Peck on a phone. He glanced at her, said "yes, sir," and hung up.

"What was that?"

"Just verifying the link." He pointed to the big screen on one wall. "It's a video conference."

Joanna didn't like the way he had trouble meeting her eyes.

"Is Dr. DeVries joining the call?"

"Not this time." Joanna took her seat at the head of the conference table. She and Peck were the only ones in the room.

"Don't you think he should be?"

"If they wanted him on the call, they would have asked for him. Besides, I have all his data."

"Still, Joanna…"

She looked at him. "That's enough, Major."

Spencer Peck held his commander's gaze a moment longer than was polite, then shuffled through his own files. He was a West Point graduate the same as her, they had both been to the War College, but of the two of them, he was the only one with combat experience. A tour in Afghanistan followed by another in Iraq should have put those silver oak clusters on his shoulder boards, not hers.

The wall screen flickered and the message STAND BY came on. Joanna was reminded of the words RECORDED EARLIER and felt a chill. She wished she had taken the time to get some Advil before the call. She had a headache that wouldn't quit.

A moment later the screen changed to a conference room similar to Joanna's, though containing more people and a lot more brass. Colonel Ferry, her immediate boss was there, and he quickly made introductions at the Pentagon end. It was an assortment of senior Navy and Army officers, several civilians and a handful of scientific types. General Laurents thanked Ferry brusquely and took over, pre-empting any further pleasantries.

"Lt. Colonel Bishop, we are three days into the outbreak, and I want to be perfectly clear on what you role is at this point. Your mission is now simply to keep the facility, and specifically the lab, on lockdown until Dr. DeVries can reverse this. Are we clear?"

"Yes, general."

"And where is Dr. DeVries? I expected he would be at this meeting."

Joanna caught Peck's smug look out of the corner of her eye. "Dr. DeVries was not requested, and I made the call that his time would be better spent in the lab working."

There was come conversation at the Pentagon table that she couldn't catch.

"And you're absolutely certain the lab has not been compromised?"

Joanna nodded. "One-hundred-percent, general. The lab is secure." She told the lie with a straight face.

"I want DeVries on the next call, Bishop. Be sure he's linked in."

"Yes sir."

And for the next two hours that was the last input Joanna had, the fact that she was not giving the briefing putting a fine point on any question about her career. Men and women at the Washington end took turns providing their own updates. L-2207 had gone aerosol, escaping through an unsecured ventilation duct (Joanna's responsibility, a fact reinforced by the way Colonel Ferry looked down at the table and how General Laurents shot a quick but hard glance towards the camera), making its first stop at the VA hospital adjacent to the Groton facility. The bug (and wasn't that an ironic term for it?) had unanticipated side effects which quickly had their way with the 3,700 patients and staff. It wasn't a simple transmission of fatal disease, as L-2207 promised, but a different class of infection. Within twenty-four hours the growth acceleration nature of the formula caused a complete, physiological change within its victims.

Those car-sized ticks scrambling over the expressway had once been human.

Infected females quickly mated and began laying eggs at thirty-six hours, around three thousand eggs each, and at forty-eight hours they were hatching. Newly hatched larva females reached maturity twelve hours later, mated and quickly produced their own eggs. It didn't take a mathematician to see how rapidly the crisis was exploding. All that was needed for the ticks to continue populating was a single blood meal, and the population of Southern Connecticut was providing plenty of those.

An Army Colonel read off civilian casualty figures to date.

Another detailed the units mobilized to combat the infestation.

A Navy officer gave a detailed account of what had happened to the submarine facility near Joanna's location. It was grim, and only a single sub had made it to sea. Whether it had been contaminated and the crew exposed remained to be seen, but Navy aircraft were tracking its slow movement off the East Coast, ready to drop a torpedo on it and send it to the bottom if it turned out the crew had been infected.

A female scientist confirmed data Joanna had on her iPad. Not only could a person be infected by the airborne L-2207, but human victims bitten and not killed outright by a tick attack were infected by a mutated form of the bacteria Borrelia. Both exposures amounted to the same thing. The victim quickly transformed into the giant, adult arachnids. It was a condition someone had casually referred to as "having *Blackleg*," and the nickname stuck. Although the creatures were driven to kill for a blood meal, believed to be instinctual, they then broke the rules of the natural world and kept killing and feeding until too bloated to move. On the surface, an observer might think this would be beneficial, making them easier to kill, but there were so many, moving and multiplying so very fast, that it didn't matter. An Air Force general was discussing carpet bombing and napalm along the I-95 corridor, which sparked some lively debate. Joanna barely heard him, distracted and staring at Spencer Peck, not knowing why. Her headache hadn't abated.

The final briefing came from an Admiral working with the Center for Disease Control. He reported the outbreak had already spread into Rhode Island, north across Connecticut to the Massachusetts border, and west to within five miles of the New York state line. Somewhere along the way his monotone voice stated that the ticks would go dormant in temperatures under forty-five degrees.

Too bad it's the middle of July, thought Joanna, forcing her thoughts - her strange and somehow sexually-related thoughts – away from her executive officer and back to the present. General Laurents took the floor again, looking into the camera.

"Joanna, no bullshit now. Does Dr. DeVries truly believe he can reverse this? Come up with an antibiotic vaccine?"

Joanna straightened in her chair. "Yes he does, General."

"Good. We'll have another call in six hours. I want him to tell me that himself."

The screen went black.

Joanna left the conference room without a word to Peck, and locked herself in her office. As she searched her desk for Advil, she called the lab. A young male tech with red eyes and in need of a shave appeared on the video link, then went to find the doctor. A few minutes later DeVries came on, looking more worn down than his assistant.

"You told them *what?*"

"I had to, Doctor. You said there was a chance."

"I said there was a *slim* chance, and that I'd need the help of another facility, and it would take months to accomplish, if it can even be done at all."

"Still, it's a chance, isn't it?"

DeVries peered closely at the screen, softening his tone. "You're exhausted, Joanna, and not thinking clearly. You should have told them the truth."

"And then they would have insisted you be on the conference link, full video."

DeVries looked down and rubbed absently at a large pair of side-by-side boils on his upper lip. The fingers he rubbed with didn't look right.

"If I told them, they'd nerve gas us without a second thought in some half-assed attempt at containment. I'm trying to buy us time to figure a way through this." The doctor said nothing, and she noticed he very purposefully kept his other hand below the table, out of sight. "How are you feeling?"

DeVries shook his head. "I'm fine."

"Good. Keep working, Doctor." Joanna disconnected.

There was minimal staff on duty for the overnight shift, only a couple of men at the consoles monitoring the complex's support systems. The screens on the wall were running new images, each more horrific than the one before, but someone had muted the volumes. Joanna saw a hysterical Hispanic woman being restrained by her husband on some suburban street, the camera soaking up her grief, then panning over to an overturned twin stroller. It was empty. Joanna was glad she couldn't hear the woman wailing.

"You never had any kids, Colonel?" Major Peck said quietly. She hadn't noticed him walk up beside her.

"No. I put my career first. You?"

"I always figured there would be time later. Any regrets?"

She stared at the image of the empty stroller. "Sometimes." Her headache was back, her joints had begun to ache, and now her lower back was throbbing near her kidneys. She closed her eyes. Peck smelled good. "New cologne, major?"

"Not wearing any."

They looked at each other, his desire apparent, and her attraction to him both inappropriate and undeniable. She took his hand and led him from the command center.

"We'll miss the Pentagon call," he said, but didn't resist her pull.

The sex was strange and savage, a wild tangling not without pain. Joanna's headache pounded through it even as he pounded into her, and the moment he climaxed she shoved him off, staggering to her feet, dizzy and holding onto a wall, her vision blurry. He reached for her but she slapped his hands away. "Get the fuck out," she said, pushing him out of her quarters.

It was a half hour before she returned to the command center, her uniform sloppy and unbuttoned, and now the left side of her face was paralyzed with Bell's Palsy, a classic symptom of Lyme. She looked like a stroke victim. There was no one here, the watch stations unmanned, and she looked towards the glass wall of the conference room. Major Peck, wearing only his skivvies, was standing at the table talking on the phone, rubbing briskly at his upper lip. It was warm in here, and a glance at a monitor showed Joanna that the complex's air conditioning had been shut down and the heaters turned up. A digital readout indicated a general temperature of seventy-eight degrees. She returned to her quarters, passing numerous closed doors, the thumping and growling of rough sex coming from behind them.

Major Peck could barely stand as he listened to the general on the other end of the phone. His heart was thudding and his respiration was ragged. A pair of hairy growths had erupted from his top lip – his knowledge of Project Blackleg's primary research subject informed him they were referred to as palps – and it was difficult to speak. Plus they itched like hell.

"Yes, general, that's correct. Completely unfit for command. Yes sir, a risk to project security." A twitch was developing in his right eye, and his body seemed to hurt everywhere at once. "No sir. No, I won't. Yes sir, right away."

He looked up to see Joanna Bishop standing in the doorway to the conference room, and his eyes widened at the sight of her. It wasn't the 9mm service pistol she held that froze him in place.

"Who are you talking to…Spencer?" Joanna wasn't feeling like herself, pain rippling through her body and her brain feeling like it was misfiring, clear thoughts replaced by dark flashes that were more irresistible feelings and impulses than anything else..

The major slurred when he spoke, still holding the phone. "I'm supposed to…relieve you…of command."

Joanna made a clicking sound deep in her throat, then managed the word, "Traitor." She shot Peck three times in the face. Stumbling back into the command center, she dropped the pistol, grunting as she started tearing off her uniform. It was so damned tight! She tried to sit at one of the terminals but her ass had grown too large for it, was still growing, and she kicked the swivel chair aside with one of the thick, black legs which had sprouted from her left hip.   Her left hand was twisting and expanding, becoming a claw, so she used her still-normal right hand to call up the lab.

Although the video link connected, no one appeared to take the call. In the background she could a constant clicking that sounded like bacon frying. Something big and black skittered past the lab camera.

Her rear and abdomen swelled, pushing chairs aside, whitish-gray and glistening, and she raised her eyes to one of the wall mounted screens. A news helicopter showed a black blanket of giant ticks swarming up the Empire State Building, trying to force their way through windows. Another screen displayed a ground level video shot from a moving military vehicle, the raucous bark of a machinegun close by, the image of a Manhattan street choked with overturned vehicles and corpses. The shot panned to show the marquis over Radio City Music Hall heavy with huge, clinging black shapes.

None of it made any sense to her.

A male tick the size of a Hyundai scuttled through the command center and disappeared through a pair of double doors. Joanna caught the scent of fresh air from that direction. Someone had opened an exterior door. She began moving in that direction, her final clear thought telling her the exit stairs were wide, and if she moved quickly she might get her swollen bulk up and through it before she was too big.

She had to get outside. She needed to find a place to lay her eggs.

TAILLIGHTS

It was four miles from Lee's Country Store to the cabin, two-lane blacktop twisting along the east side of Whitaker Lake. Patricia's headlights showed a rock face on the left, a narrow strip of trees to the right and the moonlit surface of the lake beyond. On the passenger seat sat three sacks of groceries. Her trip to the store had taken longer than expected, just enough supplies to tackle breakfast, and she was making it up now, her Mountaineer racing along the deserted road.

Patricia's window was down as she smoked, which she wasn't supposed to do with Gabby in the car, but as long as she kept it out the window she figured it would be okay. In the back her two-year-old sat buckled into her car seat, babbling and singing little songs to a plastic elephant.

The deer trotted onto the road from the trees ahead, stopped and stared at the headlights.

Patricia screamed, her cigarette falling into her lap, and stomped the brakes, yanking to the right. Tires smoked and the SUV shot off the road, headlights dancing off the trunks of pines, bouncing and rocketing down a short embankment, branches snapping at the sides.

She had quick images of wrapping around a tree, Gabby's car seat, Randy and the boys-

The Mountaineer plunged into Whitaker Lake, a wave washing over the hood and windshield, then cold water pouring through the open driver's window. *Oh God*, she thought, as the nose tipped sharply and started down, the lake quickly filling the front seat. *Gabby*. She lunged between the seats, but the belt snapped her back painfully. Patricia fumbled for the buckle as the water rose to her chest, couldn't find it.

Gabby was crying. "Mama!"

"Mommy's coming," she moaned, tugging, probing for the button. Her thumb depressed something and she was free, hauling herself up into the back seat as the SUV went vertical. She forced herself to think her way through the five point harness securing her daughter, got it open, and Gabby dropped into her arms with a splash. It was up to her chest now, and the cold water made Gabby shriek. She yanked the door handle.

Nothing.

She tore at it, pulling hard, but it wouldn't open.

The child locks were on.

"No!" Patricia pushed Gabby up and into the cargo area, then kicked and pulled herself up and in as well. A moment later the lake followed, cascading over the leather seat back. She tucked her screaming daughter under one arm and began pushing at the rear hatch, one hand groping along the surface for a release lever. She had never been back here, always opened the hatch remotely with her key fob, didn't even know if there was a handle.

There wasn't.

The lake rose to her chest again, and Gabby was crying in one ear, thrashing and kicking at the water. Patricia pounded a fist against the glass as the SUV sank. She could see the shore in the moonlight, saw a campfire and a pair of boys standing side by side at the water's edge. They didn't move.

"Help us, *pleeeease!*" She battered the glass as the water rose to her chin.

The Mountaineer went under with a gurgle, the red of its taillights shimmering briefly before being swallowed by the cold dark.

Dale and Chance stood close together, staring out at the calm surface. Their scoutmaster had just finished telling a ghost story, and they'd come out here to look. Five years ago, he'd said, a woman and her toddler, right here. "On quiet nights like this one, you can still see her taillights glowing at the bottom of the lake."

Chance looked at the dark water and shuddered. "Let's go back to the fire."

Dale nodded, and they headed back to join their friends. He looked at the water again. He didn't see any taillights.

But for a moment he thought he'd heard thumping.

WILDFIRE

It was a catastrophe being repeated up and down the West Coast, and it was quickly growing out of control. The destruction doubled every twenty-four hours, spreading outward from numerous zero-points, and the loss of human life was staggering. Only four weeks in and already Portland and San Diego had been lost, with Los Angeles wavering on the brink along with other cities.

Seattle was one of them.

Yet there remained lives to be saved, people trapped inside the urban centers, desperately needing relief and rescue. They needed heroes. They needed salvation from above.

"Tacoma, this is Bluetail. Drop was on-target, preparing for next run."

"Roger, Bluetail. Be advised, Rodeo King is inbound to your location."

Jake Fowler nodded and consulted the small clipboard strapped to his right thigh, holding a map of metropolitan and suburban Seattle, covered in pencil markings. "Tacoma, suggest that Rodeo King make his run up I-5 into downtown, heavy concentration. Tell him not to clip the Needle."

A chuckle in his headset. "Will pass it on, Bluetail."

The weather report called for scattered cloud cover and overnight temps dropping into the fifties as this part of the Pacific Northwest eased deeper into fall. Favorable flying weather, thought Jake, stretching the big aircraft north, away from the suburbs. Minutes later he banked left in a wide arc, cutting his speed and starting his descent. For a brief moment the two-hundred-foot wingspan of the *Sonoma Mars*, call-sign "Bluetail," was silhouetted against a three-quarter moon. The cold, lunar glow revealed her colors, a royal blue belly under white fuselage, and a matching tail. It also gave a glimpse of her nose art, a curvaceous, forties-era pin-up wearing blue, Daisy Duke short-shorts, the source of her nickname. Miss Bluetail would have made any WWII bomber vet grin with nostalgic appreciation.

Wearing a weathered leather jacket with U.S. Dept. of Forestry patches on the shoulders and a Giants cap turned backwards, Jake's eyes flicked across the dials; altimeter, airspeed, oil pressure, wind gauge, compass, back to altimeter... He was dropping smooth and steady, coming up rapidly on 1,000 feet, the deep hum of the engines filling the cockpit. Beyond the windscreen, forested hills in the night could be seen far to his right and left, and a flat, inky blackness waited ahead and below. A rosary swung gently from the overhead dials, the crucifix clattering against dog tags from a previous life hanging beside it.

"Tacoma Base, this is Rodeo King, I'm on station, commencing my run in zero-five minutes. Jake, you got me out there?"

Jake smiled at his friend's voice in his headset. "Roger that, Rodeo King. Negative visual, but I've got you on radar. Safe run, buddy. Don't fly into anything." Rodeo King was the McDonnell Douglas DC-10 flown by Martin Hodges, an old friend he hadn't seen often, at least before this crisis. Although they were both currently flying out of Tacoma, Martin was normally based in Spokane, while Jake's bird roosted in a slip at the old Alameda Naval Air Station in San Francisco, the base long closed but portions leased to the Forest Service.

He focused on his own work now as the Bluetail slid down through five-hundred feet, level and slowing, approaching the moonlit water of Puget Sound. He wasn't crashing, and he wasn't landing either.

Aerial firefighting was normally work carried out over wilderness areas, with the intention of stopping the threat before it could reach populated areas. Things were different now, and the targets *were* population centers, specifically major cities, with over a thousand flying tankers, water bombers, Catalinas and fire choppers running missions along the West Coast. If this tactic worked the way its planners believed (and Jake prayed it would), the heaviest concentrations of the disaster would be snuffed out, and the remaining, smaller hot spots quickly dispersed. Then the smoke jumpers – also with a new mission and new tools – would move in and take the fight to the ground.

"Here we go," he said aloud, for the benefit of the man seated to his right, his co-pilot Aidan. *Co-pilot*, he thought, grinning. A sixty-year-old who couldn't fly an aircraft and had a powerful fear of flying, Aidan looked uncomfortable in his green jumpsuit – a departure from his usual uniform – and sat without touching the controls, hands tightly clenched in his lap as he stared out the windscreen. This was their third run of the night, and the older man hadn't gotten used to it yet. So long as the fuel lasted, and with Puget Sound so convenient, they could make a run every fifteen minutes. Maybe by the end of the night he'd have found his stomach. It didn't matter much to the pilot, as long as the man did his job.

They passed through three-hundred, then two, then one. Jake hit a switch, and hydraulics opened the belly scoops in the curved hull. The JRM Mars, a sixty-year-old design commonly known as a flying boat (sometimes confused with the smaller Catalina until one got a look at the impressive size difference), roared towards the waters of the Sound at just under 100 knots. The mission of the Forest Service's Air Attack Squadron may have radically changed in the past month, but this part remained the same.

Martin Hodges's voice announced in Jake's ears that Rodeo King had delivered its payload, twelve-thousand gallons of water on target, and was RTB. Jake barely noticed, hands gripping the yoke as he brought the Bluetail down to kiss the water.

From a distance, the act appeared graceful, the aircraft skimming the surface gently and leaving a feathering white wake. The reality was more like riding a freight train over speed bumps. The Bluetail smacked the water, thudding along in a sudden, rumbling sawmill of noise as the airframe shook hard enough to rattle teeth, Jake fighting to keep her level, to keep from dipping a wing or dropping the nose, maintaining airspeed. The slightest mistake would mean an instantaneous, explosive tumble of metal and death, and he held his breath for an endless twenty-two seconds, the time it took for the scoops to draw seventy-two-hundred gallons of water into the tanks. A panel light turned green and Jake's breath exploded as he hauled back on the yoke, the scoops closing automatically, his bird now thirty tons heavier.

"C'mon, big girl," he growled, the muscles in his arms bulging as he hauled back while kicking his throttles full forward, pushing the four, eighteen-cylinder engines towards their 2,500 horsepower capacity. The props clawed at the air and the big plane rose slowly, passing a hundred feet. Jake saw the blacked-out shape of a Japanese car-carrier suddenly pass close beneath him, crewless and adrift in the Sound. He hadn't seen it on radar. Was the equipment malfunctioning, did he lose it in the surface clutter, or had he simply not been paying attention? No answer was a good one, and he shuddered, realizing that if he had started his loading run five seconds later, he would have flown broadside into the ghost ship.

Aidan had seen it too. He started praying out loud.

The Bluetail banked left in a gentle horseshoe, and Jake lined her nose up with his attack coordinates. Downtown Seattle approached in his windscreen, a far different looking target area than he had become accustomed to over the last seven years in Aerial Fire Attack. It was as blacked-out as the drifting car-carrier had been, not a single streetlight or highway stripe with white light coming one way and red going the other, no glittering skyscrapers, no field lights at the airport or even avoidance strobes atop the Space Needle. Darkness, lit only by the night sky. At his eleven o'clock, Jake could see the route Rodeo King had flown, sporadic pinpoints of fire in the streets and on rooftops to show where he had dropped.

Jake's coordinates took him slightly east of there, north of I-90 and to the right of downtown. Seattle University. He tipped the heavy bird down to five-hundred feet and eased back on the throttles, keeping her low and slow, then flexed his fingers on the yoke. He glanced at Aidan, who had his head down and his eyes closed, still praying loudly.

"Tacoma Base, this is Bluetail, I am commencing my attack run." His voice was the same, bored-sounding tone familiar to pilots the world over. It was that calm pilot's voice he'd used when the Bluetail nearly had to ditch in a Canadian forest fire the previous year, the same steady tone he used six years before that, when an Afghani insurgent with a Stinger had tried to put a missile up his tailpipe. His business voice.

Only this business was far deadlier and with much higher stakes than anything he had ever done before.

The aircraft roared in over the city as Jake made his final adjustments, and he glanced down out the left window as his right thumb snapped up to pause above a red button at the top of his yoke. Even without light he could see the swiftly passing streets below, every avenue overrun and filled with movement. A look out the front showed the sprawling campus before him as he descended to three hundred feet, and there he saw more of the same, rooftops and common areas alike, all swarming with figures. They might have been refugees, panicked survivors trying to escape the city.

Jake knew they weren't.

"Releasing," he said, triggering his payload.

Thirty tons of Puget Sound – what Father Aidan's prayers had since transformed to holy water – erupted from the belly of the Bluetail as it swept across the campus, covering a four acre area.

The vampire swarm took the full force of the hit.

They exploded in flames, hundreds of figures immolated in seconds, running and burning and collapsing in the night.

Free of its burden, the Bluetail seemed to leap into the air, and its powerful engines found altitude as Jake checked his dials and knee chart and began planning for another pick-up. Rodeo King could only make a single drop before returning to base, but Jake's flying boat could keep this up all night. As the plane rose, a wash of moonlight across the fuselage showed that the sexy pin-up painted on the nose was holding a stake and a mallet.

Jake looked at the priest in the right seat, Aidan and others like him the Forestry Service's newest recruits in a new war. He looked fatigued, drained. "We can make another half dozen runs on our fuel before we have to head back to base. Think you can handle it, Father?"

The older man took a deep breath, then nodded and smiled just a little.

"God willing."

TRAIL OF BREAD CRUMBS

They sat at the table across from each other, fraternal twins and physical opposites. He was robust, plump with rosy cheeks. She was sallow and drawn, cheeks and eyes sunken in her face, staring down at a doll in her lap. The boy was shoveling a third plate of meat into his mouth.

"You need to eat something," he said between mouthfuls.

She didn't reply.

He looked at her as he chewed on a rib. Four weeks of near-starvation had left his sister a skin-wrapped skeleton in a baggy gray dress. He shrugged. She would eat when she was ready.

After a few minutes, the girl spoke without looking up. "Father left us in the woods to die."

The boy chewed and swallowed, nodding. "Because of the famine. Mother told him we were too many mouths to feed." My goodness, he was hungry. Living on nothing but sweets had created a serious protein deficiency in him, as well as doing unpleasant things to his teeth. He looked around the delicious cottage as the old woman's raspy song played again in his head.

"Nibble, nibble, little mouse. Who's that nibbling at my house?"

He remembered the way she had pinched his cheek and said, "That will make for a nice bite." The boy went back to forking meat into his mouth.

"I hate them," his sister said, looking up. Her eyes were flat and dull. Gone was all trace of childhood, and her brother saw that although the old woman had failed to kill her, something inside his sister had died nonetheless. It made him sad.

"You were very brave," he said. "A hero. You saved me from the cage, saved our lives."

She looked at him without expression. "I don't feel bad about doing it."

The boy nodded again, his teeth crunching down hard on something. He picked it out of his mouth and examined the object. A button. Then he remembered the witch had been fully dressed when his sister pushed her into the oven. He flicked it away.

"Children!" called a voice from outside. "Children?"

The girl walked to a window and peered out, seeing the woodcutter making his way up the forest path, heading for the gingerbread house. "It's father," she said. "He's sorry for what he did, and came looking for us, just like you said he would."

The boy tossed a rib onto his plate and burped.

"It's mother's fault, too," she said, walking to the wood pile beside the oven and picking up a hatchet, then returning to stand beside the door. "I want to push *her* into an oven."

The boy sucked grease off his fingers and hopped down from his chair, bringing a butcher knife with him as he moved to flank the other side of the door. "She's quite skinny," he said, looking at the reflection of his eyes in the blade. "We'll have to fatten her up a bit."

Then he smiled. "But father first."

John L. Campbell

ZERO TOLERANCE

The Lincoln Navigator left Ashville behind as it chased the setting sun on Interstate 40. Twilight had come to western North Carolina, and Thomas Kirkland switched from his daytime running lights to full headlights.

Traffic was sparse along this section of highway, but still the Navigator stayed at a cruise-controlled sixty-four miles per hour. A big Freightliner with Piggly Wiggly emblazoned on the side rocketed past doing eighty plus, and once it moved out of sight the road was empty save for the big Lincoln.

Within the air conditioned comfort of the luxury SUV, Thomas tapped his fingers lightly on the steering wheel, keeping time with a Kenny Chesney song playing softly on a classic country station. Beside him, Bianca appeared engrossed in an old Nicholas Sparks novel, but he knew she was dividing her attention between the book and the back seat, listening to the bickering. Angela and Carl, sixteen and fourteen respectively, were debating the rightful ownership of a Spin magazine. Their Generation XII iTablets were drained and dead, and they were already bored with both the games and movies available for the rear seat video screens. Had to have something to argue about, Thomas thought. But they were smart enough to keep their voices low, knowing that if they *really* fought about it, one or both of their parents would get involved, and the magazine was likely to get tossed in a trash can at the next rest stop.

Thomas lifted his gaze to the rear view mirror and let it drift past his two oldest children to come to rest on Edwin, his nine-year-old. The boy was in the third row seat, nestled amid suitcases and propping his back against a duffel bag. Edwin had inherited his mother's love of reading, but not her taste. At the moment he was intently absorbing the contents of a thirty-one page pamphlet entitled *Summaries of Chinese Civil Defense Research Reports.* It was a booklet put out by the U.S. Office of Home Affairs, presumably so Americans could learn what the bogeymen on the other side of the world thought about preparedness, and apply some of those organizational skills to their own lives. Edwin had picked it up at the Georgia State Fair last week. Thomas shook his head, amazed for the umpteenth time that the boy was interested in – much less capable of understanding – such an obscure and no doubt abysmally dry topic. But then with two of his children running the emotional gauntlet of teenagerhood, he often felt he was long past trying to understand his kids.

The headlights reflected off a green highway sign, informing Thomas that he would soon be making the turn onto Route 215. Thank God, he thought, this had been a hell of a drive. They had a late start yesterday, and made little more than a hundred miles from their Atlanta home before stopping for the night. Today had been devoted to driving, and Thomas was sick of it. The fact that Bianca was intimidated by and refused to captain the big SUV kept him behind the wheel for the entire trip. But he admitted to himself that it was better to face a sore back and exhaustion than the tension which went with sitting in the passenger seat and watching his wife try to handle the Navigator.

Thomas watched the darkening woods slide past, trying unsuccessfully not to think about business, but as the owner of Kirkland Insurance this was a nearly impossible feat. It wasn't the actual details of the insurance business that captured his thoughts, however. It was Howard MacDonald, his former top sales agent. There was some unpleasant business.

He couldn't say he was really surprised when Howard was arrested in Los Angeles while attempting to board a flight to Venezuela. Nor was he surprised that Howard was tried, convicted and subsequently executed three days later on the gallows in front of the state courthouse, an event which was both televised and blasted over the internet. What surprised Thomas was that Howard had embezzled the money from the firm in the first place. All fear of punishment aside, Howard just shouldn't have done it. He and Thomas were friends, for Chrissake! And Howard was no moron, either. That was one of the things which was most puzzling, that Howard would even think he could get away with it, especially these days.

The volume of the bickering in the back increased, pulling Thomas back to the present.

"I said hand 'em up, you little creep!"

Bianca twisted around, slipping out from under the shoulder belt. "What's going on?"

"Mom, Edwin's hogging the pretzels, and he won't give us any," Angela said.

"Yeah," seconded Carl.

Bianca sighed. "Well, do you think you could ask nicely for things, young lady?"

Angela put on a look of astonishment. "I didn't do anything!"

"Yeah," mumbled Carl.

"Stay out of it, Carl." Thomas looked at his older son in the rear view.

"Edwin, give your sister the pretzels."

The boy peered over the pamphlet and shrugged, tossing the bag to Angela. "It's okay with me if she wants to turn into a blimp." His face sank behind the pages.

"You little geek," hissed Angela.

"Pizza face."

"That's enough, both of you." Bianca raised her voice just enough to show she meant it, turning back and ducking under the shoulder belt once again.

"Yeah," grinned Carl, as he snatched the magazine from his sister's hands.

The squabbling returned to a low roar, and while Bianca went back to Mr. Sparks, Thomas turned the radio up a little and kept his eyes on the darkening road. The Lincoln was in hill country now, indicating the turn-off was getting nearer. On the radio the station was between songs, and the drawling DJ cut to an affiliate's live news report from Toronto, for an update on the hostage drama being played out there.

Thomas listened as a reporter recapped the story. A TWA 787 had lifted off from O'Hare International this morning, bound for Pittsburgh. Shortly after it was airborne, two men claiming to be soldiers in the service of Allah took control of the plane, shooting one crew member and forcing the pilot to detour to Toronto. Thomas didn't envy the folks who would have to explain how someone managed to get firearms on an aircraft, and he was amazed that the Air Force hadn't simply shot it down. As soon as the aircraft landed, a Canadian-American counter terrorist team disabled the landing gear, immobilizing it. The terrorists demanded the release of political prisoners held in Guantanamo, along with the usual demands of troop withdrawal, safe passage, blah, blah, blah.

Now, the reporter explained, the crisis was over. In support of American foreign and national policy, the Canadian government permitted two U.S. fighter jets to enter their airspace – better late than never, Thomas supposed – and they attacked without warning. The fighters came in low over the airport and loosed a pair of smart bombs which impacted the 787's fuselage near both the cockpit and coach seating. One bomb would have been more than enough, and the big white aircraft disintegrated under the double blasts, leaving a massive crater in the runway. There were no survivors. A low-ranking spokesman for the U.S. Department of Justice made the usual, tired speech about how the United States would tolerate absolutely no terrorist activities which affected American interests or citizens, directly or indirectly, and would respond to all acts of aggression swiftly and without compromise. An unwavering message of strength, the government proclaimed, was U.S. policy.

Thank goodness that's over, Thomas thought, and waited impatiently for the regular programming to come back on. The news story reminded him of how much travel abroad had decreased since the Zero Tolerance amendment had been added to, and radically changed the Constitution. Incidents like this were regrettable and unavoidable, but it was far worse overseas.

The Navigator passed another reflective sign, and Thomas slowed the SUV as his exit came up on the right. He took the off ramp, rattled over a metal cow crossing, and turned left under the interstate. Now they were on two lane blacktop, and the leafy woods to either side crept closer to the road as they entered the back country. The hills were more pronounced here, but the big vehicle slid over them without hesitation.

Thomas's thoughts returned to Howard MacDonald. Howard's execution made him think of how clever a person Howard had been, which made him think of how he would have believed he could pull it off, which reminded him that Howard's eight-year-old son Deke had placed the call to the police, telling them about the bad thing Daddy had done, which made him think of his own son Edwin, and that made him smile.

Just before they left for vacation, Edwin was honored by his school with a citizenship award, for turning in a pair of high school boys he had seen vandalizing a car while he was walking home from school. At the PTA meeting later that week, Principal Halsey showed the assembled parents the video he took during the electrocution of the high school boys two days later. Halsey went on to tell everyone that Thomas and Bianca's little boy had served his community well, and that the nine-year-old had a big future ahead of him. Thomas's heart had swelled with pride for his youngest son.

"Tom?" He was jerked out of his reverie by his wife's alarmed voice.

"Wha...?" Then he saw the twin flashes of yellow ahead. The headlights had frozen a whitetail doe in the center of the road, and the Navigator was hurtling towards it. "Jesus!" Thomas stomped on the brakes and gripped the wheel to control the skid, the squealing of rubber on asphalt filling the car, rivaled by Angela's terrified scream from the back as she held on to the back Bianca's headrest. The Navigator shuddered to a halt, turned at an angle in the road, headlights illuminating the trees on the left side. Thomas caught a glimpse of a white tail as the doe bounded into the safety of the woods.

The smell of hot radials crept in through the air conditioning, and the only sound was the soft purring of the big engine. Thomas released his breath. "Jesus," he repeated. For once his children were speechless.

"My God, Tom, do you know what could have happened?"

Thomas looked over at his wife and tried a weak grin. "It's okay, honey. The deer's fine, and we're fine."

"But Tom!" Her voice was rising. "Do you have any idea what something that big would have done to this car? We would have been killed!"

"Honey," Thomas patted her leg, "I'm in the insurance business, remember? I know perfectly well what would have happened, and it's not as bad as you think. This is a 2034 Lincoln, built like a tank, with every possible safety feature. A broken grill, maybe a wrinkle in the hood at the most, not even a full day in the shop. It would have been fine." He kept his voice and face relaxed as he told what was probably a lie.

Bianca was shaken and not easily put off. "You should pay more attention to the road."

Christ, not another fight. Better head this one off at the pass. "Bianca, don't take me to court over it, okay?"

His wife looked away, but Thomas could see the grin spreading over her face in the reflection of her window. It was an old joke between them, one of those silly things between married people. Of course each had seen stories in the news about people who lost cases in small claims and divorce courts, or were found delinquent with their child support payments, only to be shipped to penal colonies on islands off the Alaskan coast. The thought of the two of them arguing in front of a judge about *anything* was so ridiculous it usually broke any tension between them.

"Well...just be more careful." Bianca couldn't hide her smile, and Thomas knew everything was alright. She turned around in her seat. "You kids okay back there?"

Angela spoke up, still burning over the pretzel incident. "Daddy almost got us killed, but other than that, no big deal."

"Wow, Dad," Carl leaned over the front seat, "if the car can take it, why didn't you just smash the deer?"

Thomas was about to lecture about unnecessarily damaging the car, and how it was wrong to senselessly waste the lives of living creatures, but Edwin cut him off from the back.

"Because it would have been considered poaching, fart face, and you know the penalty for that."

"Shut up, geek, nobody asked you."

Thomas looked into his rear view and saw his youngest son looking calmly back at him. If he hadn't stopped in time, if he had hit the deer, would Edwin...? He hoped this citizenship award wasn't going to the boy's head. Then he thought of Howard MacDonald. Howard's boy was younger than Edwin. He tried to shake off the goosebumps rising on his arms, telling himself they were only an after-effect of the close call, and got the Lincoln moving again.

Half an hour passed and silence filled the SUV. The kids were trying to sleep, except for Edwin who was reading his pamphlet with the aid of a small flashlight, and Bianca, who just sat quietly, watching the headlights pierce the night. Thomas allowed his mind to wander again.

He didn't usually think about the Zero Tolerance Policy. It was something that had lost its glamour long ago and taken its place alongside trivialities like shoveling snow in the winter and keeping gas in the car. Just one of the many things that makes up a life. But now, with Howard's execution only a few days in the past, he was thinking about the whole thing again.

His children weren't around when things were different. Hell, he had only just been born when the rhetoric of the presidency had been A kinder, gentler America. Presidents change, however, just like national policies and national thinking.

It wasn't really that long ago that the president who first voiced those words was in office. He was followed by a popular, two term president riding high on a fat economy (as well as a fat intern), and was succeeded by the son of Mr. Kinder-Gentler, who had to face 9/11. That had been the real start of it all, a collective ending of what was left of American innocence. Or so it seemed. As it turned out, America had another soft layer yet to be peeled away. Following the Texan, America elected its first black president, a man whom the cameras loved but who accomplished a great deal of nothing. Behind him came a one-term Republican who was even more lackluster than his predecessor, and who managed to crush the economy even further. A wave of extreme liberalism began sweeping the country, and Americans elected a far left Democrat who disappointed everyone by dying of aggressive bone cancer nine months into his term. His young vice president stepped into his shoes, and if possible he was positioned even further left. This one lasted all of four months before a man who wrote a rambling, far-Right blog lifted the top of the president's skull in Seattle with a sniper rifle.

Up stepped the Speaker of the House, another African American with extremely liberal views, a reverend who had fought hard over the years to reach the chair he now occupied. His term lasted slightly longer than his predecessor's – nine months. A man later linked to an Idaho-based white supremacy group managed to slip through the Secret Service coverage of a state dinner (exactly how he managed this would be the subject of investigation and speculation for years, and would fuel conspiracy theories for decades) and used a pistol-grip shotgun to turn the president's face into chopped meat. The assassin was captured, but was shot and killed by a black agent later that night while allegedly attempting to escape.

Race riots sparked by the killings tore the country apart for the next two years, and America entered one of its darkest periods. Liberalism was shunted aside in the struggle for survival, and the United States might just have ceased to exist had not John Sawyer arrived on the scene.

John Sawyer was a politician with a dream, and the charisma, finances and contacts to make it happen. When he took the presidential oath during a special election, he promised Americans that he was going to put the country back together again. And he did, but back then no one except he and a select few knew where his plan would lead. Sawyer adopted some rhetoric from the eighties, and put it to work in the present day. His dream was Zero Tolerance, and with the pendulum swung hard to the right again, he went about making it a reality.

The first order of business was to repeal presidential term limitations and broadly expand the powers of the Chief Executive, legislation which met with surprisingly little Congressional resistance and overwhelming public support. Americans were worn out, and bought into the idea that getting things fixed would take time and the steady, long-term commitment of a single man. The Zero Tolerance legislation which quickly followed struck a chord with citizens who were sick of uncontrolled violence and crime, and as a majority they readily and eagerly gave their consent and sacrificed most of the freedoms their ancestors died for. The plan was simple. No tolerance for crime. Period. Capital punishment became the order of the day, and when, instead of Congress, the Joint Chiefs of Staff were put in charge of approving Supreme Court Justice nominees, everyone knew that the times, they were a-changing.

Thomas slowed the SUV as he approached a railroad crossing, watching a long freight creep by. Carl and Angela had exhausted themselves with their squabbling and were asleep, but Edwin was still perky enough to count the passing cars with his mother. Once the last boxcar rattled past, the family was underway again. By Thomas's calculations they were a little less than an hour away from their vacation cabin in the Carolina woods.

The changes were dramatic and effective. When American troops invaded Colombia in order to stop the drug cartels – *Stop it at the Source!* was the bumper sticker slogan of choice - the American people stood by their president. Even after it was decided that the mountains of that country were too difficult a place to conventionally root out the drug lords, and the U.S. resorted to the use of several tactical nuclear weapons – much to the dismay of the Colombian government – the American people didn't put up much of a fuss.

As Zero Tolerance expanded from the drug trade to the everyday aspects of crime in America, the people continued to support their president. When they saw convicted murderers being executed promptly, without lengthy appeals, they rejoiced. When the death penalty was applied to rapists, arsonists, armed robbers and child molesters, and later to shoplifting and other petty infractions, the public was euphoric. The crime rate plummeted and Americans saw that Zero Tolerance was directly impacting their lives, so they proclaimed that they would support their national leader in any way possible. It was the mandate Sawyer was looking for, and certain Constitutional amendments were swiftly eliminated, modified or created anew. Concepts such as Reasonable Search and Seizure, Miranda, Cruel and Unusual Punishment became historical footnotes.

During this period, the federal government simultaneously poured staggering amounts of funding into educational programs aimed at transitioning the public into the new way of thinking. Certainly there were individuals and groups – some of them prominent and famous - who opposed the changes, but they were quickly branded as threats to national security and silenced. No one seemed interested in the details of how they seemed to simply vanish (the *why* was obvious), and the government felt no need to offer explanations anyway.

There were also protests from the United Nations (which resulted in their immediate ejection from U.S. soil) and members of NATO (which quickly dissolved after the U.S. withdrew from it), as well as countries not so friendly to the United States. Things had gone too far by then, however. America, its people supporting their president with a near religious fervor, had rapidly reclaimed a position of world leadership both militarily and economically. Those countries that protested through peaceful means were either ignored, or crushed financially. Those that protested through threats of force were dealt with in kind. In those days, America handled its problems with nuclear-tipped cruise missiles (Germany, Yemen, Pakistan) or invasion (the oil-producing nations which were now jokingly referred to as America's Middle East Mobil Station.) Popular "peasant" uprisings had long ago caused the Chinese to lose their grip on economic dominance (but not their trigger – millions of insurgents perished at the hands of the Red Army), and the Russians had surprisingly little comment. To hard-liners who longed for the good old days of the Soviet State, America had finally begun to think like a Russian. In the end, no one wanted to cross the U.S.

The country had certainly changed over the years, but Thomas was sure it was all for the better. America was prosperous and peaceful, they had a leader they could trust and respect, and they didn't take shit from anyone. Crime, though still present, was terrifically low compared to the past. And with the way citizens were encouraged to take part in the justice system, everything from reporting crimes to preventing or actively stopping them ("Vigilante" was no longer a four-letter word), crime would continue to decline while quality of life for upstanding Americans continued to improve. Sacrifices would have to be made of course, like blowing up a plane and killing two-hundred-sixteen civilians just to get at two terrorists, but that was all part of progress, and at least the message was clear to anyone who intended harm.

Thomas saw the silhouette of an old barn in a field on the right, a landmark that told him he was almost there. Only a few more miles and they would be at the cabin. Now even Bianca was asleep, and only the occasional bob of a flashlight in his mirror told Thomas that Edwin was still awake.

The Navigator rounded a gentle curve, and well up ahead the headlights picked out the reflectors at the end of the long gravel drive which led to the Kirkland's summer home. Thomas saw a man in shabby clothes and a backpack walking on the shoulder about fifty yards beyond the curve. He turned at the sound of the approaching vehicle and stuck his thumb out. In the wash of headlights, it was clear he hadn't had a decent meal – or a bath – in some time. Thomas started to ease the Navigator to the left, so as not to pass too close to the hitchhiker, when he heard the penlight click off behind him. He glanced in his mirror and saw Edwin leaning intently over the seat, staring back into his eyes. Edwin had enjoyed turning in those two criminals, and seeing they got their punishment. And he was happy about his citizenship award and his bright future as an upstanding American. Very happy. Howard's son was probably just as happy about turning in his own father.

Thomas jerked the wheel right and hit the gas. The headlights seared the hitchhiker with their glare, and he threw his arms up over his face. A second later the heavy bumper and grill slammed into him, flinging his limp form into the trees to smack against a pine, killing him instantly. The *THUD* awakened the family, and Bianca looked over at her husband, who guided the big Lincoln back into the center of the lane and slowed for the approaching gravel road.

"What was that?" she asked, her voice heavy with sleep.

"Nothing, hon." He switched on the washers, and the wipers cleared the windshield of red.

"Are we there yet?" mumbled Angela.

"Couple more minutes." Thomas guided the Navigator up the long driveway, thinking that he would have the mechanic in the nearby town take a look at the Lincoln in the morning, confident that the damage would be minimal. He glanced into the mirror and saw Edwin smiling at him. He suffered a brief chill, then forced himself to grin back and wink.

86

Hitchhiking was illegal.
But so was tolerating it, and he knew the penalty for that.

TROPHY WIFE

Everyone said she was crazy to marry Dean. The newspapers called her Cooper IV. Her mother, for whom marrying money was the greatest achievement a woman could hope for, expressed her fears and reservations. Her girlfriends told her she was not only crazy, but stupid. Even that detective from the District Attorney's office tried to warn her off. Monica held her ground, professing her love and standing them off. It cost her those friendships, and gave her no one to whom she could turn when the papers got really ugly and hurtful. It left her isolated, and the last thing Samantha, her closest friend since childhood, said was, "That's exactly what he wants, Monica. For you to be all by yourself."

That friendship ended bitterly.

After four years she proved them wrong. Dean was a loving and faithful husband. He had his serious moments, of course, and liked things the way he liked them. A forceful personality was the best way to describe it. But then a man didn't reach the pinnacle of wealth and power in the New York real estate market by being timid. It was one of the things which attracted her to him in the first place.

"NAIVE," the Post had said. "BLINDED BY LOVE," the Daily News shouted. "FATAL BEAUTY," said The Times. The tabloids were far more unkind. Monica didn't care, and Dean was patient with her, explaining how a man in his position, who had experienced so much tragedy in his life, was an easy target for the media. He was there to calm her down after that TMZ reporter accosted her on 5th Ave, shouting, "Monica, how long do you think before he strikes again?" And Dean's lawyer, Saul Kessler, took the time to walk Monica through each case, explaining all the details and answering every question she had.

Yes, Dean Cooper, real estate billionaire and New York mover and shaker, had been married three times previously. Yes, his first wife Darla had run off and never been seen or heard from again. Yes, so had his second wife Piper. And yes, Antoinette had been jumped in the dark and murdered during a robbery in the parking lot of a club. Her assailant took her jewels, and used some kind of cutting tool to snip off her left ring finger, stealing the massive diamond and taking the finger with him.

Dean Cooper was investigated in every case, and more intensively each subsequent time. No evidence of his involvement could ever be found, and he had never been charged. The police didn't buy it, and Dean told her they would never stop trying to make their case. But, as he explained, an innocent man had nothing to fear.

Monica sat on the couch in the living room, their extravagant apartment soaring around her. From the other room Dean called, "Honey? Do you want a drink?

Dean was a particular man, and very particular about Monica's appearance. She had undergone a facelift and had her nose thinned, gotten the implants, and hit the gym five days a week; yoga, Pilates, spin classes. Dean was forever in the media, and a man of his status had a certain image to maintain. The lady in his life had to be stunning. Monica did it all willingly, wanting to please him, wanting to be that stunning woman he wanted, and she was. At twenty-eight, she was the center of attention at parties, blonde and long-legged, her chiseled and enhanced figure turning heads, and her photos frequently appeared in the society pages.

After almost two years of marriage they had Ethan, but Monica was determined not to let the baby impact her looks any more than he had to, and she doubled her efforts, trimming back down in record time. Ethan was nearly three now, and despite their financial prowess, Dean wouldn't hear of a nanny, except on a part time basis or during vacations. But like their maids, not a live-in. He believed a mother should raise her own children, which Monica came to realize suited her fine. Once all she thought about was shopping and fashion, jewelry and parties and exotic travel. But she found there was something with a much more powerful pull than all that. Her heart ached for their little boy, and she loved being a full-time mommy.

A perfect life, and the kind of money to make all her dreams come true and more. After a while even the media left them alone, the scent of some other, more salacious scandal drawing off the hounds. Dean was sweet and thoughtful, and although at times he used what she called his "stern voice" with her, usually when she was being extra blonde as Dean put it, he had never once raised a hand to her.

But then Monica found the box, and confronted him.

Dean smiled, and punched her in the face so hard it fractured her nose and knocked out a tooth.

The rattle of ice in a glass announced her husband's return to the living room. He was dressed in jeans and loafers, wearing an expensive blue button up spattered with drops of blood. Monica's blood.

"Sure you don't want anything?" He smiled that billion dollar smile.

On the couch, where she had fallen after being hit, Monica could only stare at him, her vision still blurry and the thick taste of blood in her mouth. When she'd come storming into the living room with her accusation, it hadn't occurred to her that Dean was just standing there in front of the couch, as if he had been waiting. She also hadn't noticed that the couch was covered in plastic, that *lots* of the living room was covered in plastic. Monica tried to stand, found out she couldn't. Dean walked to her with a look of concern on his face, setting his drink on the coffee table.

"Does it hurt, sweetheart?" he asked. Then he hit her again, three fast blows, one to each eye and another to her already lumpy nose. Monica gurgled and blacked out.

In the darkness, her mind saw the little cherry wood box, something a young woman might keep her precious keepsakes in. There it was, sitting on her vanity in the master bath. Not there by accident. Dean had decided that tonight was the night, and knew she would open it, that she would come demanding an answer. He knew her so very well, which was probably why he chose her to be Mrs. Cooper number four.

A series of slaps brought her back to the living room, and she wheezed against her freshly re-broken nose, trying not to gag on the blood and a little hard object which had to be another tooth. Her eyes were swelling to slits. Dean was perched on the coffee table before her, leaning forward relaxed, elbows on his knees, still wearing that smile the TV loved so much. Another man sat in a chair a few feet away, looking at her with his head cocked, as if she was a curious zoo animal. Richie.

"It's been a nice four years, hasn't it, honey?"

Monica tried to shake her head, but knew if she did she would throw up and pass out again. If that happened, she knew she'd never wake up.

"But people change, they get too comfortable, and then things get dull."

Monica gurgled something.

"What's that?" He leaned forward. "You have to speak up, sweetie."

She forced herself to lift her head. It helped her breathe better. "Evidence," she said, her voice thick. "They'll catch...you."

The billion dollar smile returned. "Oh, Monica, no they won't." He held up three fingers. "They never have. You'll be no different."

She choked down a clot of blood, swallowing the tooth, and put her hands out to steady herself so she didn't slump over on the plastic sheeting. "Evidence," she repeated.

Dean frowned and nodded, as if seriously considering it. Then his bright smile came back, bigger than ever. "Richie will see to that, like always." Richie D'Agostino was ex-NYPD, a man who served as Dean's driver and bodyguard. They had been together for years. Monica knew he was a former cop. She didn't know he had spent half his career in crime scene investigation, and was a man who knew just what they would look for, and how to make it go away.

"He did a perfect job with Darla and Piper. He's got a wood chipper upstate." Dean nodded to the man in the chair, and Richie tilted his head at the compliment. "Antoinette was even better, a tragic, unsolved street crime. What is this city turning into?" He sipped his drink. "Sure, I'll take some serious heat, you being number four and all, but eventually it will all go away, just like the others." He patted the cherry wood box, now resting beside where he sat on the coffee table.

Panic was overtaking her, and Monica struggled to sit up, opening her mouth and letting out what should have been a scream, but was little more than a loud, "Gaaaaaah!"

Dean and Richie laughed. "C'mon, you can do better than that!" Dean patted her knee. "Really let it rip."

She swayed, gripping her knees to keep from falling back.

"Go ahead," Dean said softly, the good humor suddenly gone from his voice and his eyes. "Scream. Scream like you're about to be murdered. You know no one will hear you."

It was true. Their penthouse, occupying the entire uppermost level of their building, was sixty-nine floors above Manhattan's streets. Dean owned the floor below them as well, and kept it empty. "For privacy," he had said. Now she knew what he meant.

"Nope, no one will hear you." He raised an eyebrow. "Except maybe Ethan."

She went motionless at the mention of her toddler's name, and it cleared her mind a little.

"Oh yeah, wake him up with a scream. He can come out in his jammies, holding his bear, and get to watch what Daddy does to Mommy."

Despite being swollen, Monica's eyes widened and she bared her teeth. "Don't you..."

Dean slapped her then, hard, rocking her head to the side. "Don't ever tell me what to do, bitch." Then he sat back, his relaxed demeanor falling instantly into place, his blue eyes sparkling with pleasure. He opened the cherry wood box with one hand, and reached for something in a hip pocket with the other.

"Want to hear the best part of all this?"

She couldn't help but look again at the three slender fingers lying in the box, each in varying degrees of decay, each with a perfectly manicured and painted nail, and wearing an enormous diamond ring. She saw him pull out the big electrician's snips.

"The best part is that when we all get to hell, you have to serve me as slaves. Like a harem. Isn't that great?"

92

Monica saw the madness in his eyes, and suddenly wondered how he could have concealed it from everyone, from her, all this time. *"Blinded by Love,"* the Daily News said. Right. Dean leaned forward and reached for her left hand. Monica pulled it away and tucked it under her armpit. Her husband smiled patiently and reached for it again, but she squirmed and started to twist.

"Richie, give me a hand, will you?" Then he burst into laughter. Richie snorted as well, and rose from his seat, plopping down beside her and gripping her wrist painfully, jerking the hand out and forcing her to straighten her arm. Dean grabbed her fingers and quickly isolated the one with the big diamond on it. The snips came in fast. Clip. The pain was blinding, and Monica did indeed scream, a high yowling which sprayed droplets of blood into her husband's grinning face. She couldn't help it, she screamed again. He tossed something into the little cherry wood box.

Dean turned his head. "Uh-oh, is that a door I hear? Footie pajamas sliding over a marble floor?"

Monica tensed and froze, straining to listen, forgetting her finger, her smashed nose, her broken teeth and blackened eyes.

"I think," Dean whispered, "that when you run off on vacation to wood chipper-land, you'll take our little boy with you."

Confidence in a man is admirable. Blunt stupidity is not. Monica screamed again, but this time instead of a wail of agony, it was something primal, and her instincts told her body what to do. She lifted one knee high and drove her foot into Dean's chest with such force it knocked him backwards off the coffee table in an ungraceful somersault. She snapped her head to the side and sank her teeth into Richie's nose, biting down until it crunched. When his hands instinctively went up to push her away, Monica reached inside his jacket with her right hand, closed on the smooth grip of the black automatic he kept in a shoulder holster, and yanked it free. She didn't wave it, didn't threaten, just pushed the muzzle against his chest and blew his heart out with a single pull of the trigger.

Dean was scrambling to his feet on the other side of the coffee table, still on all fours, the billion dollar smile gone and replaced by a look of surprised confusion. He saw her swing the pistol towards him, and the confusion turned to a wild rage.

"Bitch...!"

Monica was never able to remember how many times she pulled the trigger. Enough to make Dean's face and most of his head disappear. The investigators said five, but who was counting.

The media went crazy, and it was a global sensation for weeks. The story dominated print and television news outlets, true crime and celebrity entertainment programs, talk shows and the internet. Armies of journalists and the curious surrounded Monica's building and hospital, and of course there was the police with an endless stream of questions. She was labeled both hero and fool.

Monica fired Saul Kessler from her hospital bed, and by that time her husband's lawyer was under investigation himself and needed an attorney of his own. She hired a firm of legal predators to deflect the book and movie deal offers, the demands for talk show appearances, and to ensure the District Attorney and the press saw her in the proper light - a victim who defended herself and her child against a monster and his henchman. The law firm also turned its considerable force to locking in Monica's claim to Dean's financial empire. Dean had never bothered with a pre-nuptial, since he had always known how the marriage would end.

Monica got it all.

She hired a private security agency. They surrounded her and Ethan with ex-mercenary and Special Forces types, the kind of men with little patience for pushy journalists or freak fans.

Home within a week, she was back in the penthouse with Ethan, who thankfully hadn't really been coming down the hall to Monica's screams. That was just Dean's game. The gunshots woke him, of course, and Monica learned something about herself. She had gone to him, battered and bleeding, and quietly put him back to bed, shushing him to sleep before calling the police.

The best surgeons money could buy set her nose and reattached her finger – though it would remain stiff and out of sync with the others for the rest of her life – and they assessed the damage to her face. Appointments with more surgeons and dentists would follow.

Monica was cleared of any wrong-doing within weeks, around the same time the families of Dean's three murdered ex-wives brought civil suits against his estate. Monica's lawyers were prepared for a battle, assuring her the families would get little, if anything, but she surprised them by directing immediate settlements, without negotiation. There was plenty of money. She also insisted on meeting personally with each family to express her own grief for their loss.

For weeks Monica kept Ethan next to her in bed at night, feeling his small warmth against her, soothed by his steady breathing and the knowledge that children are resilient. He barely asked about his father. Now the penthouse was on the market, and Ethan had finally moved back to his own room. Her security people were on duty outside, and the media was under control. Monica was finally safe.

At 2:00 am the pounding started on her bedroom door.

It woke her up, a heavy, repetitive slamming on wood, and Monica sat up in bed, her heart thumping. She could hear the door rattle in the frame.

"Monicaaaa!"

She covered her mouth to hold in the scream.

"Monica! Open the door, bitch!" Dean's voice.

The knob rattled. She didn't even remember locking the bedroom door. It was something she never did, in case Ethan got up in the night and wanted to come to her. More pounding, and her dead husband calling to her from the other side.

"Monicaaaa! Come out, come out!" There was no doubt. She knew that voice.

The cordless was in the living room. Her cell phone was in her pocketbook on the front hall table. The security men outside the penthouse in the elevator lobby would hear it, wouldn't they? The door shuddered, and she thought she heard a crack.

There was no way, she tried telling herself. It was a nightmare. It was a hallucination from painkillers. But she knew she was awake, and had stopped taking the painkillers weeks ago. Monica threw on a robe and slowly approached the door, still covering her mouth. She smelled something foul as she neared it, something wet and moldy.

"Sweetheart," Dean said, his voice no longer a yell, "I really need to see you. Come out and play with me."

Monica wanted to scream, wanted to run, hide in a closet, wish it all away. When he dragged his nails down the wood and chuckled, she thought her sanity would snap. She started backing up.

"Mommy?" A little voice, distant and muffled. "Mommy?" A tiny sob. "Mommy, I'm have a nimare!"

Her breath caught and she froze in place. On the other side of the door, Dean's voice crooned, "Oh, it's our little man, Monica. Don't worry, Daddy will go get him."

In seconds Monica snapped off the lock and jerked open the bedroom door. A wave of damp filth washed over her and she gagged, holding onto the frame. The lights of Manhattan, dazzling beyond the wall of windows off to the right of the living room, revealed what was before her. Dean stood several feet away, wearing the blood-soaked clothes he'd had on the night Monica killed him. His face - which should have been missing after five close-range hits from a 9mm – was back, though dark and starting to decay. His eyes gleamed with a dirty, bronze light.

"Hi, baby," he said, smiling that billion dollar smile. Something white and wriggling moved in a rotted open cavity in his throat. Monica saw that he wasn't alone, either. Silhouetted against the panoramic windows, three figures stood side by side, little more than shades. A collective sound came from them, a soft moan. It sounded like pain to her. She didn't need to recall their photos to recognize Darla, Piper and Antoinette.

Dean looked back at his former wives, then at Monica. "Don't you remember what I said? They're mine. They serve me in hell." His grin widened. "And so will you."

"Mommy?" Ethan's voice was more urgent, his bedroom just two doors off the living room. Monica sidestepped the corpse to get to him, but Dean was quick, and darted in front of her. Up close she thought she would vomit from the smell.

Her husband shook his head slowly. "I told you Daddy would get him."

The trio of wives moaned, swaying but moving no closer.

Dean pulled the electrician's cutters from his hip pocket. "Just need to finish up, baby, then we'll all be on our way. Mommy first." He took a step forward, as Ethan called out for her again.

Monica felt her face flush, felt a heat rise in her chest. "No!" She shoved Dean away with both hands, expecting him not to move, or her hands to sink into his rotting chest, and was surprised when the corpse staggered backwards. Not as surprised as Dean, who let out a startled cry. Monica advanced, and shoved him again. "No." Another shove. "No." Shove. "NO!" He fell back against a decorative table, and the marble statuette of a rearing horse wobbled and fell off, shattering on the marble floor. Dean made a growling noise, but the bronze light in his eyes seemed to flicker.

Monica looked at her husband, then at the three dead women. "I don't believe in ghosts," she said, her voice firm, and she clapped her hands together sharply. The shades which were Darla, Piper and Antoinette let out a sigh, and faded.

"You bitch!" Dean shrieked. What have you done?" He snarled and came at her, but Monica didn't move, just looked into his eyes as his form lunged through her, his arms grappling but connecting with nothing. Monica faced him as he turned and stared at his hands, then at her, blinking and not understanding.

"I don't believe in ghosts, Dean," she said softly, stepping towards him. "And I'm done with your games." She clapped her hands again, a crack in the open space of the penthouse, and Dean faded, the light in his eyes winking out.

The last of him was a soft, receding, "Nooooo...."

Monica strode through the space where he had been and went to hold her little boy.

John L. Campbell

PET SHOP TARANTULAS

The drugs wear off and I come around
my wrists and ankles tightly bound
and in a closet, door and shelves removed
the air filled with an awful sound

A scrape of mortar, the sight of bricks
rising and rising, I may be sick
Music plays, a country song fills the basement and she hums
along
using her trowel to seal me in to the tune of a Nashville hick

She meant nothing, I cry, it was just a fling, sweetheart, don't
do this thing
I forgive you, she says, and lays two more rows
I considered taping your mouth and your nose but that would
be quick, and I want you to see how the rest of this goes

Masonry, a skill I did not know she had, close to the top now
building her wall, my beautiful wife
so calm and betrayed and utterly mad
I can't handle tight spaces, I wail, and she agrees that it's sad

All but finished except for one last, a rectangle up near the
top,
but now comes the funnel, greased so they'll slide and won't
scamper out, 'cause she knows that they're fast and opens the
boxes, shaking them in
The moment for rational thought is long past

Thailand and Texas, Brazil and Belize, ordered from
everywhere,
shipped to the house while I played, while she knew, and came
up with a plan and now down they come, spilling into the dark
Please, please, oh God please

A hundred, she says as they fall, the big ones, they're my
favorites of all
Quick and aggressive I learn as they race up my legs, up my
chest, running over my face and begin biting while I begin
screaming and watch as she sets
the last brick in its place

EMBRACING NEPTUNE

It was supposed to miss. Anything else was unthinkable.

The government told the public and the press for months that it would be a "close call," but once they saw impact was inevitable, the authorities scurried off to their holes without warning. What would have been the point? There was nothing anyone could do to stop it.

Benjamin stood with his cube farm colleagues at the front of their top floor office, watching a wall-mounted flat screen. Video shot from a Navy aircraft over the Atlantic recorded the brilliant sparkle growing larger, filling the screen, then a searing flash and a fiery streak before the screen went to static.

Everyone felt the building shudder, and a moment later the windows blew in. Men and women in business suits – those who hadn't been cut down by table-sized blades of flying glass – started screaming and moved as a herd to the elevator lobby. They knocked over cubicle walls, crushed their co-workers underfoot, and crushed a few more against the elevator bank before turning towards the fire exit.

Benjamin allowed himself to be carried along, the only smiling face in a sea of pale terror.

In the stairwell, Benjamin broke away from the herd as it poured downstairs, shrieking and tumbling and crashing and breaking bones. From the forty-seventh floor it would take them considerable time to reach the bottom and spill out into the streets of Lower Manhattan, where the doomed from other buildings throughout the financial district would join them, packing streets already choked with abandoned cars.

Not Benjamin. He headed up.

Two flights and he was pushing out onto a tar and gravel roof. He ran to the edge, kicking off his shoes, stripping off his suit and hopping to clear his trousers. In moments he was naked, standing at the edge, a twelve inch lip separating him from the drop. Here at the tip of the city he had a clear view all around, and most importantly to the south. Far below was a chorus of honking and screaming, but it was quickly drowned out by a growing whisper, a whisper building into a roar.

The East River and the Hudson were being sucked into New York Harbor like Colorado white water rapids, and the harbor was being sucked out to sea. Hundreds of ships were carried in the surge, some turning helplessly. A Circle Line boat of sightseers slammed into a freighter and was quickly pulled beneath the surface. To the right, a massive white Carnival cruise ship had become locked against a bigger Royal Caribbean, and they rushed out to sea side by side, paper boats caught in a storm gutter.

The sharp angle of the asteroid trail hung in the air out over the ocean, sketching a smoky line from the heavens like God's finger of judgment. Benjamin started to laugh. He had been planning on stepping off a subway platform this afternoon, right in front of the express from Grand Central. This was so much better.

Within minutes the river bottoms and silt bed of the harbor were exposed, clotted with beached ships and two centuries of human trash, and the raging whisper of the now-vanished rivers was replaced with a rumble. Benjamin wept and smiled at it, a rising dark wall stretching across the horizon, moving fast, pushing the air before it. He stepped into the cold, salty wind and onto the ledge.

It was impossibly high and climbing still, bluish green and foam crested, and as it neared its rumble made him tremble. The locked pair of cruise ships, small as bathtub toys, appeared to be scaling its vertical wall, and a blue whale tumbled out of its surface, tadpole-sized against its magnitude.

101

The impact wave was over a mile high when it hit.

As it arrived, blotting out the sun, Benjamin tipped his head back and opened his arms wide.

"Come to Papa."

And it did.

COURAGEOUS LITTLE PHILOMENA'S WONDROUS BAIT

It was always midnight in Petershead.

Even before the Thorazine.

As a well-read resident, Courageous Little Agnes Philomena – 'Clap' to her friends – knew about the Before Time. She had learned of it in the library, and that was where she was headed now.

Three feet tall and bony, Philomena strode with a purpose along the cobbled street, her high, lace-up boots with the pointy little toes *Click-Clacking* on the stones, her head with the pointy little chin held high, and her hat with the pointy little…well, with the pointy little point pulled firmly over her long red ringlets of hair. Her dress was prison-matron gray, her favorite color, with little black buttons running from hem to throat.

Click-Clack-Click-Clack, like a drill instructor's measured gait.

A pig dressed in bloody butcher's whites pedaled a bicycle towards her. He rang a little bell on the handlebars as he called to her, the bike wobbling.

"Salutations, Clap!"

She smiled with her pointy little teeth and waved. "Greetings, Hamhock."

Click-Clack-Click-Clack up the street, past the tailor and the pipe shop and the mummifier. Just beyond was a little shop with a big front window and a shingle hung over the door. It showed a red and white striped candy wrapped in a bow. Philomena stopped to press her pointy little nose against a window pane. Fernando's Sweets wasn't open, but even through the gloom within Philomena could make out shelf upon shelf of glass jars, all filled with colorful, delicious, poisonous treats.

Her tummy growled.

Maybe she'd stop back by after the library. If Fernando was open for business (he so rarely was, spending most of his time asleep in a coffee can in his office), she'd spend a penny and get her favorite sweet, a Putrid Puscake. Or maybe a chocolate hemlock bar.

With a little sigh, Philomena pulled her nose from the glass and marched on, *Click-Clack.*

Once upon a time it had been Daylight in Petershead, and there had been a family and children's stories and laughter. She knew this from her reading. Then the Twilight Time crept in (but hadn't it been there all along, really?) and the laughter turned the same color. Soon Midnight came calling, and it stayed. No more family. No more stories. And the laughter turned black as a witch's asshole.

Philomena giggled and covered her mouth. She wasn't supposed to curse, even in her own mind.

Click-Clack-Click-Clack, past the burnt church where deformed rats scampered and played and ate one another. Past the bakery and the haberdashery. A cold burst of wind sent dead leaves twirling and skirling down the street, and they danced in a circle around her for a moment as Philomena jumped and clapped her hands before they sailed on their way.

At the intersection a stoplight blinked red in every direction. Philomena dutifully stopped and looked every which way. There were only three cars in Petershead; An old-timey flatbed truck with an *OOH-GAH* horn, driven by Skeleton Bob; A silver minivan with tinted windows that drove off the Petershead Bridge every day and burst into flames; a shiny white ambulance driven by The Men in White. None were in view, so Philomena crossed the street and started up the hill, *Click-Clack*.

Across the lane to her left was a big Victorian house painted purple with white trim, every window glowing with warm candlelight. In a smart little yard out front a plump woman with a gray granny bun tended to a garden of black tulips. She raised one hand, which wore a flower-printed gardening glove.

"Courageous Little Philomena, how are you dear?"

"*Agnes* Philomena."

"Of course, dear. Off to the library again?"

Philomena didn't break stride. "Of course."

The woman tisked. "All that reading will turn your brains to mush. Why not come in for some tea?"

Philomena waved, keeping to her side of the street. "Not today, Mrs. Caul, thank you anyway." It paid to be polite to Mrs. Caul. And it paid even better to stay *out* of Mrs. Caul's kitchen. Where the knives were. And the pots. And her cellar door.

The old woman went back to her tulips, and Philomena continued her march up the hill, *Click-Clack*.

At the top of the hill, the street turned right. Growing out of the cobblestones, completely disrupting and blocking the road, was the Wiggle Tree, a huge black oak with great spreading boughs, each ending in viney twists, not a leaf upon any of them. They appeared to sway, but due to wind or consciousness was unknown. The Wiggle Tree slept a great deal of the time. Its roots spread out in a riot, buckling the cobblestones and poking out of the ruptured earth, as if it might at any moment decide to go for a walk on some dread business. The only way round the corner was to pass beneath its arms.

Philomena, wise beyond the ten years she was and would ever be, took a deep breath and sprinted under the tree, pointy little knees and elbows pumping fiercely. In a moment she was past it and round the corner, and she stopped to look back. The tree hadn't moved. Perhaps it was indeed asleep. Perhaps she was simply too fast for it – she liked to believe that. Or perhaps it was already full.

In the Before Time, the Wiggle Tree had been green and leafy and happy, and the family often picnicked under its pleasant shade, the children climbing its inviting limbs. These days it liked to snatch up pedestrians and cram them into its toothy black maw.

Lots of things ate other things in Petershead.

Past the corner, the upward slope continued, though here the cobbled street was known as Twilliger's Hill. All along the right shoulder was a tall fence of iron bars with nasty spikes at the top, dark ivy hanging thick upon the rusting metal. Once upon a time this had been a white picket fence, but that was in the Before Time. On the other side was Petershead Cemetery.

In the Before Time, it had been a lush meadow of soft grass, blueberry bushes and sprawling, shady elms. Wildflowers had grown in spectacular clusters, and the air was always filled with butterflies. A friendly rabbit named Mr. Fobb had lived there in a quaint little blue cottage, tending his vegetable garden.

Then Midnight came. The flowers and the blueberry bushes and the soft grass had turned black and died, the butterflies started spinning webs and feeding on birds, and the trees turned gnarled, sentient and cruel. Gravestones began sprouting like weeds from the dead ground, old, chipped, weathered things with illegible inscriptions, some with broken angels, some with stone faces frozen in screams, all of them crooked. The crypts and mausoleums grew next, gothic masses of cracked marble and granite, iron doors yawning wide into blackness and cold. The ivy covered them like hair.

Philomena marched up the long hill *Click-Clack-Click-Clack* and stopped at the crest, standing before the gates of the cemetery. Here a stone archway stretched over a wide entrance, where a pair of spiked iron gates stood open amid high dead grass. She peered inside.

Sometimes a Reever or a Five-Legged Bandolino (the ones with eight eyes, not six) could be seen peering out from the dark entrance of a mausoleum, clicking their fangs and drooling their poison, wondering if they could skitter out and snatch up a victim before bursting into flame from the caress of moonlight. There were no such monstrosities lurking around at the moment, though, only Mr. Fobb the friendly rabbit. At present he was upside-down on the face of an old gravestone, an iron spike through his belly, pinning him there. His long ears hung limp on the dead ground, and his arms dangled over his head.

"Hello, Mr. Fobb," Philomena called.

The rabbit's whisker twitched and he opened one eye. It was bloodshot. "Well, well, how do you do, Clap?"

"Quite well, thank you. What nailed you to that stone, Mr. Fobb?"

The rabbit's left rear paw spasmed. "A Reever. Interrupted my tea. Broke my teapot, sorry to say."

Philomena made a sad little huff. "The white one with the little blue flowers? You've had that teapot forever!"

"Yes, yes, a terrible thing." The rabbit sighed.

The little girl took another look around the immediate area and stepped closer to the cemetery entrance. "Shall I pull you down?"

The rabbit waved a panicked paw. "No, no! It's still close by, I can smell it. I'd hate for it to get you too, dear. They bite, you know."

She did indeed know, and had the semi-circular scar on her right calf to prove it. And they didn't just bite. They ate. But then Philomena could bite as well, as the Reever that gave her the scar quickly learned.

"Besides, it would just nail me right back up again." He fingered the spike through his belly and wriggled his pink nose. "Off to the library again? I'd have thought there was nothing left for you to know."

Philomena smiled her sharp smile. "Oh, there's still so much I haven't learned!"

"You know about Early Twilight, and the College Girl In The Trunk?"

"Read that. They never found the body."

The rabbit wiggled his nose. "What about the Anonymous Letter Bomb To Golden Books?"

Philomena smiled. "Of course, Mr. Fobb. Got a junior editor with that one."

He gave an experimental tug at the spike. It wasn't moving. "The Christmas Fire?"

Nod.

"The Hit And Run He Thought Was A Dream Because Of The Painkillers And Tequila?"

Nod.

"Infant Sister Bathtub Accident?"

"Of course," she said. "I've even read all about you. In the Before Time you were very popular, and had dozens of adventures. An entire series."

Mr. Fobb sighed and hung limp on his spike. "Yes, those were the days. Before the butterflies became predators and my cottage turned into a crematorium." As Philomena nodded in sympathy, a black butterfly with lots of eyes floated onto one of the rabbit's ears. He flicked it off with an annoyed twitch. "What could be left for you to learn?"

The little girl looked left and right, then in a stage whisper called, "I need to know all about the Crusk."

The rabbit sucked a quick hiss of air through his buck teeth, eyes wide. "For mercy's sake, why?"

"Because I'm going to catch it."

Mr. Fobb clasped his hands to the spike and shuddered. "Oh dear, oh dear! Philomena, you mustn't even think such a thing!"

Courageous Little Philomena folded her thin arms across her ten-year-old chest and stuck out her pointy little chin. "Oh, I'm going to do it, Mr. Fobb. The Crusk has eaten far too many children for far too long, and no one does anything about it. So I will. If I don't, I'll be the only kid left in Petershead!"

"Oh dear, oh dear," the rabbit fretted, fingering the spike.

Philomena looked up the street. "Well, time for me to go, if you won't let me pull out the spike, that is."

The rabbit's ears drooped even further than before. "Please reconsider, Clap. I'd just hate to hear that you'd been eaten too."

"Not to worry, Mr. Fobb, I have a plan. Just need to figure out the right bait." And with that she was off, the rabbit sending her a slow, sad wave, her little boots *Click-Clacking* over the cobblestone, up to the crest of Twilliger's Hill.

Over the hill and just beyond the cemetery, the cobblestones ended in a great roundabout in front of the library. In the center of the circle, rising from an overgrown tangle of black ivy, was a statue of a great, chubby bear with wide eyes and a curious expression. It was heavily stained with pigeon shat. This was, of course, the Butter Bear, once a children's favorite in the Before Time. Philomena frowned as she walked around the circle, looking at the statue. A shame how that had all turned out. The rampage at the kindergarten picnic, the crazed bear eventually brought down with a bloody rag doll clutched in each paw.

The library was a gothic manor complete with turrets and gargoyles and high windows of cloudy glass, candlelight glowing from within. The wide stone steps of the entrance were flanked by flickering gaslight poles, and Philomena climbed the stairs between them and pushed through the castle-like double doors.

The main hall was a vast, cold space that smelled of dust and paper and old leather, and she breathed in the pleasant aroma as her heels echoed across the stone floor, *Click-Clack-Click-Clack*. The walls were lined with high shelves loaded with books, interspersed with dark archways which led to the special collections rooms. Candles burned in sconces and holders throughout the chamber. This was her temple, for everything that had ever happened or been dreamed was here.

At the center was a big circular desk with an enormous QUIET sign on it. Behind the desk, a creature with the head and wide yellow teeth of a mule stood eying Philomena with a sour expression. He wore a threadbare green waistcoat from the 19th century. They were the only ones here.

"Shhhh…!" The librarian held a long finger to his broad lips.

Philomena walked to the desk, *Click-Clack* over the stone floor, stopping before him. "Hello, Ass Face."

The mule-headed librarian drummed his fingers on the desk top. "What do you want, Philomena?"

"Access to the Secrets Collection, please."

The librarian scowled. "Out of the question."

"I said please."

"Doesn't matter."

"The Secrets Collection, Ass Face."

"You've already read everything in there."

"Not everything. There's one shelf left. The top shelf."

"I don't have a ladder for you."

"I'll climb."

"We're closing."

"You never close, and you know it."

The librarian scowled deeper. "That's a restricted collection. You can't check anything out."

"I'll read here."

"I don't know where the key is."

"It's on the peg board behind you. J-4."

The librarian curled his mule lip in what passed for a mule sneer, and the little girl smiled up at him.

"What if I just say no?"

Philomena sighed. She reached into the pocket of her dress slowly, holding the librarian with her eyes, like a gunfighter, then in a blur drew out her library card and held it before her like a talisman. "Out damned spot! Get thee behind me! Give up the booty!"

The librarian flinched and looked away, quickly retrieving the large brass key and slapping it down on the counter. He kept his eyes averted from the library card, and only dared to look once Philomena had returned it to her pocket and snatched up the key.

"I hope you fall and break your neck," he muttered.

"I'll be fine," she called, *Click-Clacking* away across the room towards an archway. "Thanks, Ass Face."

"Bring it back when you're done!" he shouted after her.

Before she entered the archway she had selected, Courageous Little Philomena picked up a lit candelabra from a table and held it high to chase back the darkness. She always felt like she should be wearing a long black cape when she held one of these, a ghostly organ playing somewhere in the background. She marched down a long stone corridor, *Click-Clack-Click-Clack*, until she reached a small iron door which opened with the brass key. She pushed into a ten by ten room with three full bookcases, two hard chairs and a table. The door squealed shut behind her on rusty hinges. As far as Philomena knew, she was the only one who ever came here. Probably the only one in Petershead who could read something other than comic books and tabloids, she thought.

She set the candelabra on the table and inspected the shelves.

Ass Face was right, she had read just about everything in here. The entire, encyclopedic series on childhood secrets, petty crimes and cheating in high school and college, endless lies, an affair... and of course the volumes of creepier information from the Twilight Time. These were dark tales indeed, stories of arson, slaughtered animals, girls abducted at knife-point only to vanish into the woods, never to be found. She shuddered in forbidden delight. And there was more. The top shelf, every book still unread, no doubt revealing the deepest caverns of depravity, the true onset of Midnight.

But today what she wanted was a location, directions to bait which would prove irresistible to the Crusk.

She dragged a wooden chair to the bookcase with a squeal and climbed upon it, standing on her pointed little toes and gripping the uppermost shelf as if she would do a chin up. She read the titles along each spine.

Although each intrigued her more than the one before, and she promised herself to come back and read every word (How To Cut A Mini-Van's Brakes looked especially interesting), it wasn't until she came upon a small, untitled book bound in brittle black leather that her little heart began to pound. She took it down and carried it to the table.

Running a small hand over the simple unmarked cover, she opened the book and began to read, slowly at first, then faster and faster, fingers snapping over pages as a pointed grin spread over her face.

Here it was, and the location of the bait both shocked and delighted her. She closed the book with a satisfied thump, tapping out a happy little dance in her pointy little shoes. Philomena patted the library card in her pocket. Now she needed to call her friends, and she was confident Ass Face would let her use his phone.

Johnny and Stumpy and One-Eyed Kate sat at a picnic table, the three of them on one side, watching Big Moose on the other cracking walnuts between his thumb and index finger before passing the nut meat to his companions. He didn't like walnuts himself. One-Eyed Kate was wearing her favorite red jumper, and kindly shared her walnuts with Stumpy, popping every other one into his eager mouth. Eating was tough for him, seeing as he had no arms or legs, and he wasn't so much sitting on the picnic bench as he was propped on it.

Johnny shoved his walnuts down his gullet as fast as his pudgy fingers could move, wheezing through perpetually stuffed nostrils, his swollen belly growling for more. Flies buzzed around his bloated and hairless head, and he waved at them with his beefy hands when they weren't otherwise engaged.

Big Moose concentrated on his task, tongue sticking out the corner of his mouth. The eight-year-old was six-foot-nine and weighed three-hundred pounds, was obscenely muscled and considerably hairy. Pelt kind of hairy. He would have passed for an adult had it not been for his simple, sunny disposition, speech impediment and a runny nose he was always wiping on the Sponge Bob pajamas which he was always wearing. And he had great, heavy moose antlers, one of the reasons for his heavily muscled neck. Every year on Moose's birthday, One-Eyed Kate tied a red balloon to each antler and sang to him, making him tear up and smile.

"What time is it?" asked Kate, blinking her big, blue eye at Moose. It was an old joke, but still made Stumpy and Johnny laugh.

Big Moose squinched up his face as he thought about it. "Midnight?"

They exploded in laughter. That was funnier than the question.

"That's right, Moose," said the little Cyclops girl, patting one of his big hands. Stumpy started to whine, so she fed him another walnut.

"Mmmph mmff Hmmph?"

"Don't talk with food in your mouth, Johnny."

Johnny gulped and belched. "I said, where's Philomena?"

One-Eyed Kate shrugged and ate a walnut. "She said she'd be here. Why, do you have something better to do?"

Big Moose watched Johnny closely, wondering if he did.

Johnny shrugged back at her. "My mom made a roast. It's Rottweiler. I want a sandwich."

Kate shook her head at the pale, fat little boy.

"This won't work anyway," Johnny continued, leaning his elbows on the table and slumping. "We're gonna end up getting eaten."

"You *are* eatin'," said Moose.

"No, you big dummy," Johnny said, flicking a walnut shell at the giant moose-child. "Eaten. *Eat*-en. As in, the Crusk is going to eat us."

Moose thought about that for a minute, then brightened. "Then you don't hafta go to school no more!"

That didn't seem to appease Johnny. In his opinion, his mom should keep him out of school completely, instead of putting his life in peril on a daily basis. That hadn't happened, for him or any of the kids in Petershead. Despite the fact that the Crusk caught and ate an average of one kid per week as they headed to or from school, and despite the fact that the bridge over the Crusk's ravine had to be crossed in order to get to that school, the adults of Petershead sent their young off every weekday to either learn or be devoured. And what did the learning even matter? Johnny had been in the third grade for as long as he could remember, and would always be. Perpetually nine equaled perpetual third grade.

"Grownups suck," he said.

"Philomena says it will work," Kate pointed out, as if that settled the matter.

"Uh-huh, and Phil's always right. Like when she said those wings she built would work, right before she strapped them to Stumpy and pushed him out of the bell tower. That worked great, didn't it?"

One-Eyed Kate frowned, and Stumpy shook his head vigorously and grunted. It most certainly had *not* worked, as the permanent dent in the side of his head demonstrated.

"And what about her little experiment with the woodchuck, the cattle prod and my ass? That worked like a charm, huh?"

"No," said Kate, "*that* was so funny I almost peed myself."

Big Moose chuckled at that and cracked a walnut. "Peed."

"And how about the…"

Kate held up a hand, her eye narrowed. "We get the point, Johnny. No one's making you stay. Go home and stuff your face with Rottweiler if you want to. Just remember you'll have to explain to Clap why you weren't there when she needed you."

Johnny thought about that. He thought about friendship. He thought about teeth.

Johnny stayed on the bench.

Big Moose cracked another walnut.

The night wind kicked up a storm of dead leaves that spun through the playground like a little tornado, making the kids cover their eyes to keep out the grit. Stumpy couldn't, and caught the worst of it. Big Moose opened his mouth wide to catch the grit on his tongue.

Courageous Little Philomena walked into the playground and saw her friends sitting at a picnic table on the far side. She pushed through rusty swings, making the chains creak, and strode towards them, a canvas bag slung over one shoulder.

Big Moose saw her first and grinned broadly, revealing his single tooth and showing off a severe cleft. "Mena! Mena!" Johnny and Kate ran to her, and Stumpy, left on the bench, craned his neck to see over his shoulder, grunting.

"Did you get it?" One-Eyed Kate asked, jumping up and down in excitement.

"Yep," said Philomena, unslinging the bag and setting it on the picnic table. "It wasn't hard at all."

"Where did you find it?" asked Johnny, poking a fat finger at the bag, then jerking it back quickly when the bag twitched.

"You'll never believe it. It was hiding in a corner of my Uncle Waldo's potato cellar. Can you imagine? It's been right there all along."

Johnny raised an eyebrow. "Wait a minute. The ultimate bait to catch the Crusk has been hiding in your family's potato cellar?"

"Yep."

"And no one knew it was there?"

"Nope."

"And no one ever saw it?"

"Nope"

"And it never tried to get out?"

"Uh...nope, guess not. Anything else?"

Johnny shrugged and waved at a fly.

"It wasn't hard to catch, either. I just grabbed it and stuffed it in this bag. I think it's scared."

The children watched as Philomena dumped the bag out on the table. Its contents rolled onto the splintered and initial-carved wood like a soft blob, then shuddered. About the size of a basketball, the bait was translucent, cloudy, shimmering with a soft, internal white light. It quivered now and again like Jell-O.

"*This* is it?" Johnny said, frowning.

Philomena ignored him, watching the blob of light with fascination. "Touch it," she said, and they all did, little hands – or in Moose's case big hands – crawling over its surface. It was smooth and spongy and cool to the touch. One-Eyed Kate lifted

Stumpy off the bench and held him so he could rub his head against the thing. The limbless child closed his eyes and made a purring sound.

"Did you bring what I told you?" Philomena asked her friends. They all nodded and pointed to a Red Flyer wagon they normally used to pull Stumpy around town. It was piled high with heavy chain, and something long was underneath, shiny metal peeking out between the links.

"Moose pulled it," Johnny said. "It was way too heavy for us." A fly landed on his ear and he swatted it away.

Philomena inspected the wagon's contents, then, satisfied, she re-bagged the bright blob of bait and tossed the canvas sack over her shoulder once more.

"Let's go catch the Crusk."

Petershead School sat on the far edge of town, a one room structure in the classic style, complete with shuttered bell steeple, which had once been painted a cheerful red with white trim. Now, the paint was gray and peeling (and, as it turned out, lead-based), its windows had broken panes, and the steeple which had once housed a resonant bell was now a home for crows.

The town limits of Petershead were clearly marked in all directions by a sheer cliff with crumbling edges, and beyond was only misty darkness. Petershead was literally an island. At this edge, a finger of land had splintered off at an angle, forming a smaller island, and it was upon this that the Petershead School rested. A creaky wooden plank bridge with broken railings was the only way across the hundred foot gap, known as the Ravine, and it was deep within this slash of darkness that the Crusk made its home. The travelers across the bridge supplied its meals.

No adults came here, except for the School Marm, simply referred to as Miss Marm. A stick-figure of a woman, she never left the school, slept on a cot near the chalk board, and ate who knew what. Crows was the best guess any of her pupils had. Therefore the only visitors were the school children, doomed to trudge out here from town each day and take their chances crossing the bridge, hoping that a hungry black mass didn't lunge out of the darkness below and carry them down to a brief and horrible end.

Courageous Little Philomena and her pals made their way up the path towards the bridge. Here and there, old chestnut trees grew along the ravine's edge, some leaning precariously out over the nothingness, roots straining to keep their grip on the stony bank. Others were set back and solid-looking, and it was towards one of these that Philomena headed, leaving the path and motioning for her friends to follow. Stopping at one tree in particular, she planted her hands on her pointy little hips and looked it up and down.

One-Eyed Kate, carrying Stumpy in her arms like a baby, stood beside her, and Johnny, sulking, shuffled a distance behind, not at all happy to be here. Big Moose pulled the heavy wagon up to the girls.

"This one should do," Philomena pronounced, pointing at the tree and looking over at Moose, who began unloading the Red Flyer.

"Do you really think this will work?" Kate asked, hugging Stumpy close.

"It has to, Katie."

One-Eyed Kate nodded and wiped at a tear that rolled down from the big blue eye in the center of her face. Petershead was dangerous enough for children without the Crusk thinning out their numbers even more on a weekly basis. She was proud of Philomena, and happy to be her friend.

"Why do you think it will work?" demanded Johnny, one hand digging deep into a pants pocket. He thought he felt a piece of hard candy down there somewhere. Or it could just be lint.

Philomena explained her plan. Kate and Big Moose and Stumpy thought it was a good idea. Johnny thought about his Rottweiler sandwich.

"But why *this* bait?" Johnny pressed. "What makes it so special?"

"Because the book at the library says it's one of a kind, and irresistible."

"It seems to like kids just fine," he said.

"Well, I don't think using a kid as bait is okay. Do you know of any extra kids we could use, Johnny?"

One-Eyed Kate elbowed her fat friend. "I can think of one."

Philomena carefully paced off the distance from the tree she had chosen to the bridge, then returned and had Big Moose lay out the chain in a straight line. She paced this off as well, then instructed Moose to anchor the chain to the tree at a particular point. Moose did as he was told, then heaved all his weight against it, grunting and making a big vein stand out on the side of his head. The chestnut tree creaked and the bark splintered a little, but the chain only dug in deeper to the wood, holding fast.

Next, Philomena pointed to the remaining item in the wagon, an enormous steel fishhook, five feet long, weighing close to a hundred pounds. Moose had found it in the barn behind his house, hanging on a wall between a snow shovel and a dried-out garden hose. It had a wicked-looking barbed head, and appeared sharp enough to cut a person in half. Under the little girl's direction, Big Moose clipped it onto the loose end of chain, tugging to make sure it too was secure.

"And now for the bait." Philomena upended the bag, dumping the glowing blob onto the ground.

Johnny tapped her on the shoulder. "Uh, Clap? I still don't understand how this is supposed to work. Even if it does take the bait, how are we gonna pull it up? It'll be too heavy, even with Moose pulling."

"Didn't I go over this already?"

Johnny pressed on. "And if we do get it up out of the ravine, what's to stop it from just eating us right here by the edge?"

"Johnny..." Philomena said, clenching her fists.

"And Phil, what if...?"

Philomena grabbed the fat boy by his shirt and hauled him in close, pushing her nose to his. "Ever see a running dog reach the end of a short leash?"

Johnny blinked at her. "No."

Philomena gasped and dropped her chin to her chest, letting him go. "Nevermind."

"But Phil..."

She pointed a finger at him. "Another word, fat boy, and we're using different bait."

Johnny closed his lips tightly and went digging for lint or candy.

Philomena picked up the luminescent blob, and without ceremony impaled it on the fishhook's barb. The midnight sky shattered with a dozen forks of lightning in that instant, and the thunder immediately after sounded like a scream, shaking the ground and then fading off to a whimper.

The children huddled together, wide eyes staring up at the sky, which had transformed to a tumult of charcoal and ebony clouds, roiling against each other. A bitter wind kicked up and made the trees sway, plastering their clothing against them.

"Did the book talk about that?" whispered Kate.

"No," Philomena whispered back, her little body shaking, not feeling particularly courageous anymore.

"Wanna go home," said Big Moose, starting to cry and holding one of Johnny's hands so tightly that a bone cracked and Johnny squealed.

Philomena bit her bottom lip, straightened her back, and forced herself away from her friends, still trembling. "We've come this far. If we don't do this now, we'll never be brave enough to come back."

"I'm not brave enough *now*," said One-Eyed Kate.

"You broke my hand," Johnny wheezed at Big Moose.

Philomena looked at each of them, and then told them what she wanted. Kate set Stumpy gently against a smaller tree before they all stepped to the big fishhook and picked it up, even Johnny, who was holding back tears of his own. Together they walked to the edge, the impaled bait pulsing before them, with Big Moose paying out the chain.

An even colder wind curled up out of the ravine, bringing the pungent smell of dead things, making them shiver and wrinkle their noses. Dried leaves spiraled up into the turbulent sky as they eased the hook and bait out over the edge, then as a group, began to lower it by the chain. As the glowing hook descended it began illuminating the walls of the ravine, revealing rock formations shaped like tortured faces, each twisted into a rictus of pain or horror. Some appeared to scream soundlessly, others to stare blankly, mouths agape, and still more appeared to be laughing, deep in the clutches of some unknown madness. But nothing moved as the hook was lowered deeper.

Once the hook reached the end of the chain, the children let go and lined up at the edge, peering down. The glow from the bait was much smaller, moving back and forth slowly as the hook swayed in the wind. They waited a long time.

Nothing.

"This is dumb," said Johnny, deciding there was no candy to be found in his pockets, exploring one nostril with a pudgy finger instead.

"Maybe it's not hungry," offered One-Eyed Kate. Stumpy was back in her arms, and he grunted his agreement. Moose just stared into the ravine.

Philomena frowned, tapping the tip of one pointed shoe against the chain in annoyance. "I think we need to get its attention."

Johnny shook his head. "You said the bait was *irresistible*. You said!"

"I know what I said, and it is."

"Uh, I think it's resisting, Phil."

"Someone's gonna find out how deep that ravine is," Philomena sang softly, and One-Eyed Kate punched Johnny in the side of the head.

They stood there in silence for a while, except for Johnny, who couldn't decide if he wanted to whimper about his hand or his head or both. Then Big Moose looked up from the ravine.

"Saturday," he said.

The children just stared at him.

"Saturday," he repeated. "No school."

Philomena snapped her pointy little fingers. "He's right! It's Saturday! The Crusk has to know his food doesn't come out here today!" And then she was off, sprinting towards the bridge, pointy knees and elbows pumping once more, red ringlets of hair flying in the wind. She started making loud, hooting noises. Her boots hit the wooden planks and she pounded across, *CLICK-CLACK-CLICK-CLACK!*

"Cruuuuusk! Come and eat me, Crusk! Lunchtime, big fella!"

The kids watched in horrified amazement.

Courageous Little Philomena reached the other side without being eaten, so she turned around and ran across again, boot heels slamming the planks, hollering and waving her arms. "Cruuuuuusk, Cruuusk, here Crusky! Yummy crunchy din-din!"

A rumble from deep in the ravine. A black mass speeding up through the air, spines and tails and teeth, oh, so many teeth.

Philomena reached the center of the bridge and stopped, gripping the weak railing and jumping higher and higher, screaming into the ravine. "Come and get it, you big BOOGER!"

A mighty mouth yawned open as it aimed at the morsel on the bridge.

Then suddenly the mass jerked left, its attention pulled by the wriggling, glowing, *irresistible* blob dangling by the ravine wall. It hit the hook, jaws crunching down, and a moment later the chain snapped taut. The chestnut tree creaked against the weight, but Philomena had chosen well, and it held, roots deep and solid in the ground. The moment the Crusk hit the bait there was another deafening, inhuman shriek and the sky was once more split by lightning. The creature banked away from the wall of the ravine and roared towards the little girl on the bridge, but a full thirty feet before it got there it was jerked up violently short and let out a terrible yelp.

Like a running dog on a short leash.

And Johnny understood.

The Crusk thrashed at the end of the chain, the hook sunk deep in its jawbone, never to come out, the bait deep in its gullet. It wailed and jerked and hit the end of the chain again and again until finally, exhausted, it sank back into the darkness, trapped and impotent.

At the ravine's edge, the children clapped and cheered. Out on the bridge, Courageous Little Philomena swept her pointed little hat off her pointed little head and took a bow.

Laughing, One-Eyed Kate cupped her hands to her mouth and shouted across to her friend. "Philomena, what *was* that bait?"

In an Indiana mental facility, a man lunged against the full restraints which held him to no more than a sitting position. Former celebrity children's book author Peter Thomaston opened his eyes and gasped.

"My soul."

THE HOUSE ON MOHAWK

It rested on a corner, a large cape with two upstairs dormer windows and a one car garage. A giant beech tree dominated the front yard, one of its roots buckling the cement walk that led from the step to the mailbox. A hedge, brown and dying, shielded the front and side yard from the road, marching in an uneven line with the asphalt as Iroquois met Mohawk. The flower beds were untended, and the curtains were drawn. The house appeared vacant.

Jennifer knew better.

She sat in a rental car half a block up Iroquois, the heater running against the early November chill. The sky was indigo as the sun settled, and a street light a block away clicked on, casting the front of the house in a deeper gloom.

She watched, hands clenched in her lap. Beside her in the cup holder was a single key on a ring with a silver heart. Her eyes never left the house as a rising breeze made the tree branches sway like arms, dead leaves chasing across the browning lawn. She watched the curtains for movement.

How many years had those limbs cast shadows on her bedroom wall? She'd been two when they moved in, so it had to be fifteen years? Until she went away to college. But the bedroom had still been hers for years after that, and the tree wasn't the only shadow that crawled in there.

As she'd left their little Connecticut town for A.S.U. – a place as far from here as she could get - she had sworn to never put a foot inside again. That hadn't lasted, of course. It was her home, where her parents lived until Mom passed away two years ago, and where Dad had lived alone until he joined her two days ago. Since going away for school she had been back inside exactly three times. Jack had only been there once, and little Collin had never been, nor would he ever be, inside that house.

"I hate you," she whispered.

Jennifer wasn't supposed to be here until tomorrow. She and Keri were going to meet some aunts and cousins for coffee, go to the mortuary to make arrangements, then come back here to plan for the house and Dad's things. In the daytime. Not that the time of day had ever really mattered on Mohawk.

She turned the heater knob up one setting.

Jack and Collin were back in Phoenix, despite her husband's protests that he should be here to support Jennifer and pay his respects. She had been firm, however, and Jack relented. Over the years she had told him everything, and though he didn't believe it all, or even most of it, he knew that she did.

People say we don't remember events from early childhood, but Jennifer knew she had dreamed about the house before she ever saw it. Dark dreams of watching windows and rooms that listened. Jack smiled his patient smile and told her they were false memories. He meant well, but then he'd never heard his name spoken when he was alone in the house.

It started shortly after they moved in, two-year-old Jenny in her high chair while Mommy was in the kitchen. A glass of orange juice two feet away on the table had floated slowly into the air, then up-ended and crashed to the floor. Little Jenny had cried at the breaking glass, and Mommy had yelled at her for somehow causing it. The next day she was back in the high chair, and this time it was a glass bowl of fruit that lifted, shuddered, and shattered on the linoleum. Again, well out of her reach, but she had gotten a spanking for it just the same.

It wasn't the last floating object, or the last spanking. Books shot out of her bookcase and hit the far bedroom wall, and her parents had been angry, thinking she was throwing a tantrum. Jars of finger paint rose from their tray on her little easel as she watched, hurling themselves against the walls and ceiling to explode in rainbows of dripping color. Her toy box lid banged open and shut, open and shut, making her run from her room, crying.

They never saw any of it.

Jennifer watched the house, knowing it watched her back. Hadn't it called her tonight? And hadn't she come?

The footsteps in the hall outside her door would wake her up at night, pounding feet running back and forth. At first she had actually had the courage – or the lack of sense – to open her door to see what her parents could possibly be up to, but the hallway was always empty. Worse was when the footsteps approached her, like when she was in the family room watching TV or reading in a living room chair, slow, heavy steps coming up behind her and stopping. The hairs on the back of her neck lifted as she looked back to see nobody there.

Then there were the lights, flicking on and off in empty rooms, or sometimes waiting until she turned off a wall switch and walked away before snapping back on. Her father grumbled about his electric bill constantly. She almost got used to the lights, and the house must have sensed that, for they started going *off* when she was alone in a room, leaving her in darkness.

Then something would whisper her name.

Jennifer cranked the heater knob all the way over, warm air blasting into the car as she hugged herself against a cold she knew the heater couldn't chase away. The dark blue had all but faded, and the house on Mohawk sat quietly under a starless sky.

When she was a teenager she found any excuse in good weather to spend nights out on the lawn in her sleeping bag, often with friends. She felt better there. At least in nature you knew what the noises were. At least outside you didn't have to listen to the basement stairs creak as someone walked up them, aware that both your parents were in the same room with you.

And it was the basement which frightened her the most.

Keri was three years younger. For a little sister, she was a good listener, and always believed what Jennifer said she heard and saw. But she swore nothing ever happened to her.

Even at a young age Jennifer saw the lie in her little sister's eyes.

Keri said she never heard her name called. Never heard the stereo turn on in an empty room. Never saw a smoky blob lurking in ceiling corners.

Jennifer did, and more. It escalated around the time she turned twelve. That was when her name, once whispered from the end of an empty hall, would instead be screamed in her ear. That was when her bed began to shake in the night, vibrating and slamming the headboard against the wall hard enough to leave marks. At first Mom and Dad yelled about rough-housing, then adolescent tantrums, and once in high school, Mom even accused her of somehow sneaking a boy into her room.

On nights the bed didn't shake, her pillows would slide from under her head, down between the mattress and the headboard, slowly, steadily, as if someone under the bed were pulling them down. Jennifer grabbed for them...once...and had them *jerked* out of her hands, *SNAP*, under the bed. Something shrieked her name in her ear, and the bedroom lights flicked on and off like a strobe until she fled to the living room to cower in a corner of the sofa.

She never fought for her pillows again.

Jennifer shut off the engine and sat in stillness for a while. Then she took the house key from the cup holder and slowly climbed out of the car. A night breeze lifted her hair about her face as she shut the door, putting the key in her jacket pocket.

The people started showing up in her mid teens, at first only when she was alone in the house. Once she had looked out the front windows and seen an old man in a straw hat standing on the lawn, arms limp at his side, looking at the house. She opened the front door to see if he was lost, but then he wasn't there. Another time she had been alone at the kitchen table studying and saw a man in a white dress shirt pass by the kitchen doorway in the hall, not looking at her.

Then her bedroom door slammed, and the snarls of an animal started from inside.

It was four days before she slept in her room again, and then only with the lights on.

Until the house switched them off.

They grew bolder. She and some friends had been in the living room, Jennifer in the recliner in the corner, with Dennis, one of the boys from the neighborhood, on the couch across from her. He had been talking, laughing, and then just stopped and stared towards her as a dark stain spread across his crotch. He ran from the house, and Jennifer chased him three blocks before she caught up to him. He was crying and embarrassed about wetting himself, and it took nearly an hour of talking to him and calming him down before he managed to tell her he had seen a wrinkled, bald man slowly peek out at him from behind the chair Jennifer was sitting in, like he had been curled up and hiding back there.

Dennis never came back to the house, and stopped talking to her at school.

Jennifer started up the street, walking slowly, her loafers crunching small gravel underfoot. The big tree in the front yard stopped swaying for a moment as the wind died, as if the house was holding its breath at her approach.

She turned sixteen, got her license and a part time job, and bought a used Mitsubishi. One Sunday afternoon she was driving home, taking a back road, and glanced down a side street. There she had seen Lisa Portman, a thirteen-year-old friend of Keri's, half a block up. She was straddling her bike and talking to someone in a dark van which had pulled to the side of the road. Lisa was wearing pink shorts and a blue top. Jennifer took it all in as she passed; the little girl, the van…she slammed on the brakes in the middle of the road, threw it into reverse and backed up.

The van was gone. So were Lisa and her bike.

Jennifer shot down the side road, checking driveways and cross streets, seeing nothing. This was pre-cell phone, so she raced home to call the police and report the abduction.

As the Mitsu roared into the driveway, there was Lisa's bike lying in the front yard. Lisa was inside with Keri in her sister's room listening to the Backstreet Boys, and had been there for hours.

And Lisa was wearing pink shorts and a blue top.

That same year, Jennifer was awakened early one morning to her bedroom door slamming open. She sat up to see her mother in the doorway in a nightgown, her hair wild and her eyes rimmed red, smoking a cigarette and pointing a finger at her.

"Do you know what you've done?" her mother screamed. "I hate you! I wish you would just *kill* yourself!" Then she stormed into the kitchen.

Jennifer sat sobbing on her bed, calling to her mother, begging to know what she had done but afraid to go to her, afraid she would make her more angry. He father had stumbled to her bedroom doorway, rubbing at sleep-filled eyes. "What the hell? Why are you crying?"

Jennifer buried her face in a pillow, but managed to choke out, "Daddy, why did Mommy say that? Why is she so mad at me?"

Her father looked confused. "When? Why did she say what?"

Jennifer shook her head, not wanting to repeat the words. "Just now!"

Her father frowned. "Jenny, what the hell are you talking about? Your Mom's in Tampa at a sales convention. She flew out last night, remember?"

The memory made Jennifer stop in the road. She gripped the house key in her pocket and stood there, squeezing until the key dug painfully into her palm, looking at the hateful house.

"Why?" she whispered.

It didn't respond, but she knew it heard her.

She had long suspected that Dad had been the only one to get it. Mom didn't have time to listen to her nonsense, and Keri was in complete denial. But Dad stopped yelling and blaming her for loud noises, and although he teased her the few times she told him about things that happened, she thought she had seen the lie in his eyes, too. What had *he* seen and heard, she wondered, never asking. And despite his apparent refusal to believe her, he was always good about allowing her to sleep over at friends, or go with him on errands that kept her out of the house, or encouraging her to join every after-school sport and activity she could.

As she neared eighteen, the tempo rose, as if the house was suddenly in a hurry. More footsteps, more whispering, her name being called from the basement. Sometimes it was her father's voice, or her sister's, but Jennifer had grown wary over the years. Then came tugging at the back of her shirt, a shove into a wall, and then a slap out of empty air that left a red handprint on her face and had her father in a rage that evening demanding to know what boy had done this to her.

The shadow people came, standing in corners, peeking out from open closets. One was a little girl who stood silently in the hallway looking at her.

Jennifer always felt that if she hadn't gone away to Arizona when she did, the house would have taken her. Not simply driven her mad, though she often feared it would and still wondered in a small way if it had, even just a little. No, she was afraid it would actually take her. One afternoon, while she was alone, just snatch her away into whatever cold, dead darkness it was that lived there.

But she had cheated it of its prize.

It wanted her back.

There were times she couldn't avoid coming home. The first was during summer break between freshman and sophomore year. It had been waiting for her. Touches on her back and neck, followed by painful hair pulling. Each summer afterwards she applied for internships that kept her in Phoenix.

When Mom got sick she came back for a week. Knowing the house was waiting to catch her alone, she had been careful to keep people around her as much as possible. Still, it found moments…a suddenly dark room followed by caresses, a shadow figure watching her from under a table, the cellar door swinging open silently when she went near it. That was where it really wanted her. Down there in the dark.

When Mom passed away she brought her husband, not realizing at the time she was already six weeks pregnant with Collin. The bed shook violently their first night there, but Jack slept through it. In the morning, however, he told her it had woken him up, then asked, "Is that the kind of thing you lived with?" She nodded, and he held her tight for a long time. Jennifer was elated that finally, someone had caught a glimpse of the house's true nature. That night in the shower, the house paid her back for her small victory. The water turned suddenly to a frigid blast, and then a hand she couldn't see pushed through the shower curtain and raked deep, red scratches across her belly, making her scream.

They spent the rest of their time at a hotel. Her family chastised her that she was breaking her father's already wounded heart, but Daddy had helped them load their bags in the car, and then looked his daughter in the eye and just nodded.

Jennifer's feet scuffed up the buckled sidewalk, past the tree, right up to the front step. A curtain moved in the front window just the slightest bit, a peek. It had been waiting, knowing she would come, needing to settle all debts and claim its own. All her life she had been trying to get away from here, but kept coming back, as the house knew she would.

And now she was here for her final visit. She knew what it wanted, could imagine the cellar door swinging wide in anticipation. What would be waiting for her there, she wondered? Her sister and cousins would wait for her in the morning, but she wouldn't be showing up. They would call her cell phone, but she wouldn't answer. They would come to the house, but wouldn't find her. She wouldn't be making any arrangements, wouldn't be at the funeral.

Jennifer pulled the key from her jacket pocket, holding it before her eyes. It looked black, and she could almost feel it tremble in her fingertips, just as she knew the house was trembling. She took a deep breath.

Then she dropped the key on the mat.

"We're done," she said, her voice clear and strong.

She turned and strode back up the walk, back to her rental car. With luck she could catch a late flight and be in Phoenix in time to have breakfast with her boys.

She knew her Dad would understand.

SOMEPLACE THE WIND BLOWS THROUGH

It sounded like the sea. So she imagined, having never left Oklahoma. It came in waves, making the treetops sway and the leaves flicker, a soft rising and falling like a never-ending whisper.

Hope sat on a bench in Filson's only park, a small square ringed by shops with the town offices at one end, a dull bronze statue of a soldier at the center. Her twin sister Faith sat beside her, both little girls swinging their legs slowly and holding hands.

"It's quiet," said Hope.

Faith nodded.

A tendril of breeze spiraled down from above, ruffling their hair and blowing a windshield flier across the fresh-cut grass. Hope loved that smell.

Nothing moved on the streets, no cars or farm trucks, no folks passing by to say hello. No squirrels played chase-me games up and down the tree trunks, and the branches above were silent in the absence of birds.

"I miss the sounds."

Hope looked at her sister and squeezed her hand.

"I miss mommy and daddy." Faith's eyes welled up again, and so did Hope's.

"Me too."

They sat that way for a while, staring out at the park, their tears turning pink as they tried to understand. They didn't want to think about the people lying on the sidewalks, slumped over steering wheels in motionless cars. Didn't want to think about their little house three blocks away, just past the intersection with the blinking yellow light and the Dairy Queen that closed just after Labor Day. Daddy in the front yard by his grass fertilizing machine, mommy on the floor of the small living room with a spilled glass of tea.

Faith started coughing. So did Hope.

Filson, Oklahoma was quiet all over. The big trucks by the grain silos were still, the high school gym with its orange and blue decorations for Homecoming was silent. Only a couple of small oil wells chugged slowly on at the west end of town.

Faith covered her cough with her hands like mommy had taught her, seeing crimson droplets on her palms. Hope's chest rattled and she leaned against her sister's shoulder, her eyes glassy.

"Do you think Jesus will be here soon to get us?" Faith asked.

Hope didn't answer. She was already gone.

High above the waving treetops of Filson, a large aircraft left a lonely white contrail across a cornflower blue sky. Serious men and women aboard Air Force One spoke with authority and confidence about biological warfare and acceptable losses.

Faith's body shuddered with coughs and she put her arm around her sister, their heads touching.

"Goodnight, Hope." She closed her eyes.

And the wind kept on.

RISING SUN, SETTING SUN

A pearly mist hovered over the field, making ghosts of the gnarled trees and hiding the large buildings of the school. With the sun not yet above the horizon, the damp sea air cast a morning chill. Three wooden posts were placed close together on the field, each topped with a cloth bag, bamboo helmets strapped to them. From within the mist an impatient horse snorted and stamped. A pair of whispers in the mist, and a pair of arrows slammed into two of the posts. Next came a rattle of armor and the pounding of hooves.

A phantom charged into view, a man in elaborate armor wearing a horned helmet, his horse thundering over the field as the rider smoothly drew a weapon with a long shaft and curved blade. In a moment of sound and speed the horseman was at the posts, his *naginata* flashing in a deadly arc as he sped past. The helmeted bag on the third post was cut in two, splinters of wood sent flying as the horse reared and turned, shaking its head and snorting steam in the morning air.

"Speed," announced the mounted samurai, "is the sister of surprise." He waved a gloved hand. "In such an environment you must take advantage of the elements, conceal your location, choose when and where to attack. This tactic will be useless, however, unless you close quickly with the survivors."

131

Fifty feet away from the posts, twenty young men in gray kimonos and shaved heads bowed as one.

Zenki Mokinoto, samurai and *sempai*, instructor-student in the House of Itto, dismounted as one of the students came forward to take the reins of his horse. He handed his slender halberd, longbow and quiver to another boy before approaching the group, tucking the ornate helmet under one arm. Zenki had been born into a noble house, his father a general who died in war during the boy's seventh year. From birth he, like his brothers, had been trained to follow his father's path. The general's station assured his sons the finest instruction, here at the Itto Ryu.

The samurai led his group back to the courtyard of the great house. Without a word they formed ranks and waited while he moved to a low veranda to remove his armor. Nearby, another group of students was practicing the basics of swordsmanship, using oak *bokken*, practice swords. They were novices and clumsy, but their instructor – a man in his late twenties wearing a green patterned kimono – was patient, explaining techniques and working slowly.

Zenki ignored the group of novices as he performed the slow ritual of removing the many layers of armor, tying it into a tight bundle for storage. This was practice armor, not the elegant suit for war, which would instead be placed upon a stand and set in a place of honor. At thirty-five, the samurai had already fought in five campaigns, from repelling Chinese invaders as a teenager to enforcing the Shogun's rule in smaller actions. He was a master of the sword, a superb horseman and highly skilled in the *naginata*, a difficult weapon to use when *not* on horseback. Yet despite his abilities and experience, he understood that every samurai was a student throughout his life, and so Zenki kept coming back to the Itto School.

His reasons were not altruistic, for he was an ambitious man. He had fought beside Itto Ittosai, the founder and sensei of the school, had helped him put the Tokugawa clan in power. Zenki was popular at court, and he understood the intricacies of politics and noble honor. At one point he was offered a post in the Shogunate, second-in-command to a *Daimyo*, a noble lord, but he turned it down, insisting humbly that he was merely a student and unworthy. Instead of being an insult, it made him that much more desirable and favored, as he knew it would. It was all part of the game.

Ono looked up from his teaching at the samurai kneeling on the veranda, then at the man's ranks of silent pupils. He frowned. Zenki had put on an impressive display for the youngsters, showing them skills which one learned only after many years of actual application. The demonstration had little practical use here, where fundamentals must be mastered before advanced training took place. Zenki's group would have been better served by performing a thousand repetitive cuts with their swords than being an audience to the horseman's prowess. Ono turned back to his class, annoyed with himself. They were equals, both *sempai* charged by the headmaster with instructing the students. Each would follow his own philosophy of training, and who was Ono to dispute Zenki's methods?

"Ono-san," one of his pupils called.

"Please," said Ono, frowning, "you must show respect by addressing me as *sensei*."

The student bowed his head at the shameful error.

"What is it, Kano-san?" Ono liked the boy, a youth of fourteen mired in the clumsiness of puberty. Kano was one of Zenki's sons, and Ono knew that if the boy had made such an error in his father's presence he would have been beaten.

"*Sensei*, forgive my stupidity, but will you please show me the placement of the feet during *chiburi?*"

Ono stood beside him and slowly demonstrated the technique of snapping blood off the blade, the boy paying careful attention. Kano thanked him and bowed, then concentrated as he repeated the move. Ono nodded, moving on to another boy who was having trouble.

Ono was the son of a samurai in charge of a small village and monastery, his early life one of quiet simplicity. Due to the proximity of the monks, he was raised in a spiritual environment and had come close to becoming a holy man himself. When bandits attacked the village, however, slaughtering the monks and half the village samurai – his father included – Ono learned that such a tranquil life could only exist so long as there were swordsmen to safeguard it. Rather than be one who reaped the harvest of peace, Ono chose to stand among those who defended it.

His father's position gave him the opportunity to train at the legendary Itto Ryu.

He was eleven when the Tokugawas came to power, already training to be samurai. At thirteen he was recruited as a spearman to defend the Shogunate against a coup attempt. At twenty he was part of a force tasked with enforcing the Shogun's will with a *Daimyo* who refused to pay the full amount of required tribute. This short and bloody campaign ended with the *Daimyo's* samurai lying dead throughout his castle, the feudal lord himself choosing the honor of ritual suicide. It was during this battle that Ono gained the reputation of a natural swordsman, an honor which embarrassed him, for he saw himself as a mere student who had much more to learn. He believed surviving that skirmish had been luck and divine providence rather than skill.

The samurai stopped the practice and had his pupils kneel for meditation designed to still their spirits, to let them absorb what they had learned. He looked over to his counterpart, seeing that Zenki had organized sparring among his group. The older man strode up and down the lines of battling young men, correcting errors with painful cracks of a bamboo cane and shaking his head in disgust.

One of Zenki's students tried to parry the downward strike of his opponent, and the jarring contact of wood on wood knocked the practice sword from his hand. The *bokken* pinwheeled through the air and struck Zenki's foot. Practice came to an instant halt as the samurai strode to the offending pupil and slapped the side of his head, hard. He fell to the ground, and with the bamboo cane, Zenki began whipping the boy's back savagely. The other students dropped to their knees and pressed their foreheads to the earth.

The beating was short and mean, yet the youth bit back his cries and endured the master's anger. At last the cane broke across his back, and Zenki stood over him, barking about clumsiness and the dishonor of losing one's sword in combat. He ordered the boy to retrieve his *bokken* and resume practice, even though he was clearly in great pain, lines of blood seeping through the back of his kimono. The boy obeyed, and the other students quickly returned to their sparring.

Ono watched the incident quietly, arms folded. The boy essentially belonged to Zenki, and if the samurai chose, he had every right to inflict whatever punishment he desired, for any offense, or even no offense at all. His methods, however, were distasteful to the younger samurai, and it was no secret that Ono objected to Zenki's harsh manner. Neither was the fact that both men intensely disliked the other.

As he watched the other *sempai,* Ono reflected on this. Was it jealousy? Clearly Zenki was a far better swordsman, and was without question an exceptional horseman. Horses frightened Ono, a shameful fact he tried to hide and which left a large gap in his skills, making him incomplete. Zenki was famous, favored at court, adept in the subtleties of bureaucracy, another area which held little interest for Ono, and in this modern day of 1620 a necessary skill. The older man's flower arranging was inspiring, and his silk paintings were much in demand. One piece – a spidery sketch of two cranes – was rumored to grace the Shogun's private chambers. What was Ono compared to Zenki, the perfect samurai?

Perhaps it *was* jealousy, shameful and bitter, an emotion unworthy of the teachings of his father and the monks. And yet, Ono truly believed Zenki lacked the proper humility of a samurai, lacked the spirituality that would lead to enlightenment. Zenki did not understand Itto's philosophy.

Arrogant ass, Ono chastised himself. *Do you dare to believe you understand the old man's philosophy? Who are you to judge another man's spirit? Who are you to say who is a fit samurai and who is not? Tend to the gardens of your own failures before casting an eye upon your neighbor's field.*

Ono closed his eyes in shame, then dismissed his class. They joined the weary students of Zenki's group, filing into the great house to bathe before more studies. As they left, Zenki stood across the courtyard, fists on his hips and his stance wide, silently challenging the younger instructor to say something about the whipping.

Ono bowed respectfully and quietly left the training ground.

The sun was below the mountains, the coming night clear and pleasant. A soft breeze rattled the wooden chimes on the veranda, making a row of colorful paper lanterns sway. Ono and Zenki, dressed in comfortable silk robes, knelt on soft bamboo mats, enjoying the open air and peacefulness. Itto Ittosai, seventy years old with a balding head and weathered face, knelt beside them. He was dressed in simple white robes with a silk sash, sipping the *sake* being served by Ono's wife Maiko. The old man's face was serene, his eyes gentle as he thanked the lovely young woman.

Zenki held out his cup, ignoring Ono's wife as she served, as was customary. He did not notice her beauty, did not notice her at all. Nor did he often take notice his own wife, whom he kept tucked away tending to his house and children, never passing up an opportunity to remind her that she was plain and undesirable. His two concubines, however, were quite beautiful, and his wife could never hope to match their grace. She had given him two sons, however, and for that he was somewhat grateful. But then it was her duty. Kano and Mifune would one day bring honor to his name.

The samurai breathed in the night air, closing his eyes. Something important had happened this afternoon, an event which was of consequence to him. Shortly after noon, an emissary from the Shogunate had arrived at the school bearing a message from the ruling Tokugawa. The Shogun desired a master swordsman to teach his first-born son the way of the sword, a great honor to the man selected. Naturally Ittosai was being considered, and the emissary inquired if the headmaster was open to such a proposal. Itto had yet to give his answer. For Zenki this meant that the Itto School – and its best *sempai* – was favored. It also meant that the time was quickly coming for Zenki to make his bid for power, to take a worthy place in the Shogunate. Such as a *Daimyo*. With his master as *sensei* to the Shogun's son, Zenki would be the natural selection for such a post. His noble birth, skill at arms, favored status and spiritual purity made him perfect for the rank.

This was what Zenki had worked towards his entire life, the reason he strove for perfection, his own road to enlightenment. He honed his skills so that he could best serve the Shogun and protect Japan, and it indeed needed protection. The harsh experience of war with the Chinese had taught him that, and his hatred for them was great. Once *Daimyo*, he would lead a campaign against mainland China as his ancestors had. He would make them servants of the rising sun, as they should be.

And of course, with the position would come the expected wealth and influence, the comforts to which such a post was naturally entitled. That, too, was as it should be.

Ono accepted the wine from his wife, nodding politely. She smiled in a way that was for him alone, lowering her eyes before retreating into the house. The samurai loved her very much, and she in turn had borne him four beautiful children, the oldest only seven. And just as Zenki pondered his own ambitions, Ono considered what he wanted. Good marriages for his daughters, training at the Itto school for his sons, peace for his family. And for himself, a quiet road to enlightenment, a desire formed during his childhood near the temple. That was not to say that a part of him did not desire privilege and a measure of authority, the respect of others, and the opportunity to share the things he learned. Any man who claimed otherwise was either a liar or a monk, and Ono was neither.

He looked at his master, who appeared relaxed, his thoughts far away. Ono remembered one of the few times in his life when he had seen his master truly angry. It was shortly after he had arrived at the school, himself a child. The Itto Ryu was visited by Japan's legendary swordsman, Miyamoto Musashi. Ono had been supremely disappointed, for this legend had matted hair and wore soiled robes, was unwashed, ungroomed, and left a trail of sour odor everywhere he went. Musashi and Ittosai had *sake* on this very veranda, while Ono hid under the porch listening. His discovery would have meant at the very least a severe beating, and at worst expulsion, an unthinkable dishonor. Yet he found he could not stay away, risking everything to lie motionless in the dark and the dirt, peeking up through the wooden slats of the veranda at Japan's greatest hero.

Ono remembered how they had argued. Their discussion was of spiritual matters, none of it comprehensible to the boy, and the debate had grown heated. Ono was fearful that the exchange would come to blows, but just when it seemed violence would erupt, both men simply laughed and continued their argument at a more subdued pace. It wasn't until years later that Ono had the courage to ask Itto about the hero's appearance. It turned out Ittosai had known of the boy's presence under the veranda all along, but had said nothing. He explained that Musashi was so slovenly because his devotion to his art left no time for trivialities such as hygiene. And the fact that Musashi subsequently gave up the sword to pursue a solitary, spiritual life attested to this. That his master could carry on enlightened conversations with such a person said much for Ittosai's spirit.

I desire one more thing for myself, Ono thought. I desire to serve you, Itto Ittosai. Ono would be forever grateful that the old man had shown him the true path of life. Without being able to put it into conscious thought, he knew he would obey any request, any demand, without hesitation. Ittosai would have slyly pointed out that this was the true embodiment of the perfect samurai.

Ono had seen the Shogun's emissary too, but it was of small importance to him. Itto either would or would not agree to teach the Shogun's son. There was no shame in refusing, except perhaps for the Shogun. What made Ono curious was the other visitor to the school. A Buddhist monk had spoken with Itto for most of the day, and this was quickly becoming a regular visit, the holy man showing up several times each month. Ittosai was a spiritual man who spoke often of the need to follow Buddha's teachings, but the frequency of the visits was unusual. Was Itto thinking of making the monk a regular part of the school? Or perhaps weighing whether or not to use some of his considerable wealth to build a temple?

His musings were broken by Zenki's voice. "Ono-san, this morning you appeared distressed. Was it the beating?" Typical Zenki, Ono thought. Just couldn't let it lie.

"Why do you ask?"

Zenki laughed. "Your thoughts are always on your face. You must understand that we are not training farmers here. He was in error, and such an error in combat means death and the dishonor of failing your liege."

"There is no dishonor in dying in battle," said Ono.

"If you are killed before your obligation to your lord is fulfilled, there is great shame."

Ono shook his head. "There is only shame if one does not do his best. That is the center of the matter. Victory, death, they are inconsequential. Certainly victory is more desirable, but it is secondary to the mind and spirit."

"Very poetic, Ono-san, but not something I would say to my lord before entering battle. And unrealistic in these times. Our master has taught us we must be able to adapt."

"That is not what he meant," said Ono, his eyes hard. Both men looked to their *sensei* for confirmation, but he remained silent, sipping his *sake* and staring into the cool night.

It was quiet for a long while, and then Itto spoke softly. "You are both honorable men, *neh?*" An answer would have been impolite, and none was expected. "Neither of you would dishonor me by refusing a gift?"

Both samurai shook their heads. Unthinkable.

Itto nodded, a decision made. He rose slowly, bowed, and bid his senior students a pleasant evening before going into the house. Both men bowed until he left, then sat with their own thoughts, wrestling with a mixture of excitement and confusion. It was one of the things which bound them to the old man, the attraction of peeling away the mystery of his words like the skin of a fruit, working towards the sweetness of the truth beneath.

The night air was growing cold now, and both samurai rose to leave. They said a perfunctory good night to one another, then returned to their homes.

The sun was barely upon the courtyard when Itto walked out onto the veranda. Every student was gathered before him in ranks, kneeling in respect. Zenki and Ono knelt in front of them, closest to the veranda. This was how school began each day, and sometimes Itto would have some small words of inspiration, but more often than not would simply nod and give them over to their teachers for the day's training. This morning, Itto Ittosai had something to say.

He knelt on a mat and looked out over the young faces, seeing the future before him. The future of his teachings. "I am in my seventieth year," he began, his voice reaching even to the last rank of students. "I have seen much of the world, have participated in historic events. Yet nothing I have done is as important as what I do now. The time has come for me to leave the world of normal men, to devote the remainder of my life to Buddha. I will join the monks in Kyoto, where I will live out my days serving my master."

His words were startling, yet none showed it.

"The school I have founded," he continued, "the Itto Ryu, must be passed to the next generation. It must go into capable hands." He extended his palms. "Zenki-san, please stand."

The older samurai stood, flushing with pride.

"And Ono-san," the old man said, gesturing that the younger man should also stand. Ono did so, slowly, not seeing his fellow *sempai's* flush turn from pride to rage.

"My two finest students," Itto said, "are skilled and capable, spiritual men worthy of being my successor, of leading the Itto Ryu. So it shall be. Only one, however, may be headmaster. The other must not face the humiliation of service to the first. I will not choose between them. Their spirits will decide."

Itto paused, looking into the eyes of both samurai. "This morning, we three will go to the field which overlooks the sea. There, Zenki-san and Ono-san will face each other with the sword. He who falls will leave this world an honorable man, destined for the mysteries of the next life. He who lives will receive my scroll, which contains the secrets of my teachings. He will receive my sword, which is alive with the souls of over three hundred years of samurai. He will receive the Itto Ryu."

Zenki, Ono and the rest of the students bowed deeply in unquestioning acceptance of their master's will. The winds of change were upon them all.

It was just after eleven, and a sea wind blew across the high meadow, scenting the air with the tang of salt. The murmur of waves lapping against rocks far below was in harmony with the buzzing of bees among the wildflowers. It was warm and peaceful. Itto had chosen his spot well.

Zenki and Ono faced each other, six feet between them. Their swords were bared, held low in their right hands with the edges facing up. Neither man moved. Ittosai knelt in the high grass some distance away, his bare head warmed by the sun, his eyes narrowed in meditation. At his side lay his sword, and before him was a simple wooden box containing his scroll.

The two samurai had been this way for over an hour, neither man moving, each watching the eyes of the other. Time unspooled between them, but actual contact was certain to be quick and final.

Zenki wore a loose-fitting cotton kimono, tied at the waist. The wind stirred his baggy skirt and a bee buzzed past his eyes, but he did not stir. His mind was in motion, however. At last he would receive the recognition he truly deserved, for as headmaster he would realize an undreamt-of ambition. Better than *Daimyo* – those lords would come to him. Now he would become indispensable to the Tokugawas, sought out for wise counsel, molding the policies and philosophies of the Shogunate just as he molded their sons into samurai. Strengthening Japan. As headmaster he would shape the Itto Ryu into something for the new century.

First, Ono had to die.

Making that happen should not be difficult. Ono, for all his pretending, was spiritually weak, lacking the fire needed to lead the school, to train young samurai for war. Pretty words and poetry was fine, but meant little compared to the need for unstoppable, obedient warriors. Ono lacked confidence and desire, thinking he followed Ittosai's teaching, but missing the true messages.

Another hour passed without movement, the sun making Zenki uncomfortable under the kimono. Sweat trickled from his forehead into one eye, but he did not blink, did not notice the distraction. Itto's voice was in his head. *Even if one has a strong body but his mind is weak – because he is scared or unsure – then he is weak. If one has a weak body but a strong mind, he is strong.* Zenki had both a strong mind and body. He would kill Ono.

Ono wore the same, simple gray kimono he had worn during the daily lessons nearly every day since becoming sempai. Unsure and up against a more experienced swordsman, he was unable to control his thoughts. Visions of his children and his wife came to him, and he struggled to banish them. He had to win, if for no other reason than to keep the school out of Zenki's hands, to preserve the Itto Ryu. Yet the responsibilities of a headmaster were tremendous, and he knew he was not the man Ittosai was. How could he lead generations down Itto's path, when he himself did not truly understand the man's philosophy? And what of the obligation he would have to the Shoguns? Zenki was far more qualified for such duties. His doubts confused him, and for a terrifying moment he was certain they were revealed on his face –

just as Zenki said – a clear sign for the other man to strike a blow which Ono could not hope to parry. But the moment passed without a strike, and Ono's spirit calmed itself a little.

Itto's voice spoke to him as well. *A fox can run very fast to escape. Yet if a dog attacks him and the fox thinks too much about how to escape, he will not. Don't use too much thinking, as it causes doubt.* Ono tried to close his mind to the random thoughts assailing it.

Hours passed, still without a single movement from either man. The sun crossed the sky, heedless to the confrontation below.

For a brief instant, Zenki had the urge to strike, but he resisted the impulse. The passage of time meant nothing, only the outcome. The moment had to be right, and Ittosai had explained when that moment was. *If one can find the opponent's mind and control it, then victory will be easy.* Zenki searched for Ono's state of mind through his eyes for over an hour, but it was in shadow. Instead of further struggle, he sank into himself, concealing his mind in its own shadows.

The pain of standing still, anticipating for hours, was a dull sensation in the background of Ono's mind. This was not war, full of movement and noise and endless exertion. This would be decided in a single cut, and if it was not timed with absolute precision and executed with perfection, then failure and death would instantly follow the error.

Ono considered the central point in Itto's philosophy, *aiuchi*, mutual destruction. It was the acceptance that death was inevitable, and the resolution to strike a killing blow even while receiving one. This was what made Itto Ryu samurai so deadly. It was *aiuchi* that Ono now pursued, mentally eliminating the weak points in his mind, his fears for the future, thoughts of his family, worry or failure or dishonor, belief that he was strong, even a desire to win. Nothing mattered, only that he strike true regardless of his own death. Finally, the younger samurai slipped into *mushin*, a state of no-mind, free of emotion and conscious thought, a virtual dead man with every sense aware, yet seeing nothing.

Zenki achieved an identical mental nothingness at the same time, and at that moment, there were no two more dangerous samurai in Japan.

Seven hours had passed since Ittosai led them onto the field, and the sun was setting, a dying orange blossom over a flat yellow sea.

Then the tense of a muscle.

A glimmer of lowering sun on steel.

A flicker of dead eyes.

The lethal blur of two swords in motion, a ring as metal kissed, a soft whisper of parting cloth and parting flesh.

One man remained standing, as motionless as before, his sword now held aloft where it had finished its arc, stained red. There was the slow snap of a wrist to clear the blade of blood, then a respectful bow to the fallen man. The victor approached Ittosai wordlessly and knelt, bowing. The bow was returned, and the master presented his ancient sword and scroll, bowing again. Then the old man rose, breathed deeply, and slowly walked from the field.

The new headmaster secured Itto's sword in his belt, tucked the box under one arm, and began the long walk home.

Three days later, the students of the Itto Ryu were once more assembled before the veranda, two newly-promoted *sempai* at the front of the ranks. An honored guest was present, the Shogun's emissary kneeling beside the new master of the Itto Ryu.

"Honorable Headmaster," the emissary said, "my lord the Shogun has been informed of the recent events, and he is satisfied. He instructs me to ask if you will be *sensei* to his eldest son, and honor the House of Tokugawa by teaching him the mysteries of the sword."

After an appropriate pause, Ono bowed slightly. "I will."

143

John L. Campbell

GIRL ON A PLATFORM

Denny Pellet had the stairway to himself, and his shoes scuffed over the cement steps as he left the street above and descended into a subterranean subway world. It was a place of graffiti-marred tiled walls and advertisements, the echoing voice of a P.A. and a vague odor of urine.

The laptop bag over one shoulder was heavy enough to make him sag slightly to the right as he made his way slowly through the corridors. His brown suit was rumpled from a long work day, and he didn't move with the frantic briskness of the commuters at earlier hours. There was no need, for it was just before midnight, another sixteen hour day.

As he approached the turnstiles he glanced left to where the musicians usually sat, finding their customary place against the wall vacant. *Musicians* was a generous term. Vagrants in dreadlocks hammering out beats on overturned, white pickle buckets, coffee cans set out to collect bills and change. But even those guys were smart enough to go back to whatever passed for home this late hour.

A rush of distant air and a squeal of metal on metal announced the arrival of a train pulling in beyond the jail-bar partition. He checked his watch. He'd missed it again, seemed to always miss it, and knew he'd have to wait another ten minutes for the next

144

one. He swiped his MetroCard, pushing against the rotating bar, but it didn't move. The green digits on the reader reported $0.00. With a sigh, Denny backtracked to the card venders against the wall and used his debit card to get a new pass, looking around carefully before pulling out his wallet to be certain no one was watching. He needn't have worried. There was only an old black man in a blue MTA jumpsuit pushing a rumbling trash bin, and he paid Denny no mind.

He passed through the turnstiles and reached the platform, the long day pulling down on him like the laptop bag, wanting a shower and shave but knowing he'd be too tired for either by the time he got home. He eyed the two benches against the wall opposite the tracks. One looked sticky, the other was occupied by a snoring lump of stained coat and soiled jeans, hugging a backpack behind which was tucked a bearded face.

Denny decided to stand, thought about leaning against one of the tiled pillars near the tracks, but didn't want the grime to rub off on his suit, even though it was long overdue for dry-cleaning. Instead he shoved his hands in his pockets, slumped a little further and looked up the black tunnel. He wondered how long it would take before the ghost appeared.

Down the platform to his right stood an older Puerto Rican woman with a long coat buttoned up to the neck. She was gripping the handle of a collapsible shopping cart as if it might suddenly try to get away. Farther beyond her, a young man with a shaved head and a Yankee jacket was shaking a cell phone, yelling, "Can you hear me?" and then shaking it some more. The platform on the far side of the cement trench was vacant.

Denny was a practical man. His job as a mid-level facilities manager at the Garden kept him firmly grounded in the realities of maintenance, electrical and HVAC systems and personnel issues, and didn't leave much room for entertaining fantasies about the supernatural. He didn't believe in those things, or at least he hadn't. But when it was right there in front of you, with no other explanation, what else was there to think? He'd been seeing her for weeks now, right at midnight. Work had been keeping him consistently late, and it seemed he never managed to catch the 11:50, so he was always here when she made her appearance. At first he decided it was fatigue from the long days, and to some extent that was right. The routine was starting to get blurry, his ride to and from Queens barely-remembered, the grind of work, the exhaustion at the end of the day. It was making him clumsy and distracted, and tonight he had almost stepped off the curb in front of a racing cab. Wouldn't that be a stupid way to buy it, he thought? Living and working in the city his entire life, developing the necessary alertness and survival skills, then getting smashed like a stray tourist looking up at the tall buildings.

Fatigue wasn't the answer, though. Every night he dragged himself down those steps from the street, his laptop just a bit heavier than the evening before, and every night he saw her on the platform down to the left, right where the tunnel emerged from the wall. She wore tattered jeans tucked into black boots, a leather jacket and a messenger bag across her chest, decorated with silver studs in the shape of a skull. She had a lot of piercings, and her jet black hair hung in her eyes. She looked about twenty, and Denny could tell she was very pretty behind all the Goth. Actually, he thought she was beautiful.

And then there she was, stepping from behind a pillar, nervous as a doe and looking around, biting a thumbnail. She was dressed just as always, her milky skin a sharp contrast to the black leather jacket. He checked his watch. Midnight on the dot.

She cut her eyes towards Denny – not really looking at me, he thought, because she's not really there – then wrapped her arms about herself and stared down at the tracks. As she did every night.

He was so curious about her. Had she been a jumper? One of those desperate wretches hurling themselves in front of a subway train, knowing it was incapable of stopping and that it would be quick. Had she wondered if it would hurt? Worried about what it would do to the motorman who had to go home with that on his conscience? Not that NYC subway drivers lost sleep over that, he mused. He suspected they'd all had it happen, and perhaps it was some dark bit of humor among them, like a special club, waiting for the new drivers to be initiated in that gruesome fashion before they could be a part of it. He wondered if they kept score of their jumpers.

Denny shook his head. He *was* tired if he was daydreaming about that kind of nonsense. But then was it any crazier than what

146

was standing just down the platform from him? He was unable to take his eyes off the girl. What had been so terrible in her life that she considered this a solution? He was more convinced than ever that she was a jumper. Why else would she appear here night after night.

Then she turned her head and looked straight at him. Denny felt a shudder race through him, and now it was he who wanted to wrap himself in his own arms to ward off the sudden chill of having something from the other side truly see you.

He looked away. She caught you staring, he thought.

She can't catch you staring, he argued. She's dead.

Staring at a dead girl, thinking she's pretty. Almost as creepy as a forty-year-old man staring at a live girl half his age. A sudden panic hit him. What if she wasn't a ghost? What if he was just over-tired, his weary mind making up things to amuse itself in the face of the daily grind? He'd actually been considering saying hello to her, just to prove his theory one way or the other, but he quickly dismissed it. If she was a spirit, might that not invite some malevolent act on her part? A dozen movies about possession zipped through his head. And if she was real, not a ghost, then the creepy old man might very well catch a face full of pepper spray, writhing helplessly on the filthy platform while she screamed for a transit cop.

The rumble of the train filled the black tunnel, pushing warm air before it, and a dazzling light in the darkness grew steadily brighter. Denny looked back at her, and now there was no question. She was staring right at him, the heavy makeup around her eyes making her look even more dead. Heart suddenly thumping, he turned away, but he moved too quickly and the laptop bag swung out, the weight throwing him off balance. He stumbled, choked out a surprised little yell, and then he was falling, the tracks coming up fast, and the train roaring in faster.

Madeline watched the ghost in the brown suit fade as he fell, and she shivered. It had been weeks since she'd seen the man fall in front of the train, and though the actual impact had been below eye level and out of view, she flinched every time she thought about it. It had happened right about this time of night, after she'd hustled down here after getting off her second shift job as a barista and bookseller. A memory she just couldn't shake, that instant of surprised expression, and then... In her dreams she heard him scream, but she told herself it was probably just the brakes of the subway train as the driver tried to stop, knowing he couldn't.

Worse was the fact that he showed up again, and now she was seeing him every night at this time, his movements and death replayed over and over again. And the way he looked at her, so intensely, had her freaked out. As if her life wasn't crappy enough. Sometimes she found herself envying him, darkly attracted to the idea that all of life's hurts and disappointments and betrayals could be over with just...a...single...step.

The train was coming, a howling mass which could make it so very simple.

Just...a...single...step.

Over on the bench, the bum watched first the man in brown, and then the punk girl fade from view as a phantom train squealed through the station. He snuffled and rolled over. Goddamn ghosts. He rubbed his chest, uncomfortable with the increasingly painful ache of his untreated heart disease and his numb left arm, and tried to drift off.

A current of cold air spun out of the empty tunnel, and the Puerto Rican woman gripped her shopping basket more tightly and crossed herself, watching as the man, the girl and then the bum all faded from view. A quick glance to the right gave her a glimpse of the young man with the cell phone walking right through the tiled subway wall. She shook her head and whispered a prayer to the Blessed Mother, deciding that from now on she'd risk getting mugged and make herself walk the extra six blocks to another station, hopefully one not as haunted as this.

And then she faded too.

AMERICAN TRAGEDY

The situation room under 1600 Pennsylvania Avenue was crowded. All the civilians had their jackets off, ties loosened and sleeves rolled, but the Joint Chiefs looked starched in full uniform, chests heavy with medals. At the head of the table, the president sat with his palms on the polished wood, staring at the video feed at the far end of the room, entranced. How was this even possible?

Sherwood, the top ranking Air Force general in the country, slid a dark blue folder in front of the president. Its cover read, TOP SECRET, Z-71. On screen, the president watched one of the living dead drift in zero gravity through the shuttle's cargo bay. Its face was half gone and it was missing an arm. The name tag on its blue jump suit read, CMDR. MARKHAM. The president had shaken the man's hand only weeks ago, wishing him well before his launch. Another body floated in the background, a woman trailing her intestines from a gaping rip in her belly. She was clawing the air in slow motion and gnashing her teeth.

"Mr. President," said Sherwood, "Z-71 represents our best choice scenario. We all concur." The Joint Chiefs nodded.

The president scanned the folder's contents. "Dear God, you actually have scenarios for this?" He gestured towards the screen.

"We have multiple scenarios, sir."

The president read. It was brief and to the point. "Those are our people up there, General. We should try to bring them home."

"They're not people anymore," said Sherwood. "You saw what happened in the earlier video."

Something had become lodged outside near the shuttle's tail, out of view of the exterior cameras. Mission Specialist King went out on a space-walk to clear the debris, and minutes later there was a scream over the intercom. When the crew hauled King back inside, they discovered his suit had been ripped open, and a large piece of his abdomen torn away. Loss of oxygen, pressure and the deep cold of space had killed the man almost instantly. But he came back minutes later, and started biting. The entire crew of seven was lost inside thirty minutes, and now they floated up there, dead but somehow not as their craft traced a lazy orbit around the planet.

"We can see they're highly infectious and aggressive, Mr. President. Some have suggested they could be contained and studied, but the overall consensus is that we cannot risk allowing even one of them to get down here. If it got out, our government, our country, would cease to exist."

The president reread the scenario, then closed the folder. "Are we ready for the questions?"

The general nodded. "We have scenarios to handle that as well, sir."

"Do it," the president said, pushing the folder away and walking out.

A phone call was made. In Houston, a shuttle pilot entered a highly restricted room which looked like a flight simulator. Using a satellite link, he tapped into the Explorer and flew it by remote, lining up its glide path around the planet, then guiding it through its descent into the atmosphere. At a predetermined point, another general inserted a red aluminum key into a panel and turned it.

Shuttle Explorer burned up at high altitude, raining small bits of debris across Texas. The blast was captured on video and replayed repeatedly for the world. The president addressed the nation to mourn the loss of their heroes, and investigations were begun. Carefully fabricated video and flight recordings blamed a structural malfunction which the crew could not have detected, and no hint was ever given of how close mankind had come to extinction.

Twelve years later, a Boy Scout hiking with his troop outside San Antonio discovered a charred, round object wedged between a rock and a cactus. When he pulled it out and turned it over in his hands, Commander Markham's blackened and sightless head moaned, and bit the boy in the palm.

SALTY

Cornelius LaBauve was eighty-seven and missing somewhere in the Louisiana bayou. The passenger in the big pickup was worried that the old man had run into a local myth, but the driver had his money on liquor-induced drowning or gators.

Cole Doucet arrived at the LaBauve place around eleven in the morning, carefully navigating the black Dodge 2500 down a long, muddy lane crowded by blackgum trees and green ash on either side, trying not to clip one of the side mirrors. Low-hanging branches scraped across the light bar on the roof, and curtains of Spanish moss trailed over the windshield as he drove down what was little more than a pair of parallel ruts. Even in daylight and over the noise from the bouncing truck he could hear the calls of bullfrogs in the rushes, his window open and his elbow cocked outside. The air conditioner was on low simply to keep the heavy, humid air in the cab circulating.

Southwest of the towns of Bayou Cane and the adjacent county seat of Houma, this area was part of Terrebone Parish, an expansive wilderness of swamp, wetlands and forest punctuated by small communities. It was the kind of place where the waterways ran alongside the roads, where you could see the boats of shrimpers and oystermen lined up at the banks, or in wider sections, graveyards of submerged vessels, masts and the tops of cabins peeking above the surface. Here on the southern tip of Louisiana, it was a place which had been ravaged by Katrina not so very long ago. Ten percent of the population spoke French, and the people of the parish were a mix of Cajun, Choctaw and Creole, fishermen and trappers and hunters who lived well below the poverty line.

The LaBauves were these people. Cole passed between a pair of wooden posts which at one time supported a chain between them, but the wood was past rotted and now it just lay in the mud, rusting and sinking into the lane. The Dodge went slowly around a long curve, and then the road ended at a wide, open area of packed clay and black mud, choked with junk. No less than half a dozen cars, stripped, without glass and sinking on their rims, rusted away along one edge of the space. Several washing machines sat jumbled in high grass next to a dented refrigerator, and a shopping cart without wheels was filled with bottles and cans. A low, tin-roof shack with a sagging covered porch was at the far end, and to the right, up against the tree line, a 60's era school bus sat with its once-yellow paint now faded nearly white and streaked with trails of black mold. Fishing gear and frog gigs leaned up against it. As Cole put the truck in park, a broad-chested, black pit bull wiggled out from under the bus and started forward stiff-legged, its flat head low and its lips peeled back from yellow teeth.

He ran up his window and draped an arm across the seat, looking at the dog. It stopped ten feet from the truck and just stood there, menacing. Cole scanned the rest of the area. There were some rusty oil drums, rows of muddy Coleman coolers, a wash line with a few flannel shirts and some shorts hanging from it, bullet-pocked highway signs leaning against the shack's porch, and a battered outdoor grill with a dozen old propane bottles scattered in the weeds nearby. Near the shack, several lines had been strung between the trees. One held gutted catfish, another had four gator skulls dangling from it, the teeth removed.

Cole tapped on the horn and waited. He didn't want to try getting out with the pit in the yard, because he'd probably have to shoot it and that would start a whole new kind of trouble. Louisianans, and southerners in general, had a strong relationship with their dogs – sometimes more than they had with their own wives – and had been known on occasion to seek vengeance for the killing of their four-legged companions. He tapped the horn again.

Brick LaBauve appeared from the interior of the school bus and eased down onto the steps, slouching against the frame with his hands in his pockets and staring with open contempt at the Louisiana Department of Wildlife and Fisheries truck in his yard. He spit and folded his arms. Brick was shirtless, wearing cut-off camouflage shorts and muddy work boots. His head was shaved in a close crew-cut, and his muscled upper body was covered in tats, including a big piece across his chest depicting a voluptuous, naked she-devil with wings which stretched back up to his shoulders. At twenty five, he and Cole were the same age.

Cole buzzed down the passenger window. "Brick, need you to chain your dog, son."

Brick chewed whatever he had in his mouth, probably tobacco, and spit again but didn't move from the bus doorway. "He ain't gonna hurt you."

"C'mon, now, put him on a chain. I'm not going away."

"Ain't nothing here for you today, warden. Wasting your time."

"Glad to hear it. Means this won't take long."

The Cajun sighed deeply, and then called to his dog. "Cephus! Over hear, now." The pit bull reacted immediately, trotting to its master and pushing its big head against his leg until Brick scratched at his ear. Then it sat, tongue lolling out and watching the truck while the man clipped a heavy chain to its thick leather collar.

Cole got out and walked towards the dog's owner, a Sig .45, collapsible Asp nightstick and oversized can of pepper spray all secured to his service belt. The LDWF Enforcement Division had a federal commission, a six month training academy said to rival Marine boot camp (though Cole knew personally it fell short of the curriculum at Paris Island,) and had state-wide jurisdiction not only over hunting, fishing and boating, but rural law enforcement as well. Its agents were trained in tactical night assault, drug interdiction, and could operate boats and quads and even some aircraft. Yet swampers like Brick LaBauve insisted on calling them Game Wardens. It was not a term of endearment.

Bayou people saw the agents as cops poking their noses in a hard-working man's business, telling him what and where and when, in a place their families had called home since the first white men appeared in the area. A nuisance. An infringement on their personal liberties and right to live in and harvest what they chose from the swamps. And of course, the agents were the enemy when it came to the fact that sometimes a man out here had to do a little more to take care of his kin when times were hard, like hunt out of season or sell some guns or even cook a little meth. Most didn't, of course, but even the ones not involved in illicit activity had no love for the LDWF.

Brick stepped down from the bus and met Cole half way to the truck. They shook hands and nodded, young men who had known each other on and off over the years, and had even attended the regional high school together for a time until Brick dropped out at sixteen. They had never actually been friends, but there had been no bad blood between them. That changed somewhat as they got older. Cole went into the LDWF right after a four year tour in the Marines, eighteen months of it spent in Iraq, and it didn't take long before he was reunited with his old schoolmate under different circumstances. Brick LaBauve was one of those who saw the law as an obstruction, something to be considered and then quickly dismissed. An original Crazy White Boy.

"What you want, Cole?"

"Just checking up. If I don't, you won't get your licenses back."

Brick shrugged. His gator tags and buck permits had been pulled after Cole caught Brick spotlighting gators. State law demanded that alligators could only be harvested between sunup and sundown, and two satisfactory inspections by the charging agent – validating that no additional laws were being broken - was required before he could apply for reinstatement.

Cole walked towards the row of coolers and began looking inside, Brick walking sullenly behind him. They held mostly catfish, with a few frogs and a good-sized turtle. Nothing to worry about.

"So what happened with that TV show?" Cole asked, poking in another cooler.

"Shit," Brick spat into the grass, "those pansy-asses. Ain't none of them a straight-shooter, scared of everything, ya know?"

A month before Brick was caught spotlighting, a popular reality show about colorful swampers hunting alligators had come to Terrebone Parish, and after some research the directors selected Brick LaBauve to participate. Brick played it up for the cameras, enjoying the pay and basking in the glow of instant celebrity for a short time. Before long, however, what the show's producers had originally thought to be a colorful backwoods redneck turned into the Crazy White Boy the locals knew him to be. He drove his boat too fast, wrecking it and hurting a cameraman. He drove a quad too recklessly and totaled it, along with another camera. He showed up for filming drunk or high or both, slurring and pawing at the female crew members, picking fights with sound technicians, arguing with the director and blurting obscenities. He told impossible lies about himself and even tried to light up a joint during filming. Most of this could have been forgiven, as reality TV was constantly pushing the envelope; over-the-top made solid ratings, and the truly inappropriate stuff could always be edited or bleeped out. But Brick was also an unapologetic racist, and loud about it, something which didn't sit well with the network's executive producer, an African-American who'd had his own life experiences with wild southern boys. Most of the Brick LaBauve footage would turn out to be useless, and the decision was made to cut him loose from the show with a minimal contract payoff.

"Them Hollywood assholes just don't know what real fun is," he said as Cole inspected the gator skulls on the line. "And it ain't right to promise a man all manner of things, then take it all away over nothing. Left me piss broke."

Cole nodded, and decided the directors and producers had gotten off cheaply. Brick was the kind of man who might get liquored up and show up on set with a shotgun, hunting for camera equipment and windshields and maybe a kneecap or two.

"That's a tough break," Cole said.

"Yeah. Fun while it lasted, though. Had myself a makeup girl." He grinned.

"What about these gators?" Cole asked, tapping one of the skulls.

"Those ain't mine, they's Pappy's. His tags are still good."

"How's Pappy doing these days?"

Brick's eyes cut away and he started chewing a thumbnail.

"He alright?"

A shrug. "Yeah, he's good."

Brick's expression said something else. Cornelius LaBauve (don't call him Cornelius unless you wanted a broken nose, Pappy will do just fine) was Brick's grandfather, a crotchety swamper in his upper eighties who had been the kind of hell raiser in his younger days as to make Brick's antics seem tame. He liked his bourbon and his beer, and even at eighty-seven could be found in the blues taverns, ready to square off over something said which he didn't like. He had even less regard for the game restrictions of Louisiana than his grandson, and no one was going to tell him how to live in *his* swamp. He was crafty, and kept to the laws when folks were looking, but every LDWF agent knew Pappy LaBauve was always working an angle somewhere. At least that had been the case in the past. Pappy's name came up less and less often these days, and it was generally agreed that age was finally slowing the old man down.

Cole looked at the Cajun for a long moment. The other man glanced up to his eyes, then looked away, still chewing that thumbnail.

"What's going on, Brick?"

A shrug.

"He in some kind of trouble?"

Brick looked as if he was wrestling with something, and then his shoulders slumped. "I'm worried about him. He's been gone two days now, took the truck and the boat. Ain't been back."

"Where'd he go?"

Brick looked at the enforcement agent. "Out to Devil's Hole. Said he was going to find Old Nick."

Cole whistled. "Gone two days to Devil's Hole?"

"Uh-huh. Too far for me to go walking to find him. He ain't young no more, Cole."

The agent looked hard at LaBauve, and saw no deception in him, only concern. He knew it was difficult for a man like Brick to ask for help, but that was surely what he was doing, and a man as old as Pappy had no business in a place like Devil's Hole. It was absolutely the meanest part of the bayou.

"I don't see any violations, don't see any reason we can't get you your permits back." He jerked his head towards the Dodge. "What do you say we take a ride out there, see if we can find him?"

Brick squinted. "You bust me and pull my tags one day, then wanna help me look for my Pappy the next? What the hell?"

Cole shrugged. "The law's my job, Brick, and I won't apologize for it. You were in the wrong. But that's the past, and this isn't about that. We know each other, and I know your Pappy." He stuck out his hand. "C'mon, let me help."

Brick eyed the agent's hand as if it might bite him, but then gripped it firmly. "I appreciate it. Let me throw on a shirt and get my rifle."

Cole shook his head. He didn't think he had anything to fear from Brick, didn't think the man had any cause to jump him out in the swamp, but he also didn't need him to be armed. "I got that covered." In the rack against the Dodge's back window hung a Remington 12 gauge and a Sig .223 assault rifle, something the department had begun issuing to agents since Katrina. "Let's go see what Pappy's up to."

It took an hour of traveling back roads, transitioning from asphalt to gravel to dirt to ruts, and now they bounced along a narrow track with high grasses and views of blue water to the left, and sprawling black willows on the right, growing half in and half out of stagnant pools. A flock of low-flying cranes swept by in the distance, their white shapes a startling contrast to the jungle-like background, graceful and seemingly slow as their big wings beat at the humid air. A few fishing shacks were nestled among the willows here and there, decaying, thrown-together places with bowed porches and crooked docks right on the water. Dogs and chickens could be seen, but no people. They would all be out on the water, making a living.

Cole braked as a family of nutria scurried from the grass on the left and crossed the road in front of the LDWF truck. Both men watched the housecat-sized, oily furred rodents disappear into the brush, hairless tails following after.

"You getting any these days?" Cole asked, gesturing towards where the animals had been and getting the Dodge moving again.

"Hell yes. Since ya'll pulled my tags and licenses, been the only way to make any money. I don't eat 'em, though. Ain't sunk low enough to eat swamp rat. Pappy has a taste for 'em."

Nutria was a breed which landed somewhere between rat and otter, an aquatic rodent with webbed feet and long orange teeth, brought to the U.S. for the fur trade long ago. Like nearly every other imported species, it had found its way into the wilds and thrived. When the market for furs died off in the eighties, the nutria grew unchecked and flourished in the food-rich environment of the bayou. Breeding as often as common rats, they fed on roots and vegetation, the very structure which held the bayou together, and Cole's agency estimated that as a result, twenty-five miles of Louisiana wetlands disappeared into the Gulf of Mexico each year. They were considered the most invasive species in America.

"Couple weeks ago, got me a hundred of them little bastards in one day. That was a damn good day."

Cole agreed that it was a nice payday. Nutria were such an infestation that the LDWF paid five dollars for every tail brought in, and was extremely generous in granting no-bag-limit licenses to locals. Brick's claim of a hundred in one day seemed a bit inflated, though, even considering the out-of-control population.

"I heard the Chinese was interested," said Brick.

"Yep. The mayor of Beijing came to Baton Rouge to look into importing them as a meat source. Nothing ever came of it, though."

Brick laughed, a harsh bark. "Goddamn Chinese're stupid enough to invite them little bastards into their country, I say let 'em take all the swamp rats they want. See how they like it."

Cole nodded as he drove, unable to argue with Brick's simple logic. And that was the one thing which made this job difficult sometimes. He had grown up with these people, he understood the bayou and their way of life, saw how hard they had it. His training and schooling had well-educated him on the need for conservation, and his loyalties were firmly in place, but it was still tough to tell a father trying to feed a family of six that the state was taking away his boat for thirty days and suspending his tags because he shot a gator an hour after sundown. It didn't help that he knew most of them by their first names. He had to enforce the law, it was something he wanted to do and for which he had volunteered, but he couldn't help quietly believing that there was more than enough deer, opossum, fish and reptile meat in the bayou to feed these simple folks and their families, and still have plenty left over to supply New York City with alligator skin for their shoes. And he couldn't really picture anyone on Park Avenue wanting to dine on opossum.

The open wetlands were increasingly broken by submerged stumps and bald cypress, thickening into woods once more, the overhead canopy steadily blotting out the sun. They were getting closer to Devil's Hole, or at least one of the few places that part of the bayou touched land.

"What was Pappy doing out here, Brick?"

The other man shook his head. "Got it in his head he was gonna find Old Nick."

"He believes in Old Nick?"

"Damn straight," said Brick, "that big bastard's out there too, I guarantee."

Cole looked sideways at his old schoolmate and tried a smile. "C'mon, really?"

"You can think whatever you want, *warden*, (they were back to that now) but he's real, and he's out there. A hundred years old, raised from an egg but escaped to the bayou when he was a baby after he killed some little girl on a farm. Been living in Devil's Hole ever since."

Cole said nothing. He knew the legend.

"I'm just hoping Pappy nodded off drunk in the truck, and didn't try to go out after him. He's always saying if anyone could ever find Old Nick, he could."

The wildlife agent didn't want to get into a debate over a mythical swamp monster with a hot-tempered redneck, and didn't bother to argue that the local reptiles were dangerous enough for an eighty-seven-year-old without bringing Old Nick into the equation. The American alligator averaged eleven or twelve feet long, and weighed between three and eight hundred pounds. Normally they steered clear of humans, but they were also opportunistic, and Devil's Hole had more than its fair share of the animals. An old man struggling to put an aluminum boat in the water might prove tempting for an attack.

"I'm sure he's fine, Brick. Probably be more pissed off that you brought a lawman to come look for him."

Brick grinned. "He would be at that. But I'll take the sharp end of his tongue and a slap up-side the head so long as I know he's okay."

They drove deeper into the darkening bayou.

Old Nick wasn't an alligator. He was said to be a "salty," a saltwater crocodile native to Northern Australia, India and Southeast Asia. Salties were the largest reptiles on earth, and Old Nick was said to be a real monster, between twenty-three and thirty feet long, weighing in at two tons, capable of pulling boats under and biting the tailgates off pickup trucks, unaffected by gunfire and able to choke down a full grown man. The tales of Nick's size and exploits enlarged in direct proportion to the amount of beer being consumed, and Cole had once even heard an enforcement agent quietly say that he had seen Old Nick kill a man twenty years earlier, but had been unable to get off a shot. Swamp tales.

Cole didn't believe in the legend himself, but there was just enough truth to make it plausible, and that was why the story lived on. Salties lived as easily in freshwater swamps as they did in open ocean. They were apex predators and masters of ambush, aggressive, territorial and physically powerful. They could swim for short underwater bursts at up to 18 mph, exploding onto shore even faster, and by using their immense tail could propel themselves their full length vertically out of the water. And they were smart, believed to be smarter than lab rats, and capable of learning. A salty who had survived over a hundred years would be a crafty predator indeed. If one existed in Louisiana, Devil's Hole would be the place for it; infrequently visited, dark and filled with prey, undisturbed and remote. The perfect lair for the undisputed King of the Bayou.

But Old Nick was a legend and nothing more. No matter how stealthy the creature might be, no matter how impassable the bayou could get, there was simply no way a reptile the size of a bus could have avoided being spotted and hunted down, or even photographed after all these years. Hell, something that big could be seen from the *air!* He was more elusive than Bigfoot. Of course that didn't stop the airboat tour guides from spinning yarns about him for the tourists, that was good for business. And the nature channels regularly came down to do stories on him, interviewing locals who had "lived to tell the tale" and taking pictures of plaster casts of his supposed footprints and doing extended filming of the creepiest sections of the bayou. T-shirts and television and tall tales. But no giant crocodile.

The sides of the road grew marshy and spotted with pools of standing water as the bald cypress trees closed in, branches heavy with gray-green clumps of Spanish moss hanging limp in the close air. It was a twilight place, the sun neatly tucked away above, the low light intensity resulting in little undergrowth. Between the trees was flat mud which led to the water. A thick cottonmouth wriggled across the track in front of the Dodge.

They found the truck a few minutes later, parked where the road simply stopped in the trees, only a few yards from the water's edge. A trailer was hooked up to Brick's old Ford, and an aluminum fishing boat was still strapped into its mountings. Cole stopped and Brick jumped out at once, running up to the cab to look inside, then turning in a circle and yelling, "Pappy! Pappy!"

Cole got out and checked the truck as well, finding the cab empty, crushed beer cans and filthy overalls on the floorboards. He had so wanted to find the old coot passed out in the front seat with an empty bottle. The boat still on its trailer wasn't a good sign, either. He looked out into Devil's Hole, a deep, shadowy expanse of algae-filmed water, rotting stumps and cypress vanishing into the distance. Nothing moved to disturb the surface, and though mosquitoes drifted through the air, nothing else did. There were no birds, no croaking bullfrogs. It was a silent place.

Brick climbed up into the back of Cole's Dodge and stood on the equipment box, cupping his hands to his mouth and yelling, "Paaaaappy!"

Cole looked at the muddy bank and shivered despite the heat. Even in the half-light he could see a pair of bare footprints making their way from the Ford straight to the water. The old man was a suicide, had finally lost his mind and walked straight into the swamp. Cole had no delusions about what would have happened next.

"Brick," he said quietly, turning to look at the other man, "I think we..."

162

His companion was sitting on the Dodge's equipment box, swinging his legs comfortably against the side of the truck, looking at him with a weird grin.

Old Nick erupted out of the water and onto the bank at just under twenty mph, hitting the back of Cole's right leg with open jaws and snaggled teeth. The impact threw him face-down in the mud and he screamed as the croc whipped its massive head left and right and tore his leg off at the knee. It snarled, deep and throaty, advancing on the prone man. Cole flipped onto his back and used his arms to scramble away, dragging his stump, slipping into shock as he watched it spurt blood across the croc's snout. Thirty feet *at least*, his brain screamed. Two tons easy. Three feet tall at the shoulder.

It bit down on his kicking leg, crushing the shin bone and making him scream, and then it started backing rapidly towards the water. Cole clawed for his sidearm, got it free, and then lost it in the mud when the croc gave him a sharp jerk. It shook its head and tore away the remaining leg.

"Brick help! Shoot it shoot it shoot it help me heeeelp!"

The salty, mottled black and green, covered in leathery scale ridges and looking very much like the dinosaur it was, gulped down the leg, a boot still on the foot. Then it looked at Cole and croaked, staring with one big blue eye, and one which was a milky, blind orb.

"Don't think I can help ya, warden," Brick said casually, pulling out a tin of chewing tobacco and fingering out a large dip, shoving it into his mouth. "You're on your own."

Cole started pulling himself backwards again, both severed legs pumping blood and his vision starting to gray. "Brick, I...I...help me. Please!"

The giant salty began walking towards him, its bulk swaying side to side.

"Nutria ain't the only nuisance out here for us poor folks. Nuisances gotta be put down."

Cole didn't take his eyes off the advancing croc as he struggled to back up. "They know I'm here, Brick." His voice was breaking, like high-pitched puberty. "They know I went to see you."

"Sure, your buddies know you come out to check up on me, I believe it. But you didn't use your radio to tell no one we was coming out here. I'll say you come seen me, said I was gonna get my permits back, then went on your way. Pappy will swear to it, too. Don't know what happened after that."

The croc opened its mouth with a grumble.

"Brick, please…" Cole's strength was gone, and he could no longer crawl backwards, only lie propped-up on his elbows, wheezing for breath as he bled out, turning the black mud a glistening red.

"They'll find your truck eventually. Then it'll be, 'No sir, I don't know what made him go out there. Didn't say nothing to me.'" Brick chuckled. "They'll give your mama a flag and maybe put your picture up in the county building."

"Goddamn it Brick help me!"

Old Nick struck then, lunging forward and snapping down onto Cole's torso, cracking bones, making him babble and shriek before his air was cut off, and then swiftly turned and trotted back into the black water, Cole flopping in his jaws. The surface boiled as Nick rolled in the shallows, finishing off his prey and tearing it apart. Within minutes the creature was gone and the rippling water began to still.

Brick LaBauve sat on the LDWF truck for an hour, swinging his heels and spitting tobacco into the mud, humming and watching the water. In time the surface broke again, a bald head followed by narrow shoulders, the pale, thin body of a naked old man, wet and muddy. He picked his teeth as he walked to the Ford and began dressing.

Brick hopped down and climbed into the Ford's driver's seat.

"You brought a warden out here, boy? Pretty damn reckless."

A shrug. "They'll think a gator got him."

Cornelius LaBauve looked at his grandson with one eye blue and winked with the milky white one, smiling. "Close."

GRAND CENTRAL

Her name was Alixis, and she was a long way from home, a place of fire and endless pain. Here only a few hours, already she was homesick for the screams of the eternally damned. Still, there was work to be done, an important task assigned to her by the Dark Royalty. She would not fail.

Grand Central's lower level was a place of snack bars, shops and restrooms. At its heart was a lounge with a ring of Alice in Wonderland chairs, red oversized things which tourists loved and sleeping bums loved even more. She wore black like an old Italian widow, perched on the edge of a chair, pocketbook on her knees. Her eyes were black and soulless behind a veil as she murmured phrases in a tongue not uttered among men for thousands of years. Something squirmed inside her purse.

At the bakery kiosk, a woman dropped dead from an aneurism. A vagrant in a nearby seat vomited in his sleep and quietly choked to death. A man with a briefcase and a coffee decided tonight was the perfect time to strangle his wife, and an NYU student walking upstairs checked the time and realized she would have to hurry if she was going to throw herself under the wheels of the 2:15 to Connecticut.

Alixis smiled with yellow teeth, still speaking softly, as the unleashing spread outward.

*

The crush of morning commuters poured off the 4 train and onto the platform. A broker in a rush bumped Karen hard, and she stumbled in high heels against the filthy metal side, almost falling into the gap. She swore as more people pressed past, mindless of her.

Karen shoved off the train, using a hip to push another woman out of the way, clenched her laptop handle and joined the herd. She cursed the bag's weight as she moved with the crowd. The surge carried her to a wide set of steep stairs packed with bodies. It looked like a mountain.

"Screw that," she said, turning right towards where a grimy ELEVATOR sign was fixed to the wall. The lighting here was poor, but at least she'd have the place to herself. Of course the elevator would smell like urine, but that was city life.

The doors opened and she stepped inside. They were waiting for her, black and deadly, clinging to the ceiling of the car like wild-eyed bats. Karen felt a stringer of drool drop onto her hair and she looked up as the doors closed.

They fell upon her, and no one heard her screams.

*

Leland pushed out of the terminal and onto the street, gritty and loud, choked with speeding cabs which wouldn't stop for anyone. The train had been late, he was tired and hungry, and there was the hotdog cart.

Ellen would shriek if she knew. The fifty-year-old was not supposed to eat hotdogs, especially dirt water dogs from street vendors, but at this point he didn't care what his wife thought.

"One with mustard," he said. The Phillipino vendor grinned and nodded, and Leland lifted a metal flap to get himself a Pepsi.

From within, a small black hand caught him and black teeth crunched down hard, biting his finger off clean. The little demon choked a bit on the wedding ring, but managed to get it down.

A honking cab drowned out Leland's cries.

*

He could always be found here, on the landing where the stairs turned as they descended to the 6 Train. Filthy, concealed within layers of coats, a vagrant huddled on the floor with a hat in front of him.

Commuters flowed past, few looking at him, fewer still dropping change or bills into the hat. He didn't move, didn't look up, and appeared to be sleeping. Within the layered coats, six small creatures feasted on his opened chest, black fur matted with blood, talons ripping greedily at the soft, juicy organs.

On the wall above, a PSA bulletin announced in bold letters, "If you see something, say something."

*

She was perfect, hunched and shuffling with age, dressed in black, her handbag hanging loose and unprotected. The crackhead smiled, pacing her slowly from behind. He wiped a trembling, dirty hand at his mouth, his need all-consuming. A glance around for cops.

She was in a scattered crowd when he crowded in close beside her. God, she smelled *bad!* He gave the purse strap a brutal yank. It snapped easily and he was moving, tucking the bag under his coat and slipping quickly into the rush hour crowd, while behind him people stopped to help a fallen old woman.

No one saw him. The old lady didn't even scream.

Minutes later he was in a men's room stall, perched on the bowl so his feet wouldn't show. He smiled and opened the bag to get his prize.

The pocket demon burst out, talons sinking into his chin and ear, needle-like teeth ripping into his throat. The crackhead's hands fluttered helplessly as blood jetted across the graffiti-covered partition. The small creature pulled out his larynx.

Out in the terminal, Alixis chuckled behind her veil.

*

The priest needed a shave, and his eyes were wild and feverish. The ancient scrolls had predicted the day and location of the old woman's arrival, and he had come to Grand Central ready to put an end to her with the sacred dagger blessed at Saint Pat's. But now the cop had the dagger, and he was handcuffed, being hustled out onto the sidewalk of 5th Avenue.

"You have to listen to me!" he shrieked. "She's come to usher in the End of Days!"

"Right, Father," said the beefy cop, pushing the priest into the waiting Bellevue-bound NYPD van and slamming the door behind him. It pulled away, and the cop took the opportunity to light up a

167

cigarette, wrinkling his nose at the worse-than-usual odor coming from the storm drain.

A RANCH IN NEVADA

Let's talk about money and limousines. And murder. I know a lot about the first two, and more than I want about the last. If the wrong people hear this, I suppose I'll learn about life expectancy, too. But a man can stay quiet only so long.

Nineteen-ninety-three, and there was sex in the White House, a thriving economy, terrorism a thing of the past. People in California were willing to spend on luxury recreation. My philosophy as a businessman was, "Give them what they want." Nothing illegal, mind you, not at first anyway, just a higher level of service than most people were used to, and the highest level for those who expected it. It's the little things that make a difference, and that reflects directly upon the tip.

Simple things, like spending the money for some quality suits, then keeping them crisp and dry-cleaned. Making sure you were always freshly showered, shaved and lightly cologned before picking up a client. Seems obvious, right? But I can't tell you how many drivers I knew who showed up for a run looking and smelling like slobs, then drove away sour with a bare minimum tip. I don't believe in bare minimums. I believe in excess. Other things you might assume drivers would do (and you'd be wrong) included punctuality, I'm talking ten minutes early punctuality. Having your routes mapped out in advance, or at least a current map in the front seat (remember, this is pre-GPS.) A clean car, inside and out, with ice in the bucket and the glasses sparkling. It's where I learned how to open wine bottles and champagne – though I did pop a bride in the eye with a cork before I learned to wrap the champagne bottle with a linen napkin. She and the groom laughed it off, thank God, but I never made that mistake again. I learned how to pin flowers to lapels, to carry a lint roller for young gentlemen picking up prom dates or nervous executives heading into meetings. I knew how to give twenty dollar handshakes to maître' d's and bell captains, valets and bouncers to ensure my clients got into "impossible" places. It was worth it, because they were always so impressed they upped the tip *and* covered the twenty. I gave them the full treatment, what they'd always dreamed a chauffeur was, and they ate it up. Lots of guys didn't. They didn't make shit.

For the up-scale clients, I really turned it on. Figuring out what they wanted most was a ticket to cash, so I became a student of attitude. Some celebs just wanted quiet, others wanted a slow drive with the window down so people could see them. Some wanted conversation, others flattery. I had rich bitches who wanted to be followed through stores by a well-dressed, obedient servant in black leather driving gloves. There were executives who wanted to look like they had a bodyguard, someone imposing, and six-foot-four in a double-breasted dark suit, reflective shades and no smile fit that nicely. I had an earpiece like the Secret Service use that I would wear just to complete the look. The wire went to nothing, I tucked it in an inside jacket pocket. A few contracted for an actual bodyguard, and they got it. I had my concealed weapons permit for California (what a bitch it was to get that thing!) and I carried a 9mm Beretta all the time, whether it was an executive protection gig or not. It wasn't for them – I wasn't taking a bullet for anyone – it was to keep me safe. Limos did, and still do, a big cash business, and they draw attention. Sometimes from rip-offs, more often from nuts. The point is, everyone got what they wanted.

And everybody paid.

At the time, an eight-seater stretch ran you sixty-five an hour, and I saw fifteen-percent of that. It was crap, but it was there to satisfy Uncle Sam. The real money came from tips, and side deals worked out with the owner or client, all of it under the table. If a client specifically requested me, I earned an extra fifteen-percent of the run (the reason I *always* sent a polite thank-you card to every client.) An executive protection contract was all mine, and I charged one-twenty-five an hour with a four hour minimum. If I was on an overnight run, the client had to cover a room, a hundred dollars in expenses, and give me a minimum of eight hours down time. That was to satisfy D.O.T. requirements, but I functioned well on five hours sleep. And then there were the tips, the real cream.

A limo contract informed the client they were expected to give the driver twenty-percent of the total cost as a gratuity. My first year I saw a lot of twenty-percent and under, and even got stiffed a few times. It forced me to learn and adapt to their needs. After that, I never saw twenty again. And I was meticulously honest in recording time and paying the owner exactly what he was entitled to from the run, no playing games. Again, you might expect that, but again you'd be wrong. Drivers shave time and juggle numbers and screw owners every chance they get, and owners know it. When they find one who plays it straight, and gets rave reviews from clients? Well, guess who gets the wine country tours and who gets stuck with the airport runs?

That isn't to say I didn't do my share of those, along with weddings, the staples of the limo business. But I made my money off the longer, service-oriented gigs; proms, San Francisco night tours, bachelor and bachelorette nights, dinner and theatre evenings, executive outings. Let me tell you, there's money to be made on an eight hour run through the Napa Valley with a carload of ladies, especially when the wine relaxes inhibitions and loosens pocketbooks. Why do you think the booze is free at casino tables? It loosens thighs, too, and sex plays a part in this story as well, but maybe not how you think.

It's important I remind you that limo drivers are working class guys. Being around the glitz all the time can have a strange effect on people, and sometimes drivers forgot who they were, started believing it was their lifestyle too. Those are the guys who end up broke, unemployed or worse. I never forgot that this was a job, I was here to get paid, and I was only a prop in their luxury life. Careful with the money, that was my philosophy.

About the money. Probably your idea of good money and mine are different, and I don't want to give you the impression I was carting home suitcases full of cash every night. Working class, remember? But even in my late twenties I was pulling in better than what a pair of thirty-year, union auto workers put together could earn, and all of it tax free. Plus I rarely got my hands dirty. I drove *all the time*, and I learned to love those hundred dollar bills I was seeing on top of the basic tip, on top of the run percentage and the by-request percentage. I learned to cultivate whales.

That's where the real payoff was, the steady, repeat high-rollers. People who owned their own businesses and wanted to impress clients. The rich elite who wanted to show off. B and C-list celebrities who acted like A-listers. Foreign tourists. You've heard people say, *"They didn't get rich by giving it to people like you."* I say bullshit. These were the kind of people with no real concept of how much they had, tossing it around freely because there was always more where that came from. I had a monthly, two-night run to Carmel and Pebble Beach with one old bag who inherited an airline. She liked vodka with cranberry and paying too much for jewelry and clothes she wouldn't wear. She also didn't like to deal with the "little people" (that's actually how she worded it) and would start the run by handing me four-hundred dollars so I could take care of all the tipping, and she wouldn't have to be bothered with it. I'd break it into tens and fives and take care of everyone from bellhops to doormen to bartenders, even the kid in the hotel garage who I'd pay to wash the car and fill the ice bucket. Of course one of those hundreds went right in my pocket. The best part? When the four-hundred was gone, I'd tell her and she'd hand over another four hundred. No questions asked, no need for accounting. And the runs were always by-request, with sixteen hours of executive protection contract per day. Sweet, sweet runs. I only had to do "executive protecting" one time, when she got really drunk and nasty with another patron in the hotel lounge, a guy who looked like he was getting ready to smack the shit out of her, old lady or not.

"Go take care of him," she slurred at me.

I walked over to the guy (who stood up and clenched his fists), smiled, and peeled off a hundred-dollar bill. "I'm really sorry my client is such an asshole," I said, and shrugged. "What can you do?" Then I offered to buy a round for the table.

He smiled back and shook my hand. Conflict resolved. When I got back to her I said, "I straightened him out, told him who you were, said I'd break his head if he said anything else."

The bartender winked at me, then poured her four fingers of Grey Goose to shut her down. She was snoring in her room fifteen minutes later, and the bartender earned himself an extra twenty for that. In the morning she gave me five-hundred dollars for being "her hero."

By far my heaviest whale was Big Al, owner of a small oil company in central California. Because of him I made a fortune. And because of him I surrendered my soul to eternal damnation. Here's where we talk about *real* money, and sex, and murder. And since you might be suspicious, no, I didn't procure young girls for him to sexually brutalize and dispose of in some horrific manner.

Big Al was a monthly, by-request client who lived in Sacramento. Like clockwork, his assistant would call me and set up an overnight to Lake Tahoe for Al and a couple of business associates, with the executive protection option. The first time we met, he decided he didn't care for my real name but announced that I looked like a "Rocco," so that's what he called me. Not a problem. Give them what they want. His business associates and friends started calling me Rocco too, and after only a single Tahoe run, so did the pit bosses.

"Good evening, Mr. (we'll leave his name out.) Good evening, Rocco."

Those guys don't forget a thing. And they treated Big Al (and his buddies, and consequently me) like royalty. He'd hand the pit boss fifty grand to put on his account, and draw from it all night. If it ran out, they'd put him on a tab without a word. The bosses ensured he and his guests got first class service, never had to call for a drink, always had a fresh pack of smokes. No one ever gave me a hassle about the bulge under my left armpit (my carry permit was for California, not Nevada,) and they let me sit at the table even though I wasn't playing. It was the best place to be, because when Al was winning, he'd slide green, twenty-five dollar chips towards me to put towards the tip fund. Of course that was just extra. I never came away from a Big Al run without a grand, plus the thirty-five percent, plus the chips. If he was *really* hitting, those sliding chips turned into black hundreds. Regardless of the color, I'd say thank you and tuck them away.

Of course the chips slid a lot less frequently when he wasn't hitting. Big Al didn't like to play blackjack. He liked to *win* at blackjack, and if he was losing, he turned into a monstrous prick. It didn't bother me, and it didn't bother the pit bosses. We were in the service industry, and the smile you got was the same, rain or shine. Win, lose, fall off his chair with a stroke…we were there to get paid.

On my third run with him, he steps away from the table to stretch and I step away with him.

"Rocco, we wanna get laid."

"I'll take care of it," I said.

Between you and me, I wasn't sure how I was going to deliver on that casually given promise, but I figured if you couldn't find a hooker in a Tahoe casino, you weren't really looking. I've learned that the best place to find anything in a hotel, especially things people won't talk about, is from the bell captain.

I gave him a twenty-dollar handshake, with more ready just in case. "I have clients looking for a little companionship." I probably didn't come across as smooth as it sounds. I'd never done this before (though once I did stop in Chinatown so a hooker could climb in and blow a group of college freshmen out for a night on the town. I told them I needed a fifty first, and then pulled over at the first skank I saw.)

The bell captain reached into his little podium and pulled out a photocopied map, handing it over like it was a tourist brochure. No shit. I thanked him and examined the map. It had the route from Tahoe to Carson City highlighted, with half a dozen smaller side roads also marked, each ending in a circle with the name of a cathouse written next to it. That was when I first learned prostitution was legal in Carson City. Of course my clients would never be permitted to learn that I had just discovered this amazing tidbit of information. It paid much better to be that smooth, "Rocco will make it happen" kind of character they expected me to be.

"We're in business," I said when I went back to the table. He collected his buddies and we were off, driving out of the mountains, me following the map in the front seat where they couldn't see it.

"Rocco, where we going?" Al shouted from the back.

"To get you guys laid!" I shouted back. They roared their approval and started giggling like junior high boys. It was just the line Al wanted his friends to hear, and it earned me an extra hundred on the spot.

I chose the "Double D Pleasure Ranch" because it was close to Tahoe, and I liked its name better than the "Velvet Pussycat" and the "Ride 'em Cowgirl." I'd never been to a cathouse, had no idea what to expect, and was immensely let down when I saw it was a cluster of connected double-wides surrounded by chain link, under a flashing neon sign showing a voluptuous woman with neon pasties that blinked from stars to nipples every second. Classy. Ours was the only car in the gravel lot. Of course it was close to two in the morning, so not very surprising.

Inside, however, it was just like I'd imagined it would be. There was a main greeting room with mirrored walls, naked gold statuary, red carpet and red, crushed velvet couches. Vera, the madam – I guessed they were called that – was a full-figured, older gal with pale skin, platinum blonde hair and a leopard print top, likely someone who had earned her position here after years on her back. She gave us a warm greeting and called out the girls.

They came out of a doorway and lined up so Al and his buddies could choose their favorite flavor. I heard them quietly coming to arrangements for what the guys wanted and what it would cost, and then they all disappeared. Before my clients left, they each handed me a fat money clip, Al's the fattest of all. It must have been close to forty grand in total, and I told them they were smart. It wouldn't do to fall asleep in a room with a whore while carrying that kind of cash. You'd wake up broke, and she'd be long gone. It was safe with me. I never screwed a client, and I certainly never stole from one.

While they were in back, I sat in the lounge and chatted with a pair of girls who hadn't been selected, one dark haired and one light, neither more than eighteen. It was friendly conversation, I didn't ask judgmental questions and they didn't try to sell themselves to me. We just talked like real people. It was nice.

At one point Big Al showed up in the doorway, bare-assed with half a hard-on. "Rocco, you want a spin with them?" He pointed to the girls. "I'll spring for both, my man."

The girls raised their eyebrows.

"Thanks anyway, Al," I said, "but I'm working."

He shrugged and disappeared again.

About now you're ready to call bullshit, right? I'm in a cathouse in the middle of the night, and someone is offering to pick up the tab so I can screw two eighteen-year-old hard bodies at the same time, and I say no? I know, I know, but that's how it happened. I was working, I was there to get paid, not laid, and now I'm carrying all their money and an unlicensed firearm. Better to stay right where I was and jerk off later.

Two hours go by, and I'm beyond sleepy, even though the girls have been bringing me coffee. I told them they should just go to bed, but they said they'd keep me company. Out of another doorway comes this guy who's not smiling, and my brain says *muscle*. I even got up from the couch, suddenly not so sleepy anymore. He's bigger than me, wearing a black turtleneck, a real goombah type, and all I can think is, *What did those assholes do? I'm just working, man! I'm not their babysitter!*

He asks me to step inside with him and I go, but I unbutton my jacket. Then he shows me into a well-lit business office, and there sits this young woman with glasses in front of a computer screen with a green spreadsheet on it.

"Can I have your business card?"

I give it to her, ready to tell her that the limo service – and especially its driver - can't be held liable for any damage or harm these guys might have caused. Instead she files the card in a Rolodex, taps out some numbers on an adding machine while she's looking at the screen, opens a drawer and starts counting out cash. Then she hands the cash to me. It's a little over a grand.

This is the part where I should say something smooth, but I just stare at the cash with this dumb look on my face. She laughs. "Drivers get ten percent of the action when they bring in clients."

"Right," I manage, and she laughs again.

"You didn't know. It's okay, it's your first time here. I won't tell anyone."

I fanned through the bills, then tucked them away. "You're serious. Ten percent?"

"Yep."

"These guys have had ten grand worth of sex tonight?"

"And you get a piece of every sick twist their little heart's desire."

I couldn't help but smile. Only in America.

She looked over her glasses. She was really pretty, much prettier than any of the girls who had lined up earlier, and I had a tough time believing she got her start in the trailer rooms. She looked more like NYC Business School.

"We like new clients and repeat business. Make a few more runs and we'll up your percentage. If we decide we like you, we'll discuss more...lucrative jobs. You seem like a man who appreciates being well-compensated for delivering that extra level of service."

It didn't occur to me to wonder how she'd managed to peg me so well after only a few minutes, but I guess she knew a whore when she saw one. I told her I'd be happy to bring her as much business as I could arrange.

"Ladies!" I heard the madam yell, her voice carrying throughout the trailers, and immediately there was the sound of opening and closing doors. I started out the door to see what was going on, but the office girl gripped me by an arm and pulled me down into a chair – she was a lot stronger than she looked – and said, "Wait here with me for a bit." I did.

Half an hour later I met my three clients as they shuffled back into the entry lounge, shirts unbuttoned, hair skewed and looking exhausted. I got them back to Tahoe as the sun was coming up, then home. They slept through the ride, and when I dropped Al off last he hit me with a three grand tip and a "See you next month, Rocco."

You bet your rich white ass, Big Al.

Al wasn't the only client I took to the ranch. I knew I had locked into a good thing, and started putting all my efforts into bringing in customers. Bachelor parties were the easiest, drunk and horny young guys eager for some action. I always warned them to bring plenty of cash, and they obliged. More importantly, they came back for more, and I made out. Thirty-five percent on the run since of course they asked for Rocco, a healthy tip, and ten percent of the action at the ranch. It didn't take long before the girls were calling me Rocco too, and the pretty accountant (her name turned out to be Veronica) quickly bumped me to twenty, then twenty-five percent. My boss was happy. He thought I was doing Tahoe runs, had no idea about the Double D, and he certainly had no complaints about the business I was bringing in. He gave me my choice of gigs, so when I didn't have a group for the ranch, I was working money runs. And of course there was Big Al and his blackjack every month, my number one whale.

I saved almost all my cash, wrapping it in tight bundles and hiding it in my apartment.

And every time I was at the ranch, just as the night was winding   down,   Vera   would   yell, "Ladies!" and there would be that opening and closing of doors. Veronica always kept me in her office during that time. I asked her what was going on, but she just smiled sweetly and shook her head. I was starting to get sort of a crush on Veronica, and even asked her out once. She gave me a polite but firm no, and I didn't ask again.

One morning at the ranch, right around four a.m., I was sitting in Veronica's office while my clients - a gang of seven frat boys from U.C. Berkeley - were busy in the back. Veronica had stepped out for something, and I was alone when Vera called, "Ladies!" Opening and closing doors, as usual. I looked outside the office, didn't see anyone, and decided to have myself a look. I went into the back hallway where the girls had their rooms.

Curiosity. A truly unhealthy condition.

Just a peek, I told myself, quietly opening the first door I came to.

One of the frat boys, a redhead with a lot of freckles and a woven bracelet with Jamaican colors, was naked and spread eagle on the bed, his eyelids fluttering. Two of the girls – one was the pretty, dark-haired one I'd chatted with in the lounge – were flanking him in kneeling positions, hands pinning him down, grunting as they worked their mouths at each side of his neck. I must have gasped, made some sound, because the dark-haired girl's head snapped up, and suddenly I was looking into a pair of yellow eyes with pinpoint pupils. Her face and neck were smeared with blood, as were her fangs. Not the canine-types you'd expect, these were incisors, side by side and long and sharp, like a Nosferatu in a black and white movie. Her black tongue flickered out and she hissed.

"Oh, shit..." I stumbled backwards out of the room and into the hallway, where a single hand caught my shoulder and spun me around. Another hand gripped my throat, slammed me against the wall and lifted me off my feet. I started choking, couldn't breathe.

Veronica wasn't so pretty anymore, with her yellow eyes and Nosferatu fangs and generally pissed-off expression. She held me up there effortlessly, staring at me, as the girls came out of the room behind her. In the hallway, more doors opened and the ladies emerged, all with the twin fangs, all wiping their palms and forearms at the blood on their faces. Even Big Vera appeared in the hall. They were hissing, and a few snarled.

"Why didn't you stay in the office?" Veronica asked.

"I...I'm sorry...so sorry..." I wheezed.

Veronica looked over her shoulder at the others. "Finish up," she snapped, and they responded, quickly disappearing back into their rooms. Then it was just me and Veronica. She slowly lowered me so my feet touched the floor, and the pressure came off my throat. Her fangs slid back in and her eyes shifted once more to dark brown. She shook her head, a bittersweet smile on her face.

"Why?"

I was trembling. I didn't know, didn't have an answer.

"We make the marks go away, we make them forget after we feed," she said. "They just go home tired. Maybe they have some bad dreams for a while, but no damage done."

"Please, Veronica," I said, beyond being ashamed at my little boy's voice. "Make me forget, too."

She seemed to think about it for a moment, then slipped her arm around my waist and walked me slowly back to her office. She gently pushed me into a chair, and sat across from me. "I don't think I will. I think you should remember everything tonight."

I shook my head, started to speak, but she held up a hand and shushed me.

179

"You've been doing a terrific job, and your client list is growing. No sense spoiling a good thing. I'm going to up your cut to a full fifty percent of the action. Plus, if you can bring us someone disposable, like a prostitute or a runaway...no vagrants...you'll get ten grand per head."

"Disposable?"

She nodded. "Someone who won't be missed. It's easier that way. The girls get tired of always having to use restraint, to let them live. Sometimes they need to blow off steam, really rip into something."

Vera and the muscled goombah walked past the office door then, carrying a long, limp shape in a bloody white bed sheet between them. An arm slipped lifelessly out of the sheet, knuckles dragging on the carpet. The wrist wore a Jamaican friendship bracelet.

Veronica giggled and looked at me. "Accidents happen. We'll make your clients forget he was with them. You're the only one who will know." She smiled, and the tips of her fangs lowered just the smallest bit as her eyes took on a yellow tint. "And you *will* keep working, and you *will* keep bringing them here. Do you understand me?"

I didn't respond, and she rolled her office chair over to me and placed her palms on my thighs, leaning in close, her lips brushing my ear. Softly she said, "I want you to remember what happens here, and remember something else. If you try to quit, or run away, or tell anyone...I *will* find you." Then she teased my ear with her tongue, and gave my earlobe a playful nibble before standing up, still smiling.

"Off you go, now."

How big of a whore was I? This was the question I asked myself all the way home, my half-empty clients dozing in the back. I asked myself the question all morning, sitting in a Denny's and drinking coffee, then again later, on a park bench in the sunlight, too tired and scared to sleep. How big a whore?

Twenty years. I've been living here just about that long.

It's a Catholic monastery in upstate New York, close to the Canadian border. We get a lot of snow. No, I'm not a monk, but the brothers let me live here in a small attic room, and don't ask questions. Brother Tobin is sympathetic but not pushy. He says we all wrestle with our own demons. Brother Tobin doesn't know the half of it. I dropped off the limo and left California that day, drove east until I couldn't see straight, somehow managed to pull off to the side of the road and catch some sleep, then just kept on going. All those tightly-wrapped bundles of cash went to the brothers as a donation. That could be the real reason they don't ask questions, but I like to think they keep me here as an act of charity. I attend mass in order to be polite. I read the bible looking for answers, and still haven't found anything satisfying. I pray, even though I know no one is listening. I'm pretty sure I sold that privilege in Nevada. No one here knows my background, and no one calls me Rocco. I left it all behind.

I'm not here seeking absolution.

I'm hiding, nothing more. The 9mm Beretta is the only reminder of that former life, and I keep it under my pillow.

Twenty years of trying to forget those images, forget what I did.

It hasn't helped.

There's tapping at the glass now, way up here with a four story drop below. Tap, tap, tap. I ease the Beretta out from under my pillow as Veronica, smiling and floating outside, pushes the widows in with a rush of cold air, and steps barefoot onto my wooden floor.

The barrel has an oily, metallic taste, and as she reaches for me, I have a fingertip's worth of pressure to wonder if it will hurt when it goes off.

181

EATER OF STARS

The Mayans were right. And wrong. As the crowning achievement to his postgraduate work at MIT, Lawrence Singh intended to prove both.

It was a Friday night and he sat at his work station on the third floor of the Media Lab, an intense young man in need of a haircut, six screens working in front of him as his fingers danced over a pair of keyboards like a concert pianist. Eleven empty Mountain Dew cans filled a wastebasket beside the work table, the lab quiet and empty around him.

On one screen there was a close-up color image of a stone with four columns of ancient glyphs carved into its surface. It had been digitally altered to become a graphic where each column could move up and down independently. Currently they were scrolling upwards at different speeds. Four other screens were busy flowing through rapidly-changing series of complex formulas and algorithms, and the last and largest displayed another graphically-modified representation of a huge disc covered in rings of strange, carved symbols.

"Their calendar is based on twenties, with repeating sets of nine and thirteen, and four-hundred being a pure number." His eyes didn't leave the screens as he spoke. In a swivel chair beside him, her high heels propped on the work table, Kiera yawned.

"I thought we were going for drinks."

"We are, in a little bit."

Her taut stomach was bared by a tight belly shirt, and she placed her hand on the smooth skin and played with the little jewel piercing in her navel, tracing a red fingernail slowly around it. She looked at her boyfriend and bit her lower lip.

No reaction.

She sighed. I should be dating one of the guys from crew, she thought, muscled upper bodies and shoulders, big arms hard from rowing. Lawrence was brilliant but not much else, and as soon as he got her through her math requirements she was gone.

Lawrence pointed at the screen with the disc. "This middle ring maintained a five-hundred-eighty-four count Venus cycle, and it's geometrically aligned with these nine symbols placed closer in, called the Lords of the Night."

"Lords? The Mayans were Catholics?"

He made a face. I should be dating one of the chicks from Anthropology, he thought. Of course none of them looked like Kiera, a sultry mix of Polynesian and black, with dark eyes and waist-length black hair. And he doubted the Anthropology chicks were as flexible. He had noticed her toying with the piercing, but he tried not to. He was so close to completion, and he had to stay focused.

"No, they were about as far from Catholic as you get. The Nine Lords feature in their mythology, the Aztecs had them too, representing their gods, each ruling over a particular, rotating night. But that's just part of their religion. What's significant is the number nine, repeating sets of nine. The Mayans were mathematicians."

Kiera looked at her nails.

Lawrence's fingers tapped, and he began nodding. "Nines, thirteens, twenties...the core of the randomized algorithm. It's going to be worth an Order of Magnitude."

Kiera, a med student at Harvard, blinked at the screens. Her own studies required a considerable amount of math, but this was so over the top it might as well have been in Martian. "And what exactly is going to win you an Order of Magnitude? In English, please."

"Remember when I told you the Mayans were right, and wrong?"

"Thousands of times." She could feel a lecture coming, and leaned further back in her chair. It might even sound like new information, since she had paid so little attention the last time.

"The Mayan calendar stops on-"

"December twenty-first, twenty-twelve," Kiera said, "the end of the world, right?"

"Wrong, and any Mayan who thought so was wrong too. That's all Hollywood and media bullshit. Twenty cycles of the Mayan long count calendar equals a *Baktun*, 144,000 days. December twenty-one, twenty-twelve, is simply the day the calendar rolls to a new *Baktun.*"

She tipped forward. "That's it?" He actually had her attention now. "The calendar just starts over?"

"Yeah, that's pretty much the only significance of it. If it didn't have the capacity to refresh, and you were a Mayan, you'd end up having to carve that monstrosity again and again. It's pretty clever, actually."

"No end of the world?"

"Nope. The last time it happened was the year 1617. No end of the world."

"If it's no big deal, then why all the hype and panic?"

Lawrence grinned. "Because you don't sell movies and books and newspapers with the mundane."

She leaned back, feeling a little disappointed that the epic catastrophe she had half believed in was explained away by something as simple as throwing out your old day planner at the end of the year and picking up a new one.

"So," he continued, "wrong about the end of the world, if they ever even thought that. But right with their other calculations, the hidden ones."

"You lost me."

Lawrence switched his right hand to the mouse while his left tapped keys, his eyes rapidly tracking the moving images on screen. "The Mayans had their own algorithms concealed within the symbols of the calendar, and it's taken me two years to uncover them. I also discovered that *this Baktun*, the one we're in, is mathematically different from any that have gone before. On the final day of our current *Baktun*, the hidden Mayan equation finally falls into place."

"Which means what?"

He looked sideways at her. "Every mathematical operation leads to something. Sometimes it's an effect, usually it's another equation, but there's always something at the end of it. I don't feel like waiting until it comes around by itself, so I've set up this program to simulate the final day of the *Baktun*, and apply the hidden algorithm, right now."

"What's going to happen?"

Lawrence shrugged. "Can't say." A massive calculation began scrolling across several screens, and the graphic image of the calendar itself, crafted so each ring could be turned independently, began rotating. "When they make me the president of MIT you can say you were here to see it first."

"I don't think you should be messing with this, Lawrence." She was suddenly very uncomfortable.

"Will you relax? It's only a computer model, all just theoretical. I need to test it before I present to the board." The equation reached its terminus, and he hit the enter button with a dramatic flourish.

Lawrence Singh was right. And wrong.

Right about there being a hidden calculation which would trigger under precise conditions.

Wrong when he said theoretical.

At the moment he struck the enter key, five of his screens went black. On the one remaining, the one showing the calendar itself, an interior ring stopped rotating with the symbol of one of the Nine Lords of the Night in the uppermost position. The carving depicted a squatting skeleton with the head of a mantis.

If Lawrence had been dating an Anthropology major, she might have been able to tell him this symbol represented *Mictlantecuhtli*, a deity named by the Aztecs, and one to which the Mayans paid homage but dared not speak of or name for themselves. Both cultures regarded him as the God of the Dead, the King of the Underworld, and the Eater of Stars. Both cultures believed he waited just beyond this world to greet the dead and rip their souls apart, and worship of *Mictlantecuhtli* involved ritual cannibalism on a broad scale. Most others cultures in the world, past and present, had their own name for him.

One was Lucifer.

The gateway erupted not as a computer graphic on a flat screen, but as a vertical, nine-foot slash in the air just yards in front of them. It bowed at the edges, forming a sort of pulsing oval with red, meaty-looking edges and an absolute darkness within. A sickening odor spilled into the lab, making Lawrence clamp his hands to his mouth and nose and causing Kiera to vomit between her knees. The sound of a frantically-played violin running up and down the chromatic scales filled the air, almost a metallic hum, and then a black, seven-foot tall praying mantis scuttled out of the opening, claws clicking on the tile floor, barbed forelegs held in the classic prayer pose. An articulated head moved slowly in a three-hundred degree arc as it surveyed the room with its glistening, compound eyes. Its razored beak clicked, and it let out a long hiss.

Kiera crawled under the console and tucked into a fetal position, whimpering and biting her knuckles to keep from screaming. Lawrence couldn't move, one hand resting on the useless mouse, eyes wide and locked on the thing before him.

The mantis let out a high-pitched squeal and skittered across the lab, quick and agile, banging through the double doors at the far end. Dozens more spilled out of the gate, hissing and shrieking, following the first, and still more emerged. Within seconds a steady stream of black-bodied giants was pouring out of the throbbing portal, flowing through the lab in a clicking, ravenous mass that had no end.

One of the black screens blinked to life, and announced it was processing a calculation to determine portal output. Simple calculations began to form, mostly multiplication and numbers Lawrence was familiar with; nines, thirteens, twenties, four-hundreds. His finely-tuned mathematician's brain reached the sum even before the computer did, as a river of hungry insects chattered past and out the door.

Fifty-four billion.

He blinked, his lips moving soundlessly. Was that even possible? Without meaning to, he broke the number down in his head. If a thousand giant mantises emerged from the gate every hour, twenty-four hours a day, it would take about eight years before the sum was achieved. Eight times the planet's population. What would be left of mankind?

Screaming from the campus beyond the glass walls of the lab building answered that question. Praying mantises were among the most efficient predators in the insect world, so utterly ruthless that – like the Mayans who worshipped their dark patron – they did not hesitate to turn to cannibalism when other prey wasn't available. Boston was just across the Charles River, with the whole world waiting beyond that. There would be no shortage of prey.

So involved in his calculations had he been, that Lawrence didn't notice when one of the shiny black killers, a big female, stepped out of line and pranced quickly up behind the desk, head pivoting with sharp, quick movements as she hunted. Finding what she sought, she squealed and used her front legs to drag Kiera out from under the desk. The girl screamed and babbled and flailed at her attacker until the mantis disemboweled her with the slash of a foreleg, dropping her jittering body to the tile.

Lawrence kicked violently backwards in his swivel chair, ramming into the edge of the workstation table, staring up at the monster towering over him. The female rocked from side to side, antennae twitching as she regarded him with her big eyes.

A single, organized thought managed to cut through his fear. If the computer had caused the portal to open, might shutting it down cause it to *close?* The whole system fed to a big surge protector under the desk, and he risked a glance down to see that his right shoe was only inches from the glowing red kill switch.

He glanced up and saw she had her head tilted, staring at him as if curious. His foot moved-

-and the mantis bit his head off as if he was a mate who had performed his primary task.

The body slumped to the floor, and the female quickly joined the flow towards the exit doors, one more player in the final act of the world.

OF CRIMES AND CROWS

In the moonlight, the coyote was just a shadow against a desert backdrop. It stood at the edge of the road, head lowered and motionless, looking at the man who had come to a halt twenty feet away. The coyote made a noise in its throat which was part growl, part whine, and took a single step onto the asphalt.

Thomas Jumping Crow stood as still as the animal in front of him. He licked his lips, tasting the whiskey, and clutched the bottle close to his chest as if the coyote might wish to take it from him. He was almost upon the animal when it stepped from behind a clump of sagebrush, looking as if it intended to cross the highway. It had startled him.

"Go back," he whispered, and saw one of the animal's ears flicker. "Let me pass."

The coyote lifted its head, sniffing the night air, fragrant with the tang of alkali and the softer scent of sage. It took another step, and Thomas tensed. Coyote, the Trickster, was without question an evil spirit, but it could also be playful. Was that what Coyote was doing now? Playing with him? Testing him? Every Navajo knew that if a coyote crossed your path, you must turn back. To continue would lead to injury or even death. He believed, but enough to walk back into the night, return to...nothing? Not that anything was waiting for him ahead, either. Did it really matter whether this scrawny desert dog walked across the road now or later?

The night had no answer. It was silent and empty, isolated. Like the two living things on the road.

"Do as you will," he muttered, taking a step forward. The coyote yipped and darted across the road, disappearing into the shadows beyond. For Thomas to go on would be a serious taboo, not broken lightly. He hesitated, suddenly afraid. Would this be the one, he wondered? Would defying Coyote be the final trigger? After a moment he forced himself to move forward, pretending he didn't feel an involuntary shudder when he crossed the path the animal had taken. Nothing happened in that instant, but then it wasn't supposed to. Coyote would work his tricks at his own pace, in his own time. Under his broken boots, Route 191 stretched on under a cool-eyed moon.

He passed a gravel turn-off which led to White Mesa, a cluster of shacks encircling a trading post a mile or so beyond the high sandstone hills. Thomas Jumping Crow was not welcome in White Mesa, just as he was not welcome many places in San Juan County. He was what his people called a Shadow Man, one who had no place in either the Spirit World or the world of men. Over his forty years – though his wind-burned face made him look closer to sixty – he had drifted across the southeastern corner of Utah, in and out of Colorado and Arizona, working menial, labor-intensive jobs, mostly on ranches. Each stay was usually brief, ending once his alcohol consumption became unbearable, or when his nature came to the attention of his employers, as it always managed to do.

The year he worked for the Bureau of Indian Affairs hadn't helped his reputation, either. In 1935 the Bureau – citing soil erosion and overgrazing – ordered the Navajos to slaughter vast quantities of their herds, compensating them with only a fraction of their worth. Jumping Crow signed on with the government, and aided its agents in going after those Navajo ranchers who were reluctant to comply, entering their lands and driving their sheep off cliffs by the thousands. To him, a job was a job, and in these times he took whatever he could get. But to the Navajo people, who measured wealth by the headcount of sheep, he was no better than a white man.

Yet regardless of his time among the whites, and despite being a drifter and petty thief frequently unable to work due to drunkenness, it was his *nature* which drove him out of communities and onto the road again and again. And that was something he could not change.

He shuffled over a rise, boots scraping the asphalt as he walked the yellow line, a man in dusty jeans and denim jacket, his long hair tied back under a blue bandana and a single crow's feather tied into his braid. As a child he was told that he must forever wear the black feather, so that the people would know what he was. He was also told that if he did not wear the feather, he would be taken by a whirlwind, where he would spend an eternity of pain spinning within it.

The desert unfolded before him, a barren sea painted in shades of gray and black, a near-full moon riding high above. Jumping Crow didn't look at the moon, knowing it would follow him if he did. He did not look at the stars for fear he might see one falling, bringing him bad luck. He did not eat corn when it was raining, for fear of being struck by lightning, and he did not whistle because it would summon the wind. There were many taboos among his people, and he, like all Navajo, had long ago been educated that breaking them could expose one to evil spirits. This was especially dangerous for someone like Thomas Jumping Crow.

And yet I crossed Coyote's path, he thought. Do I fear death less than wind and lightning? It was yet another point of confusion in a life both complex and simple at the same time.

He spotted the car pulled off the road about a quarter mile down a dirt trail, partially hidden by sage, its curved white roof gleaming under the moonlight. Abandoned, perhaps? It would be worth a look. There might be something of value inside, something he could trade. The car itself would be useless, of course. Jumping Crow had never driven an automobile.

Within fifteen minutes the highway was behind him and he was scraping along the trail, his boots kicking at the tire imprints in the rocky sand. Theft was a taboo too, of course, but one he had broken before without ill effect. There were greater worries, like avoiding high places because they were home to the Holy Ones and monsters, and the prohibition against killing a spider without first drawing a circle around it and saying, "You have no relatives." Handling crow feathers was said to cause boils, but he knew this wasn't true. Perhaps for other Navajo, but not for him, which made sense. He drank from his bottle as he walked, relishing the liquid burn as it went down.

The car came into view from behind the sage and Thomas staggered to a halt. A '33 or '34 four-door Pontiac, it was white with black fenders and doors, and on the door facing him were white block letters reading SHERIFF'S PATROL SAN JUAN COUNTY curving over and under a white star. The car was shaking.

Thomas turned and began walking briskly away. Then he heard the girl scream. He told himself it was a cry of passion, and then it came again, young, piercing, in pain. His legs kept moving. It was white man's business, none of his business. Another scream, long and shrieking, filled with terror. He was running now, not thinking, not wanting to think, and suddenly realized he was running *at* the car, boots sliding in the sand and dirt. He saw figures moving in the back and jerked open the rear passenger door. The man – *boy* – in back was naked from the waist down, his pale rear end pumping furiously as his arms fought to restrain the figure beneath him. Jumping Crow caught the strong whiff of sex and fear, and he gripped the boy's ankles and heaved backwards. Years of ranch labor, days spent slinging hay bales and the strength which came with it, sent the boy flying through the air with a frightened squawk before he landed on the desert floor and tumbled across rock and cactus. Within the car, a Navajo girl of sixteen, wearing only a torn blouse and nothing else sobbed and crawled backwards against the far door, trying to cover herself.

Jumping Crow stood unsteadily, looking at her, unsure of what to do and not believing what he had already done.

"You filthy Nav!" Jumping Crow turned to the voice just as a fist connected with the side of his head. He fell to his knees, the scene spinning, trying to make sense of the boy in a khaki shirt with the star pinned to his breast, looking comical with his skinny legs and shriveling privates, and at the broken whiskey bottle on the ground nearby. When had he dropped that?

The deputy wrenched open the driver's door, cursing and fumbling inside, as Jumping Crow climbed slowly to his feet, head pounding. He heard the car door on the other side creak open.

"You stop right there!" The boy's voice was high and frightened, and it was followed a second later by the *BOOM* of a gunshot. Jumping Crow flinched, seeing the boy standing near the hood of the Pontiac, his gun belt in one hand, pistol in the other. Beyond, the girl was running into the desert. *BOOM-BOOM!* The white muzzle flashes lit the night, and the girl fell.

Jumping Crow felt the whiskey coming back up, and he vomited into the sand as the boy turned towards him. The Navajo wiped a palm across his lips and started to straighten, seeing the boy's face contorted into a mask of hatred, his lips peeling back from his teeth in a snarl. He raised the barrel of the pistol, and Jumping Crow lunged forward, grabbing his wrist and slamming his larger body against the young deputy, crushing him against the Pontiac's fender, the pistol between them.

BOOM! They both jumped, and Thomas saw the boy's eyes go wide a moment before his body went slack. Jumping Crow released him and stepped back, and the deputy slid to the ground, dropping onto his side next to a whitewall tire. The belly of his shirt was a spreading darkness which quickly darkened the sand beneath him. His eyes stared sightlessly up at the stars.

Jumping Crow stood over him, trembling, his own blue work shirt wet with the boy's blood. He looked at his palms, dark and glistening in the moonlight, and somewhere in the distance a coyote howled.

He started to run.

San Juan County sat in the extreme southeast of Utah, part of the "Four Corners" territory where Utah, Colorado, Arizona and New Mexico met. It was bordered on the south by the Navajo Nation, and was as desolate and remote as the southwest got, a place of wind-carved canyons and strange sandstone sculptures, deserts and mountains, sagebrush and lonely stretches of desert. Its isolation made it attractive to Bad Men, and it was the Mormon Church who first sent in settlers to establish the county, creating a "point of interception" for bank and train robbers, horse thieves, cattle rustlers and renegade Indians. It was a place which quickly established a tradition of men rushing home – even from church services – to get their horses and guns to take up the chase of outlaws. In its history, gunfights between lawmen and outlaws were far more common than in more notorious locations like Tombstone and Dodge City.

Sheriff Edgar Bybee was proud to be a part of that tradition, proud of the star on his chest and the big handled six-shooter on his hip. As he drove along Route 191 in his 1936 black and white Pontiac – purchased new for him by the county two years ago – he cocked an elbow out the window and enjoyed the pink glory of a desert sunrise. The little town of Bluff wasn't too many miles down the road, and his plans included an easy day checking in on Glen Parsons, along with a meal and a slice of apple pie at Rawling's Luncheonette.

At forty-three, Bybee made $1,830 a year, plus the car, gas and a uniform allowance. In these hard times – the papers were calling it the Great Depression – he considered himself lucky to have a stable, good-paying job and a place to live when so many across the country didn't. Bybee was grateful for his many other blessings, as well. Last night he had taken his wife to see the new Spencer Tracey movie "Boy's Town" in Monticello, and after the movie he basked in her affection over ice cream. He had the respect of his deputies, the county and the church, his daughter Jeanie was set to marry a fine young man, and FDR was in the White House setting things right. All was well in his world.

Maybe it was the wink of early morning sunlight on chrome, maybe the circling crows, but his eyes picked out the car in an instant. A chill hit him when he saw the white roof. Few folks out here had cars, and he knew of only one with a white roof. Bybee slowed and turned onto the dirt trail, and a minute later pulled to a stop behind Deputy Glen Parsons' patrol car. As he stepped out a cloud of crows lifted off a shape lying in the shade near the front tire, screeching their indignation at being disturbed in their meal, black feathers drifting down from the abrupt departure. Sand and rock crunched under his boots as he approached his fallen deputy, and he felt a blackness surge within him. He crouched beside the twenty-five year old, his eyes welling as he took the pistol from the stiff grip and checked the cylinder. Good boy. He'd gotten off four rounds before being gut shot, and though Bybee hoped he had hit his killer, he could see that someone had stripped Glen naked. It was a depraved defilement which he struggled to understand.

The sheriff sighed deeply, the sound of a much older man, and stood, turning slowly and squinting, trying to make sense of it. An auto stop gone wrong? Why so far down this dirt track, why not the side of the road? Had Glen seen something out here and pulled in? Bybee checked the ground, looking for tire tracks and finding only the Pontiac's. He saw the broken liquor bottle, saw a confused shuffle of boot prints and bare feet which didn't add up. Inside the car he found Glen's uniform trousers wadded up on the front seat. In the back was a long, Navajo skirt with a torn waistband.

As he looked around once more, a scrap of color out among the sage and cactus caught his eye, a flutter of movement. More crows took flight as Bybee approached, and he ached to find a dead man, a stranger who had murdered Glen but then succumbed to his deputy's bullets. Instead he found himself standing over the body of a girl lying face down. One bullet wound low in her back was exposed, much picked-at by the crows. The other was hidden behind a bloody shred of blouse. What in the world had happened here? He didn't like the answer which kept coming back to that question.

"I trust in your strength, Lord," he whispered, and then began the grim task ahead of him.

An hour later he was once more on the road, his heart heavy, his beliefs violently shaken. The Pontiac ran low at the rear, and the tarp covering what was in the trunk couldn't keep out the rising smell. Bybee drove with all the windows down.

He might have missed the man sleeping in the shade of a rocky outcropping beside the road, had it not been for the coyote. The bone-thin animal, patchy with mange, darted out into the road from the right, making the sheriff stomp the brakes and lock the tires in a smoking skid. The police cruiser came to a stop at an angle on the highway and stalled out, Bybee gripping the wheel so hard it could have cracked. Through the windshield not ten feet away was the sandstone outcropping, a figure stretched out beneath it.

The sheriff left the car in the road and walked over, nudging the sleeper with a boot. He was a Navajo, a farm worker or drifter

194

by the poor condition of his clothes and faded jacket, and as the man snorted and rolled over to face him, Bybee saw the blood on his shirt.

The sheriff gave the man a sharp kick to the leg, his pistol in hand. "Ease up out of there real slow, fella." He clicked the hammer back. *"Real* slow."

Jumping Crow squinted at the harsh daylight and raised a hand to shield his eyes. A white man with a gun. A lawman. He did as he was told and climbed to his feet.

Sheriff Bybee recognized him from around the county. Tom-something? Crow? "Turn around, hands behind your back." The Navajo turned slowly, and the sheriff rammed the muzzle of the revolver hard against the base of his skull. "Gimme some trouble. I'll put your brains on the rock."

Jumping Crow didn't give him any trouble, just put his wrists together slowly so the white man could lock on handcuffs. Then he was pushed to the back of the police car and shoved inside, the door slamming hard behind him.

"Gimme your name, fella," Bybee said, getting the Pontiac moving towards Bluff again.

"Thomas Jumping Crow."

"You kill my deputy?"

A long pause. "Yes, sir."

Bybee struggled not to take the Lord's name in vain. "He caught you doing something awful, didn't he?"

Another pause. "No, sir."

"Liar!" Bybee pounded the steering wheel. "He caught you raping that girl. Then you killed him and her, and made it up to look like something else. Right? You answer me!"

Jumping Crow began to weep. "I...I did such a bad thing."

"You're flippin' right you did, fella!"

Jumping Crow was crying harder, his head down. "I'm sorry."

"I don't give a gol-durn for your sorry. You just shut up back there before I decide I'm not a decent man." Bybee was flushed and his hands trembled on the steering wheel, his mind filled with the images from the deputy's car, the crows rising from the girl's corpse, wondering how he would explain it all to Glen's folks, to his own wife. And there were darker thoughts, ones which he forced away.

The morning desert rolled by. The sheriff spoke in a quieter voice. "You're gonna swing for this, Navajo. Gonna tie the knot myself." Utah had two approved forms of death penalty for aggravated murder; hanging and firing squad, though there hadn't been a hanging since 1912. The most recent murder of a police officer was in 1923, a Salt Lake City patrolman named David Crowther, shot down by a man with a concealed .32 revolver. It took three years before the shooter was tracked down in California, returned to Utah and convicted. Bybee was a young deputy himself then, and accompanied his sheriff on the long drive to Salt Lake to show rural law enforcement's support of the execution by firing squad. They waited outside the county courthouse with a large contingent of lawmen from across the state, while sentence was carried out in a fenced lot out behind the building.

For a time, from 1851 to 1888, Utah had a third method of execution; beheading. In theory it was to be carried out by the sheriff of the county in which the condemned was convicted, but there was no record of it actually being used anywhere in the state. No official record, that was. In law enforcement circles there was a well-circulated story – accepted as fact – that in 1887 a man known as Navajo Frank was beheaded by the Kanab County Sheriff after being convicted on a charge of "Raping a white woman." The weapon of execution was said to be a common axe the sheriff retrieved from his own woodpile.

Bybee glanced up at his mirror to see the man seated behind him. Jumping Crow was quiet, his head down, shoulders slumped. He didn't even deny the murder. The sheriff had no illusions of how a jury would receive all this, for though the white communities were neighbors with the Navajos, there was no great love between them. In the eyes of San Juan County's residents, the Indians took their rightful place among the other dusky-skinned folks; people of low moral character, ignorant, dirty and prone to savage abandon. If there was one story which articulated this feeling it was the well-known tale of Latigo Gordon.

In the late 1800's, Gordon was a cattle company foreman who specialized in harassing farmers by burning hay sheds and barns and even houses. When summoned to the county seat to answer

196

for his offenses, he took a shot at a county commissioner's son. He missed, and was charged with both mayhem and attempted murder. A jury acquitted him, citing that no one had ever impeached Gordon's reputation before this one event, and that even though he fired his pistol at a man, he hadn't meant to do any harm. As far as the mayhem charge, well, they were mostly Navajo farms he burned. Latigo Gordon went free.

Several years later, Gordon courted a young lady in Blanding, and received permission from her father to marry, but not before insisting Gordon have a conversation with the bishop.

"Have you ever killed a man?" the bishop asked.

"I don't think so," Latigo replied, "unless you count the nigger I caught bathing in a watering hole, and kept pushing his head under until he didn't come up again. But that probably wouldn't count." Apparently it didn't, because the wedding went ahead as planned with the bishop himself presiding over the ceremony.

No, there would be little sympathy for a Navajo drifter who murdered a well-liked, church-going deputy.

Bybee's patrol car bumped over railroad tracks, the sign that he was within the Bluff town limits. "When we stop," the sheriff said, "I'm gonna move you inside to a cell, and you're gonna be as nice and quiet as you are right now, understand?"

Jumping Crow said nothing, just kept his head down.

In his law enforcement career, this was the worst Edgar Bybee had seen. Twenty years earlier he had been a much younger man, fighting the Kaiser in the trenches of France. The things he had seen still lived within him, though somewhat tempered by time and peace, wife and home and church. Still, they were awful sights, and he had no trouble recalling them. Yet somehow, the sight of that murdered boy and the half-naked girl out in the sagebrush was worse. The carnage of war was to be expected, but this...this violation... It was something beyond sin.

Glen Parsons had been a San Juan County deputy for five years, hired by Bybee personally, as much a son as an employee. His parents had a tidy little farm in Blanding, and Glen could have worked the land beside his daddy if he'd wanted to, but he chose the law instead. A single man with good prospects, he lived in a little apartment attached to the Bluff Jail, provided by the county. Glen was a deacon in the church, a scout leader, even pitched in with church-sponsored food and clothing drives for the Navajos. A good boy, a respected boy. A fine deputy.

And a rapist and a murderer. These words had been circling the edges of Bybee's conscious thought like coyotes watching a sick antelope, waiting for it to weaken before pouncing. Now they burned before him, not to be ignored.

Edgar Bybee was a simple man, but no fool by anyone's definition. Despite what he had said to Jumping Crow, words spoken in anger and grief, he knew what he had seen. Those bare footprints bore undeniable testimony to the fact that Glen Parsons was bare-assed *before* being shot. His nakedness, plus the girl's, the torn clothing, the car out on a remote trail in the middle of the night...bullets fired, and bullets finding their marks. No, Edgar Bybee was no fool, but he was confused. How did the Navajo man entered into all this, and why did he admit to killing the deputy?

Rapist. Murderer. It was all just too horrible to be true. Glen Parsons? He'd sat beside Bybee and his wife in church, taken Sunday meals together. The county had trusted him. Bybee trusted him. *Dear Lord.*

He needed guidance, and knew he would find it in the little town of Bluff.

If there was a word to describe Bluff, *dry* was it. The little cluster of brick and tin roof structures, straddling the road with a population of seventy, boasted a single cross street with a four-way stop sign. It baked still and silent under the morning sun, heading for a July high of ninety-five degrees, a pocket of humanity in an expanse of grey-tan monotony. By noon the road would be simmering with a curtain of distorting waves.

Wind blew down the street, making the ESSO sign swing over the town's only gas station, and kicking up a pair of dust devils which danced across the pavement. In the back of the Pontiac, Thomas Jumping Crow looked at them. He would never name a whirlwind, nor would he throw a rock at one. Both invited evil spirits.

The sheriff pulled behind a low, flat brick building and into a packed dirt yard, easing the car into a stretch of shade cast by a detached garage. He pulled Thomas from the back seat and gripped his upper arm tightly as he walked him inside. The Bluff jail was a single room with a creaky wooden floor, a desk and several well broken-in wooden chairs, a pair of file cabinets and a padlocked rifle locker. One corner of the room was dominated by a large, iron-barred cell with a small barred window. The door to the attached deputy's apartment was closed.

Bybee produced a big iron key from the desk drawer and unlocked the cell, moving Thomas inside before taking off the handcuffs. The door made a hollow, metal bang when he closed it behind the Navajo. Thomas sat down on a bare cot next to a toilet bowl.

"I'll be back," the sheriff said, shoving the cell key into a pants pocket. "Don't you get up to any foolishness, Tom Jumping Crow. You're in enough trouble already." Jumping Crow stood on his cot to look out the window, watching the sheriff as he walked across the hard-packed yard and out of sight, his head down.

He sat back down and looked out at the deputy's office beyond the bars. A calendar showing a photo of a sleek black car on the street of some big city hung over the desk, JULY 1938 beneath it. On the desk was an empty inbox, a pencil cup and a coffee mug with a blue rim. Dust motes filled the sunbeams falling through a pair of windows, and outside a desert wind buffeted the brick building. Thomas hadn't whistled, hadn't looked up at moving clouds or pointed his finger at a rainbow, but the wind had come just the same.

"A wind blows through every man," the Elder told him long ago. "Your wind is a dark wind, Jumping Crow." He was eight when that was said to him, and not for the last time. He could still picture the leathery face and dark eyes of the Elder, towering over him and looking as old as a weathered mesa. It was easy to summon up the image, but it was quickly replaced by the running girl falling to the ground, and the face of the boy the moment the pistol went off. He wished he still had his bottle. It was the one magical elixir which could chase away the spirits of his past.

Thomas was born in 1898 at a trading post in Cortez, Colorado. There was much anticipation over the birth, for the tribal medicine man claimed to have seen signs and portents which predicted the child would be special, touched by the spirit world. This was both a source of pride and fear for his parents, for it could mean many things in the Navajo culture, not all of them good. For this reason the medicine man insisted on attending the birth, standing in a corner and chanting throughout the delivery.

Thomas had no sooner been placed in his mother's arms when a crow flew through an open window and landed on the infant's head, wings flapping, black feathers dropping onto the bedcover, and one landing on the baby's chest. The Navajos recoiled, and the medicine man bellowed a string of angry chants, waving his arms. The bird screeched and lifted off, circling the room once and flying back out the window. A moment of silence followed, and then Thomas's mother burst into tears, thrusting the infant out at arm's length and shaking her head. The others in the room, even her husband, stepped back, refusing to take the child.

It was the medicine man who named him *Nizah Ga'gii*, Jumping Crow. Navajo do not point at anything, for it was considered an act of aggression and a serious taboo, choosing instead to make a kissing gesture with the lips in the intended direction. But there in the hot little birthing room the medicine man did point, leveling a bony finger at the crying infant and whispering, "Skinwalker."

And with that single word, Thomas Jumping Crow was condemned.

He stared out through the bars, watching a stink bug slowly trundle over the plank floor, passing through a patch of sunlight. "Where are you going, brother?" he asked. "Home to your family?"

The beetle chose not to answer, and kept walking.

That young girl in the car must have had a family. He wondered if they would be missing her. Had she run away with her head filled with dreams of California and movie pictures, hitchhiking on a desert road? Her family would be worried, certainly, but even more ashamed of what she had done, and how she had met her end. Navajo were a complex people, easily disgraced.

The stink bug left the sunbeam and wandered towards the bars. Thomas sat and watched.

Shame. It was a concept he understood well. To the Navajo, everything was sacred, and had its place in the world. They believed it was man's responsibility to respect that balance.

Skinwalkers were an abomination, as obscene disruption to that balance, and despite how they might appear on the outside, they could never be trusted. The Navajo avoided and often would not speak with them, and they were not permitted to marry. No one would accept a skinwalker as a neighbor, and they were not welcome at tribal ceremonies. And yet the Navajo stopped short of completely shunning them, permitting a solitary existence on the fringe of their communities until the skinwalker chose to move on by his own accord.

Skinwalkers, Navajos who held an evil spirit, capable of taking the form of animals in order to do harm to men. Crows were especially reviled, as they were considered the spies and helpers of witches. Not that Jumping Crow had ever changed into an animal, or anything else for that matter. But as the medicine men taught and the Elders maintained, a Navajo so afflicted, who broke the laws and beliefs of the people, was forever in jeopardy of the evil spirit gaining control and pulling him into the Night World. The difference between man and beast was only a broken taboo away, but which taboo and how often broken remained a mystery.

"I have broken taboos," he whispered to the stink bug, which had stopped at the bars. "I have blown on hot corn, and not lost my teeth. I shook a pinion tree but a bear did not get me, and I put salt on the pinion nuts but it did not snow." He looked at the floor. Jumping Crow had killed a porcupine and waited for a nosebleed which didn't come. Once he even came upon a rattlesnake curled up on a nighttime rock, drinking in the heat of the day. Snakes represented the Lightning People, and were to be respected and avoided. Thomas laughed at the snake, but his legs didn't go crooked. Then he killed it with a rock, which should have triggered a drought, but the rains continued to fall and the rivers continued to flow. In fact, before he was twenty, he tried to break nearly every Navajo taboo he had been taught, hoping to bring about the dreaded change and end his angry, lonely existence. Nothing worked, and in the process he fell away from his beliefs entirely.

Then in 1918 an influenza epidemic swept through the Southwest, wiping away entire Navajo villages and families. Thomas was living in White Mountain at the time, in a shack at the edge of sheep lands, scraping out a living helping with the flock – butchering, mostly. The influenza killed every living soul in the village, leaving Thomas untouched. It was then that he began to believe again, began to understand the powerful darkness waiting silently inside him, strong enough to resist disease and death. He stopped breaking Navajo taboos after that, stopped trying to provoke the skinwalker, turning to drink in order not to think about what he might become.

Only there was no *might* about it anymore. Jumping Crow had violated the gravest taboo of all, committed the ultimate act of evil by killing another man. There would be no stopping the skinwalker now.

"Journey in peace," he said to the stink bug as it turned from the bars and wandered away. Outside the window, he heard a crunch of gravel and muffled voices. Jumping Crow stood on the bunk again and looked out.

The sheriff was walking slowly across the yard, a tall, thin man wearing a white shirt and suspenders walking beside him, a wide brimmed hat keeping the sun off his fair skin. They were talking, although the Navajo could not make out the words. They went to the back of the sheriff's car and opened the trunk. The tall man staggered backwards and put his hands to his face, and then the lid slammed shut once more. They spoke for a time, leaning in close together like men not wishing to be overheard, and at one point the sheriff gestured towards the jail and took several steps, trying to lead the other white man. The tall man shook his head, glancing at the jail and then looking quickly away. They talked some more.

Thomas felt a soft tremble course through his body, felt a tingling in his arms. And so it begins, he thought, a single tear rolling down one lined cheek.

The sheriff went into the garage and returned several minutes later with a pair of shovels, putting them in the back seat of the police car and climbing behind the wheel. The tall man hesitated, then got in on the other side and they drove away, leaving a cloud of dust which the desert wind quickly carried away.

Look out for whites. They have something on their mind. The words of his Elder came back to him over the years. Thomas sat back down on the bunk to await the change.

Sheriff Bybee and Bishop Johnson rode in silence for a long time, the windows of the cruiser down and air heated by a noon-day sun rushing in. It helped a little with the smell. Around them the sand and rock and scrub rose and fell. Johnson's hat rested on his lap and he mopped his brow with a handkerchief.

"This is a terrible thing," he said at last.

"That's why I came to you first, Bishop."

"Such a thing..." he shook his head. "Imagine the trouble it will cause with the Navajo. We'll have federal agents, godless bureaucrats poking through our affairs, second-guessing our business and treating us like backwards Mormon pioneers."

The sheriff nodded. He'd had enough contact with the feds down here to know he didn't care for them or their way of looking down on regular people.

"The Parsons boy's parents are good, church-going folks. This will destroy them, not to mention the reputation of the church and the community. It's the kind of scandal that people remember forever." The bishop sighed and looked out the window.

They were quiet again for a long time, and as the miles unfolded Sheriff Bybee's frown deepened. "Can this be right, Bishop? What we're doing? I fear what the Lord will think of this."

Johnson looked back at him. "A terrible thing has been done, Edgar, an evil thing. Nothing can bring that poor girl back, or excuse the Parsons boy's behavior. Is this the right thing? I've been asking the Lord since you told me, and of this I'm certain. Allowing this sad incident to cause further harm to this town is the wrong thing. Do you understand, Edgar?"

The sheriff nodded slowly, not entirely sure he did.

"We're shepherds, you and I," the bishop continued. "Just because a wolf comes among us, doesn't relieve us of our responsibility to protect the rest of the flock." He gave the sheriff a long look with his soft blue eyes. "After today, we'll never speak of this again. It will be the burden you and I will carry alone, as good shepherds."

"And what about Glen?"

"He often spoke about leaving small town life and heading out to Alaska to look for gold." The bishop looked out the window again. "I'm sure he'll write, eventually."

The small deputy's office was close and hot from the sun beating down on it throughout the day, and Jumping Crow was suffering from thirst. There was no water in the stained toilet bowl, or he would have gladly scooped it into his mouth. Despite the heat, however, he was chilled, and unable to control the shudders which came over him without warning as the change came on.

Skinwalker.

Doomed to succumb to the evil within him, and travel the earth in animal form.

What he was changing into was clear. Already a loose black feather rested on the cell floor in front of him, a black shape in the fading red and purple light coming in through the windows. Thomas only hoped he would not hurt anyone else in the process.

Headlights washed across the window and he climbed back onto the bunk, seeing two cars roll into the hard-packed yard. The dead deputy's car stopped against the side of the garage, the other pulling up near the officer door, the engine still running. The tall man got out of the first car and walked in front of the headlights, wiping at his brow and walking slowly out of view. The sheriff watched him go, then removed the shovels from his car and returned them to the garage. Thomas heard the squeal of a pump, and a few minutes later the sheriff walked in and switched on a single, overhead bulb. He carried a pistol belt in one hand and a tin cup in the other.

"Here." He handed the cup through the bars, water sloshing over the rim, and Jumping Crow took it at once, draining it.

"Thank you," he choked, but the sheriff had turned his back and was putting the pistol belt in the locker across the room. Thomas saw that he no longer wore his uniform shirt, and his white undershirt was brown with sweat and dirt, his hands and arms filthy. He didn't smell good.

The sheriff walked to the desk, pulling the deputy's six pointed star from a pants pocket and tossing it inside a drawer. He moved slowly, his eyes turned down, then approached the cell and produced the handcuffs once more, passing them through the bars.

"Put them on. Make them click."

Thomas did as he was told, locking the steel on his wrists. The sheriff opened the cell door and guided Thomas by the arm out to the running car and put him in the back seat. A minute later they were headed out of town, the evening sky shifting from purples to a deeper blue out over the desert.

His chills made him tremble, and now the bones in his shoulders and arms began to ache as the transformation to wings began. He wondered if his clothing would simply fall down around him when it was over? Or would he turn into some hideous, man-sized crow creature, tearing the sheriff apart with a massive beak. He hoped not. He didn't want to hurt anyone else.

In the front seat, Bybee seemed not to notice the change coming over his prisoner, driving in silence with both hands gripping the wheel, eyes forward where the headlights bathed the asphalt. After half an hour the sheriff turned off onto a rough track which wound back into the hills, the springs bouncing over the rough surface.

"We don't harm the flock because of the wolf," Bishop Johnson had said when they drove out here earlier. *"We get rid of the wolf."*

"But Glen Parsons is already dead," Bybee replied.

The sheriff's Pontiac came to a stop near a cluster of high, sandstone rocks with clumps of rabbit brush at their base. Bybee shut off the engine, had Jumping Crow step out of the back, then took him by the arm and walked beside him through a narrow gap between the rocks. Above, starlight began poking through a deepening blue curtain, and a cooling wind rustled the sage. Still the sheriff didn't speak, and Jumping Crow was afraid to, fearing it would come out as a screech. His entire body was shuddering now, and he knew the skinwalker was about to appear.

Please, he asked the Holy Ones, *do not let me hurt this man.*

The desert holds many secrets, Jumping Crow thought. No one knew this better than the Navajo. Beyond the rocky gap was a small sandy clearing where fresh earth had been turned in two places off to the left, and to the right a large rectangular hole yawned in the earth. Sheriff Bybee walked him to the edge, stopping him before it.

"Yes," the bishop had said, *"Glen Parsons is dead, Sheriff. But he isn't the only wolf who poses a threat to our flock."*

Jumping Crow felt a whirlwind of energy explode inside him, a force he was powerless to resist as the skinwalker twisted away the last of his humanity and brought about the change. His clothes did indeed fall away as he unfolded his great, black wings, buffeting the air and taking flight with a triumphant screech.

The Navajo stood still and silent before him as Edgar Bybee slid the revolver from his holster, placing the muzzle against the back of the man's skull. He pulled the trigger, then hung his head.

Jumping Crow didn't feel the bullet, didn't feel his body fall into the grave. He didn't hear the coyote barking in the hills, making a sound like laughter.

His spirit was already soaring into an evening sky filled with stars.

SOCIETY

When the bad news came, Deanna was at her desk in her 27th floor corner office. A view of the bay, sparkling and blue in the summer sun, stretched beyond her floor to ceiling windows. It was a large room, but a visitor would be hard-pressed to find the carpeting or even a place to sit, since it was choked with clothing racks, cardboard boxes and stacks of catalogues and advertisements. Deanna was the senior executive west coast buyer for Macys.

Her assistant told her she had an important call, and closed the door on her way out. "Deanna Sansone," she answered.

There was a long pause. "D, it's Shelly. Can you talk?"

Deanna frowned, the tone in her friend's voice putting her instantly on guard. "I'm alone. What's up?"

Another long pause. "Scotty is dead."

Deanna blinked, processing.

"Are you still there?"

"How? What happened?" Scotty was a regional vice president based in Miami. Deanna had dated him casually on and off over the years since her divorce.

"Have you been watching TV?" Shelly asked. Deanna could tell she'd been crying.

"I just got back from Taiwan yesterday, I've been completely unplugged. Shell, what happened?"

"It's all over. The news, the internet, papers. Scott went crazy, D." She started crying again. "The Miami police caught him…caught him eating a homeless man's face. While the man was still alive. He was naked and in an alley and…eating a person."

Oh my God.

Shelly choked back a sob. "The cops shot him three or four times in the arms and legs, but he wouldn't stop. They said he just growled at them and kept…doing it. They shot him in the head to make him stop. The homeless man died too." She was snuffling and her voice was garbled. An Ugly Cry, Deanna had always called it. "Oh, D, it's on every channel."

Deanna clenched her fists to keep her hands from shaking, and her eyes welled up. "Do you know anything else? About Scotty?"

"I talked to his boss, Bill Delloite. Bill said Scotty had been missing a lot of work, and when he was there he acted strange, distracted." Another sob. "The news said Scotty used some kind of file to sharpen his teeth, that he did it himself, probably last night or this morning. Deanna, what *happened* to him?"

Deanna didn't answer. She was still trying to figure out how she felt about Scotty's death. They had never been a serious thing, didn't even speak that often. It was just for fun when one or the other was in town. He'd seemed fine the last time they were together, but this? To die that way, doing *that* to another person while they were still alive…

"Shelly, I've got to go."

"I'm sorry to be the one to tell you, but…"

"It's okay, I'm glad it was you. I'll talk to you soon." Deanna disconnected and stared out at a perfect afternoon. While she was overseas she'd heard the other stories about cannibalism coming out of the U.S. this week; a man in Montana eating his stepson, a woman dining on her own sister and a gay porn star beheading and consuming one of his lovers. The media was eating it up, and hadn't *that* unintentional pun already made the rounds? Of course those victims were already dead. Scotty had attacked and tried to eat someone while they were alive. As if that was any worse, she thought. It was too bizarre to get her head around, and she felt the office walls closing in on her.

"Lenore, I'm gone for the day," she told her assistant on the way out, pocketbook over a shoulder. Minutes later she was on the sidewalk, sunglasses hiding her wet eyes as she headed down Geary. She needed a drink.

The street was crowded with cars and sightseeing buses, cabs weaving among them, and the sidewalk bustled as well. There were executives from the many business towers and hotels, tourists, and the people she considered locals, both the well-heeled shoppers and the regular folk who catered to their needs. Deanna wore Gucci and Prada, and counted herself among the former. The city, infamous for its large homeless population, did a good job keeping the vagrants out of this part of downtown, for which she was happy. It was bad for the high-end image, and an annoyance for those who had to fend off their aggressive begging. Thinking of vagrants made her think of Scotty and his victim, and she wiped tears away under her sunglasses.

She loved this part of the city, and just walking in it made her feel a little better. Before reaching the enormous Macys up ahead, she crossed at the light and turned down Powell, the trees of Union Square Park to her right. There was Victoria's Secret and the Westin St. Francis, and across the park was Louis Vuitton. Neimans, Fendi, Donna Karan...temples of the elite. She was known in all of them as a customer to be given special attention. Deanna might have worked in the world of retail, but her private life was one of money and exclusive privilege. A hefty divorce settlement from her ex – a senior partner in one of San Francisco's top law firms – ensured she would never go without the finer things. It made her Macys salary feel like pocket change.

She considered Scala's Bistro another block up, but decided she needed more privacy. Before reaching the end of the block she stopped at a dark mahogany door with polished brass fittings, flanked by a pair of dark leafy plants. A discrete bronze plaque over the door read simply, *Society*. She started towards it but was cut off by an Asian woman tugging on the arm of a wailing and uncooperative five-year-old. Deanna's frequent overseas announced that the woman's strange, barking language was Vietnamese, though she couldn't understand the words. Kids were difficult in any language, and she was happy never to have had any. She let them pass, and the pair went through an adjacent doorway. Deanna pushed through the mahogany door and into darkness.

"Good afternoon, Ms. Sansone." An attractive young woman in a tight black dress and heels greeted her from a small podium set with a brass reading lamp. She was pretty enough to be a Vicky's model herself.

"Hi, Cassandra," she said.

"Tough day?" the girl asked, linking arms with her and walking her inside. A sitting lounge with enormous chairs and a fireplace was off to the right, a room which would be at home in a gentleman's club, and the clack of billiards came from somewhere beyond. Cassandra steered her down a dark paneled hallway.

"You can tell?" Deanna asked, and the girl nodded with a sympathetic smile.

"Probably too early for dining," Cassandra said, "but I'll bet you could use a cocktail."

"Or four."

A soft laugh. "Main room, or the back?"

Deanna took off her sunglasses, the red of her eyes and smudged mascara mercifully hidden in the low light. "Ladies room first, then I'll go on back."

The hostess gave her arm a reassuring squeeze and left her in the hall, retreating to the podium. Minutes later Deanna had fixed her makeup and felt at least presentable. She continued down the hallway, passing a luxurious dining room and a long polished bar, stopping at another mahogany door neatly tucked in a corner. An electronic card reader was mounted beside it, and over the reader was a brass plate, again with the word *Society*. From her purse Deanna extracted a small card wallet and flipped through her black and platinum plastic, pulling out one which was midnight blue, *Society* in raised silver lettering down one side. The reader accepted it, and the door clicked open.

Exclusive, the operative word in Deanna's life. She was known and welcome in every VIP boutique, nightclub room and private club worth visiting in the city, and recognition alone was usually enough to get her past whatever discrete attendant or security watched the door. The inner room of Society was beyond

210

exclusive, a members-only club where would-be entrants had to be referred by a current member in good standing before being subjected to an in-depth pre-screening and background check. It was the kind of place which, if you didn't know it existed, you weren't their kind of person to begin with.

"Good afternoon, Ms. Sansone," said Dimitri, a handsome thirty-something in a five thousand dollar suit, waiting just inside the door. They exchanged a friendly kiss on the cheek, and he also took her by the arm in the comfortable way of old friends, leading her inside. "Are you joining anyone?"

"No. I think I'll just sit at the bar."

"Of course." He took her past the tables, and held a high-backed barstool for her while she sat. The bartender, a man who could be Dimitri's twin in youth, good looks and rugged sex appeal, appeared at once.

"Peter, I'll have a cosmo."

"Right away, Ms. Sansone."

Deanna pulled her iPhone from her pocketbook, toyed with it for a moment, considering, then shut it off and dropped it back into her bag. She didn't want to look at the news reports. She'd heard enough. The drink appeared, and Peter moved away to give her some privacy. She raised the glass a little. "Anthropophagy," she said softly, and sipped.

The media was going crazy over cannibalism, as if it was something new. Deanna knew differently. She'd met her ex while she was getting her MBA at Yale, but the degree in psychology came first. It was where she'd first encountered the term anthropophagy, the practice of eating the flesh of other human beings. She had done an extensive paper on it for her abnormal psych class, fifty percent of the semester grade. There were many lessons from college which she no longer remembered, or even cared to, but this was a topic the years hadn't been able to shake.

Before the scent of money called out to her so strongly, she'd thought to become a clinical psychologist specializing in the kind of mental instability which led to disorders like anthropophagy. Deanna made a little snorting sound into her cosmo. A headshrinker for headshrinkers. That brought on a tiny giggle. The whole idea was both repulsive and darkly attractive, and the fact she had been secretly dating her aby-psych professor at the time – who thought the study of cannibalism was just *fascinating* – nudged her in that direction. Her dorm mates warned her not to leave her grisly research photos lying around, her friends didn't want to even *hear* the word cannibal, and her parents were distraught over the idea that their daughter was going to throw away her high-priced education on a bunch of whackos. Deanna did the paper, got an 'A,' broke up with the professor shortly after the semester ended, and did not become a psychologist. It wasn't that the field or the research wasn't intriguing, but she decided not too many of them wore Dolce Gabbana or had private bungalows in St. Martin.

Four incidents of cannibalism in a week, and the news would have everyone believe it was the start of a zombie apocalypse. It reminded her of the zombie flash mobs which popped up in San Francisco on occasion, thousands of people in makeup and bloody clothes shuffling through the streets and dining in sidewalk cafes. Ridiculous. But there was nothing even a little amusing about Scotty, and what he had done. Thinking about him brought her to the verge of tears again, so she drained her glass and motioned for another. Peter was swift and efficient, both in his delivery and retreat.

Cannibalism – and society's abhorrence of it - was an old story, and few people other than those who had actually studied it knew just how old. The Roman god Saturn was said to have devoured his own son. The bible spoke of it during the sieges of Samaria and Jerusalem. It was reported during the Holy Crusades, and Pope Innocent IV, seeing its widespread prevalence during the famines in Europe, declared it a sin deserving to be punished by force of arms. Shakespeare addressed it in *Titus Andronicus*, and the native Algonquin people's Wendigo was said to be a malevolent, cannibalistic spirit. Many of the indigenous people of the Pacific, Polynesia and Meso-America indulged in it as part of religious and cultural celebrations. The Aghoris of Northern India, a splinter sect of Hinduism, believed consuming human flesh gave both physical and spiritual benefits, which eventually led to supernatural powers and immortality. Its place in the world ran from the Romans to Hansel and Gretel, from Borneo to Hannibal Lecter.

None of them, however, fit the profile of a smart, successful 21st century urban executive who had filed his teeth and tried to eat a bum face-first. Scotty had lost his mind, and gone native. Deanna finished her second, and Peter quietly replaced it without her asking.

At Yale she had learned cannibalism wasn't just something from the old world, and it was often found to have starvation as its root cause. From 1609-1610, there were reports of several Jamestown colonists eating the flesh of both the dead and the living, and one man was burned alive after confessing to killing, salting and eating his pregnant wife. In 1820 the whaling ship Essex was sunk by a sperm whale, and its captain and surviving crew spent ninety days at sea in a small, open whaling launch, dining on each another one by one until only two men remained. Their rescuers found the pair sucking marrow from femur bones, eyes locked and refusing to look away from the other. That event was Melville's inspiration for *Moby Dick*. Hunger was blamed for instances of cannibalism within the Donner Party, Flight 571 in the Andes, during the siege of Leningrad, the Great Chinese Famine of '58-'61, and for the five American fliers who were captured and eaten by starving Japanese troops in 1945. The offenders were subsequently tried for war crimes and hanged.

Deanna turned in her seat, drink in hand, and looked out at the private room with its expensive but tasteful décor and subdued lighting, only a scattering of patrons at the tables, each with a personal waiter hovering nearby. On one wall hung close to a hundred photos of celebrities and high-profile politicians posing with chefs and bartenders and maitre Ds, all of them members. Scotty had come here with her on several occasions, and he loved the place. She had sponsored him, and remembered warmly how impressed he had been, both with the club and with her and the people she knew. It made her sad, and she started wondering if he'd meant more to her than she thought. She turned back to the bar, glancing at a small clock next to a bottle of Grey Goose, surprised to see she'd been here for two hours already.

Peter appeared. "Another, Ms. Sansone?"

She pursed her lips. "If I don't get something else in my stomach you're going to have to pour me into a cab. I'll take it at a table."

Peter motioned, and Dimitri appeared beside her, guiding her to a corner seat. She settled in, feeling the cosmos, as a fresh drink appeared. "I'll bring around a menu in a few minutes, Ms. Sansone." She was feeling a little better, and knew the pink concoction was the reason. Still, she forced herself to take smaller sips.

Scotty. In the times they'd come here together they had never sat at this table, and that was at least a small relief. Suddenly she wondered if he had ever come here without her. He was a member, after all, and they had no strings. Had he sat in this room with another woman, enjoying the fine dining and each other's company before retreating to a hotel suite for dessert? She was surprised to find herself feeling a tinge of jealousy, and again wondered what he had meant to her. Deanna remembered his touch, the heat of their bodies together, and felt a flush which didn't come from the cosmo.

Then the image of him crouched naked in an alley with sharpened teeth and bloody face reared before her, and she shook her head sharply. That wasn't the man she had known, and it reminded her there were motivations for cannibalism which went beyond hunger.

Politics and anthropophagy went hand in hand. Throughout the age of colonialism, accusations of cannibalism had been used to demonize indigenous people – whether it was true or not – and justify their destruction. Certain island kings were selected for their culinary prowess, and a few Central African leaders had used it to demonstrate their ferocity and dominion over their subjects, as with Idi Amin in Uganda, though it was never proven and he was never held to account for it.

Scotty, though, seemed to fall into the last category; mental illness. Again, despite the media's attempt to depict the recent spate of incidents as "increasing at an alarming rate," cannibalism was nothing new in the modern age, and popped up in all sorts of places, like Australia, Venezuela, the Ukraine and Germany. There were American serial killers like Albert Fish in the 20's and 30's, and Jeffery Dahmer in the 90's. In 2003 rap artist Big Lurch ate a friend while under the influence of PCP. A London man ate an acquaintance in 2004 just days after being questioned and released in an unrelated murder case. In 2007 a Turkish man stored human remains in his fridge and fed them to his unknowing parents. 2008 saw a man who was sleeping on a moving Greyhound near Toronto, killed and partially eaten by another passenger while the other riders dozed around them. As recently as 2011, in separate events in Pakistan, Slovakia, Brazil and Haiti, modern cannibals were caught selling the meat of their victims at local markets cooked into pastries and pies.

Someone approached her table, rousing her from her ruminations. "Deanna?"

She looked up to see a well-dressed, slender man with dark hair. He had started out doing stand-up, and then gone on to be a raging success with a sitcom which shared his last name, one of the first comics in the industry to start pulling down a million dollars per episode. "Oh, hi!" She rose and gave him a kiss on the cheek. "I didn't see you here."

He smiled. "You looked lost in thought."

"Are you in town for a show?" She knew he lived between LA and New York.

"Yeah, two nights over at Cobb's. If you want to swing by I'll leave tickets at the window."

She nodded, knowing she wouldn't. His face turned somber. "I'm sorry to hear about Scotty. Everyone liked him."

She thanked the comedian and they exchanged a few awkward pleasantries, then he touched her on the arm and made his exit. Deanna looked around the room. It was no real surprise that he'd heard, they likely all had. The members list of Society wasn't all that large, and this was big news. She felt like crying again and drained her cocktail. Peter brought over another, and Dimitri quietly set a leather-backed menu on her table, murmuring that he'd be by when she was ready.

For most, whether forced into it by starvation or those isolated acts of madmen, consuming human flesh just made people sick, similar to a moderate to serious case of food poisoning. It generally passed without further effect, although it would be even more severe these days, as it was believed the modern diet was so filled with chemicals and additives that human meat was just short of toxic.

Deanna supposed it depended on the chef. She giggled unexpectedly, loud enough to make a few of the dining room's patrons look over, and she hid behind her fresh cosmo. She was getting loopy.

The real risk came from *Kuru,* an incurable degenerative neurological disorder caused by the prions found in humans. This was the risk for long-term cannibals, and could take anywhere from five to twenty years before the onset of symptoms. Body tremors were a classic example, and as the fatal disorder entered its final twelve months, a victim often began to experience increasing weakness and inability to stand, slurred speech and mental instability. Tribal people called it the *Laughing Sickness* due to the afflicted person's pathologic bursts of laughter.

She opened the menu as Dimitri arrived, standing patiently nearby with his hands folded.

Is that what happened to Scotty? Had his diet led to a fast onset of *Kuru,* and driven him mad? Was that what the members of The Society had to look forward to? Her right hand trembled ever so slightly as she held the menu, and Dimitri pretended not to notice. Inside was a pair of fine parchment pages in script, the entries all without prices. *If you have to ask, you can't afford it.* And the cuisine here was expensive indeed. Clipped to the upper right corner was the daily special, a photo of the Vietnamese boy she'd seen outside being pulled into a doorway by his mother.

She tapped the picture. "I'll try the veal."

"Excellent, Ms. Sansone." Dimitri tucked the menu under one arm and disappeared into the kitchen.

Deanna sipped her cosmo and let out another unexpected giggle, covering her mouth with a shaking hand. Nothing to worry about. It was all about the chef, and she could afford the very best. Everyone at Society could.

JACK'S FOLLY

This wasn't working out as planned. Not at all.

Should have kept the cow, he thought.

Smooth porcelain walls rose about him on all sides, and he was unable to scale them, even after he'd shucked off his boots and tried it with bare feet. He kept sliding back to the center of the bowl. Still, he tried again, getting a short run at the wall, charging up, lunging, hoping to catch a grip on the rim.

Over a foot short, again, and he tumbled back to the center. The metal bar running up his back and hidden beneath his clothes gave him a sharp jab. Jack let out a cry that was part frustration and part fear. He wouldn't have many more chances.

As he eyed the sheer white walls – and the wood beamed ceiling impossibly high above – he cursed himself once more. What had he been thinking? Just a simple trip to market, sell the cow, any idiot could do it.

Stupid peddler. Stupid trade.

The bowl shook as the footsteps returned, throwing Jack onto his bottom. A moment later an enormous face filled the space above the bowl, eyes with heavy lids, a broad flat nose over thick, pouting lips.

The face rumbled, "Fee, Fi…"

217

"Oh, shut *up!*" Jack screamed, scrambled to his feet and shaking a finger at his captor. "Just let me go and I'm out of here! Won't trouble you again!" His voice was raw. Could the beast hear him up there? Did it even understand?

This should have been a no-brainer. A little climbing, a little creeping, nick some gold while the big bastard was sleeping. But he'd barely circled the room before it snatched him up and dropped him in this goddamn bowl.

"Fee, Fi..."

"Yeah, yeah," muttered Jack, then his annoyance turned to fear as he saw a huge thumb and forefinger reaching into the bowl. He backed away as far as his confines would allow, fumbling behind him, pulling the long piece of metal from its hiding place. It was the only thing he'd been able to grab before being grabbed himself. Jack planted his feet and held the giant sewing needle like a spear before him.

...Fo, Fum," said the beast, but suddenly the little snack struck out with something, something *sharp!* A bellow of pain erupted from its gap-toothed mouth and it jerked back its wounded hand, yanking the needle from Jack's grip. It howled in agony, the little piece of steel imbedded in a cuticle.

"That's what you get!" Jack shouted.

The face reappeared, contorted with pain, shaking with sobs. It began to wail and cry. Giant tears splashed into the bowl, and to Jack's alarm, the water was up to his chest in moments, huge drops landing like rain, hammering him. The giant carried on, and Jack found himself immersed to his chin, kicking his feet and waving his arms.

I'm swimming, he thought suddenly. I'll float to the top and just climb out!

Then, still sobbing, the giant thundered, *"Bad!"* and jabbed its finger down into the bowl, pinning a thrashing Jack to the bottom.

Stupid beans, he thought.

He drowned choking on salt.

CORN OF CORTEZ

Amber cirrus clouds crept overhead. They did not gather and darken as they once had, did not bring the rain, only marched on to distant places without touching the land. The winds came instead, sweeping over peaks and ridges, hooting past openings in the rock, laughing down the canyons. When it reached the open land it became a great shushing sound, pulling at the soil and gathering it upwards in masses of fine particles, turning the red sky brown.

Traces of water vapor and dust, but no rain, and in the fields the soil cracked and powdered. Squat stalks of blackened corn lost their grip on the land and fell against one another, brittle, their leaves curled and crisp. Dust fell upon the corn, adding its weight and bearing it to the ground.

High summer, and twenty-three degrees.

Cortez stepped from his domed house and felt the wind. It blew cold against skin which was leathery and blackened from the ultraviolet, and the calloused hands he thrust into the pockets of his hooded parka were large and lined with the red earth. He walked to the wire fence, boots kicking up red dust, and leaned his forearms on a post. He wore scratched goggles and a dirty pink mask to ward off the dust, which nonetheless found a way in to grind between his teeth and wear down the enamel, just as it wore down the land.

A three foot stalk had fallen against the wire, and he snapped off a small ear, stripping away the flaking leaves and brittle silk. Martian corn was black to begin with, the same shade as his skin, but these kernels were so hardened and devoid of moisture that they gleamed like the silica glass so common on this red world. The ear was only a few inches long, killed well before maturity. He pitched it into the field as he squinted out across the acres of withered crops, the wind kicking up swirls of dust between the fallen rows and making the leaves crackle.

"Is it all gone, Papa?" said a small voice beside him.

He hadn't heard her come up, and didn't look down at her, only stared into the field. "Yep."

"Won't none of it come back?" She coughed, a long dry hack he didn't care for. She'd picked it up over the winter, and it had hung on. Sometimes he found dark brown spots on the pillow in the bed she shared with Isaiah.

"It's all gone. Where's your brother?"

"He's playing in the dooryard." She wore goggles and a mask too, her small, dark face barely visible within the hood of her coat, the ring of synthetic fur worn down and looking patchy like a dog with mange. Not that he had ever seen a dog, except in pictures.

"Crawler all packed? You bring the water jug and your blanket?"

"Yes." She used the tip of her boot to draw a circle in the dust.

"You pack the satchel?"

Her boot moved in a slow circle and she nodded. "There's only the two foil packets of bread and the can of onions."

Cortez stooped and picked up a clod of rusty soil, slowly rubbing it between his palms until it crumbled to a powder which the wind carried away like smoke. Magnesium, potassium, sodium and chloride, high alkaline pH. Its nutrients could support life, the hardy Martian corn in particular, but as tough as it was it still needed moisture to save it from the wind, needed a sturdier anchor than the iron oxide dust. He'd plowed these fields his entire life, had crawled on his hands and knees picking out iron and nickel asteroid fragments to keep from breaking a blade, had worked in wind which could carry a man away and cold which turned his black fingers white. He'd buried his kin out here, had buried Eve. This was his soil, but even he couldn't make it rain.

"Happy Glory Day, Papa."

Cortez just nodded at her, and she walked back towards the house, coughing. He hung his head and tightened his fists, then just let his arms hang by his sides as he looked up at yellow clouds without promise. Beyond them, pale and muted behind the rusty smudge of sky, the twin, irregular shaped moons of Phobos and Deimos hung close together. A gust lifted the surface of his fields into the air and clouded them from view.

He turned back to the house, and a Martian wind blew over dead, black corn.

The crawler trundled along the Cape Road at 50 km/h on ribbed, hard rubber balloon tires, kicking up a billow of red dust for the wind to take. The crunch of gravel beneath the wheels was louder than the hum of the power plant, and not even enough sound to echo off the high walls of maroon thoeliitic basalt rising into foothills on the right. Sweeping out to the left and disappearing over the horizon was Plantation 216, a thousand square miles of geometrically placed rows of pyramids, each a hundred feet high. They were covered in flat panels of blue silica glass, and would have once looked like a blanket of sapphires sparkling in the thin sunlight. Now most of the panels had fallen in, leaving blackened titanium skeletons spotted with cobalt blue where panels had held on. Many centuries ago this was one of ten thousand plantations where early Martian corn was cultivated, before it was sturdy enough to grow out in the open. Back when Mars was Earth's breadbasket.

Now it was a place for the wind to whistle. The soil was ruined, and the ancient irrigation systems – along with the knowledge of how they worked – had disintegrated over the endless years.

It was a half day's drive from Cortez's farm to Cape Verde, and he would leave 216 behind and pass all of Plantation 217 as well before he got there. The crawler had the road to itself, and would not pass another vehicle for the next ten hours, its only company the cold wind buffeting the enclosed cab.

Dinah played in the back with Isaiah, a simple game with a pair of polished sticks, something he could keep up with. Isaiah was eight, only three years younger than his sister, but he struggled. In the front seat Cortez watched the gravel track unroll ahead of him. If the wind kicked up much more he'd need the headlights, but for now the dust was thin enough and he had no trouble staying on a road his people had traveled for over a millennium.

A hymn, *How Great Thou Art,* came softly from a speaker mounted overhead next to the comm set, which hadn't worked since he'd acquired the crawler. Not that there was anyone to talk to. No one had a working comm set. He supposed he should have pulled it out, gotten rid of the excess weight, but it was small and besides, throwing it away felt like giving in. It was something he'd never be able to articulate, but he felt that every piece of technology discarded brought them closer to the inevitable, an acknowledgement that eventually it would all be gone, and his people weren't the kind to give up like that.

Although staying on the road was easy, keeping his eyes off the digital fuel gauge was not. There was only one bar left, a dark red color, maybe enough to run the crawler until the end of the summer. Once it was gone there would be no way to re-energize the fuel cell, and the vehicle would become a relic of plastic and metal wherever it came to rest. That would mean the journey to Cape Verde would turn into a ten day walk through the cruel landscape, a brutal proposition for a man on his own, never mind with two children. Once the Martian winter set in, with temperatures dropping to minus one-hundred-twenty degrees and winds of up to 400 km/h, it would be an impossibility, even in an emergency. He thought about Dinah's cough. Not that there was anything to be done, there were no doctors left since folks moved on. People lived or they died, and that was just the way of things now.

After a few hours, Dinah sang Isaiah to sleep and then nodded off herself. The speaker played *The Battle Hymn of the Republic,* and Cortez drove. Outside, the distant sun climbed towards midday and a summer high of twenty-seven degrees. The wind rocked the cab gently as the crawler spit gravel and bumped along the road. He drove with the sounds of Jesus and solar winds, and thought about Glory Day.

Cape Verde sat a kilometer back from the rim of Victoria Crater, a massive depression created by a meteor four billion years earlier. There were many like it on Mars, the planet's proximity to the asteroid belt and the unstable comets hanging in Jupiter's orbit the reason it was covered in ancient impact basins. Although nothing of significance had hit the surface since colonization, two-thousand years was but a blink to the red ball, and the planet would certainly be struck again.

The city, a once thriving capital, was now a sprawl of bare titanium bones and broken blue glass. East and west of the ruins stood the decaying cone shapes of atmospheric processors rusting back into the land. A tiny cluster of intact buildings hugged the ruins at the edge nearest the crater, all which remained of Cape Verde. The muted yellow of lights glowed from a handful of these structures, at the center of which stood a low building which the sand had scoured down to bare metal. A glowing purple sign on a pole outside said LEVI'S.

Elson Willard stood next to the well in his back room, arms crossed over a narrow chest, wearing an apron which had once been white but was now closer to ivory. He listened to the asthmatic wheeze of the motorized pump, watching the conveyor belt of scoops rise empty from the depths. The pump coughed and began to stutter, the belt slowing, and he gave it a good kick. It settled back to its normal rhythm.

"You're gonna put your foot through that thing one day," Helen called from the other room.

"Yeah, the last day," he yelled back to his wife, not taking his eyes off the slow-moving scoops. They went by empty, one after the other, each clotted with red soil. Was today the day it ran dry, he wondered? The pump stuttered again and he gave it another kick. Over the chug of the motor he heard the bell at the front door ring, and a man's voice saying, "Happy Glory Day." His wife responded in kind.

A scoop emerged with a red blob in it, giving off a faint pink smoke. "Hallelujah," he muttered, quickly dumping it into a bin. Five more full scoops appeared, and he emptied these as well before shutting down the pump. As always, he wondered if it would ever start again. Elson used a rusty trowel to transfer the dry ice into a pressurizer – it worked better than the pump, at least – and minutes later he had four liters of red fluid. The pressurizer piped it into a filter to separate the soil, and after a few moments of whirring pumped cloudy water into a plastic jug. Elson carefully capped the jug and placed it on a shelf with a dozen others, next to the last sack of beans, and then headed out front, wiping his hands on his apron.

A cadaver of a man with a thin ring of white hair was hanging his parka on a hook beside the door. "Happy Glory Day, Brother Elson," he said, smiling with black teeth. "May the Lord bless and keep thee."

"Happy Glory Day to you too, Preacher, but it's a little late for blessings. The corn's gone."

Helen shot her husband a dark look, as the Reverend Amos John took a stool at the long counter. To the right was space for the general store, full of empty shelves. To the left stood the empty, cracked red plastic booths of the diner. The preacher set a dog-eared bible on the chipped counter beside him.

"Haven't seen you in ages," said Helen, pouring a cup of weak coffee and sliding it in front of him. "Knew we'd see you today, though."

He gave her a mildly disapproving look. "You'd see me if you came to Meeting." She looked down, embarrassed.

"Folks still go to Meeting?" Elson asked, taking a stool two down from the preacher.

The man sipped his coffee, frowning over the rim. "Not so much, and it's a pity. There's much need for prayer these days."

Elson snorted. The shaded bulbs overhead made their tightly-pulled, blackened skin look almost blue. Helen leaned on the counter. "Seems the thing worth prayin' on most is Glory Day, ain't that so, Reverend?"

"Amen to that, Sister."

Elson rolled his eyes. His wife might still put stock in all that foolishness, but he had no use for it. All the praying in the world mattered not a speck to the fully-automated re-supply ship in orbit overhead, and computers didn't give a damn about Jesus. So much so that last Glory Day, twenty-four months ago, they hadn't seen fit to send down their blessings at all. It had been a crushing blow to the community, and now it was the equivalent of four Earth years since they'd had a drop. Plenty of folks hadn't made it as a result.

Amos John rested his long fingers on the bible. "May the Lord look kindly upon us, and grant us a plentiful Supplement. Amen."

"Amen," said Helen, as Elson rose to get a bowl of beans off the steamer in the kitchen. The preacher would of course expect a free meal in exchange for his prayin'-over, and Elson knew that insisting upon payment would only get him in nitters with his prayerful wife. Not that the preacher, or anyone else for that matter, had anything with which to pay, and other than beans Elson had nothing to sell them.

Folks started to arrive shortly after Amos John tucked into his meal.

The crawler rolled to a stop outside Levi's just as evening was beginning to settle over Cape Verde, the small sun throwing a crimson twilight across a dusty sky as it dropped along with the temperature. Through his windshield Cortez could see Olympus Mons silhouetted in the distance, the highest mountain in the solar system, and at twenty-seven kilometers three times the height of Everest. It looked black against the bloody sky, a lonely monolith which cared nothing for the plight of men like Cortez.

Around him stood a half dozen crawlers of assorted design, all parked as close to the front of the building as they could be, each as battered and used up as his own. A few figures emerged from the vehicles and hustled inside as the wind brought down the cold.

Dinah pulled Isaiah in close as the three hunched into their coats and made the short walk, hurrying to get inside. Levi's was bright and warm, and smelled of beans and coffee. Helen was serving up small, steaming bowls on the counter, but as soon as she saw Dinah and Isaiah she descended upon them, smothering them in hugs and kisses, making Isaiah giggle, and then guiding them into the kitchen where she'd hidden away some hard candy. Cortez watched them go, grateful for the way Helen had taken to the children after Eve passed.

He shook hands with the men, who were drawn off to one side by a little glowing heater. Someone produced a small plug of tobacco, a treasure squirreled away from the last Supplement, and passed it around to appreciative noises. They talked on the dealings of men in low tones, and that meant the crop, for they were all croppers. Had anyone's survived? No, not a bit of it. Were the rains gone for good, do you think? Is there enough seed for spring planting? Was there anything left in the community stockpile? They all knew the answer to that. Did anyone have any food put up? Not much was left.

They looked over at their families, the women clutching together and talking about food and illness and death, with Amos John moving among them. He was not included in the discussions of croppers. Their children sat in a circle and played games on the floor. All were skeletons hugged tightly by leathery, UV blackened flesh, cheekbones and knuckles and ribs jutting outwards, lips peeled back tightly from black teeth in perpetual smiles. Their torn clothing hung on them like sacks, and more than a few were coughing.

Talk turned to the Supplement. "There's so many less of us than last time," said Elijah. "The Supplement's sure to go further. Plenty for all, an answer to our prayers."

Cortez frowned. The only answer he'd ever received had been, "No."

"The drop not coming last year," said Samuel, an older man who carefully dropped his spit into a bucket near the heater, "that was nothing more than a technical thing. A glitch." He nodded wisely. "It'll come for sure this time."

"That's right," said a cropper named Remus. "And I'll bet you Elson's beans they double it up this time, on account of missing it last time."

Yes, that sounded right, they all said. None of them managed to look at one another as they said it.

"How's your young-uns," asked Samuel, pointing his chin at Cortez. Their farms weren't too far from one another.

Cortez chewed his lip. "Dinah coughs." He shrugged. "Isaiah is as he is."

The men looked past him at the children playing on the floor. Isaiah sat among them trying to track the progress of a red ball

226

being passed from hand to hand, a glassy smile on his face. When the ball came to him he didn't reach out, just looked at it.

Eve Cortez died while giving birth to the boy, and her husband had gone through a hard patch trying to raise a child with difficulties, a three-year-old girl and his crops all by himself. Privately some of the men wondered at how the boy had managed to survive, and thought the real blessing might have been if he hadn't. Still, they knew the kind of man Cortez was, and that he'd sooner plant himself in that red earth than give up on his kids or his crop. And yet his tenacity hadn't kept his corn standing, and they wondered if it might be what finally broke him. They wondered this of themselves, as well. Their corn was gone, too.

Samuel changed the subject. "Heard Caleb's boy Aaron made some good finds in the city. Heard he brought back a few tools and even a halfway decent pair of boots."

"I heard he found medicine," offered Remus, immediately drawing frowns from the other men. If anyone had found medicine, they all would have heard about it. They didn't doubt the tools or the boots, though. Aaron had been scavenging in the ruins since he was a child, and had a particular talent for uncovering useful scraps.

"And I heard," said a cropper named Zion, who's wife was friendly with Caleb's wife, "that he didn't come back the other day, and Caleb went in to look for him, and he didn't come back neither."

There were glances exchanged and solemn nods. That was likely true, as neither man was here at Levi's, and no one missed Glory Day unless they were dead or dying. Caleb's wife was sitting in a chair in the corner, crying and being comforted by some of the women, turning the question mark into a period. The ruins were dangerous, filled with unstable metal and rotten flooring, and an incautious step could send a man plunging through to impalement, broken limbs or the equally final fate of simply being trapped in a hole. There was no question of men gathering to go look for someone lost in such a way, it just wasn't done. Kin might risk themselves, but that was expected, a search party was not.

Dinah appeared next to her father and tugged on his sleeve. "Papa, Missus Forbes says I can have Chloe's sweater, long as you say it's okay."

Cortez looked across the room to a drawn woman with vacant eyes, whose dark skin had gone ashy. Sarah Forbes had lost her daughter, a girl Dinah's age, only a few weeks ago. No one said exactly to what, she just hadn't woken up one morning. Most suspected starvation. Dinah coughed and Cortez cupped her narrow face in one hand, looking into eyes which had purple smudges under them, and were slightly more sunken than they had been a week ago.

"Of course. Mind you tell her thank you."

He looked up to nod at Chloe Forbes, but the woman was staring at the floor. Dinah skipped away, and Cortez drifted off from the men, wandering into the empty half of the building which had been Levi's general store. No one knew who Levi was or had been, including Elson, whose ancestors had been running the place for two centuries. The shelves and clothing racks were bare except for some dusty shelf tags, and a hand-lettered sign so yellowed and curling with age that it could barely be read. *Sorry, COKE out of stock.* Cortez didn't read too well, and didn't know what coke was. For his whole life he couldn't remember the store being anything but empty. He passed through and stopped at the big window in the far wall.

Standing before it, watching the night descend, his breath made a little cloud of fog on the cold glass. From here there was an impressive view of the receiving field, with one of the ancient atmospheric processors in the distant background, visible only as a great cone shape against a darkening sky. His eyes lifted to the heavens, immediately picking out the bright light high above. It wasn't a star or a satellite; it was the *Glory*, hanging there in orbit, matching the rotation of the small planet.

He looked just to its right, at a dark spot which hadn't always been there. Cortez remembered his father first pointing it out to him when he was a child, a brilliant blue speck which glittered like a far-off jewel, the cradle of human life and a technological wonder so bright that it radiated like a star. Earth went dark without warning when Cortez was ten. There had been no communication with it or anyone since.

As he watched the sky he wondered if once upon a time the people of Earth had looked up at Mars, entranced by the agricultural marvels which fed them all. It started when they – *They* were the scientific wizards and all-powerful thinkers of Earth – discovered glaciers of CO^2 on Mars, which fit considering its topography was covered in river and lake depressions, an indicator of past surface water. Unfortunately Mars also had a thin atmosphere and no magnetosphere, resulting in low atmospheric pressure. Lack of sufficient pressure meant that when the six month Martian summer arrived, the increasing temperatures caused the ice to sublimate to gas instead of transforming to liquid water.

To make matters worse, solar winds tore at the poorly protected planet constantly, stripping away atoms from the outer atmospheric layer, causing it to become thinner and thinner. This made it difficult to store heat, and allowed in heavy levels of ultraviolet. The stripping of atoms was so severe that Mars left a dirty cloud of ionized atmospheric particles behind as it moved through space. Cortex had heard this called the Pigpen Effect, but didn't understand why. Finally, "air" which was heavy with carbon dioxide and the methane which leaked from old volcanoes made colonization unattractive.

But they did it anyway. They built the enormous processors and manufactured an atmosphere, forcing the sky to cloud up and rain while developing irrigation at the same time. Settlers were slowly exposed to increasing levels of the natural environment until, over the many generations, their bodies had evolved so they could breathe in the open, their skin pigment darkening and toughening to protect them from the UV. They invented a breed of corn which eventually took hold and thrived in the open soil, commenced farming on a global scale, and solved the hunger problems of an Earth bursting with overpopulation.

Cortez used his index finger to draw a circle in the fogged glass, then tapped a pair of moons off to one side. He stared at the image.

Something had happened back in his ancestors' times. They stopped running the processors, and people started leaving for Earth in great numbers. The city emptied rapidly, leaving no one to maintain the sprawling plantations or the sophisticated technology of Cape Verde. Cortez didn't know what became of them, and couldn't imagine they fared well outside the carbon dioxide and methane environment of Mars, upon which their biology relied.

Those who stayed were croppers, folks who had a kinship with the land, who had buried their people in the red soil, raising their children, living and dying amid that black corn. They couldn't leave, wouldn't leave, even as year after year the atmosphere bled off unchecked, the UV rising and the temperatures falling as Mars hurried back to its former state. Each generation saw less rain, smaller corn, higher winds and the unstoppable decay of technology, the knowledge with which to replace or repair it lost over the long years. Still the croppers stayed, tightening their belts in order to feed their children, clawing their lives out of the red soil.

They eventually sent the *Glory* into a Mars orbit, an unmanned supply vessel packed with everything the croppers could need; food, medical supplies, clothing, spare parts and fuel cells, even educational and training materials. As the corn continued to fail, the croppers became increasingly dependent upon the Supplement, dropped once every twenty-four months in the middle of Martian summer. *They* had once appointed administrators to measure out the supplies amongst the remaining population, but that practice had moved on as well, and now the people divided the supplement as a community, according to need. It was fair, and there were few disputes.

Cortez looked at the receiving field, a large, wind-scoured stone pad ringed with lights which hadn't worked since he was a boy. On each of the four edges stood over a hundred of the empty supply landers, big cubes which had once been white but were now pink from embedded dust. They had been stripped of anything useful, even wiring, and pushed off to the side. A person could just look at the many landers and tell them apart, old from more recent, by their condition.

He felt a pair of bodies press close against him on either side. Isaiah stood on his right, sucking his thumb, and on the other side Dinah's small hand crept into his own. They all looked out the window.

"Will it come, Papa?"

"Can't say, honey. I hope so."

230

Isaiah's thumb popped out and he breathed on the glass, fogging it. Cortez waited to see what the boy would draw, but he just went back to sucking his thumb.

"It has to come, doesn't it, Papa?" Dinah squeezed his hand. Cortez knew his daughter wasn't talking about launch programming, but about their mortality. He didn't reply.

Outside a bitter wind kicked up a dust devil a hundred feet high, and it marched across the receiving field before twisting into the night. The bright spot which was *Glory* hung silently in the heavens, and Dinah coughed, a few raspy barks ending in a rattle. He squeezed her hand back. An hour passed, and one by one the folks of Cape Verde gathered quietly at the window around them, eyes turned upwards. A few of the youngest children fidgeted, but everyone else was still, all wondering the same thing.

"Let us offer up a prayer," Amos John said at last.

Some of the men frowned at him and shook their heads, but Cortez turned to the preacher. "I think that would be a good idea."

Fifty people linked hands and lowered their heads as Amos John spoke, his voice soft, lacking its usual jump and holler. "Dear Lord, we thank you for letting us come together as a community. We ask you to watch over our sick, and welcome home the loved ones we've lost. We know you have a purpose for our hardships, and we accept your mysterious ways and trust in your divine wisdom. Lord, we pray that you deliver the Supplement unto us, so that we can continue your work a bit longer. Help us to be strong. Help the corn. Amen."

"Amen," they repeated. Amos John nodded at Cortez, smiling at Dinah and her little brother as they all went back to watching the sky.

Another hour later a pinprick of light separated from the *Glory* and moved away, then slowly began to grow brighter. The group sighed and many began to weep, men and women alike, embracing one another as the Supplement descended towards Mars. Soon the men were shrugging into their parkas, pulling on gloves and goggles and masks, hugging their wives and children again before pushing out into the cold.

The wind hit them hard, icy and full of blowing grit, and they bent against it as they piled into the crawlers and drove in a line towards the receiving field. Headlights cut thin beams through the dust while above them, the Supplement lander flared blue as it burned through the atmosphere. The cube fell quickly, and then rockets fired a dazzling white, slowing its descent. The lander, the size of a small building, thumped onto the field amid a burst of smoke and white fire, the roar of its rockets reverberating through the cabs of the crawlers as they arrived. The rockets shut down and the wind tore the smoke away. Floodlights at each corner of the lander snapped on, creating pools of light.

The crawlers approached and spread out, stopping in a line as the men climbed down to the pavement, heads tucked. The powered lifts and loaders were now petrified relics in a forgotten garage, so the men would have to unload by hand and pack the goods into their vehicles. They huddled together for a moment, then approached as a group. The square outline of a big cargo door was set in one side, and it was Cortez who opened a small panel beside it, exposing a keypad. He removed a glove and tapped in a numerical sequence, the same code used since the drops began, and memorized by every person on the planet once they were old enough to speak or understand.

"Praise God," Amos John yelled over the wind, his voice muffled behind a dust mask. The men nodded. A moment later there was a hiss, and the men stepped back as the door lowered itself into a ramp, revealing darkness within. Boots thudded on the ramp as the group walked up and in, relieved to be out of the wind. They stopped and waited.

Lights flickered for a moment, slow to ignite, but then they started snapping on in rows along the ceiling of the high cargo bay, where the full, strapped down pallets waited for them in orderly rows.

It was empty.

Wall to wall, the smooth floor was bare. Not a box, not a bin, not a barrel.

The croppers started cursing, and Elson wailed. Amos John fell to his knees, clasping his hands and crying, demanding to know why the Lord had forsaken them. Cortez could only stare. After long minutes, he turned and walked back down the ramp, starting his crawler. The lone bar of the fuel gauge glowed at him from the dashboard. He drove back to Levi's and collected his children without speaking, ignoring the panicked questions from the women, helping Dinah into the crawler and then handing Isaiah to her.

Cortez drove into the night, back to his farm, back to his dead corn. His daughter coughed, and he wondered which of them would be the first to go into the ground. He told himself to remember to leave a shovel by the door for Dinah, in case it was him. Above, the speaker softly played *What a Friend we have in Jesus.*

TEN RULES OF WALTER

Walter followed the rules.

He'd been doing it his entire life, careful to stay within the lines, keeping a low profile and staying out of trouble. It didn't make him particularly happy – that wasn't a state he experienced often – but it avoided a lot of hell, and he supposed that was a sort of happiness all by itself. Rules. The pillars of structure and civilized life which kept the world stable. And it was his unshakeable belief in that rigidity which attracted him to his current field.

Recently, Walter had come to a startling realization. He'd decided that of the millions of rules which existed, in the end, only ten really mattered at all. Several he had known and accepted all along, and others he had discovered only within the past few weeks. A few came up just today.

So Walter followed the rules. His rules, and though he kept them numbered in his head, it was only to satisfy his need for structure, not to place them in any particular order. They were all equally important, and equally true.

1) The U.S. Mail Is Still Reliable. The internet was amazing indeed, and there was no denying its ability to instantaneously reach millions. But for a physical delivery, the U.S. Mail was the ticket. A dependable organization, they could still get your letters or packages anywhere in the world within days. And really, Walter thought, there was nothing like personal correspondence you could touch and feel to get your message across.

2) Four Day Weekends Breed Carelessness. The protocol said no one was ever to be alone in the work space. With a four day Christmas weekend about to start, however, people were anxious to leave and had in fact been slipping out early all day. By three o'clock, only Tom Jenkins and Amanda Carroll remained with him, and they were in a hurry.

"Walter," Tom said, "wrap it up and let's get out of here."

"Yes, come on Walter, we'll all walk out together." Amanda had her coat on, her purse over her shoulder.

Walter waved at them from behind his computer screen. "You two go on ahead. I'm running a program, and it's going to take at least a couple more hours."

Tom and Amanda exchanged looks. They knew the protocol, but they also knew they had people waiting for them. "Please?" said Amanda. "We've all been working so hard. *You've* been working so hard. Can't it wait until we're back on Tuesday?"

"Yeah, c'mon sport," said Tom. Walter despised being called 'Sport.' "We can't go without you, and our families are waiting. You don't want to be the reason they're disappointed, do you?"

Walter peered from behind his screen. "I don't want to hold either one of you up, but it's only three, and like I said, I have this program." He gestured at his screen, which they couldn't see from across the room, and which currently displayed a screen saver of cartoon chickens laying eggs which hatched into dinosaurs, which promptly ate the chickens.

Tom shot Amanda an annoyed look, and she sighed and rolled her eyes.

"Listen, as soon as it's done running, I'll shut down the lights and make sure the place is secured on my way out. I won't tell anyone, it'll be my Christmas gift to you."

They exchanged another look, then smiles, and in that moment all the detailed training on security procedures went out the window. They thanked Walter – Amanda blew him a kiss – and wished him a Merry Christmas as they hustled out the door. When it banged shut, Walter smiled towards it. "Fuck you very much."

That was over two hours ago.

3) Psychological Screening Is An Imperfect Science. It was all about belief, he'd decided. Not believing in your own answers – only an idiot would believe the bold-faced lies necessarily told during psychological screening. No, where belief came in was in the tester's belief in the accuracy of the tests, and the effectiveness of their Q&A model. They believed it couldn't be beaten, so they weren't prepared for someone to do just that.

Not only could Walter defeat their tests, he was an ace at out-foxing polygraph as well. Belief. His was stronger. What it really came down to was their *desire* to believe, not in the actual screening, but in the idea that it would protect them from having that one highly motivated individual slip inside and…do the unthinkable.

Walter wasn't sure if his next rule stood by itself, or was an extension of number three. He decided it was certainly in the same theme, but deserved its own number.

4) Top Secret Security Clearances Are Given Too Easily. A solid work ethic with no disciplinary actions, no criminal record, a perception of being stable and a moderate level of patriotism; all easy enough to achieve or fake. Presto, access granted to all manner of dark knowledge and dangerous toys. It was foolishness, and another example of people putting their heads in the sand out of a desire to not believe. To be sure, there were some who *did* believe in monsters. They were the ones who created the screening and testing procedures, and designed the multi-layered security precautions. Sadly, these guardians were delusional as well, not about the idea that it could happen, but in their faith in their clever protective systems. The security they dreamed up was Walter's friend, because once a person was past the impressive defenses, no one really worried about him anymore.

5) One Man Can Make A Difference. Despite all evidence to the contrary – a pervasive attitude that teamwork could overcome any obstacle, that no man is an island, and the belief that individuality, while admirable, was not to be taken seriously – Walter knew different. Was the loner rejected and often reviled? No argument. And when that same loner was bright but lacking in social skills, people tended to avoid contact, and their behavior isolated the individual. A perfect combination, and for Walter it created both time and space to think, to dream, and to engage in his pursuit, a project which would change the world. What greater achievement for a man?

6) Picking On Co-Workers Is Bad. Walter was awkward. He wasn't attractive, and simply couldn't see the point in all the effort it took to master social niceties and develop relationships. All that energy was better spent on work, and so he lived an isolated existence with his computers. He was a nerd and a geek, had been told so most of his life, and he was okay with that. The fact was this facility was filled with them. So why then should Robert Rawley ("Uh, it's Bobby, bro.") single him out for torment? Robert was good-looking and friendly, and said things like, "Let's do some softball and get our drink on," or, "You look great, Karen, but you'd look even better on my boat. What are you doing this weekend?" But for Walter, Robert was school all over again; the mocking, being the butt of jokes, the juvenile pranks.

His intellectual brain – and dear God was that a big part of him – told him that Robert Rawley was just acting out his insecurities, and that he felt threatened by the depth of Walter's mind, by his frighteningly brilliant grasp of complex theories about which he spoke so casually. The inner-intellectual said Robert was forever fighting against the idea that at his core, he would never be anything more than a well-educated jock, and once his college days had ended, his best days were then behind him.

Walter's more primitive, emotional brain, however, was still the clumsy little boy who got tripped on the bus and shoved to the floor in school hallways, a wedgie target for the Robert Rawleys of the world, sentenced to eat lunch every day with only his hurt feelings for company. It was this part of Walter which made sure Robert Rawley was on the mailing list.

7) People Are Easily Distracted. Walter's position gave him access to The Vault, but not unlimited access. Although he was entrusted with the codes, he was still required to have written authorization to go inside, and had to be accompanied at all times. This was true for each of the carefully chosen few who were granted such access. The Army corporal on duty near the big, pressurized door and armed with an intimidating black automatic was the human back-up to The Vault's complex, computerized security system, and he knew the rules. Not Walter's rules, but his own set of orders by which he lived.

But he was young, and he was bored.

Walter had approached him carrying his iPad. "Scott, I found a You Tube video of two women having sex in a JC Penney fitting room." The kid grinned and came out from behind his desk. While he was engrossed in the video, Walter slit his throat with a carpet knife he bought at Home Depot, then accessed The Vault and removed what he wanted.

8) Calligraphy Is A Lost Art. Children who spend a lot of time alone – especially bright ones – master obscure skills which most of the world has forgotten. Walter had many of these skills, including chess, trivia, bird identification and juggling. The one he was using for this project was calligraphy, something he had started teaching himself in junior high with a book from the library, and still did to this day as a means to amuse himself. He knew how to use the old-fashioned fountain pen, but he had discovered that the craft stores carried a selection of fine, chisel-edged markers in a variety of sizes, which looked just as nice but were less messy than the jars of ink.

He had done the original letter in Old English script, and when he was done it looked like something a medieval sheriff might have nailed to a castle door. The text was simple, and not personalized for the recipient, just a few paragraphs covering Walter's views on justice and equality. From the original he had made five hundred copies, the few remaining sitting in a Staples box on the desk beside him, next to a scattering of pre-addressed business envelopes. He had let the printer make the peel-and-stick address labels, and putting them on along with the stamps had been the most time consuming and boring part of the process.

Walter lifted a letter from the box and gave it a single spritz with the cut glass atomizer on the desk, the fancy kind with the tube and the little squeeze ball. Beside it was an empty glass vial with a red label on it, a tiny bit of clear liquid still pooled around the open mouth. The atomizer had been his mother's, used for her many perfumes over the years, and was one of her few remaining possessions he still had. It worked nicely, puffing out a tiny mist which settled invisibly on the paper. As he folded it neatly into thirds and stuffed another envelope, he was struck by how similar this was to some lonely girl in the forties sending a love letter to her G.I. fiancé in Europe, adding a touch of fragrance to give him a hint of home.

But this wasn't perfume, and it wasn't a love letter.

Across the top of each photocopied page in tall, Old English script stood the words, DEATH WARRANT.

9) Intelligent People Don't Necessarily Do Intelligent Things. And here was a perfect example of that. Biochemistry was a field filled with bright young talent, highly educated and creative. And those minds dreamed up – then cooked up – Poveglia V, naming it after an island in the Venetian lagoon which had been used over the centuries as a place to dispose of plague victims. How clever. Poveglia V was *highly* contagious, spread by both physical contact and airborne transmission, with flu-like symptoms followed by sudden paralysis appearing at seventy-two hours, and death occurring twenty-four hours later. It was a hardy little bastard, too, and didn't break down when it hit the air or sunlight as many other organisms did. PV was capable of living outdoors in a virulent state for up to two weeks and had a 97.6% mortality rate. There was no vaccination for it, and no way to halt its brief but fatal journey once it entered the body.

God knew what they ever thought it could be used for. Unless you wanted to end mankind, of course. For that it was the perfect agent of change.

10) Insane People Should Not Be Allowed To Work With Contagious Bioweapons. He stuffed his last envelope, then opened his mouth and gave his tongue a spritz. Yummy. He decided his last rule needed no elaboration. It was self evident.

Walter filled a nylon duffel bag with his envelopes, hung it over his shoulder, grabbed his coat and shut off the lights in the lab as he had promised. It was only Thursday, with two more mail service days before the holiday. The people in charge wouldn't find the murdered corporal for hours, and wouldn't find Walter for days. By then he would have visited four mailboxes and three different post offices, and PV would be well on its way to spreading its holiday cheer.

At the main doors, bright desert sunlight streamed into the facility lobby. The Army sergeant at the watch desk looked him over, then gestured for Walter's bag to be placed on a nearby table. He unzipped it, and began pawing through the envelopes.

239

"What's all this?"

"My holiday newsletter. I'm late getting it out." He gave what he hoped would look like a sheepish grin. "I used some of Uncle Sam's time to get them ready to mail." The sergeant raised an eyebrow, still sifting through the envelopes, and covering himself, the table, the lobby of the lab building with Poveglia V particles. Within an hour, the forty-nine people still working in the building would be infected, and they would bring it home to their families, their neighborhood grocery stores and gas stations, restaurants and holiday parties. About half would be flying to other parts of the country for the long weekend, and not one of them would notice a thing until Christmas.

"Don't worry, Sergeant," Walter said. "All the envelopes and paper are mine. I didn't take any government property for personal use."

The sergeant zipped up the bag and pushed it back to Walter. "Merry Christmas."

Walter walked out, and looked back through the glass doors. He threw the sergeant a wave and a smile. "Fuck you very much."

KING OF THE MONSTER HOUSE

It was a small place, neat and tidy, simple and empty. Except for Carla, who sat alone in her kitchen with only the light over the stove to chase away the night. On the table in front of her sat a birthday cake with eighteen lit candles. Beside it in a 5x7 silver frame was a photo of a seven-year-old girl with dark hair, a school picture. In it, the girl was smiling without her front teeth.

"Happy birthday, sweetheart," Carla said to the picture. "Eighteen. A real milestone." Carla raised a glass of vodka to the cake and took a long swallow, her last remaining vice. She'd kicked smoking, wrestled through a tough patch with sleeping pills and come out the other side, and was eating right and keeping fit. July twenty-third was the only day she drank, and always alone.

"We'd be getting you ready for college, baby." She smiled and tipped the glass again. "You'd be excited and nervous, I'd be happy for you but so sad inside, not wanting you to go. I'd try to keep up the smile but you'd know how I was feeling, wouldn't you?" It was now nearly impossible to see her daughter's face when she closed her eyes. She needed photos to remind her.

Anita stopped having birthdays just after she turned seven, but that hadn't stopped Carla from celebrating them. She sat and

241

looked at the vacant chair across from her, wishing she could see her, even just a glimpse, a smile, a reassurance for mommy that she was happy in Heaven.

"I'd be so proud of you, off to become a doctor, a professor, maybe a business executive...maybe a..." Carla started crying then, softly at first and then building into great wracking sobs, squeezing her eyes tightly against the tears which fell onto the tablecloth, clenching her fists until her nails dug moons in her palms. She gasped for an endless breath, then let out a long, rising and falling moan, rocking back and forth, red eyes staring at the ceiling as if searching for an answer to the unanswerable. There was only the empty kitchen.

She snatched the vodka glass off the table and hurled it at the refrigerator with a snarl, exploding it, her clenched teeth bared. "Why?" she screamed. "Why? Why her, you fuck?" At first Carla wasn't sure which sadist she meant, but decided she was screaming at God. He chose not to respond, so she began drinking from the bottle, staring at the picture as her sobbing turned to a dull ache in her chest, getting quietly drunk. Just before she passed out, she thought she heard the mobile of ceramic hummingbirds over the kitchen sink tinkle softly, could swear she felt the soft touch of a little hand on her back. And then there was the sweet oblivion of nothingness.

In the morning, Carla took a shower and scrubbed the bitterness from her mouth, did her usual five mile run, showered again and got ready for work. On the drive in, she stopped for coffee and spent the rest of her ride thinking about Kelvin Finch.

Deacon Valley Correctional Facility sat in the northeast corner of the state, surrounded by miles of flat, open prairie. Both the prison marksmen and the inmates behind the wire referred to that open space as the killing fields, for there was no place to hide from and no way to outrun a bullet fired from a tower. Deacon Valley, or simply DV, was made up of the administrative wing, engineering and motor pool areas, and the main building itself, broken into ten structures home to dining and kitchen facilities, recreation rooms, a small medical center, and housing for the inmates themselves. They were numbered DV-1, DV-2, DV-3 and so on.

No one thought it was a coincidence that the Protective Custody unit segregating the violent sex offenders from the rest of the population was numbered DV-8. Administration and official documents called it PC. The inmates and COs at Deacon Valley called it the Monster House.

Twenty-eight men were housed in two tiers of fourteen, single occupant cells against one wall, the upper level reached by a catwalk with a stairway at both ends. The common area, filled with metal tables and benches cemented to the floor, sat in front of the cells, and a shower area was off to the left. It looked like every other corrections housing unit built since the 90's, each cell door secured by a steel, motorized rolling door with a reinforced glass window and a food slot with a locking hatch. The only way in or out of the block was through the Bubble, an octagonal control point of armored glass and steel with a separate airlock-style passageway for people to move in and out. The Bubble was staffed 24/7 by a pair of corrections officers who controlled the locks and movement of each cell door, as well as the access passage. Officers only went onto the block when it was time to serve meals, and they never left the Bubble unmanned.

In many prisons, this area would have been called the SHU, for special housing unit. Deacon Valley did indeed have a SHU, but it was elsewhere, and much larger. Those cells had back doors which opened into small, individual, heavily fenced exercise yards where the inmate occupants were allowed to go for one hour a day. They were locked down the other twenty-three. Inmates in the SHU were the most violent, and posed the greatest threat to staff.

Also in many prisons, sex offenders found themselves housed in general population, where they had a hard time of it, enduring physical and sexual assault, enslavement to other inmates, and living a life of paranoia and fear, never knowing from which direction the next attack would come. They were the absolute lowest life form on the prison food chain.

Deacon Valley was a little different. The garden variety sex offenders and rapists were still housed in GenPop, and their existences were no different from others like themselves around the country. But the State of Oklahoma decided that the most violent sexual predators would be housed together in the PC. This wasn't any acknowledgement that they were special, and most posed no risk to staff. The state, however, knew these men were the most reviled, and the most at risk of being murdered by other inmates. Such instances meant weighty investigations and second-guessing by review boards, politicians and the media, all of which interfered with the smooth day-to-day of the facility. And so they were kept in the Monster House to keep them alive, the worst of the rotten eggs in one basket.

In DV-8, the ground level cell on the far left was where the King lived.

Because of what he had done, he couldn't have survived on any other block, and while the inmates in PC might have been hated, the King was despised above all others. Yet here within the Monster House, he was a celebrity. Several years ago, TRU TV had done a ten minute piece on his exploits and included it in an *American Predators* episode. When HBO announced its intention to put together a full hour documentary on him, titled "King of the Monster House," Kelvin Finch was elevated to the status of rock star.

King Finch VIII, eight for the number of his victims. Or at least that was how many he'd confessed to. Investigators across five states suspected there were many more, but Kelvin wasn't talking. Everyone believed he was holding back information which he intended to parlay for future attention once his fame started to dim. He certainly had time in which to play his games. Initially facing lethal injection, Finch's lawyer negotiated life without the possibility of parole in exchange for his client leading them to the remains of his seven previous victims, and providing full disclosure of the details of each case. The opportunity to close out so many disappearances and bring a measure of peace to so many family members was impossible to pass up, and so Kelvin Finch bought himself a lifetime, after ending so many others.

Right now the King was out of his cell and sitting at one of the tables playing chess with another inmate, using a soft felt game board and plastic pieces. Across from him was a heavyset black man named Linus James, doing twenty-five-to-life for abducting a fourteen-year-old runaway and sodomizing her for four days in a hotel room before smothering her with a pillow. Pretending to play chess – a game Linus neither understood nor cared about – the inmate gave a casual look around, and then carefully passed a dog-eared wallet photo under the table to the King. It was a picture of a girl at a birthday party.

"Like we agreed," Linus said softly.

The King glanced down at the picture before tucking it away. He smiled, revealing a missing front tooth, his lips still yellowish purple from the bruise. Several weeks ago, a rookie CO named Granger had been assigned to the Monster House, and made the mistake of talking with another officer about his six-year-old daughter Katie, with Kelvin Finch close enough to hear it. For weeks Finch took every opportunity to whisper vile comments about what he wanted to do to Katie when only Granger could hear. The rookie acted like a professional, writing Finch up repeatedly and ensuring his privileges were revoked as long as was permitted. Finch kept at it, each softly spoken remark more twisted than the last, and it began to wear at the young man. Finally, one afternoon when the inmates were lined up at the rolling food service carts, Finch whispered to Granger the specifics of how he would murder Katie and what he would then do with the body. Granger snapped, turned on him and punched Finch in the face, knocking him down, knocking him out, and knocking out a tooth.

Granger lost his job.

Finch filed criminal charges, and the prison scheduled him for a dental implant.

Finch's lawyer hastily drew up the lawsuit.

Everyone knew Granger had been provoked, but the assault was witnessed by thirty people, and there was no way around that. Although threats were made by the administration to shut down HBO's access and interviews, Finch's lawyer suggested that it would most certainly be construed by a civil jury – as well as the media – as retaliation and abuse of power, not to mention a possible violation of First Amendment rights. Reluctantly, the administration withdrew its threat, and the special was still a go, much to the King's delight.

Linus nodded to Finch. "Talk to me." The deal was a picture of Linus James's young niece in exchange for Finch's detailed telling of his fourth abduction and murder, a grade school girl in Kansas City named Lilly Barnes.

The King smirked. "It's all about the preparation, my friend," and went into his tale. When he was done, Linus James was sweating and wanting to spend some time alone in his cell.

"You one sick motherfucker, King."

"Better believe it, son."

Carla kept her life simple. It was the best way she'd found to hold it together. She kept to routines; grocery shopping at the same store, the same day of the week; oil change for her Nissan on the 3rd of every month; apartment cleaned room by room in the same order; closets neat and organized, with hangers one finger's width apart; running every day, regardless of the weather. Some would have labeled her behavior OCD, but that just wasn't so. It was how she pushed back the images which wouldn't fade, the grief which chewed at her soul day after day.

At first, though, there was nothing but helplessness, a raging sadness which threatened to sweep her away in a storm of bitter anguish, a great hollow left in her heart which she knew would never be filled. Her doctor, with the best of intentions, prescribed sleeping pills, and although she had the temptation to simply swallow the bottle and chase it with vodka, she resisted, and got hooked instead. It led to four months of barely leaving her bed, and shuffling like a confused zombie when she did. Yet something – she liked to think it was Anita – talked her back into the world, and she kicked the pills.

Her marriage wasn't so successful, and within six months of Anita's death – the discovery of her remains, actually – she and Emilio were finished. The counselor Carla was seeing in order to deal with it all was compassionate, and gently told her that divorce was extremely common within a year of losing a child, under any circumstances. There was simply too much guilt, blame and second-guessing of one another that few could survive it with an intact relationship. The counselor went on to say that parents with other, surviving children fared better at staying together, statistically anyway, and in some cases because they threw new energy into their other kids, the death sparking a renewed appreciation for their family, and one another. This was rare, she pointed out. Frequently the grieving parents became so wrapped up in the loss and feeding off one another that it was the surviving children who suffered, moving through the house and their lives like ghosts, unnoticed and forgotten by their mothers and fathers, often ending up resentful towards the lost sibling who had not only died, but taken their parents with her.

Anita was an only child, so there had never really been much of a chance for their marriage.

Carla stayed in the house for another year, quietly losing touch with her family and friends. She'd lost her job months earlier when her supervisors, although sympathetic, could no longer tolerate her long absences. Once her savings ran out, it was time to find new employment, but she had no desire to return to the retail jobs she'd held her whole life. All that time alone, all the thinking, eventually convinced her that a complete change of life was in order, including a career which could mean something. She landed a job which required a move, and had no regrets as she left behind a town she had come to despise, a house where happy memories turned black, a tomb which she haunted all by herself.

Kelvin Finch was fifty-three, and had been incarcerated at Deacon Valley for nearly ten years. He'd taken the first of his eight victims almost twenty years earlier, and the idea they had about him that he had suddenly decided at age thirty-three to abduct, sexually torture and murder young girls was laughable. They were supposed to be so smart, these clinicians and psychologists and profilers. The cops were a different story, suspicious to the bone and not believing it for a second. Eight indeed. Kelvin's real number was nineteen.

He'd been twelve when he took the first one, a six year old in a city park who'd wandered away from a babysitter. Kelvin had been fantasizing about this for as long as he could remember, and that afternoon he'd seen his chance and lured her into a cinderblock restroom building. When he was finished, he'd held her face in a toilet until she drowned, then slipped out and ran home. No one ever suspected him.

The following ten were spread out over the next twenty years, both in his home town and then out of state once he was older. Some he left where he'd killed them, but most were deeply buried, and he became very skilled at not only hunting, but avoiding leaving behind evidence and artfully disposing of the bodies where no one would ever find them. What was significant about the eight was that was the time when he'd started sending letters and photos to the families.

Kelvin was a very intelligent man, and he knew why he'd done that. Some of it came from a need for attention. The bigger reason, he knew, was that after so many he'd begun to grow bored with the actual acts themselves. Taunting the families gave him a thrill he hadn't felt in a long time. It aroused him to imagine the expressions and reactions of the parents when they opened the anonymous letters and read his calm description of what he had done, along with an admonishment that, had mommy or daddy kept a better eye on their little angel, none of this would have happened. Sometimes the photo was an action shot, or a carefully-crafted scene involving restraints. The panicked eyes were key in those. Sometimes he led the parents to believe their daughter was still alive. A few times he sent them a picture of the child crumpled in their grave hole, about to be filled in.

It was the letters – none of them signed – which made him so famous, as well as making him the most hunted man in the western U.S.

Only seven of the girls prompted letters. He never got the chance to write to mommy and daddy about number eight. Three days after he'd snatched her from a crowded flea market, she was dead and wrapped in plastic in the trunk of his Taurus, and he was on his way to a remote, pre-dug hole. Driving carefully and obeying the speed limit and all traffic rules hadn't prevented an Oklahoma trooper from pulling him over, though. Kelvin methodically checked out his vehicles before traveling with a body, in order to avoid the stupid mistakes which got most serial killers caught. Bad luck found him that night, though, for his right tail light went out while he was driving, and he didn't know it. The trooper hadn't suspected a thing as Kelvin handed over his driver's license, registration and insurance card – all spotless, of course – but the cop had still asked to look in the trunk.

Had he seen Kelvin swallow hard, noticed the bob of his Adam's apple? At that moment Kelvin knew it was all over. He didn't carry a gun in the car, and even if he did, he would probably have come out on the losing end of a gunfight with a trained officer who was already on edge from making an after-dark stop on a lonely road. Kelvin popped the trunk, and that was that. Years later, he found the whole thing comical. Oklahoma had a serious problem with people trafficking methamphetamine along that stretch of highway, and the state troopers had been instructed to ask to see inside the trunk on every traffic stop, regardless of how the drivers appeared. Refusing the trooper just earned you cuffs in the back seat while he investigated, impounded the vehicle and searched it anyway.

It was just bad luck. Kelvin wasn't bitter. It just meant that his life was different now.

Carla moved through the days, through the years. She did well at work and was promoted to supervisor. Her running made her exceptionally fit, and she could have easily competed in any number of marathons, but she only ran alone. She didn't socialize, and politely avoided her neighbors, made excuses not to attend workplace get-togethers and annual Christmas parties. She didn't date, not because she had no desire for male companionship – there were nights when her desires and loneliness threatened to overwhelm her – but because it felt like a betrayal. The idea of going out and having fun, of having a relationship to satisfy her own selfish needs while her daughter vanished into the earth, and her killer kept drawing breath, was offensive. She wouldn't do that to Anita.

She did, however, eventually give in to a repeated dinner invitation from Dean Frye, another supervisor at work. Carla told herself it was only to get him to stop asking, that it was just a work-friends thing, just a meal with a colleague. She didn't want to think about how much she liked being around him, finding him funny and confident, a down-to-earth man. She told herself she wasn't attracted to him, and hadn't entertained thoughts of sharing her bed with him. No, she was just being nice to someone she had to see every day. They kept it simple, and went to an Outback.

Dean Frye was the same age as Carla, had been married briefly, and let his work fill his life in much the same way she did. He'd come to the job after her, and they had been working together for over eight years. He still knew little more about her than the day he started. She was divorced and she didn't get involved in work gatherings. He didn't know where she was originally from.

Carla was a private person and Dean respected that, and he believed the reason she kept to herself was hurtful to her. He suspected she had been deeply injured in the past, probably by a man.

Despite her outer coolness, Dean enjoyed being around her. She had a clever wit, was talented and capable at her job, and genuinely cared about the people who worked for her. He didn't want to be pushy, wasn't looking to save her from whatever pain she lived with, he just wanted to get to know her better. Behind all those rationalizations he admitted that he was also in love with her.

Dinner was a disaster, and it was Dean's fault.

The evening had been going well; the food was good and the conversation safe and pleasant, about work for the most part. She had laughed a few times – music to him - and he was happy inside, aware that she liked him too. She'd even opened up a bit, talking a little about her childhood and telling a funny story from high school. He'd learned she was from Tulsa. The plates had been cleared, he was having a beer and she had a Diet Coke. He didn't know why he asked the question.

"Do you and your ex have any kids?"

The muscles in her neck tensed visibly, and he didn't see it. "What?"

"Do you have any kids?"

There was a long silence, and the hardening of her eyes immediately told Dean he had screwed up.

"No. Let's get the check."

They hadn't gone out again, and although she continued to be polite at work, that relaxed feeling between them was gone. He tried to apologize, to draw her out, but a curtain had fallen between them which he knew would never open again. Dean would forever have to be satisfied with a "just friends" relationship, and that did little to comfort his broken heart. It hurt worse that he was the reason it was broken.

For her part, Carla went home that night, changed into sweats and athletic shoes, and went running. She cried as she ran, at first because Dean was stupid, then because she was stupid for letting him in. As her feet slammed the pavement she wept because she knew there would be nothing between them, that the light of any hope she might have had for a future had been blown out, leaving her in the darkness. She pushed her body, running through the late night streets faster and faster with tears streaking back across her face. Her legs and lungs burned, but she didn't notice. She was thinking about the lengthy questionnaire.

Have you ever been the victim of a violent crime?

No.

Do you know anyone who has been the victim of a violent crime?

No.

Have you ever gone by a different name?

No.

Do you know, or are you related to anyone incarcerated in a correctional facility?

No.

Have you ever abused prescription or non-prescription drugs?

No.

Have you ever been convicted of a felony or misdemeanor? If so, explain.

No.

Carla wasn't in the darkness alone. She had Kelvin Finch for company, and she had her rage. It was something she had come to understand quite well. Hatred is a difficult emotion to sustain, and if one doesn't really work at it, it will slip away a bit at a time, unnoticed. If a person does manage to hold onto it, they eventually learn that it is an animal, eternally hungry and all-consuming, devouring happiness, hope and physical well-being. As it eats, it leaves behind a hollow shell, a person so drained and weary that they just don't have the energy to hold onto the animal anymore.

Unless a person really applies themselves and nurtures it, feeds it. Carla Mendez had been feeding her hatred animal for eleven years. It was a ravenous beast, and only one thing would satisfy it. Kelvin Finch had a reckoning coming.

And she had a plan.

Trent Whitsome sat in the warden's office with a thick clasping file on his knees. The man behind the desk in front of him was paunchy, in his late fifties and balding. The expression on his face was one of sour contempt.

"I'll tell you up front I don't like any of this, Mr. Whitsome. I said as much to your superiors, and I said it to the governor."

Trent nodded. "But the governor *did* support it, Warden Epps." The older man's face flushed, and Trent hurried on. "Sir, I'm not here to make anyone look bad, and I'm not here to turn Kelvin Finch into some kind of hero."

"That's precisely what you've done already, Mr. Whitsome."

Trent shook his head. "I know what he is, and I'll be certain our viewers know what he is."

Epps leaned forward. "And what do you think he is, exactly?"

Without hesitation, "He's a monster. And nothing he says during the interview will portray otherwise. I've done my research on him, and I've already filmed the segments with the abnormal psychologist, the FBI profiler and two of the investigators who worked his case. Those conversations and opinions will all appear. I also did the piece with the D.A. and even interviewed Finch's lawyer."

The warden raised his eyebrows. "And how did that go?"

"After we got through all the, 'My client is a victim of an abusive childhood and an unfair criminal justice system' crap, I saw a man who was happy to be representing someone infamous and nationally known, but even happier that his client is locked away in your facility." He paused. "I think Finch scares the shit out of him."

Epps snorted. "Unless he's a little girl, he has nothing to fear."

Trent shook his head. "It's more than that. I think what scares him is knowing Finch is…simply evil."

The warden rotated his chair and looked out his office window. He didn't speak for a long time, but then he said, "You're about to see evil up close, Mr. Whitsome. I hope you're ready for it."

"This isn't my first serial killer, Warden."

The older man turned back around and opened a thick file on his desk. On the top was a letter signed by the governor, permitting HBO to film a documentary on Kelvin Finch, using the prison, and instructing the warden to extend all courtesies which did not jeopardize the safety or security of the facility.

He tapped the file. "I have a lot of leeway here, Mr. Whitsome."

The producer had a copy of the same letter. "Yes, sir, you do, as you should. It's your prison."

"I could decide this event constitutes a clear security risk and deny the whole thing."

They both knew he wouldn't. In order to grease the wheels, HBO had arranged to interview the governor, and edit clips of his Q&A into the special. The man was very excited about the opportunity, and the warden knew it. Epps drummed his thick fingers on the file.

"I want to clear any footage before it airs."

The producer shook his head. "You know that's not going to happen." He said it as respectfully as he could, but inside he wanted to ask this bureaucrat if he had ever heard of the First Amendment. He didn't, of course. That would spin this interview into territory more hostile than it already was, and besides, the man was right. He had a lot of leeway, and could choose to make things so restrictive that Whitsome would never get the kind of candid interview he needed.

Warden Epps scowled at him for a moment without speaking, and then his face changed to a look of resignation. He knew he wasn't going to win, and he would cooperate because he had been directed to cooperate. Inside, Trent was rejoicing.

"Alright, Mr. Whitsome. There are some things you need to understand, and rules by which you will abide. Violation of any one of these rules constitutes a felony in the State of Oklahoma, and if you disobey them I will personally turn the key on the cell where you will await trial for breaching the security of a state correctional facility. Do you understand me?"

"Yes sir."

"That goes for your people as well. Our facility houses over five-hundred of the most violent felons in the State of Oklahoma, and I want you to appreciate the potential dangers." He opened the file. "I see you're requesting a crew of four."

Trent nodded. "Myself, my cameraman and sound technician, and one lighting technician. I could also use an assistant..."

"Four will suffice, Mr. Whitsome." Epps leaned back in his chair. "You and your crew will be subject to searches when you enter, when you leave, and at any time my officers choose. Your equipment will be thoroughly inspected. You will not bring weapons or contraband into my facility. You will not go anywhere unescorted. You will not give anything to or accept anything from an inmate. You will follow the instructions of all COs at all times."

The producer nodded.

"You can film in hallways, common areas and cell blocks only after you request and receive permission. Anyone other than Finch whom you wish to interview on camera must first clear it with me. Anyone who doesn't want to talk to you, or have their face on TV…"

"We're very respectful about that, Warden. Not a problem."

Epps nodded. "I'll arrange for a secure room for the interview. You can have Finch for two hours only, so you'd better make it count. There won't be a second interview. He will be in restraints, and there will be two officers in the room with you at all times. If they decide Finch is getting out of line, or poses a threat to you or your crew, the interview is over. That's their decision."

Trent nodded that he understood. He didn't argue about only getting access to Finch the one time. If the bosses at HBO determined Trent should have another go at him, then they would romance the governor and make it happen.

"One last thing, Mr. Whitsome, and this is very important."

The producer waited.

"In the event of a crisis at the facility, we will do what we can to get you and your crew to a secure area. However, among the many waivers you and HBO will have to sign, it clearly states that should you be taken hostage by inmates, you will be considered a casualty of war. We do not negotiate, and we retake compromised areas by force."

Trent Whitsome wanted to smile, but when he saw that the warden was serious his grin wavered and he swallowed hard. "I understand."

"Good." Warden Epps rose from his desk and guided Whitsome out.

It was 6:50am, and the rows of seated corrections officers listened as the sergeant announced the assignments for first shift.

This was the busiest shift of the day, since all the inmates were awake, off to their jobs or receiving visitors, going on sick call or facing disciplinary or parole review. There was intake, a small amount of out-processing, and of course this was the time when the highest amount of civilian workers were in the facility. "Carson and Karst, you're in the bubble at DV-3. Dingham and Gianetta, bubble at DV-4. Stroeham, you're at medical..."

Sergeant Carla Mendez continued reading. She wore a crisp white shirt with sergeant's stripes, and had her hair tied back under her blue ball cap. Sergeant Dean Frye leaned against a table nearby.

"...Wininngham, Crosby, Pope, Esperanza and Wales, you're on the yard. Poplin, you're on review board escort. Levins...ah, glad you're awake this morning, Officer Levins."

There was some chuckling, and an embarrassed CO sat up straighter and rubbed his eyes.

"Levins you're on food service with Triest." She flipped the page. "SRT officers, we have a meeting at 0730, then you'll get your assignments." The SRT, or Special Response Team, was the prison's SWAT team, specially trained officers who handled violent cell extractions, manned the rifle towers, and were on constant standby in the event of a riot or similar disturbance. They wore black and bloused their trousers into their boots, military style. All wore taps on their boots for added psychological effect. The inmates, who dressed in orange jumpsuits, called them Orange Crush.

As well as being a sergeant, Carla was the team leader of Deacon Valley's SRT.

She stood at her podium handing out assignments as she did every day, and like every day, inside she was amazed at the wonder of it all. There was no way she should have gotten away with it, no way she should have been able to slip past all the screening and background checks without someone throwing a flag. And yet she had. At first, she told herself her attempt to enter corrections was an effort to keep society's predators locked away, preventing them from hurting others. Of course that was all bullshit and she knew it. She wanted to get close to Kelvin Finch. She fully expected that going back to her maiden name and lying on all the questionnaires, lying during the polygraph, would not stand up.

They hired her.

She knew that even though she had gotten in, someone would soon find her out.

They didn't.

COs have no say in where they are assigned, and go where they're told. There was no chance at all she would be assigned to Deacon Valley.

That was exactly where they put her.

For years she struggled with the fear of discovery, the sick feeling that she was betraying her fellow officers with her deception, waiting for that moment when the warden would summon her, toss a file on the desk in front of her and demand to know how the mother of a murdered girl had managed to wiggle her way into the facility where that killer was kept. Her anxiety didn't originate from any concern over punishment. Her fear was that she would be found out before she had the chance to avenge her little girl. But that moment had never come.

Carla had played out variations of that vengeance thousands and thousands of times, and had almost as many opportunities to carry it out. As a sergeant, getting a weapon into the prison was a simple matter, and getting close enough to Finch to use it was just as easy. In her nine years at Deacon Valley, however, she had yet to act. Somewhere along the way she came to the decision that a simple ambush, a quick death, would not do for Kelvin Finch. She wanted him to see it coming, to experience the fear of knowing death was on its way, and that there was nothing he could do to stop it. Like Anita. So she resisted the urge, devising a more fitting plan and waiting for that one, unique moment when everything came together, reconciling the fact that the man living in the Monster House continued to draw breath while her daughter did not. Sometimes she anguished over the idea that the moment might never come, that her plan was too complex and relied upon a set of events which mathematically would likely never occur. Those were her lowest points, when she wavered and nearly gave in to the idea of simply ending him the next time she got close. But she endured, convincing herself it would happen.

"You've all been briefed on the HBO film crew coming today. They're scheduled to arrive at 0900, and may be here filming as late as 2300. Acre and Falstead, you're assigned as escort until second shift relieves you at 1500 hours. Orders from the warden are to wear them like a shirt. No screw-ups."

The two men nodded.

"Finch's interview will be at 2030 hours, after everyone is down for the night. I'll let you know where and give you the specifics later." She finished up with the briefing, passed out the rest of the assignments, and then dismissed her officers. Dean Frye was just getting off the phone over by the table.

"That was Epps," he said.

"And?"

Dean looked embarrassed. "He says you're on mandatory overtime. He wants this HBO thing to go smoothly, and says you're on the escort detail and in the room during the interview."

She just stared at him.

"I'll take the SRT watch today so you can focus on our guests." Dean was her assistant commander on the team.

Carla only nodded, her face revealing nothing, but inside she was caught in a whirlwind.

Kelvin Finch sat in a hard wooden chair, wearing a clean orange jumpsuit and a white tee shirt. Although his hands were free, his ankles were shackled down below the camera view, and the chain ran through a steel ring bolted to the floor. The room, located in the administration building and normally a storage place for boxes of files, had been completely emptied, and now only a blank wall painted in institutional gray served as a backdrop. Finch sat in a relaxed pose, hands resting on his knees with a small microphone clipped to his collar.

Trent Whitsome was not so relaxed. It was 9:30pm, and he had been inside Deacon Valley for over twelve hours, long enough to know he never wanted to come back. It wasn't the prison itself – he'd done work in several, and they were all about the same – it was the men locked up within it, muscled and lean and covered in tattoos and scars. They watched like wolves sizing up a weak calf. Trent was careful to stay close to his escort.

He had the prison footage he needed, and a couple of interviews with inmates willing to talk to him about how they felt about the residents of the PC, and Kelvin Finch in particular. Now he was an hour into his chat with the King, referring to prepared notes on a legal pad.

"Let's talk about the letters and photos. You sent them to the families of seven of your victims. Before we talk about why, tell us how you even got that information."

Finch smiled. "Everything I needed was on the news after the girl was taken."

Trent noticed Finch spoke in the passive voice; *the girl was taken*, as if he'd had nothing to do with it.

"The family's name, the address of their house, the news put it all out there. I got more details off the internet."

"Why send the letters, why inflict more pain?"

He shifted in his chair. "I was different then, full of hate, not thinking clearly. I just wanted to hurt people." His smile returned. "I know now that it was wrong. I've been saved, and I put my faith in Jesus Christ. I've received his forgiveness, and hope the families can do the same."

Unlikely, Trent thought, ignoring the remark. He'd heard it from every killer he'd ever interviewed. "Those letters did some damage, didn't they? Two suicides, the mothers of Kelsey Wallingford and Fran Petra, numbers four and six, I believe."

"Well, like I said, I was a different man."

Against a wall out of view of the camera, Carla Mendez stood at parade rest with her hands folded behind her, staring at Kelvin Finch. She'd gotten two of those letters, the first six months after the abduction, the second a year later. The first contained a graphic explanation of what he was doing to "Number Seven," accompanied by a shadowy photo taken of the girl when she was still alive. There was duct tape and plastic zip strips and terror in her baby's eyes. The second letter apologized that his plaything was all worn out and no longer of any use to him. The photo with this one showed a black lawn and leaf bag at the bottom of a hole in the woods.

Carla wanted to kill someone when she received the first correspondence. The second one made her want to die.

"Tell me about Anita Rodriguez," Trent said.

Carla stiffened, but kept her face a stone mask. *No, please don't.*

"She was your seventh victim," the producer went on, "and you kept her the longest. Why?"

Kelvin Finch's eyes looked past the camera and into memory, and the faintest ghost of a smile crossed his lips. "I was drawn to her," he said, his voice wistful, as if he was a man talking about a love affair from his younger days. "I thought she was beautiful, and she had the most amazing, big dark eyes."

Finch proceeded to talk about Anita Rodriguez, and what he had done to her. Trent Whitsome had advised him before they started that anything too graphic would simply be edited out and never see any screen time, and so far during the interview Finch had kept it vague. Now, however, it was as if he could no longer contain himself, and he explained in heartbreaking detail his "romance" with and ultimate disposal of the seven-year-old.

Against the wall, Carla's eyes bored into her daughter's killer. His words washed over her in great, crashing waves of pain, and she was unable to stop him, unable to not hear about the things he had done, of which she had mercifully never known until now. Somehow, she managed not to cry.

She saw Finch was getting an erection as he reminisced.

Concealed in her right boot was a box-cutter, a heavy silver device with a razorblade which could be pushed out by thumbing a lever forward. When she learned she would be standing here during the interview, mere feet away from Finch, she retrieved it from a locked box of contraband weapons confiscated from the inmates over the years, now used during officer training. She had placed it so she could reach it easily, and now its weight and shape was an irresistible presence.

Carla's life was one of despair. One of those many despairs was that the combination of events she needed in order to exact her detailed revenge would never come. It was a feeling which had become a constant, and the items hidden in a small black nylon zipper bag, locked in a bottom drawer of her desk, untouched and unused for so many years, were a constant reminder of this. How many chances would she have to get him in this position, defenseless and unsuspecting, within easy reach? In the years he had seen her at Deacon Valley, he never once recognized her, even though she was sitting in that courtroom when the DA told the judge a plea of guilty had been obtained in exchange for life without parole. She had even been on the TV news, standing next to Emilio at the end of their driveway, surrounded by supportive neighbors and clutching a school picture of Anita – the same one she shared the annual birthday celebration with – crying and begging anyone who had seen her daughter to please come forward. No one recognized her now. Then again, that had been many years ago, and in a different part of the state. Finch wouldn't recall her because he cared only about himself.

The King was talking about circular saws and Hefty bags.

Carla was going to do it, the hell with her grand scheme. Finch could have a heart attack tonight and die in his cell, or run across one of the general population lifers with nothing to lose and a hatred of pedophiles, and having him taken away before she could avenge her daughter would be more than she could endure. It was going to be now. She would slit his throat from ear to ear right in front of the camera, and scream Anita's name at him as he bled out.

Yet she didn't move from her place, remaining motionless as a grave marker.

When the King was done with his story, Trent signaled to his crew to cut and wrap it up. He'd come in here thinking he was thick-skinned and hardened enough to hear whatever this man had to say without reaction, a cool professional who could separate his emotions from the job. He was wrong, and now he just wanted to go back to his hotel and try to shower off Kelvin Finch.

He nodded to the lady sergeant, a woman with a lean face and hard eyes who might have once been attractive. Since being introduced to her this morning he had the recurring feeling that they'd met before. Her name tag simply read MENDEZ, and that was no help. Once during the day he'd expressed this idea, but she had said no, they'd never met. During the interview she'd had no reaction at all to Finch's horrific stories and casual commentary on the destruction of young life, and the producer figured she was probably numb to all this, exposed to it on a daily basis. That was the kind of professional demeanor he'd come in here incorrectly thinking he had.

Carla instructed the other CO in the room to return Finch to his cell. Once he was gone, she waited while the crew members packed their gear, used her radio to inform Central Control that they were coming out, and led Trent Whitsome and his people into a hallway. They made it twenty feet before Carla brusquely excused herself and pushed into a ladies room, barely making it into a stall before she threw up.

Carla's kitchen was in shambles. The table was overturned, one of the chairs lay broken under a ragged hole in the sheetrock, shards of glass and ceramic littered the linoleum floor from where she had hurled plates and glasses against the refrigerator and walls. She stood in the center of it all, fists clenched, screaming as tears streaked her face.

Why didn't she kill him when she had the chance?

How could he have done those things to her precious, tender-hearted little girl?

Memories of pregnancy, of changing diapers and cooing nursery rhymes, night lights and cuddling after bedtime terrors spun through her head. Anita learning to walk, the first time she said "mommy," crayon drawings and laughter and wrestling in the grass. Singing ABC's, endless questions and favorite toys. The first day of school, Christmas mornings, a play in kindergarten where she was dressed as a sunflower. The random "I love you's."

"Oh, God!" she wailed, failing to her knees and cutting them on the fragments, hugging her chest and rocking, a long moan of animal pain escaping her. *"You did that to my baby! You took away my baby!"* She fell on her side, curling into a fetal position as the tears exploded. Yet another birthday would come and go while Kelvin Finch moved day to day through life, another sad little cake, another bottle of vodka, the years stretching out before Carla like an accusation.

"Mommy's sorry, baby," she choked. "Mommy's so, so sorry."

It had been her third day of second grade, and Anita had begged to walk to school on her own because she was a big girl. The school was only three blocks away, the street didn't see much traffic, the neighborhood was safe and friendly, and Anita was a smart girl. Emilio had left for work already, and Anita had taken her time getting dressed and ready. Carla knew she'd be late for work if she spent the extra twenty minutes to drop her off, and gave in.

Yes. A single spoken word, a product of her own selfishness, her misplaced sense of importance in wanting to avoid a scolding at the store where she worked instead of protecting her only child as a mother should. For eleven years, that knowledge reminded her daily that it was her fault. She thought about it more than she did Kelvin Finch.

No one saw him take her. Carla never knew how it happened until this evening, a nagging question answered by the killer himself. He had been driving slowly through the neighborhood and saw her on the sidewalk, ponytail and bright yellow backpack bouncing along behind her as she marched to school. He pulled to the curb half a block ahead of her, got out, and started looking under his car.

"Here kitty, kitty," he called. "Here kitty."

Anita stopped, crouched and looked under the car too. "Here kitty," she said, always a helpful little girl. His hand clamped her mouth and she was inside the back seat of his car so fast that no one heard or saw a thing. He bound her, sealed her mouth, and drove away. The entire abduction took less than sixty seconds.

Carla stared across the kitchen floor at the fragments of glass, some tipped with fresh blood, and gasped for breath, the tears still flowing freely. "So sorry," she whispered. "Mommy's so sorry, baby."

Trent Whitsome followed his GPS and drove his rental car down the main avenue of Levi, Oklahoma, a burg sitting on the prairie twenty miles from Deacon Valley Correctional Facility. It was a small, nondescript town which probably wouldn't even have existed except for a large stockyard and rail center, and the fact that it was home to most of the people who worked at or provided services for the prison.

It was ten days since the Finch interview, and he was the new favorite with the HBO brass. They loved what he had put together, and even after plenty of cutting the interview was chilling. It would be the centerpiece of the special. Whitsome would oversee the final editing process, dishing up pieces of the Kelvin Finch interview and intermingling it with the details of the case, archive footage of cops emerging from wooded areas with small body bags, interviews with investigators and neighbors, as well as a psychologist's views on Finch's letters and the events which led to his capture and incarceration. There was talk that they had landed Gary Sinise to provide the dramatic narrator's voice, and the audio department had given him a preview of the documentary's haunting soundtrack.

Also key to the special, to provide the heartache and connect with the audience, was the interviews with the parents. The two single moms had committed suicide, another couple had divorced and died during the intervening years of a car accident and cancer respectively. A fourth couple, also divorced, refused to participate. But Trent had already conducted and filmed interviews with three of the remaining families, only one of which was not divorced. One more to go.

Carla Rodriguez's husband couldn't be located. The woman herself had vanished as well, simply dropped out of existence. Trent spoke with anyone he could find who knew her, hitting repeated dead ends. She had broken off all contact, and hadn't been heard from since the whole, terrible thing came to a close.

He got lucky with Shay Downing, however, the realtor who handled the sale of Carla Rodriguez's house. After some polite conversation and Trent's assurance that he would keep her name out of it, Ms. Downing offered that Carla had left Tulsa right after the sale was completed, but before the check for the equity – and there wasn't too much of that, she said – could be cut. Carla left her realtor a forwarding address, an apartment in Levi, Oklahoma.

Trent believed it was the one and only loose end of a woman who clearly did not want to be found. And he thought it was beyond intriguing that she had relocated to the town adjacent the prison where her daughter's killer was spending his life. That by itself was a story, and Trent had busied himself during the long drive from Tulsa to Levi with questions. Why did you vanish? Why move here of all places? Have you ever visited him, tried to contact him? What have you been doing for eleven years?

He turned into a residential neighborhood of small frame houses and little stucco-walled apartment complexes, stopping when directed by his GPS. Grabbing a legal pad off the front seat, he headed across a dry lawn towards one of the buildings.

He would ask her all those questions in person.

It was her day off. Carla was coming out her apartment door with a bag of trash for the complex dumpsters, and saw the man trotting up the concrete steps, his head down. They passed each other on the stairs with a brief "excuse me," and then the man stopped on the steps above her.

"Mrs. Rodriguez?"

She froze, and he skipped back down the steps until he was in front of her.

"Mrs. Rodriguez, I'm…" He stared at her, his mouth open in mid-sentence. "Oh my God," he whispered.

Carla looked at the HBO producer, her jaw clenched, the hand not holding the garbage bag trembling. She wanted to tell him he was mistaken, wanted to tell him to go away, forget he had ever seen her. She knew he wouldn't.

Trent shook his head slowly. "You look different. From when you…back then. You're thinner."

"I run."

He paused. "Yes you do." He raised an eyebrow.

She took a deep breath. "When did you recognize me?"

He let out a short laugh. "I didn't, but now I know why I thought I knew you. I have the footage from when you and your husband were on TV. You've changed a lot, not just because of the years."

She unconsciously put a hand to her face, and he saw the tremble. "It's the prison. It changes a person." She set down the trash bag. "What are you going to do?"

Trent hefted the notepad. "I have a lot of questions for you. Will you…?"

"No. I have nothing to say."

"C'mon, Carla. All this…" he waved his notepad in a circle, "…is very unusual. What you've done is unusual. Talk to me, tell me your side. Give *me* a chance to tell your side."

She shook her head. "You couldn't understand it."

"You were in that room," he said, "you had to stand there and hear the things he did. I won't pretend to understand how painful that was, but you can help me to understand."

"No."

He shrugged. "The story gets told either way, I just..."

Carla moved up the steps and into his face, her voice tight between clamped teeth. "Listening to that sick fuck talk about torturing and killing my girl wasn't enough? You need more pain, Mr. Whitmore? Is that what turns you on, like those *things* that live in the Monster House?"

Trent retreated from her sudden fury until his lower back was hard against the iron railing, leaning away from her. "Wait, I..."

"Fuck you, Whitmore. Fuck your questions and your story." She said the last word like she was spitting out something nasty. "The story's over. It ended when he put my child in the ground." She snatched up the trash bag. "Now get away from my house."

Trent watched her go down the stairs and around the corner of the building, suddenly realizing that for just a moment, he *knew* she was going to kill him right there on the stairs. He went back to his car faster than he would have liked, quickly pulling out of the neighborhood.

What was he going to do about all this? Carla Rodriguez...Mendez, whatever she called herself, wasn't just near her daughter's killer, she was on top of him. Why? Then he thought about her burst of rage and realized the real question was, why hadn't she done it yet? Surely that was at the heart of it all. Where to go with this? It was a game-changer, an explosive turn of events in an already spectacular story. What to do? It was a question he wouldn't try to answer alone, and so once he pulled out onto the highway he called the brass at HBO. Let them make the decision. He already had a good idea what they would say.

Ahead, lightning flashed on the horizon, and thunder rolled across the sky.

Carla wasn't on again until third shift the following night, and from the moment she met Trent Whitmore on her steps until she pulled into the staff parking lot at Deacon Valley, she didn't sleep. The storm which had been threatening since the previous day had arrived with a vengeance, and now, at a quarter of eleven, it was punishing this entire corner of Oklahoma. Rain hammered the roof, and curtains of water marched across the parking lot, driven by a high wind which made the car shake.

She sat for a while with the engine off, watching the storm, thinking of what was to come. She had received a call late this afternoon from Warden Epps – and he never called officers at home – which she let go to message. The warden's voice was low, without a trace of humor, and he called her Sergeant Mendez, instead of the familiar Carla he had used with her for years. Epps instructed her to report to Lt. Dykestrom, the third shift watch commander, as soon as she arrived at the prison. He gave no further details, and hung up without saying goodbye.

So this was the end of it. Trent Whitsome reported what he had learned about her, and that was that. She would be fired, certainly. Would they prosecute her for falsification of her employment and background records? Probably. The state didn't have a high level of tolerance for misconduct from its employees. It didn't matter. What did matter was that she had missed the many chances to exact revenge for Anita's murder, and tonight would be the last time she would ever be allowed inside the facility. She would never get another shot at Kelvin Finch, and there was no way they'd let her get near him tonight.

She had failed, and she started to cry. She didn't tell Anita how sorry she was, again, didn't tell her daughter how much she loved her. She simply cried. When the internal storm had wrung her out, Carla stepped into the downpour and hustled towards the entrance. There was no point trying to avoid the consequences of her actions. By the time she got inside she was soaked and shaking.

The on-duty officer checking in staff gave her a pleasant good evening as she passed through the metal detector. He didn't look at her funny or order her to wait for an escort. She passed half a dozen more officers in the corridors, all exchanging greetings, none of them acting unusual. Carla struggled to act the same. One officer told her that the power from OMPA, the Oklahoma Municipal Power Authority, was down and the prison was running on its emergency generators. He said there were tornado warnings as well.

Carla ducked into the ladies locker room to towel off and rub at her hair before going into the Pen, the central ready area for COs. Outgoing second shift officers were mixing with oncoming third shifters, some sharing the day's stories, but in most cases talking sports or families or anything other than about the prison. None of them acted any differently with her. She headed into the briefing room, where all that changed when Dean saw her.

"Come over here," he said softly, taking her elbow and leading her over to the cluster of desks the sergeants used. She went without protest. He looked around, keeping his voice low. "Dykestrom called me into his office a few minutes ago. He said he got a call from the warden, who got a call from some HBO executive."

She just looked at him.

"What the hell, Carla? You've been lying to everyone? To me, all these years?" He frowned at her. "What's your real name?"

"Mendez is my maiden name. When I was married it was Carla Rodriguez." There was no sense trying to keep up the charade.

"And your daughter...Finch..."

"Kelvin Finch abducted my daughter eleven years ago," she said, surprised at how calm her voice was. "He held her for three months, repeatedly raping and torturing her, and when he was finished he killed her, cut her into pieces and buried her. It was almost a year before we knew she was dead, and not just missing. We didn't recover her body until after Finch was caught."

Dean stared at her, slowly shaking his head at her words, too stunned to speak. How was it she was still sane after something like that? And then she had worked so very hard to position herself inches from the man who had done it all. For what purpose? The easy answer was revenge, but over all these years she would have had hundreds, thousands of chances to kill him. But she hadn't. None of it made any sense.

"I don't even know what to say to you." Dean still had her by the arm, but it wasn't a grip, more a touch of comfort.

"I wish I had an answer that you would understand," she said, her eyes starting to well up. She saw he was hurt, and had never thought about how this would affect him if it all came out. It was

267

never meant to until it was over, and then she wouldn't be around to see it. But now here was this man whom she still cared for, wounded and confused, and she couldn't even explain it.

"Dykestrom's looking for you. He's going to suspend you and send you home."

"I know."

"Carla, you could be prosecuted on several counts, fraud for one."

She sighed. "I know. And I'll take what's coming."

He looked around again. "Or you could just turn around and walk out of here right now. No one else knows, no one will stop you. Get in your car, pack some things and leave, just disappear."

She smiled at him and touched his face. "You're a sweet man, Dean Frye. I missed out on a good one."

He started to protest, but she shook her head. "I did all this. I'll face it." She wished she felt the conviction of her words. Fired, locked up or simply kicked out, how would she face the rest of her life knowing she'd had the chance and failed to give Finch the justice he had coming? It wasn't a life worth living. But then, had it ever been? Not for eleven years now.

"I'll walk with you," he said, reluctantly letting go of her arm. His voice was thick as he struggled to keep his emotions in check. Carla nodded, and then glanced past him, her breath cut short.

Anita was standing in the corner of the briefing room.

She was like smoke, and Carla could see through her to the wall beyond, but it was Anita. Her little girl's eyes were far away and sad, and she stood with her arms loose at her sides, hair limp about her face. Carla had never seen anything so forlorn in her life, and her heart broke all over again.

Anita looked at her mother, and then turned and walked through a door.

Carla looked quickly at Dean. "I need to make a stop before we go." She moved to her desk and unlocked the bottom drawer, pulling out the nylon sports bag which had rested there in the dark for so many years. "I need to take care of some girl stuff first."

He barely glanced at the bag, and didn't notice the way it sagged in the center from the weight.

Carla hurried through the briefing room and out the door her daughter had taken. The corridor beyond was empty except for the gray little shape drifting down its center ahead of her, feet unmoving and not touching the floor. A trail of cold air followed behind her.

"Mommy's coming, sweetheart," she breathed, quickening her pace, the contents of the sports bag clanking. She knew this hallway well, and where it led. A few moments later Anita paused, turned, and passed through another door. When Carla reached it she had to flip through her keys to find the one which unlocked it. A few seconds later she was alone in a small room, the hallway door closed and relocked behind her, the only light a thin white line shining under the door from the hallway. She set down her bag and stood there in the dark, facing the outline of a steel door. If Anita was in the room, she couldn't see her.

Carla waited, her heart pounding, the room freezing.

"Mommy's ready, baby."

Deacon Valley Correctional Facility relied on OMPA for all its power needs. In the event of a power failure from that source, the prison automatically shifted to the emergency generators housed in a cinderblock building just outside the wire. Within the loud, oily smelling building sat a trio of big yellow, air-cooled 975kw Caterpillars with the capacity to produce well in excess of the roughly 2,400 volts needed to run the prison. Properly fueled, the generators could run indefinitely, or at least as long as it took to restore central power, permitting the facility to carry on without disruption. In the unlikely event the big Cats failed, a few smaller, individual units around the facility would kick in to continue providing power to the top priority areas; the main gates, perimeter and tower lights, and parts of the administrative building. There was no such third level failsafe for the majority of the prison itself, including the blocks.

The tornado dropped out of the sky without warning at ten minutes past eleven, a violent funnel as black as the devil's heart. It cut a savage trough across the killing fields outside the wire, and then slammed into the generator building, obliterating it in an explosion of cinderblock and mangled yellow metal that spun out into the screaming wind and rain. Two of the big Cats were torn apart instantly, and the lights at Deacon Valley flickered and surged. The third generator, untouched by the twister, struggled to take on the full load, whining up like a turbine engine until it was squealing louder than the storm. Unable to keep up with the drain, it exploded like a little star, and Deacon Valley was dropped into darkness.

The energy of the storm already had the prison's population awake and wound up in much the same way intense lightning and thunder will agitate zoo animals in their cages. When the power crashed and the cell blocks went black, it pushed them over the edge. Violence erupted almost immediately in most of the forty-eight man, dormitory-style housing units. Some was directed at the glass of CO bubbles, some against bunks or wall-mounted televisions protected by steel mesh. There was yelling and screaming, fires were started. And there in the dark, with only the hellish light from a burning mattress to see by, well-hidden shanks came out and old grudges were settled. Men were stabbed and kicked to death and had their heads bashed in with knees and doubled fists, rapists and pedophiles and Aryans and Crips and whoever had done something to someone else and was owed a death. In minutes the prison was rocked by riots in six of the cell blocks. The alert siren was one of the few devices able to run on backup power, and it howled throughout the facility.

It was the series of events which Carla had needed, had waited on for eleven years. In that little room, she used a big brass key on the steel door and opened it, heaving it to the side. A wall mounted, battery-powered emergency light on one wall lit the arsenal in black and white, and Carla went to work with the speed of someone who had drilled for years. Her fingers flipped through the key ring with trained precision as she unlocked the assorted racks and cabinets, selecting what she would need and slinging the gear across her chest and over her shoulders. When she was ready, she retrieved the weighted sports bag, left the steel door standing open, and moved back out into the hall, taking off at a run.

Chaos. Over the blare of the siren, men were running in the dark, orders were shouted, and in the distance was the muffled roar from the cell blocks. Thunder shook the prison as the storm descended in force, and outside the shooters huddled in their towers as the twister shredded a hundred yards of fence and razor wire, then lifted an unmanned patrol jeep and spun it away into the night sky.

Dean Frye met Lt. Dykestrom in the hallway, both of them carrying mag-lites.

"DV-2 through DV-6 is coming apart," the Lt. said, "and they're almost through the bubble at DV-4. Looks like the sprinkler system is still working, though. Three's bubble reports the fires are out." Both of their radios crackled with shouting voices and confusion.

"Any losses?" Dean was opening the outer door to the arsenal as running COs started forming up in the hallway behind him.

"Negative. All bubbles have reported in." The Lt. looked around. "Where's Mendez?"

"She came this way a few minutes ago," Dean said, pushing open the door. The Lt. followed him in. They saw the open steel door immediately, and then they were both inside, panning their lights around. There were only three people with keys to the arsenal, and two of them were standing right here. They looked at the unlocked weapons racks and open lockers, then at each other as officers pushed past them. The COs started pulling on body armor and helmets, arming themselves with shotguns and batons, gasmasks and Plexiglas shields.

Mendez did not respond to the repeated radio calls from either Dykestrom or Frye.

The two men quickly geared up. "Send the SRT to DV-4," said Dykestrom, "I'll get the rest of them moving. Then go find Mendez."

Dean quickly assembled the Special Response Team in the hallway, giving instructions to the senior man before they ran off as a unit. Then he headed down another corridor, gripping his shotgun in one hand and his flashlight in the other, its white beam leading the way. He had a good idea where she was going.

Officers Pico and Moore were buttoned up in the bubble at DV-8, listening to the chatter on their radios, broken by frequent bursts of static, glancing occasionally at the ceiling. It sounded like the storm would peel back the roof at any moment. Beyond the armored glass, the Monster House was still, all the inmates locked safely away in their individual cells, a single box of emergency lights high on a wall casting long shadows across the common area.

Banging at the glass to their backs made them jump, and they turned to see Sgt. Mendez in the hallway beyond, holding a mag-lite. For a moment they were confused, because the SRT sergeant wasn't wearing her riot gear as they would have expected. She wasn't even wearing her baseball cap, and her wet hair hung loose about her face and shoulders. She was armed, though, and carrying equipment bags.

She rapped the mag-lite against the glass. "Open up."

They did, using the manual lever to unlock the power-driven door, pulling it open on its tracks. She moved inside and dropped her bags.

"Both of you report to the arsenal and Sgt. Frye. I'll man the PC until I'm relieved." She handed them her flashlight.

They glanced at each other. Shouldn't she be leading an SRT squad somewhere? Pico looked at her. "Sergeant, you know we always need two in the bubble, no matter what."

Carla glared at the younger man. "Get your asses to the arsenal, *now.*"

"Yes, Sergeant!" They ran from the bubble and down the hall.

Carla pulled the door shut and watched the bouncing light disappear into the darkness. Once it was gone, she picked up her bags and went through the interior door, into the common area of the housing unit, pulling that door shut behind her as well. She crouched and unzipped the bag which had rested in her desk for so long, removing a pair of steel wedges and a hand-held sledge. She placed the wedge under the door to the bubble and slammed it home with repeated hits of the sledge. The *PING, PING, PING* of metal on metal reverberated off the concrete walls. Then she moved to the door to the airlock passage and did the same, *PING, PING, PING.*

The storm had already awakened half the men in the Monster House. Carla's hammering woke the rest, and faces appeared at small windows.

Carla tossed the sledge back at the sports bag, then slung the other bag over a shoulder as she raced across the room, weaving in and out of the tables, going straight to Kelvin Finch's cell. He was at the door, staring out at her through the glass, his face puffy with sleep. She opened his food slot at crouched in front of it.

"Wake up, Finch. You don't want to miss this."

Before he could reply, she was moving from cell to cell, unlocking the individual food slots and leaving them open, ignoring the questions from the men inside. A minute later her combat boots thudded up the metal stairs to the second tier, where she moved down the row doing the same to all fourteen cells.

"Finch, can you hear me?" she shouted, her voice echoing through the big room. She unslung the evil-looking, black Mossberg combat shotgun and pumped a round into the chamber. "Her name was Anita Rodriguez. She was seven years old."

"What's going on, Sergeant?" asked the man on the other side of the door. *Parker Dunn; molested a five-year-old boy in the men's room of a Chucky Cheese, and when he cried out, strangled him.* Carla shoved the barrel of the Mossberg through the slot and into Dunn's soft belly, pulling the trigger. It nearly cut him in half.

The weapon's blast sounded like a bomb going off, and as one the men in the Monster House started yelling. Carla moved to the next cell. *Eldon Whitley; serial child rapist who used a hammer to forever silence his victims.* He was kneeling in front of his food slot, trying to see what was going on. Fatal curiosity. He saw the looming muzzle of the Mossberg inches from his face a second before it went off.

"She was my little girl, Finch," she yelled. "My baby."

Tyrone Lawrence; tied his girlfriend to a kitchen chair and forced her to watch as he sodomized her nine-year-old daughter before killing her with a kitchen knife. Tyrone had pulled his mattress off his bunk and was holding it against the inside of the door, blocking the food slot. The Mossberg roared, shredding the mattress and blowing Tyrone's spine out through his back.

The inmates were screaming, calling for help, hurling obscenities and mindless questions.

"Are you listening, Finch?" Carla shouted.

Leon Smith; raped and murdered his two stepsons then set the house on fire with his wife inside. He tried to hide back under his bunk. The Mossberg found him.

Donald Poleski; abducted a girl from a sleepaway camp and held her for a weekend in a cabin, alternating between raping her and forcing her to play board games with him until he decapitated her. Donald hugged the near corner of his cell, keeping back from the food slot and any angle the Mossberg might have on him while he screamed "No!" over and over. Carla dug a flashbang grenade out of the bag over her shoulder and dropped it through the slot, stepping back and looking away, covering her ears. The blast and white light was like a moment of suspended time, followed by a void of silence. Carla used one of her big brass keys to manually unlock the cell door, pulling it open on its tracks. Donald Poleski was crumpled in the corner, hands pawing weakly at the air. She stepped inside, and blew his head off at close range.

"She was my baby!" she screamed.

Below, Kelvin Finch pressed his face against the food slot. "You're crazy, you bitch!"

Dean Frye ran, the echoes of his boots following him. Ahead of him, a light followed by a pair of running men appeared, Pico and Moore from the PC.

"What are you guys doing?" he demanded. "Why aren't you at your post?"

Moore, overweight and breathing hard from the exertion, bent over and put his hands on his knees, unable to speak. Pico was puffing too, but between breathes managed, "Sgt. Mendez relieved us. Told us to report to you at the arsenal."

In the distance behind them came the ghostly boom of a shotgun.

Dean gritted his teeth, jerking a thumb. "Get moving, gear up and find the lieutenant." Without waiting for a response, he ran past them.

Tommy Lee Halsey also tried hiding under his bunk. It didn't save him. Anthony Braccio, a car mechanic who violated his wife's restraining order and beat and murdered both her and their daughter, stayed in the near corner and tried the reason with the murderous sergeant. It took a flashbang to get him out of the corner, and then the Mossberg spoke.

Carla's head was ringing and she had to grip the railing as she stumbled down the stairs from the upper tier, pausing at the bottom to regain her balance before feeding fresh rounds into the shotgun.

"Halfway there, Finch," she yelled, her fingers fumbling a shell and dropping it. No matter, she had plenty.

"You're out of your fucking mind!" Finch screamed from the other end of the block. "I don't know what the fuck you're talking about!"

"You remember number seven. I stood there while you told HBO how much fun you had with my little girl. I read your letters a thousand times." She chambered a round. "You made me think there was some chance, made me think she was still alive even after you had her in the ground." Carla moved to the first cell. *Sampson Jeffries; a hospital orderly who over the course of a year molested three children in a terminal ward before smothering them with their pillows.* He was tucked in a corner.

"Crazy bitch. They're gonna kill you!"

Carla used a flashbang, but caught a fair amount of it herself. She managed to open the cell door, but then fell to her knees in the entrance, her head spinning and her vision a tight little cone. Sampson Jeffries moaned on the floor nearby, trying to climb to his hands and knees.

Dean Frye reached the outer door to the bubble and used the manual release to pull it open, quickly moving to the inner door. He had heard more shooting, recognized the sound of the grenades, and now in the dimness of the emergency lights beyond he could see Carla lying in the open cell doorway on the first level at the far right.

The door wouldn't open. He heaved against it, felt a little play, but it was jammed.

"Carla!" he shouted through the glass, banging a fist against it to get her attention. "Carla, stop! Stop this!"

Carla got to her hands and knees as Sampson Jeffries got to his feet. He made a growling noise and kicked her, landing a bare foot in her ribs before stumbling, still dazed from the blast, waving his arms to keep his balance. Carla grunted and fell onto her side, seeing the big man looming over her. She clawed the 9mm automatic from her hip holster and fired six rounds at a range of three feet. Two whined off the cement wall behind him, but four found their mark, slamming into flesh. From the low angle, one caught Jeffries under the chin, and blew out through the top of his head.

Her head felt like it was filled with wet cotton, and she shook it as she got to her feet, recovered her shotgun and staggering to the next cell.

"How do you feel, Finch?" Her own voice sounded far away. "Helpless? Knowing no one is coming to save you?"

At the other end, Finch shrieked an animal noise out into the common area.

"That was how Anita felt," Carla called. "Helpless. Frightened. She couldn't understand any of it."

"Crazy bitch! Crazy bitch! Crazy bitch! Heeeelp!"

Edward Quince; abducted a little boy from a church picnic, and after he was done with him, pushed him off the top of a construction site. Quince tried to block the food slot with his mattress as Tyrone Lawrence had done. The Mossberg blew apart both the mattress and Edward Quince.

"All she knew was fear, Finch! All she knew was that she wanted her Mommy, and was being hurt by a monster." They were all monsters in here. Beyond serving her purpose of terrorizing Kelvin Finch, Carla had long ago decided that they all needed to die.

The King was wailing, a high, hysterical sound. "It's not my fault! I'm sick! I can't help it!" His fists thudded against his cell door. "She loved me! She loved me and she cried for you at the end!"

Carla pumped another round into the Mossberg, her teeth clenched so tight she thought they might crack, and took a step towards his cell and finish it. But then she moved to the next door. "Be right with you, Finch."

Larry Colt; after online pedophile sites no longer gave him the kick he needed, he snatched a little girl from a mall and raped her in his trailer for two days before chopping her up – as well as his own mother – and burying her in the back yard. Another flashbang was needed to get his out of his corner, but this time Carla was more cautious, stepping well back and covering up before the blast. Larry actually tried to pick up the grenade before it detonated, and when it did, it blew his fingers off. He was curled in a fetal position on the floor, choking and pressing his bloody stumps to the sides of his head when Carla rolled the door open. She put the shotgun's muzzle against his upper lip and fired.

Dean Frye roared in frustration as he threw his weight against the door, again and again, feeling it give a little with each yank. "Carla, stop!" he shouted through the glass. Stop, honey, stop!"

"Death is coming for you, Finch. Can you feel it?"

Lamar Templeton; caught with a murdered infant. A flashbang put him on the floor, and the Mossberg sent him to hell.

Carla's face was wet with tears. "She was my baby, Finch. She had a life and you took it away. You made her die in fear." She pumped a new round. "And I'm coming for you."

Kelvin Finch's wails turned to shrieking sobs for help.

Ruben Marquis; a skinny, former accountant with thick glasses, who once took vacations to Southeast Asia in order to purchase and use young boys. Back in the U.S. he grabbed a neighbor's five-year-old in his apartment building, sexually asphyxiating him. Marquis was found crying over the body. Now he was crying again, just sitting on his bunk with his face in his hands.

Carla cut him down without a word.

"Almost done, Finch," she called, only one door down from his cell. "Almost there."

The king was screaming himself hoarse.

"Shut the fuck up!" Linus James bellowed through the adjacent food slot. "Sergeant! Hey Sergeant! It's Finch you want, I ain't did nothing to your little girl."

Carla walked to his cell.

"Go on now, blow that motherfucker away and leave old Linus alone. He's the one done it." Linus stared at her through the slot, his eyes rolling like a panicky horse. "Please, Sergeant, go on finish that sick motherfucker."

Carla thrust the Mossberg through the slot. Linus James squealed and tried to run the eight feet to the far end of his cell. The Mossberg blew his spine out through his belly, and painted the wall.

"How does it feel, Finch?" she said softly, feeding shells into the shotgun with little clicks. Her fingers moved slowly. She was so very tired.

Dean gave a tremendous heave, his muscles straining and face darkening to the point he feared he would pop a blood vessel.

With a grinding squeak the wedge slid free and the door rolled open.

"Carla!" He ran towards her across the common room.

She approached the King's cell.

"Carla, stop right there!" Dean slid to a stop and put his own shotgun to his shoulder, aiming it at his friend.

She paused and looked at him, her eyes sunken in a drawn face. "He took away my baby, Dean."

"I know he did, honey." The muzzle of his shotgun wavered. "But not this. You have to stop." What was he doing! He loved her, and she was doing what every CO had fantasized about in every prison in the world. A final accounting for the dead and destroyed. Was he going to shoot this woman, who by every definition of the word was putting *justice* back into the justice system?

Still he didn't lower the shotgun.

She looked at him a moment longer, gave him a sad smile, and turned towards the King's door.

"Carla, no!"

She put the Mossberg's muzzle to the food slot.

From twenty feet away Dean fired. The double-aught buckshot hit her in the back and shoulder, throwing her forward into the cell door. Her Mossberg fell with a rattle and she slid to the floor, face down. Dean ran to her, dropping his own weapon and falling to his knees beside her, turning her over. Even in the shadows from the emergency light he could see her face was gray, her eyes distant and blinking slowly.

"Oh, honey, I'm sorry," he said, cradling her head as the tears came. What had he done? She choked and tried to say something, but it only came out as a wheeze. Then she was gone.

"God*damn!* Thanks, man, you got here just in time!" Kelvin Finch pressed his face to the food slot, turning his head so he could see the fallen sergeant. He laughed, a shaky, nervous sound. "That was one crazy bitch."

Dean said nothing.

Finch, the terror over, started talking from the adrenalin. "Man, she got 'em all, didn't she? Every chickenhawk in here, dead as dead can be! Gonna be hell to pay. Crazy bitch. How'd she get in here, anyway? Man, I think I'm gonna throw up."

Dean looked down at the woman he had just killed, eyes wet, feeling sick inside, and empty as well. He suddenly understood some of what she must have felt over those long years, that dead void inside. He brushed the hair away from her face. Sleep now.

"They should give you a medal, Sergeant. You saved my ass, you really did! I don't mind telling you, I thought she was gonna get me."

Dean stood up with Carla's Mossberg in his hand, and he turned, shoving the barrel into the food slot and against Kelvin Finch's face. "She did."

The King had a tenth of a second to gasp before the blast took his head off. Dean set the weapon back on the floor beside Carla, knelt down and took her in his arms, rocking her slowly as he wept.

A touch of cool air crossed his neck, but he barely noticed. Behind him, a shade in the shape of a little girl was joined by that of a woman. They joined hands, and faded.

SOON TO BE RELEASED

OMEGA DAYS

&

A JUDGE FROM SALEM

by
John L. Campbell

Made in the USA
Charleston, SC
14 August 2014